CONQUEST

CONQUEST

Daughter of the Last King

Tracey Warr

First Published 2016
by Impress Books Ltd
Innovation Centre, Rennes Drive, University of Exeter Campus,
Exeter EX4 4RN

© Tracey Warr 2016

Typeset in Garamond by Swales & Willis Ltd, Exeter, Devon

Printed and bound in Great Britain by TJ Books Limited, Padstow

British Library Cataloguing in Publication Data

A catalogue record for this book is available from the British Library

ISBN: 978-1-907605-81-9 (pbk)
ISBN: 978-1-907605-82-6 (ebk)

For Lola

CONTENTS

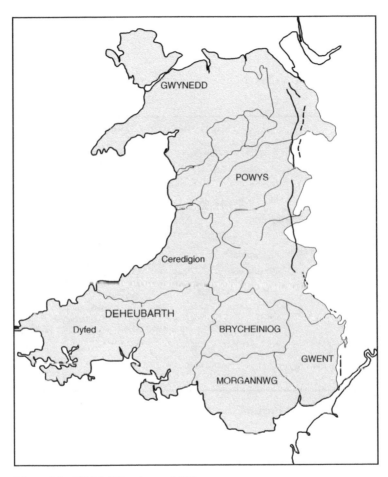

Map of the Welsh Kingdoms, 1093

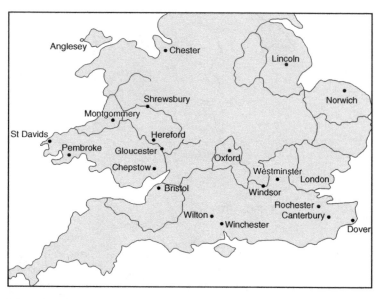

Map of Wales and England

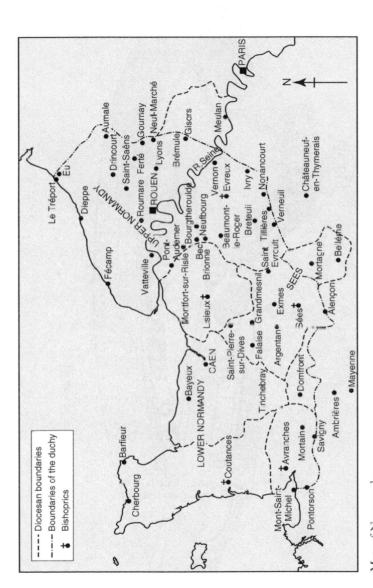

Map of Normandy

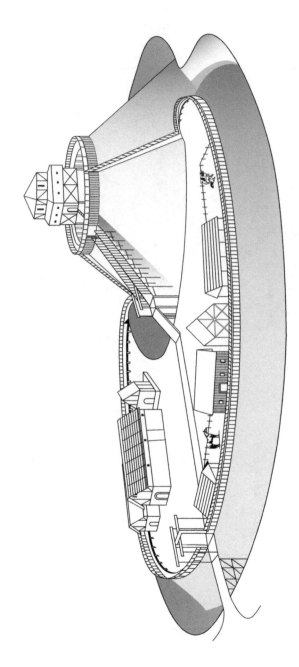

Sketch of the Motte and Bailey Castle at Cardiff

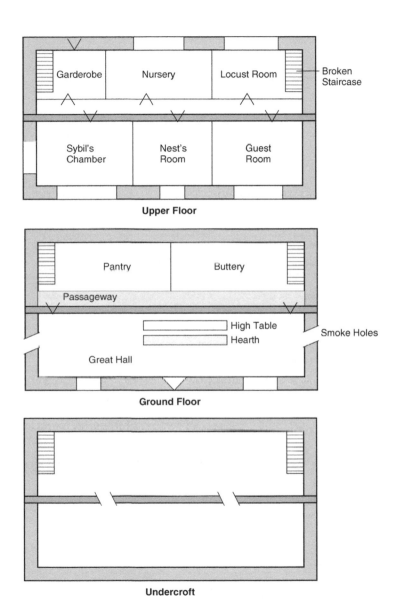

Floor Plan of the Great Hall at Cardiff Castle

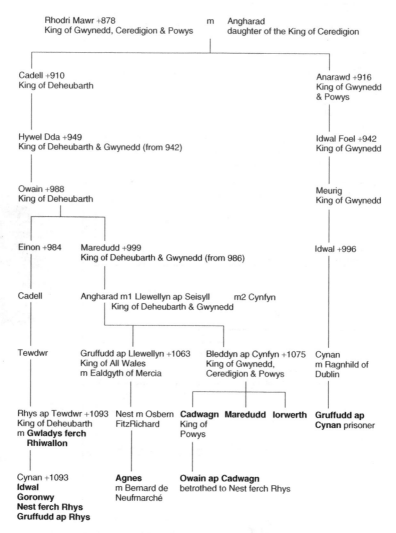

Rhodri Mawr +878
King of Gwynedd, Ceredigion & Powys

m   Angharad
daughter of the King of Ceredigion

Cadell +910
King of Deheubarth

Anarawd +916
King of Gwynedd
& Powys

Hywel Dda +949
King of Deheubarth & Gwynedd (from 942)

Idwal Foel +942
King of Gwynedd

Owain +988
King of Deheubarth

Meurig
King of Gwynedd

Einon +984

Maredudd +999
King of Deheubarth & Gwynedd (from 986)

Idwal +996

Cadell

Angharad m1 Llewellyn ap Seisyll   m2 Cynfyn
King of Deheubarth & Gwynedd

Tewdwr

Gruffudd ap Llewellyn +1063
King of All Wales
m Ealdgyth of Mercia

Bleddyn ap Cynfyn +1075
King of Gwynedd,
Ceredigion & Powys

Cynan
m Ragnhild of
Dublin

Rhys ap Tewdwr +1093
King of Deheubarth
m **Gwladys ferch
Rhiwallon**

Nest m Osbern
FitzRichard

Cadwagn
King of
Powys

Maredudd   **Iorwerth**

**Gruffudd ap
Cynan** prisoner

Cynan +1093
**Idwal
Goronwy
Nest ferch Rhys
Gruffudd ap Rhys**

Agnes
m Bernard de
Neufmarché

Owain ap Cadwagn
betrothed to Nest ferch Rhys

Genealogy of the Welsh Royal Families, April 1093

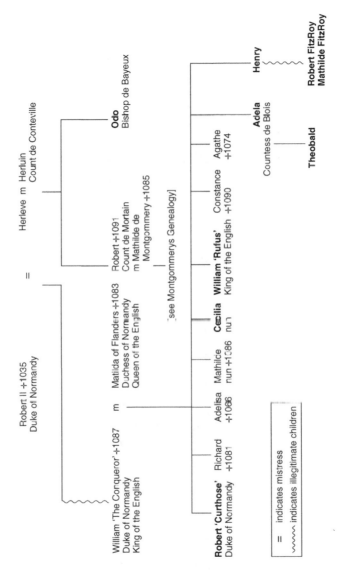

Robert II +1035
Duke of Normandy

=   Herleve m Herluin
             Count de Conteville

William 'The Conqueror' +1087
Duke of Normandy
King of the English

m   Matilda of Flanders +1083
     Duchess of Normandy
     Queen of the English

Robert +1091
Count de Mortain
m Mathilde de
Montgommery +1085

[see Montgommerys Genealogy]

Odo
Bishop de Bayeux

Robert 'Curthose'   Richard   Adelisa   Mathilde   **Cecilia**   **William 'Rufus'**   Constance   Agathe   **Adela**   **Henry**
Duke of Normandy   +1081   +1066   nun +1086   nun   King of the English   +1090   +1074   Countess de Blois

Theobald

Robert FitzRoy
Mathilde FitzRoy

=   indicates mistress
〰〰〰   indicates illegitimate children

Genealogy of the Anglo-Norman Royal Family, April 1093

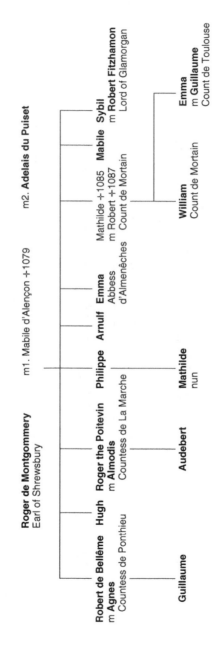

Genealogy of the Montgommerys, April 1093

Part One

1093–1094

1

A Small Massacre

I was on the beach at Llansteffan with my brother Goronwy watching the sunlight winking on the water. In April 1093, the fifteenth year of my father's reign as King of Deheubarth, I was twelve and Goronwy was thirteen. Our mother complained we were too old to play together. Goronwy should spend more time practising at the archery butts and I should be indoors, improving my very poor skills on the harp. But the sun was shining and our mother was heavy and sluggish with the child she carried in her belly, and we took advantage that she did not see us slip out of the compound and skid and slide fast down the hill to the yellow sands that we could not resist. Goronwy was building a splendid sand palace with a moat and a rivulet that ran to the edge of the sea and filled up more and more with each rush of the tide. 'It's your palace in Powys,' he told me, referring to my betrothal to Prince Owain ap Cadwgan and that I would, in time, be the king's wife in Powys, the lands adjacent to our own.

Something black was half-submerged in the sand between my feet. I bent and picked it up, blowing off the sand and turning with glee to my brother. 'Look, Goronwy! I've found a claw *at* The Claw!' We called this place The Claw because of the shape made by the three rivers that flowed into the bay here – the Taf, the Twyi and the Gwendraeth. It wasn't a shape you could see. You had to imagine it, as if you were a bird flying high above, looking down at the three blue river talons reaching up into the land. Goronwy did not reply, absorbed in his building so I turned back to the sea, twisting the bird's claw between my thumb and finger.

I remember the sun shone in my eyes as I looked out to the sea and the next trickle of surf. The breeze whipped loose strands of my black hair into my mouth and I had to hold it from my face with both hands cupped to my brow, shading my eyes and opening them as wide as they would go. 'I think I can hear bells ringing under the sea,' I said. There was no response from Goronwy, so I turned around to protest it was true and ran towards his palace meaning to plant my claw in its crest as a sort of grisly banner when something made me look up to the fort on the cliff above us. Perhaps a stone skittering down the steep rock face or a blinding flash of sun on armour. I looked up and saw flames. 'Goronwy, the fort's on fire!'

He ignored me, slapping his sandy turrets into shape, thinking I was feigning. He often teased that I was a spinner of tales.

I tugged at his sleeve. 'No, look! Really!' We screwed up our eyes to see the fort high above us. There were horseman in armour milling on the road and gouts of black smoke staining the blue sky. 'Father!' I said. Our father and older brothers had been away for the last few months, campaigning against the Norman invaders.

'No, it's not ...' Goronwy started to say but then he spun swiftly to the right, where horsemen were galloping down the long beach towards us. Not the Welsh warriors we knew but Norman warriors we had heard about, sheathed in chainmail with conical helmets and metal strips projecting down their noses. Their big *destriers* kicked up spray at the water's edge as they rapidly closed the distance between us. I pulled at Goronwy's sleeve, twisting my body towards the dense undergrowth at the foot of the cliff where I knew places we could hide. The horses kept coming. I could see the whites of their eyes battling the pain at their mouths, the foam at the corners of their black lips. Now I could hear the clanking weapons above the sound of the sea.

One of the men at the front of the group lent forward in the saddle to shout in Welsh. 'Boy! Are you the *Edling*, the son of Rhys?'

'Lie!' I hissed, still pulling at his arm.

Goronwy resisted my pulling and turned to face them. 'I am Goronwy, Prince of Deheubarth, son of Rhys,' he yelled, since he had been drilled to do so.

'We have to hide,' I said desperately but it was already too late. 'Goronwy!' I moaned, pulling at him, but he stood his ground as they were upon us, milling around in a crowd of hooves, shields and sea-spray. One of them swept me up, slung me unceremoniously on my stomach across his saddle, a hand gripped in my belt. He turned his horse back towards the path up to the fort. Upside down, the long black rope of my plait dangled. I heard a cry from my brother and I tried to see what was happening, but there was just a blur of spurs and boots, the legs of the horses, their snorting. I closed my eyes on the sound of blades grating as they were drawn from their scabbards.

My captor's horse hauled up the steep path to the fort and I tasted acrid smoke that roiled around us like thunderclouds. I felt sick, jolted and bruised in every direction, the breath knocked from me, the warrior's hand heavy on my back keeping me in place. We clattered under the gateway and I saw, still upside down, a dire scene of confusion. Servants and the few warriors my father had left to guard us lay dead, their blood congealing in dark red pools. I recognised the features of my father's huntsman, but many of the corpses were too mangled or bloodied to tell who they were. Buildings were in flames, their timbers cracking loudly, heat washing over me as we passed close to the conflagration. A roof beam lost its hold and fell with a thud that shook the earth, carrying burning thatch with it, sending out more fire spores. The beautifully carved lintel that had stood proudly over the hall door, lay on the ground splintered in half. A small group of women and children had been herded into a corner and were eerily quiet as Norman warhorses milled around them. The iron scent of blood was in the air but my nostrils seared with the charring heat.

The man who had swept me up, plucked me again by my belt and dropped me to the ground. 'Nest!' my mother screeched. I got to my feet, rubbing at my bruised upper arms, searching in the direction of her voice. She lumbered out between the horses oblivious to their efforts to corral her and grabbed me by my sore arms, causing me to cry out. Her white face was streaked with tears and smuts. Her belly was huge with the child she carried. I struggled to comprehend what I was seeing: the sudden transformation of my father's well-ordered court, his *llys*, to this wreck and chaos, the translation of my mother from stately king's wife to grimed, distraught woman.

'Mother. Sit down,' I said slowly, trying to give my numbed mind time to catch up with the evidence of my eyes, realising my legs were jellied and I needed to sit myself. We stumbled towards a mounting block and sat together, her hands roaming over me searching for injuries. Two bodies hung from the metalwork above the well which had been turned into a makeshift gibbet. Their faces were contorted and their tongues lolled but I recognised my father's bard and my playfellow, the cook's boy, and turned my face away. I had been staring blindly into space with my mouth open for a long moment when my mother asked, close to my ear, 'Did they find your brother?'. I nodded miserably and she fell against me wailing.

A man in Norman dress spoke to me harshly in Welsh, snapping me out of the shocked trance I had entered. 'Girl! Keep the woman quiet! The lord won't stand for no more screeching. He's getting a headache.' He laughed showing teeth that were brown and jagged.

'Mother, calm,' I soothed her, trying to also sooth myself. She shook against me as I stroked her hair, sobbing in a low moaning voice like an animal, rolling and rocking. I tightened my grip protectively around her, hearing hooves skitter to a stop beside us, and looked up into the face of a warrior staring down at me. He looked peculiarly pig-like with dark eyes peering around the nose-guard of his helmet and his long, brown moustache bristling on either side of it. His horse and armour were splendid so I guessed he was the leader of the attack. My eyes travelled over the fine red and gold silk of his saddle cloth, the rich red of the tabard he wore over chainmail, and finally I noticed the open golden filigree at the tip of his sword scabbard slowing dripping blood in a small vermilion pool close to his horse's hoof.

He called out, 'FitzWalter!' Another man rode up beside us in answer to the red silk man's command. I understood a few words of their language since my father at one time had Norman hostages in our household. I gathered the leader was giving orders about us, my mother and me, to the second man, FitzWalter. 'Take the girl to Cardiff and …' I missed some words, drowned out by the racket of distress all around us. 'We have most of the forts now, but I must get to Pembroke before Cadwgan.' Fitz-Walter acknowledged the commands. The *llys*, I thought, my father's forts that our household moved between: Dinefwr, Pembroke, Narberth, Whitland, Carmarthen, and here, my favourite place, my poor Llansteffan, afflame and running with blood, its elegant pillars splintered and blackened; its gold and silvery tapestries turned to smouldering ash.

My mother was gripped, pulled from me, and loaded into a cart that clattered out of the castle under escort, whilst the soldier named FitzWalter, leapt down from his horse, picked me up with ease and placed me on a small paltrey, tying my hands carefully so that I could move them enough to hold onto the reins and guide the horse but not do much else. 'I hope you can ride well, little princess,' he said, grinning. This one had a row of even, white teeth and a full red mouth beneath the nose-guard of his helmet. His eyes were pale blue and he seemed young. His Welsh was terrible but I got the rough idea of what he was saying.

'I ride better than you ever will,' I told him.

A laugh burst from him in response and he shouted to his lord, 'She has spirit, this little Welsh girl!' The lord twisted in his red and gold saddle to stare at me and when FitzWalter told him what I had said, they laughed at me together. The young soldier remounted, signalling to six other soldiers to follow us, and he led my paltrey out through the gateway and palisade and onto the road. Through eyes smarting with smoke and grief I looked around as we passed the blazing wrecks of the villagers' thatched houses and the haywains of the royal estate, the *maerdref*. The fields and garden strips that provisioned my father's court were blackened and trampled and more corpses, surprised in the midst of feeding the chickens or darning a sock, sprawled in the embrace of the land they had tilled and cared for.

Before long we overtook the cart carrying my mother and the small escort of soldiers with her. 'Mother!' She looked at me, her

7

face ashen, her mouth trembling terribly, forcing the remnant of a smile for me as we passed her.

For the first hour I shook in the saddle like an old woman with palsy and fought to quell nausea and shock. Every fibre in my body thrummed and thrashed, but slowly I calmed myself until eventually I could shout in Welsh at FitzWalter: 'Where are we going?'

FitzWalter spoke over his shoulder to me. 'Cardiff Castle. We'll be five days on the road so save your energy for riding not talking, little princess.'

'How is it you speak Welsh, though so badly?' I called out.

He turned his horse to look at me, laughing at my insult. 'We have Welsh scouts and translators in our service,' he said. 'I learned.'

'Scouts? Traitors you mean.'

He ignored that. 'I've been in Wales most of my life, first sent as squire to Lord Arnulf de Montgommery when I was seven, and lately as captain of his guard. I've picked up Welsh over the years. Now I am in such exalted company as yours, I will of course try to bring more polish to my language. Perhaps you will teach me?'

I turned my face away from him. So the man in red silk who led the attack was Arnulf de Montgommery. I knew his father was the Norman Earl of Shrewsbury with lands on the English border.

The men all called me *petite princesse,* with mockery in their voices, as they gave me water and biscuits and tied me tight at night when we slept on the ground wrapped in cloaks. Waking in the morning, I immediately longed for the oblivion of sleep to return, when I did not hear the scrape of swords extracted from scabbards as the riders surrounded my brother on the beach, did not feel overwhelming fear and grief, and remember the misery on my mother's face.

We rode through mud and rain, skirting bogs and swamps, through dense forest lined with great oaks, and cruelly carpeted with gay primroses and bluebells, and more truly with gorse and brambles.

'What has happened to my father?' I ventured to the captain when we stopped on the second night and were eating the lean supplies. He had removed his helmet to reveal a sweaty head of dark blond hair. He shook his head impatiently, too tired to mangle Welsh any more, beckoning at the scout, a turncoat Welshman who came and answered my questions.

'Dead,' he told me. 'King Rhys is dead, lady, and his son Cynan.'

I knew it already, but speaking it seemed to make it so. My mouth trembled but I blinked away tears that I did not want these men to see. 'How did they die?' I demanded.

'Rhys died in the battle at Aberhonddu, killed by the Norman lord of Brecknock, Bernard de Neufmarché, and Cynan was drowned in a lake. Afterwards.' He looked shiftily at the captain when he said that. I forced the image of my valiant brother spluttering in filthy water from my mind's eye.

'And what of my other brother, Idwal, who was at the battle?' I did not want to ask and hear that he was also dead, but I needed to know.

'He was captured and imprisoned.'

FitzWalter said something swiftly and irritably in French, and I could not understand him. 'Sir Gerald says enough talking,' the scout said, 'Sleep now, lady.'

I looked at my caretaker, Gerald FitzWalter. The sweat had dried in his fair hair and it curled softly at his ears like a girl's. He was young – perhaps only seventeen. I saw in his posture and the dullness of his eyes that his fatigue was bone-deep.

I lay awake, thinking about the words I overheard from Arnulf de Montgommery at Llansteffan: 'We have all the forts but I must get to Pembroke before Cadwgan.' My father held peace in Deheubarth for many years and had been the only Welsh ruler to come to terms with the first Norman invader, William the Conqueror. The bards sang of that old Norman king riding into our lands and honouring King Rhys with his friendship. Father also defended our lands from the aggressions of neighbouring rulers including Cadwgan, King in Powys, and promised me as brideprice to Cadwgan's son Owain to keep the peace. I had been betrothed to Owain by proxy and never seen him.

Did the words of Arnulf de Montgommery mean Cadwgan had invaded Deheubarth again, in treacherous alliance with these enemies? My father always said Cadwgan was 'tricky' and I understood this was meant as humorous understatement. The men of my father's warband, his *teulu*, spoke of Cadwgan's frequent changes of allegiance: first to a neighbouring Welsh king, then to the Norman Earls on the border. Arnulf de Montgommery said he was making for Pembroke, the greatest of Deheubarth's strongholds. If Cadwgan had betrayed my father, did that annul my betrothal? I could not be sure from the few words I had understood. In any case I was a captive and the future was a gaping, jagged hole before me. My uncle Rhydderch was my only hope since he was not at the battle in Aberhonddu. Perhaps he would rescue me on this journey, or treat a ransom for me.

I lay on the cold, hard ground thinking of my father, how he would never cup his big hand gently on the top of my head and call me 'my blue-eyed, dimpled beauty' or yell across the compound, looking for me: 'Where is that miniature queen?'. He would never again squash me to his hip when he returned weary from battle, and the gladness to be home brimming in his eyes. I determined I would be no vanquished hostage. For my father, my mother and brothers, I would be that queen in my heart no matter what came next.

On the third day of the journey my horse was lame and they put me in the back of a cart, bound with rough ropes about my hands and ankles. I heard an irritating noise, and then realised it was my own teeth chattering against the chill air. I peered into the dark trees lining the road, looking for rescue, but none came. Rain began to lash us as we moved off again. The small stony path we followed soon turned into the bed of a rapid stream. It took us diagonally across the dark green of a field towards a gateway where cows had been called for milking and churned the ground to deep mud. One of the soldiers cried out as he sunk up to his hips in black ooze. 'Jesu!'

'Don't move!' FitzWalter shouted to him. 'Stay completely still.' FitzWalter directed the other soldiers, who were laughing at their companion's plight, to lead the horses and my cart carefully around the firmer edges of the morass and through the gate while he pulled a small axe from his saddle-bag and chopped two stout branches from a tree. One, he laid down on the ground for the man to hold onto to secure him from sinking any further, and the other branch he threw to the soldier. 'Lever yourself out, slowly, that's it!' He coaxed the anxious man gently, as if speaking to a nervy horse.

'My boot! I've lost my boot to the devil's grip!'

'Never mind your boot. We can find you a new boot. Just keep levering yourself and your bootless foot out of there.'

Slowly the soldier emerged from the slimey grasp of the earth with lumps and smears of thick wet soil clinging to every inch of him, so that he looked like a mud-monster rising from the sod. His eyes and smile shone frantically through the muck mask covering his face. 'I thought it had me there!' he said, his humour on the edge of hysteria, as FitzWalter yanked him to the drier land, clapping him on the back.

We resumed our progress through the rain and mire, eventually finding a drier path and FitzWalter called a halt to the tramp of horses and men. The cart I sat in stopped abruptly and tied as I was I toppled over in it, banging hard against the edge of a wooden chest. Later black bruising bloomed from my shoulder to my elbow. FitzWalter, hearing me whimper, slid from his horse and climbed into the back of the cart to right me. He propped soft bundles of blanket-rolls around me so that I could not fall again. He took off his cloak and wrapped it around my shoulders, looking with concern into my face. 'I have a sister your age,' he said. You would call his actions kind but in those days, on that journey, I had no notion there could ever be such a word or feeling.

He leapt down from the cart and stepped back up into his stirrup, his movements fluid and assured, giving the order for the cavalcade to move off. FitzWalter's cloak had a well-lined hood but my hands were tied and I could not lift it to cover my head. I blinked at the water melding my eyelashes together. FitzWalter glanced back at me and rode swiftly again to the cart. His horse walked slowly alongside as he lent across towards me. Tutting and frowning, he lifted the hood over my draggled head and shook his own. My face streamed with rain. He took off a gauntlet and wiped my cheek gently with the back of his hand and then carefully, peering at me like a mother with her child, swiped his thumb under my wet eyes. He tried to get me to look at him,

11

cupping his hand under my chin and turning my face to him, but I kept my eyes away from his. 'You *are* a beauty,' he said, 'even soaked to the skin.'

'You might speak thus of a horse, or a whore,' I told him in Welsh, around my chattering teeth, 'but I am the daughter of a king and you will speak to me with respect.' Now I stared at him.

Since he had given me his cloak, his hair was plastered to his head and water streamed down his cheeks. His mouth was open and then began to curve at one side into a smile, as it took him a moment to absorb and understand what I had said. One pale brown eyebrow arched. He inclined his dripping head to me. 'Well that I will Princess Nest, for you have spirit and a sharp tongue as well as very fetching dimples.' I frowned, but he laughed and turned his horse back to the cavalcade before I could think of another retort to his impertinence.

We were riding across the lands of Morgannwg, that the Normans call Glamorgan. After the downpour the sky cleared quickly to blue and sunshine. We rode through fertile fields with crops starting to push green through the mud, and now and then I gained a glimpse of the coast and distant harbours. We were about a mile from the sea, following a large river. Beyond the bend of the muddy waters, across a wide flat plain, a fortress was built on a rise in the land, surrounded by trees and shrubs, and all around the foot of the fortress were numerous thatched houses. It was one of the largest settlements I had ever seen. We rode up the main street between houses and shops where people cowered away from the soldiers and horses and craned with curiosity at me and my bindings, until we were suddenly confronted with an immensely long, high wooden palisade that stretched further than the eye could easily comprehend and was fronted by a deep water-filled ditch. 'Cardiff Castle,' one of the soldiers told me, noticing how I had twisted round in the cart to look with amazement at this vast structure. 'It's built on top of what's left of an old Roman fort. King William the Conqueror founded it.' I rearranged my face to an unimpressed expression but kept my eyes fixed on it. The men encouraged the horses and my cart onto the drawbridge, across the ditch, moving towards the shadow of the three-storeyed wooden gatehouse that bristled with soldiers armed with bows and spears.

* * *

The truth of things done should be committed to writing. Now, many years since those grievous events, as I look back on them as an old woman instead of the naïve girl I was then, I see how this story began long before I was born, in 1066 when the Norman Duke, William the Conqueror, crossed the English sea from Normandy, killed the Anglo-Saxon king Harald at Hastings, took the kingdom of the English for himself and parceled out those lands to his Norman barons. To begin with the Norman earls on the Welsh borders were stationed to guard against Welsh incursions into the English realm, and amongst them was Roger de Montgommery, the Earl of Shrewsbury, whose family features large in my story. Working with the policy that attack is the best defence, those Norman lords began to advance their territorial claims into Wales and there they met with fierce opposition from the Welsh kings and their kin.

William the Conqueror, or William the Bastard as he was also known, died in 1087, not long after I was born, and left behind him three sons: Robert Curthose, the eldest, who became Duke of Normandy; William Rufus, the second surviving son, who became King of the English; and Henry, the youngest, who was bequeathed only money and received no lands or title. For years to come those three sons fought each other and struggled with divisions and rebellions amongst their Norman barons. Peacefulness and loyalty were not Norman traits but then neither were they the habits of the Welsh warrior aristocracy from which I sprang.

A few days before I had stood all unthinking on the beach at Llansteffan with Goronwy, William Rufus, King of the English, lay on his deathbed in Gloucester. The King's younger brother Henry sat just outside the sick chamber, away from any possible contagion, listening to his brother's stertorous, salivaed breaths, reading Xenophon's manual on hunting. Henry would rather have been outside in the sun-striped forest chasing a hart instead

13

of just reading about it, still it could not be helped. William, it seemed, was going to die and had no heir. Henry waited calmly. In the event, if it came to it, he knew exactly what he would do and who he could count on.

Around the same time and some sixteen miles west of Gloucester by the Welsh reckoning, the tall, fat, Norman lord, Bernard de Neufmarché, stood in the mud before his partly built castle at Aberhonddu, close to the Black Mountains where the river Usk meets the river Honddu, looking down at the bloodied corpse of Rhys, the great King of Deheubarth – my father – laid out before him like a gutted trophy stag. I imagine Neufmarché nodding his blood and mud tousled dark head to himself, thinking, good, very good. King William must be dead by now and Duke Robert would soon cross the Channel from Normandy and claim the English throne. The Duke would be grateful to Neufmarché for taking this initiative. He might reward him with the dead king's lands in Deheubarth and that would make Neufmarché as mighty a Norman baron in Wales as Roger de Montgommery. Still staring at the corpse, Neufmarché, I suppose, allowed himself a satisfied grin that creased the folds of his fat face.

Three days later and fourteen Welsh miles further west into Wales from Aberhonddu, Arnulf de Montgommery, the fifth and youngest son of the Earl of Shrewbury and therefore hungry for his own conquered lands, was concealed with a small band of warriors near Llansteffan in the woods known as The Sticks. One of those warriors, Gerald FitzWalter, had recently been knighted and meant to demonstrate his mettle to his lord in the coming skirmish. Arnulf's spy sped the message from Aberhonddu of King Rhys' death. The truce William the Conqueror made with King Rhys held for twelve years, but now Rhys was dead and Arnulf saw the whole of south-west Wales for the taking. He would be damned if Cadwgan or Neufmarché would beat him to it. He would take the fort at Llansteffan, then Carmarthen, then Pembroke and prove to his father and Duke Robert that he had enterprise. He believed he deserved to be rewarded with the kingdom of Deheubarth – the kingdom that belonged to my family.

2

Cardiff Castle

As we moved across the drawbridge to enter Cardiff Castle I shivered uncontrollably from so many wet hours on the road. My damp woollen clothes clung coldly to me like riverweed. Two porters strained to push open the huge doors to allow us to ride into the bailey, then the doors were banged shut and barred behind us. Four large dogs on chains lunged barking and were called to heel by a stableboy. Inside, the castle was a great rectangular compound surrounded by a high wooden palisade with several thatched wooden buildings that did not look so different from my father's *llys*, but what *was* different was the great grassy mound that rose some forty feet high, occupying the far left quarter of the compound and with its own moat and wooden wall. A steep causeway could be ridden up but ended abruptly in air several feet before the palisade surrounding the three-storeyed keep on the high, green mound.

We rode towards the largest building in the lower bailey which I guessed to be the main hall. A woman on an upper storey was beating a blanket slung over a window-sill and she stilled her labour to look down at us. Another young woman, richly dressed in green and miniver sheltered from the wind in the doorway. She watched FitzWalter lift me from the cart and carry me towards her. Like my mother, her belly was swollen huge with a child. She stood aside and he carried me in with the woman following, speaking swiftly to him and without pause. I was too tired to try to comprehend the torrent of her words but I watched her, my chin bumping on his shoulder. Her most prominent feature was her stomach, straining the costly green fabric of her gown, advancing before her, as she walked with her feet placed flat and pointing away from each other in a V shape. Her feet and hands were large and broad like a man's.

FitzWalter set me down on a bench close to the central hearth sunk in the floor. Slowly I began to feel human again. Blood returned painfully to my extremities, rushing round the outer circuits of my ears. The woman tutted at the ropes on my wrists and the sores beneath. She said something angrily to FitzWalter, who knelt and cut my bindings with his dagger, then stood and held his palms out in apology to the woman. Exhausted as I was I struggled to pick out the few Norman words I knew from their rapid speech together.

'Does she understand any French? *Langue d'Oïl? Français?*' she demanded, turning to me. I shook my head and Fitz-Walter frowned since he knew I did understand a little, but he said nothing. The woman rolled her eyes and turned away to supervise the reception of the men. She had ale and bread waiting on the trestle for them. I watched three servants fuss around Fitz-Walter, one holding a brass bowl beneath his hands, while another poured water over his hands and the third handed him a towel. A maid set bread and a beaker in front of me but I did not move to touch it. I flexed my whitened fingers as they recovered from their constraint.

The woman said something more to FitzWalter and he lifted me up and carried me upstairs to a chamber where a fire burned in the hearth. He placed me on the large bed, gave me a wave that I did not respond to as he squeezed out past a maid in the doorway. The chamber was finely decorated with tapestries and gilded candlesticks and I guessed it was the lady's own quarters. She soon came and joined the maid in stripping the wet clothes from me and rubbing me dry. They pulled a warm nightgown, too big, over my head and regarded me critically. Gently the maid applied a salve to the ugly raw strips around my wrists and ankles, and wiped my face. She murmured soothing words to me in French. She tipped a little wine into my mouth and I felt it burn its way down my throat and into my stomach. Together they wrapped me in the furs on the bed. I stared into the fire whilst the women stared at me.

I must have closed my eyes and slept, for when I opened them again, the lady was sitting on a stool before the fire sewing. She exclaimed and the maid went quickly out of the room, returning with a man who bowed to the lady and then regarded me on the bed. I had not moved, only opened and closed my eyes and then opened them again. I stared at him immobile in my fur cocoon.

'The lady wants me to tell you her name is Sybil de Montgommery,' he said in Welsh, bending down to look in my face. 'She'll be giving you lessons and you'll be learning to speak the Norman tongue.'

So she was his sister, Arnulf de Montgommery, the man with the red silk trappings on his horse who had led the attack on Llansteffan. I closed my eyes again.

'No response,' the man told the lady. And for now they let me be.

When I woke the second time FitzWalter was standing in front of the fire with Lady Sybil and they did not notice at first that I was awake. Sybil was tall and fair-haired with a plain, round face and plump arms and fingers. She was young. I judged her to be less than twenty. FitzWalter, with his curly fair hair and pale blue eyes, looked handsome, now that he was dry and clean. They were discussing me and I was frustrated to understand only a few names and words: '... Arnulf ... wife'. I am going to be the wife of Prince Owain ap Cadwgan in Powys, I told myself, but perhaps Cadwgan had decided to renege on that? My stomach churned. I was of little use to him now my father was dead. A few days ago my future seemed clear, mapped out, but now I had lost all sense of who I was, all orientation. I screwed my eyes shut, trying to calm myself. I heard another word I knew. '... dead?' Sybil asked FitzWalter and I opened my eyes to watch him nod. 'King Rhys, two sons, Cynan, Goronwy ... Bernard de Neufmarché.'

I shivered on the bed. Tears leaked out of the corners of my eyes and I rolled my face on the sheet to get rid of them. My sweet brother, Goronwy, who I had played with on the beach that day, who was not even a man yet, I guessed he had died there at the hands of those devils, his blood in the sand where we had built so many castles and moats and watched the sea rush into them, where we had tussled, giggled and swum in the salty water, where he comforted me when I cried at a cut foot caused by a broken seashell. They thought they had wiped us out, done for us all, the royal house of Dinefwr that had ruled Deheubarth for time out of mind. I prayed my brother had no chance on that beach to realise what was happening, to feel terror. I hoped he had that mercy. Carefully, in my mind's eye, I stored away the name Bernard de Neufmarché, who I presumed to be the murderer, as if I were writing it on a slip of parchment, folding it, stowing it in my purse.

The sudden vivid memory of my father talking at table, with his men around him, their beakers brimming, the bard seated with a harp, the fire blazing, made me realise anew that my world had come loose from its moorings. The high wooden palisades of the *llys* had not protected us. My tall brothers, my father and his warriors were gone and I was alone with the invaders. Idwal, my half-brother, was chained in a prison, yet they could not know about my infant brother Gruffudd! He had survived the slaughter and was my father's heir now. A year ago my father's lands were briefly overrun by Cadwgan. Gruffudd was born in Dublin where Lord Torcall, my father's ally, gave us shelter. When we returned to Deheubarth, the baby had been too feeble for the crossing and my mother left him in Dublin with the wetnurse, intending to retrieve him the following summer. I remembered his huge dark eyes staring at me unblinking and his tiny fingers curling round my index finger as I stroked his cheek.

I tried to focus on the thought of my tiny brother. When he was older, when he was a grown man, he would come and take vengeance on Neufmarché, he would reclaim his kingdom, and we would sit beside one another, restored to our lands. He would rule in Deheubarth and I would be the king's wife in Powys. Perhaps. My certainty about that marriage was dissipating, and the picture I was trying to create of Gruffudd and I slipped and dissolved. All I had to cling to in this wreckage was a tiny baby, far away.

I do not know how long I slept this time. Hours or days? I had no sense of it. I slept to avoid thinking. I was dimly conscious that at some point the lady, Sybil, had come and slept beside me.

18

The maid banged through the door, startling me fully awake. She spoke to me in hesitant Welsh. 'Lady Sybil says I'm to take you to the room prepared for you and you must bathe and then go and dine in the hall.' I started to shake my head. 'It's not a choice, my lady.' I would rather slit their throats than share their meal, yet my stomach turned over on itself, consuming air and I knew I must eat or die and I was not ready to die yet. I *must* not die. I had to live for vengeance for my father, for Cynan and for Goronwy. I sat up.

The maid led me along a narrow passage to the chamber next to Lady Sybil's. 'It's yours,' she said and I had to make an effort not to mirror the glee on her face as I looked at the small room. The bed had a dark blue canopy, a gaily embroidered quilt, piles of cushions and thick blue curtains embroidered with golden suns. When I sat down to let the maid undress me I felt a well-stuffed mattress beneath me. At the foot of the bed there was a carved and polished chest. The table held a golden candlestick, a brass bowl and jug and an arched cupboard with three shelves, an *aumbry*, stood empty against the wall. The fire was burning well in the small hearth and a curtained tub was set in front of it. A small window let out onto the bailey, allowing the smoke to escape from the room and the light to filter in.

The maid and I spoke to each other in a mixture of pidgin French and Welsh. Occasionally she tried words from her own Breton language which had some similarities to Welsh and I could understand her that way. Patting her chest, she told me her name was Amelina. She was a young woman with ample breasts that were a little more visible above the neck of her gown than they should be. She was on the short side and had a very long twist of plaited dark brown hair and grey-green eyes. She told me she was eighteen years old.

Amelina pinned the curtains open on the tub and the scent of cinnamon and cumin filled the room. She unlaced and pulled the nightgown from me and I stepped into the hot water, crouched and then sat as Amelina sponged the mud, blood and tears from me.

Amelina moved over to a pile of clothes heaped on the floor near the chest, holding them up for inspection. They were the garments I had worn on my journey from Llansteffan and looked like muddied, soiled shrouds risen from a grave. 'These will have to go in the rag pile. They're beyond repair.'

'No!' I said. 'My claw.' I had slipped it into the patch pocket of my dress on Llansteffan beach when we were attacked.

'What?'

'I need to keep my claw.'

She frowned at me but rummaged in the pocket and then held up the battered claw between two fingers, a look of disgust on her face. '*This?*' she said incredulously.

'Put it on the shelf.' I closed my eyes and wanted to stay in the tub forever if only the water could stay warm and the tips of my fingers were not wrinkling more and more in pale whorls. I remembered my father drawing the shape of the three rivers in the sand on Llansteffan beach – The Claw. He had shown Goronwy and me how the three rivers reached up from the sea into the land, into the three parts of his kingdom, Dyfed, Ystrad Twyi and Gwyr. 'It's not a shape you can see, even from high up at Llansteffan fort,' he told us, 'but it's a shape a bird will see, that the red kites trace in the air as they give out their haunting whistles, swooping up and down, hunting for prey, all along the three rivers.'

'There's a garderobe, across the passageway,' Amelina interrupted my memories. I allowed my legs to float up to the surface of the water like pale logs. 'And I am yours. Your maid. Lady Sybil says,' she finished lamely, when I made no reply. 'I will sleep there,' she pointed to a low, truckle bed close to the door. Was she my jailer?

She had a clean linen shift laid on the bed for me and the dress she fished from the chest was the smallest she could find but still it swamped me, yet she managed to artfully pin it, gather and belt it so that it was passable. Or so she indicated by her pleased expression. The dress was dark red wool with a black embroidered band across the knees and similar black bands at the cuffs and around the neck. She sat me on the edge of the bed again and brushed my hair in long strokes over and over, one hand firmly on the top of my head to steady me. Finally she wove dark red ribbons intricately through my loose hair.

The bells struck the hour of eleven of the morning, the dinner hour. Amelina led me back down the passageway and the stairs to the hall where dishes were clattering and there was a loud buzz of conversation. She whispered close to my ear, 'Courage, little one,' and propelled me with a small push at my back through the doorway.

The hall was vast, even larger than my father's at his best palace in Dinefwr. Great chandeliers with dozens of candles, hung on iron hoops from the thick beams crossing the high ceiling space; two long trestles accommodated the household and castle visitors; a long hearth burnt in the centre of the hall. Sybil was presiding at the high table. I recognised Gerald FitzWalter but none of the other people sitting with her. There was an empty seat on one of the lower tables and I made for that, lifting the long red skirts of the dress so that I would not trip.

Lady Sybil's voice rang out angrily and all heads turned to me. I looked up and saw she was gesturing at the seat next to her. The heat of humiliation suffused my face. I had wanted to prove I was a royal princess worthy of their respect and had made a fool of myself already. Carefully I climbed the two steps up to the high table and sat down next to her, keeping my eyes away from the men there. 'This is my brother, Arnulf de Montgommery,' she said. I glanced up quickly and nodded my head in acknowledgement, avoiding his eyes. It was impossible to equate this suave, well-dressed man with the chaos of my memories of Llansteffan, with the mud, fire and blood and the noise so loud and cacophonous that I had felt myself somehow suspended, deafened, in the silent centre of it. I had barely looked at him but it had been enough to see that without the nosepiece of his helmet he had lost the pig-like aspect I first noticed when I saw him clad in red and chainmail amidst the flames of my home. He had a well-formed, handsome face with large brown eyes and long hair as black as a raven's wing. His drooping moustaches were a lighter brown colour.

Sybil and Arnulf were in the midst of a conversation in which I heard the name Bernard de Neufmarché again, and also the names of my father, Rhys ap Tewdwr, of Cadwgan, and of their King William. Arnulf was doing most of the talking. At one point he must have said something indiscreet because Sybil touched her fingers to his mouth. 'Shhh.' She dropped her usual strident voice to an intimate murmur. These two were close. Sybil swivelled in her seat towards me.

'How old are you, girl?' It was him, her brother addressing me. FitzWalter cleared his throat and translated the words for me. 'She doesn't understand you,' he said apologetically to Arnulf.

'Twelve,' I said, keeping my eyes on the table.

Sybil and Arnulf resumed their conversation and I glanced at FitzWalter but he did not translate any more words for me. I heard the words 'marry … Welsh … Norman … Pembroke.' Sybil nodded her head.

'I am betrothed, my lady,' I said in halting French.

Sybil looked astonished that I had addressed her and in words she could understand. She said something in a sarcastic voice to Arnulf who let out a harsh shout of a laugh and asked me a question. 'To whom?' FitzWalter translated.

I swallowed. I had hoped to avoid any conversation with any of them. I should have kept silent. 'Owain ap Cadwgan, Prince of Powys,' I said quietly.

Arnulf slammed his goblet down on the table. 'That bastard, Cadwgan!' He made a theatrical expression of astonishment to his sister. I had learnt that word from my father's Norman hostages and heard it coupled with Cadwgan's name before. Arnulf made a remark about Owain and he and Sybil laughed. I noticed FitzWalter regarding me with a look of pity. I did not want his pity. I returned his gaze stonily until he looked away, frowning.

'May I help you to some sauce, Lady Nest?' the man sitting to my right asked in Welsh. His accent garbled the words but I could make out what he was saying. He was a man in mid-life with grey hair that had once been orange judging by the traces of that bleached out colour still lingering in places. His fingers were stubby and stained with brown ink.

Relieved to be let away from the discussion between the brother and sister, I turned to him. 'Thank you.' I reached for a trencher from the pile on the table. It was Wednesday, a fish day. Bowls of lampreys, mussels and pickled fish were set before us.

'I am Richard Belmeis, clerk to the Montgommery family, and will be teaching you your letters and to speak French as if you were born and raised in Normandy,' he told me cheerfully, and then repeated his words in French for Sybil and Arnulf's benefit.

Sybil snorted. It was an ugly sound. 'Do your best, Master Richard,' she told him in a voice laced with scepticism.

In the morning Gerald FitzWalter was in the bailey below with his men, leading their saddled horses from the stables, tightening girths, loading bedrolls, readying to leave. Since it seemed I had the run of the castle, I determined to go down and ask him my favour, as he had been kind to me before.

In the bailey I climbed up onto a mounting block to keep my feet safe from the horses chafing to be out of the crowded space. 'Are you leaving, Sir Gerald?' I called out.

He turned his horse's head to regard me. He looked amused to see me on my perch. 'Yes I must return to my duty at Pembroke. Take care of yourself, little princess.' He still called me that when Lady Sybil was not in earshot. She had told him sharply that I was no such thing and he should not mislead me into thinking it. I was sorry to see Gerald go. He was the only human being who had given a kind word to me since Llansteffan. Now I would be left here with Lady Sybil who was as tender as granite.

'Can I ask you a favour, sir?'

Gerald frowned. 'What is it, princess?'

'My brother, my half-brother Idwal, who was captured in the battle. I would like to know how he fares. Perhaps I could send a letter to him?'

'I doubt it,' Gerald said curtly, starting to turn his horse away. Seeing the expression on my face, he relented. 'I will try to find out for you but it's unlikely I can bring you any good news of your family. Lady Sybil's household is your family now and you must make shift.' His cheerful expression sobered. 'I fear there is little kindness in war, Nest.'

'Another question, sir!' I called out, seeing him start to turn his horse again. 'Who killed my brother Goronwy on Llansteffan beach?'

'Neufmarché's men I suppose.' He called out a command and was gone, riding swiftly through the castle gateway followed by his soldiers. I watched his back retreating out of view, feeling pathetic in my desire to latch on to someone, like a motherless duckling, seeing him leave me and feeling more bereft than before.

* * *

Long ago Henry watched me writing. 'Always scribbling like an inky clerk, Nest!' he said and gave me this book. I smoothed the palm of my hand down the fine vellum of its blank pages and began to scribe the story of my life. It gave me comfort in the hardest times and was my constant companion, but after the Battle of Crug Mawr I had no heart to write anymore so I put the book at the bottom of a chest brimful with jumbled documents – letters, bills, writs, charters, testaments, genealogies, maps.

Now my nephew Rhys is asking me questions about the past to help him in his contentions with the Norman lords in Deheubarth, so I unearthed my neglected journal and collected together other pertinent papers in my possession including the notes scribed by Sir Gerald FitzWalter at Pembroke Castle in Wales and the copybook of Sister Benedicta containing correspondence with her brother. Rustling between these papers is the story of my life and my land.

Like an 'inky clerk' I have put them into a kind of chronological order and look with amazement on the story they tell between them which I was all unaware of at the time. You never know how the past will turn out. Henry's sister Countess Adela once wrote, 'Lest acts be confounded by oblivion through time, let us take care to recall them in memory with virile writings.'

I will give Rhys his answers distilled from these pages to help guide him, yet I will not give him this book full as it is with so much tinder that if lit the conflagration might consume the world, or at least my castle here at Llansteffan where I sit at the end of my days. Llansteffan has seen conflagrations enough already.

I never thought to be so old. The backs of my hands look like dry old parchments that might themselves be written upon. This brown-spotted tissue-thin skin was once moon-pale, my long fingers and thumbs loaded with gems winking in candlelight. In that time, long ago, powerful men did things they should not have done for the sight of me. There is relief *and* regret that my time as

24

that young woman is all over with now. From the perspective of old age, love and desire seem like a madness driving our lives; a madness that I miss nevertheless.

The shifting scenes written down here are like two parallel games of chess: with one hand Henry plays against me and my Welsh compatriots, and with his other hand he plays against the Anglo-Norman barons. Most times he won, but not always. I am so old that my bones ache and creak: my knee, my hip, my shoulder. I shift over and over at night seeking a position to hold the pain at bay and find sleep and when I cannot sleep I read and wonder at the variegated story of my life.

I insert here the first extract from the correspondence of the Flemish knight Haith with his sister Benedicta, a nun at the Abbey of Almenêches in Normandy. Haith was in service to Henry, the youngest son of William the Conqueror. The Flemish brother and sister wrote to each other in a cipher that my clerk decoded and translated from the Flemish, a book code based on a psalter their mother gave them, a copy to each. Benedicta sent her copybook of the letters to me when she knew she would write no more. I have Haith's psalter and he marked the passage for himself deciphering the code so it was not difficult for my clerk to follow and reveal their words to one another.

* * *

From the Copybook of Sister Benedicta

Gloucester, Easter, 1093

Greetings dear sister, wise mistress of the holy dishes! I picture you there in your Abbey, marshalling your pots and pans and commanding the swivels of your spoons and ladles. Here, as promised, is your next instalment of the adventures of your little brother in the cipher as you demand, but guard these papers well, Benedicta, or at least the psalter that reveals the code, for my tears would flood the land if harm came to my Lord Henry from the betrayal of any words of mine.

We find ourselves back in England after such a long sojourn in Normandy. We are in Gloucester but it has been a sorry time for we came here expecting the death of Henry's brother, King William Rufus. Count Robert de Meulan took us to ship across the Channel and then up the Severn with haste when news came that the King was gravely ill.

The King has no heir and it is in the minds of Meulan and Henry that my lord is the unspoken heir to England and would make a better one than the oldest brother, Duke Robert Curthose. This nickname for the Duke, Curthose, meaning short legs, was his father the Conqueror's invention, he taunted him with it – I heard it myself – and it sticks still. I am a biased commentator as you often chastise me but I assure you, Benedicta, Henry would be a most careful, astute king with a true sense of his responsibilities as God's caretaker of the country, whereas I have seen Curthose's court first hand and there is no proper care for the people of his lands there. You see that yourself in the poor people crowding at the alms door of your Abbey, or in your hospital, those who have lost everything in the constant warfare of the lords in the surrounding countryside.

They say that at William Rufus' court everything is for sale, including the King's love. (He is nicknamed Rufus, Benedicta, because of his ruddy cheeks. Ruddy with drinking I suppose, or fornication – I put that in to check that you are awake.) Henry's father, the Conqueror, has left behind him a sorry legacy of contention between his three sons and divided loyalties and lands in England and Normandy for his barons. I think Meulan is right to see Henry as the brother who could heal these contentions and divisions. He has a brain of brilliance I assure you. He is up hours before me and the sun each morning and when I finally join him yawning with my hair awry he tells me I look like a sleepy lion and someone should throw a bucket of cold water over me! 'Why do you rise so early, my lord?' I asked him.

'Because I wake with my brain burbling at me,' he says. 'I can lie there in bed with my head rattling through lists of things to do and sudden new thoughts that I need to write down, or I can rise and start putting those lists and ideas into action.'

'I don't have that problem at all my lord,' I say.

'I am well aware of that, my friend!' he says laughing. 'Never mind. One burbling brain is enough between the two of us.'

One morning, when we were all at Gloucester waiting on news from the sick king's doctors, I overslept and lay in a dark corner of the hall near the hearth, rolled in my cloak. I was roused awake by the rasp of a bench as Meulan and his brother Henry, Earl of Warwick, sat down close to where I lay. They did not see me, thinking everyone was about their business by that hour. When I realised the content of their discussion I stayed as still as I could, just about able to hear and see them through a bald patch in my cloak. I put this conversation down verbatim here and I passed it on to my Lord Henry later that day.

'I am glad to see you in England brother,' Warwick began. He is the younger of the two brothers and has been a solid supporter of King William Rufus.

'I think you will see more of me in England now.'

I was intrigued to know more of Meulan who has a formidable and I would say well-earned reputation as warrior and politician. He fought as a young man at Hastings with the Conqueror, gaining vast lands here in England as a result which he mostly passed on to his brother Warwick, since Meulan also has substantial lands in Normandy and France. There is an accord between these two brothers that alas, is not there for the sons of the Conqueror.

'More of you in England?' Warwick asked Meulan, surprise in his voice.

'I've tried for the last five years to give my support to Curthose in Normandy whilst you fulfilled our bargain working for the family's interests alongside Rufus here in England, but Curthose is unruly. He cannot control the Norman barons, especially Bellême, the eldest of the Montgommery brood, who arrogantly seeks autonomy for himself and has no equal in battle.'

'What then?'

'I'm minded to jump ship from Curthose's court in Normandy to Rufus' here in England, to work alongside you. What do you think?'

'I would be overjoyed, brother. The Conqueror's sons can find no condominium between them and their contentions threaten the gains of the Conquest. This divided kingdom where we are

pulled and pushed between two warring lords is in nobody's interest. They say every kingdom divided against itself is brought to
desolation. But how would we protect our interests in Normandy
and France if you are here?'

'I can continue both for now. It will be a while before
Curthose realises what I am about and by then we will have dealt
with him.'

'Dealt with him? It has come to that? What has caused this
fracture between you?'

'He threw me into prison unjustifiably over an argument concerning rights to Brionne and Bec and I'd be mouldering there
still if it hadn't been for the skilful intercession of our father.'

'You harbour a grudge from that?'

'A grudge, yes, but a doubt also at the Duke's judgement and
that doubt has grown since. The rebellion in England against
King William and in Curthose's favour in eighty-eight was a
disaster. I've seen many instances of weakness in his rule in Normandy since.'

Warwick was silent for a few moments, his fingers steepled
beneath his chin. 'You think Rufus will gain the upper hand in
Normandy as well as England.'

'He's been deliberately pursuing a policy of undermining
Curthose's rule in Normandy for the last few years. He is the
superior commander in battle and has England's wealth in his
hands, whereas Curthose is permanently impecunious.'

'Curthose is brave, successful on the battlefield. He's proved
that time and again.'

'Yes, but it's always a flash in a pan. There's no following
through with him.'

'Rufus' rule is not without its issues.'

Meulan raised his eyebrows and waited for his brother's considered response.

'The King shows no inclination to marry. At all. He has alien-
ated the English churchmen beyond remedy. The country is well
managed because of those who serve him, such as Flambard,
FitzHamon and myself, and not because of King William's own
wisdom. He's only really happy in chainmail. He is aggression
walking – when he's well.'

'Yes this marries with my own observations and that's why I persuaded Count Henry to accompany me here.'

Warwick leant forward. 'How far ahead are you looking brother?'

'Far enough.' Meulan allowed himself a small, grim smile. 'Rufus has inherited his father's belligerence but none of his policy. Curthose is his mother's son – too courteous and genial for his own good. Henry – now there are the qualities of the Conqueror melded together and breathing again.'

They rose from the trestle and strolled out of the hall together so that I was able to fight free of the cloak I was bundled beneath and go to wash my head under the spigot in the courtyard.

At any rate it has not come to any such serious thing as the throne of England for my Lord Henry and perhaps never will. King William, thinking himself about to die, took the step that Meulan and Warwick advised and appointed that famous Anselm de Bec as Archbishop of Canterbury. Anselm is strongly urging the King to marry as soon as possible now he regains his strength day by day. The King assures his advisers he will do all they suggest but that has not been his previous record. I'm not confident he will remember the fearful sweats of his sickness now he is in health again. If William does marry soon he can get his own heirs for England so then Henry and I will be able to return to our less heavy responsibilities in Domfront, giving me the opportunity to visit with you before too long and look on your dear face, with those eyes that shine as brightly as your scoured pans.

Looking forward to your chronicle of Almenêches, fare thee as well as I fare Benedicta, your loving brother Haith.

Almenêches Abbey, Normandy, Midsummer, St John's Eve, June 1093

To my dearest brother, Sir Haith, from Benedicta, nun of Almenêches, with the affection of sisterly love, greetings and blessings. You must change your picture of me. I am no longer twirling pots and pans in the Abbey kitchen. I am promoted to librarian and mistress of the scriptorium and furthermore this has given me a better place to hide my copybook with your coded letters inside along with copies of my own to you. It is concealed within the wooden covers of the dullest, dustiest old text you can think of on algebra that is of absolute no interest to anyone except moths and bugs. So it hides in plain sight in the library, under my sharp nose. Before proceeding to my chronicle I must thank you, my giant of a 'little' brother, with the most enormous hug in imagination for your delightful gift of the arm-warmers. Though I am older and of course a great deal wiser than you, my head barely reaches your shoulder, so I must send you this imaginary hug low down at chest level and hope that your unkempt head, so far above, can take some notice. You cannot even begin to know how welcome those armwarmers are in my new post since the library is a little chilly on the fingers to say the least. But scarlet wool, Haith! For a nun. You are incorrigible. Yet you are right: they do remind me of mother, her marvellous bright weavings, and our old home in dear Bruges. Thank you so much!

I could not be inconspicuous with a pair of scarlet arm-warmers poking out of my habit so I had to ask the Abbess for permission to wear them. She was all kindness, admired their softness and colour, and the even greater gift, she said, of a kind brother. It is not God's will, she told me, that her scriptorium mistress (yes, that is my new title, you oaf), that I should have frostbitten fingers. She does not know exactly who my brother *is*, of course, that you are in service to Count Henry. The Abbey swarms with the Abbess' family, the Montgommerys, as it should, since their father was our first noble patron and is our benefactor still. I judged it best to be a little circumspect on your service to Count Henry since the Montgommerys all hate him violently after he took the citadel of Domfront from the Abbess' brother, Bellême. I told her merely that you are a landless Flemish knight offering military service here and there, to various lords and sending me news from the courts and households you pass through.

I thank God's mercy King William has recovered and seen fit to appoint such a saintly man as Anselm as Archbishop. And you have met him! I thank God also, that I am blessed with such a conduit of the greatest news of the realms of Normandy and England as yourself, to enliven my dull days here (though holy of course). Tell me all about the Archbishop, won't you, in your next letter. I hear he is a very great man. I pray King William will heed counsel now from his religious men and take a wife. If only Duke Robert would follow suit here in Normandy but I fear he has little concern for the present and future of his poor kingdom where there is constant warfare and suffering.

Do you really think your Lord Henry might be King William's successor? I understood there was a mutual agreement between the two *older* brothers – that Duke Robert was William's heir to England and vice versa, King William was Duke Robert's heir to Normandy. Have they reneged on that truce already, or is it just the will of Meulan and Henry that it might change so? You write of Duke Robert and King William's nicknames. Your Henry is nicknamed Beauclerc for his learning I believe. A king must be a warrior as well as clever. I suppose Henry does have that capacity, from what I hear of his and your battle exploits in the Contentin? It would be a heavy thing to lift indeed if your lord should ascend to such greatness and responsibilities as the throne of England. How that would change your prospects and your sphere Haith! If there is something I can do from my enclosed state here to help you both, I hope you will tell me so.

Each night after supper and before the service at Vespers, Abbess Emma and I talk a while warming our toes before the good fire in her room. She was glad to hear the news of Anselm's appointment. She tells me what she hears of Duke Robert from her brothers Robert de Bellême and Roger de Montgommery who are sometimes here at our visiting window talking with her. I contrive to walk past behind her when they come to the grille to catch a glimpse of those great men. Yes, before you tease me, I have said my penances for it! Her oldest brother Bellême is a distinguished and comely man but rumour tells his soul is not as fair as his exterior. He seems the source of most of the trouble Duke Robert has to contend with in Normandy.

How strange that you and I, who are so dear to one another, find ourselves in two different camps – you holding tight and fast to your Henry, and me in a nest of Montgommerys. The Abbess' niece, Matilda de Montgommery, the daughter of another of her brothers, Philippe, recently entered the Abbey as a novice. The night before her arrival I applied grease to the hinges of our great bossed door since it had not been opened for over a year. Last time was when one of the oldest sisters died and her body was removed, so this was a more cheerful occasion. Abbess Emma produced her keys and unlocked the three locks, and two sisters hefted the door open, its wood creaking and protesting. All the sisters lined up to greet the new entrant – in silence of course – but with kind gestures and eyes. The girl, Matilda, stepped in and startled when the great door banged shut behind her. I remember that moment for myself very well, when I entered the Abbey just six years old, thinking I would never see you or the world again. I was so miserable at it I paled and threw up on the ground in front of all the nuns, and the Abbess was so kind to me instead of beating me as I thought she might.

Come again soon to our visiting window, Haith. I am longing to see your leonine head framed there and be relieved of my tedium. Take great care of your lord and of yourself, with all the affection of my heart, fare well, Benedicta.

3

Becoming Norman

Through the glimpse of the outside afforded by the castle gateway, I watched Gerald FitzWalter's troop cross the drawbridge and disappear into the early morning mist that was rising from the river and lingering in twisted, shifting swathes across the fields. Sybil's voice rang out behind me, scolding. She gestured that I must come back into the hall. I moved past her with my eyes cast down, fixed on the mound of her belly.

The elderly man from dinner, the one with orange-grey hair, stood waiting for me at the trestle. Servants bustled around the hall setting it to rights after the feast and departure of the men. Hounds wound around table legs hoping to find a last scrap. Two maids, laughing, flung a clean cloth between them to drape over the high table, disturbing dust motes suspended in the sunlight. A boy swept the dirty rushes into a pile. It was a familiar scene but I did not belong here.

I turned to the tutor. Master Richard wore costly clothes, showy even for a clerk. His complexion and build however were the clerk's: pale and feeble. 'This way, Lady Nest,' Master Richard gestured to the staircase and I followed him up to the first floor and along the narrow passageway that went past the door to Lady Sybil's chamber, then past my chamber, and then the empty guest room next to mine. On the other side of the passageway, opposite the guest room, we came to a studded wooden door opening into an extraordinary room.

Master Richard's chamber was square with a large rectangular table in its midst. A fire cracked and spat in the hearth to the left of the doorway. Directly opposite the door, beyond the table, a glass vitrine sat on a narrow bench top and filled the length of the wall, beneath a large window. Inside the vitrine were hundreds of dry, pale brown insects of a type I did not know, like small crickets. A small arched opening to the right of the vitrine was roped off. Perhaps it was Master Richard's own garderobe. Every other inch of wall space was lined from floor to ceiling with shelves of books, scrolls and piles of parchments.

Seeing me staring at the insect vitrine, Master Richard declared, 'Say hello to my locusts. All the way from the Holy Lands. I'm studying them.'

I tried not to grimace. They clambered over each other, seething behind the glass, but the most disquieting thing was that the glass was thick enough to almost entirely muffle the chirping racket that I knew they must be making. You could simply *see* the sound of them, and I heard it later in my dreams. Master Richard loved his locusts. Sometimes he would lift the lid a crack to feed them, and then their rustling and bowing would invade the room and they would trample across each other in a frenzy to devour their food.

Master Richard chuckled fondly, watching them as though he were mooning over a newborn baby. 'If I were to let them out,' he told me gleefully, 'they would swarm and fly great distances, consuming all the green vegetation wherever they settle, stripping the fields and laying all to waste.'

They are like Normans then, I thought.

'It's also possible to eat them,' he said. 'Quite a delicacy.' He stroked the glass top, stupidly licking his lips at his paramours. Above the tank, a window flooded the room with light and gave a view onto the top of the wooden palisade of the outer bailey and over that I could just glimpse the rolling green countryside beyond.

There were two chairs, facing each other across the table. Richard took his seat with his back to the locusts and I sat opposite him, trying to ignore them. I trembled at the thought that he might crack the lid too wide one day and they would fly out in a brown clicking cloud and devour us in a thrice, leaving just our grinning skeletons here, the bones of our fingers turning the pages, the books now full of holes and lacy shreds.

With Master Richard I learnt French, French history, a little Latin, and a little mathematics. Slowly and patiently he taught me to read. He was a good teacher although I found his disquisitions on Carolingian and Capetians kings in France sometimes tiresome. His speech was constantly interspersed with 'ers', so that I had to quell my impatience for him to get to his point.

Master Richard had me copy out a genealogy of the Montgommery family. Sybil had five brothers and two of them, Robert de Bellême and Roger the Poitevin, had married heiresses who would each soon inherit a county in France, greatly enriching their husbands. Arnulf evidently had in mind to play the same trick by marrying me. I resolved to do what I could to resist such a marriage that would lend credence to Arnulf's rule of my father's kingdom and mitigate against the Welsh resistance to the Norman occupation. I saw on the genealogy that one of Sybil's sisters had died in childbed and another was Abbess of a nunnery in Normandy.

'The girl is obsessed with genealogies,' Master Richard told Lady Sybil in a humourous tone, thinking to make fun of me.

'Yes, well, unlike you Master Belmeis,' Sybil responded in her usual acid fashion, 'she has one.'

When Master Richard was busy elsewhere and left me alone with parchment and ink I occupied myself with something more useful than Norman genealogies: drawing up a genealogy of the Welsh Royal Families. There was sad reading here when I con templated it. The Normans were invading our bloodlines as well as our lands and there were few of us left to eject them. I thought sadly of how my mother used to keep a family chart rolled and wrapped under her bed, along with her large bible. She brought out the family chart ceremoniously whenever the occasion warranted, marking up new births, marriages and deaths. Even a death could be a delight to her because it gave the opportunity to make a new mark on the chart and remind us all of our lineage.

The chroniclers called my father the last king and wrote that with his death the kingdom of the Britons fell to the Normans, but my infant brother Gruffudd, concealed in Ireland, was the

Edling of Deheubarth, the rightful heir and there was a Welsh king in Powys still – Cadwgan. Master Richard, however, told me Cadwgan was a 'client king', not a real one, owing allegiance to the King of the English and my father had been the last *independent* king in Wales. I thought Cadwgan would look mightily askance at that interpretation. Seeing the mere handful of surviving Welsh royalty on the pedigree I saw how fragile we were, how vital my marriage to Owain ap Cadwgan was. What could I do to bring it about?

Here I insert the first extract from the notes of Gerald Fitz-Walter, castellan of Pembroke Castle, my father's former *llys* and now usurped by Arnulf de Montgommery.

* * *

From Gerald FitzWalter's Day Book

Pembroke Castle, Michaelmas, September 1093

Up in the dark this morning with so much to do, the rain thrumming on the thatch and the waters rushing round the foot of the castle. The men on duty are coughing and cursing as I undertake my regular round on the battlement walkways at first light. The damp seeps into everything, my throat is perpetually sore and yet I love it here. My place, my first command. Everything I do here comes from my own efforts.

The rain began to clear with the first glimmers of dawn. Smoke rolls lazily from the hall's smoke-hole, a pungent black bloom staining the pale sky. Looking out across the fields I wonder every morning at the stolidity of cows, as they lie stoic in the ceaseless drizzle. A boy in the courtyard below chases a goat escaped from its tether and slips round a corner on horse dung, swearing like a well-practised soldier. He'd best catch that goat before it gets into the cook's vegetable patch or he won't be able to sit down for a week. A loud squawking catches my attention. One of the castle cats has found a nest on the riverbank and runs past with a small bird protesting desperately in its mouth. Draggled pigeons shelter beneath the buttresses.

All things considered I am well pleased with the events of this year of 1093, the seventh year of the reign of King William Rufus in England and of his brother Duke Robert in Normandy, and my first year as Castellan of Pembroke Castle. I had not expected such responsibility so soon and mean to capitalise upon it. I have written to my brother and family at Windsor Castle to tell them of my advancement. It is a lonely posting that feels some days like the very edge of the world, far from anywhere or anyone, but other days I celebrate that our banners are planted squarely at the very frontier and I am charged with keeping them there.

My lord requires me to send him regular reports so I set down here my experiences that I might distill my reports from these notes. My schooling at Abingdon Abbey, when my father intended to give me as a novice monk, has come in useful after all. If I could not scribe these notes myself I would have to be more circumspect in what is written down.

Our progress in Wales has not been as straightforward as William the Conqueror's capture of the Anglo-Saxon kingdom. Here we have more than one king to contend with and a sodden, mountainous, forested terrain besides, that prowls with wolves and rebels. The Conqueror gave the borderlands between England and Wales to the great barons, Roger de Montgommery, Hugh d'Avranches and William FitzOsbern and they used them as bridgeheads to extend the Norman domains into Wales.

Until recent times, the three strongest royal families of Wales were the House of Aberffraw, the House of Dinefwr and the House of Mathrafal. The House of Aberffraw once ruled in the north in Gwynedd but Hugh d'Avranches, Earl of Chester tricked that prince, Gruffudd ap Cynan, into a prison some thirteen years ago. Earl Hugh expands greatly in all directions – in his rule and in his immensely fat person. I know not how he succeeds in sitting on a horse or how any horse can bear it. His nephew Robert of Rhuddlan made inroads into Gwynedd but this summer he was ambushed and killed by Welsh insurgents. This mountainous, forested and boggy land is no good for our usual cavalry tactics and the western coast is still plagued by Viking raiders from Ireland and the isles.

Of the House of Dinefwr that ruled in the south, in Deheubarth, King Rhys ap Tewdwr, his heir Goronwy and his illegitimate son Cynan are lately dead. At Easter when King William was gravely ill and the doctors were sure he would die, when there was no hand on the tiller in Westminster, Arnulf, his brothers and allies in Wales rose up to take what gains they could. After the battle at Aberhonddu, Bernard de Neufmarché gave Idwal, Rhys' surviving illegitimate son, into my custody. I sent him in chains to Windsor Castle and he is imprisoned there in my brother's gaol.

Of the House of Mathrafal that rules in Powys and parts of Ceredigion, King Cadwgan gives us allegiance, but he has proven countless times to be an untrustworthy trickster. His brothers Iorwerth and Maredudd are also capable warriors and we can expect further turbulence from that quarter.

Lord Robert FitzHamon, who is married to my lord Arnulf's sister, Lady Sybil, has firm control in Glamorgan (or Morgannwg) and the Welsh there are confined to the uplands, their efforts at resistance like so many butterflies flying against a thickly glazed window. Neufmarché likewise has a firm hold on Brecknock, that the Welsh call Brycheiniog. My lord's father and brothers command the borderlands around Montgommery and Shrewsbury. Slowly we are slinging a broader and broader band of occupation that squeezes nearer and nearer to the mountain heartlands where the Welsh rebels hide out.

As soon as King Rhys died there was a rush into the absence he left behind him. Cadwgan plundered in Dyfed but retreated before Arnulf's advance. Arnulf's father and older brother Hugh marched straight into Cardigan and established a castle there and then came on to Pembroke to assist our efforts here. William FitzBaldwin has arrived by sea from Devon on orders from King William Rufus and has built a castle on the river Tywi, not far from Carmarthen.

Cadwgan is edging his territory further into Ceredigion but in the coming months I will push him back and take those lands for Arnulf. Deheubarth, where we occupy, is rich and fertile with herds on the saltmarshes and fine harbours for traders. Perhaps in time, Lord Arnulf, will gift me my own estate here. It is more than I looked for as my father's youngest son and all my best hopes lie in these Welsh frontier lands.

It was reported to Arnulf's scout at the battle of Aberhonddu that Neufmarché wanted to get the location of King Rhys' other sons from the captured son, Cynan, and he threatened him with drowning to gain the information but Cynan would not speak and so the young man was drowned by Neufmarché's men. This Cynan ap Rhys was of an age with me, seventeen. At first I flinched contemplating Neufmarché's harsh proceedings but I know I must harden my own mind on this model of necessary brutalities if I mean to rise. Yet to fight and kill honourably in battle is one thing but this .... He was already badly injured and would perhaps have died in any case, but even so, it is the knight's code to deal with prisoners in war courteously. William the Conqueror severely punished a Norman knight who desecrated the body of the fallen Anglo-Saxon King Harald at the Battle at Hastings. 'Are we butchers or knights!' he asked in fury but it is not always easy to see that distinction. Neufmarché argues the Welsh are not even half-civilised and cannot merit chivalry, but I saw their *llys* before the destructions we wrought on them, I heard the poems and singing of their bards and I cannot say I am fully in agreement with him, though I keep my opinion to myself.

At Llansteffan we had to dispatch the young *Edling*, Goronwy. Where one Welsh King is extinguished another one rises from his kin, so Arnulf tells me we must exterminate the Welsh nobility if we mean to gain and hold these lands. He hopes he will be confirmed as Count of Pembroke soon. Rhys ap Tewdwr's queen is in the custody of William FitzBaldwin at Rhydygors Castle near Carmarthen and was with child. If she bears a boy it will not be allowed to live.

Arnulf ordered me to convey the dead King's daughter, Nest, to his sister Sybil de Montgommery at Cardiff Castle for educating. When I arrived after a wet journey and mucky roads, Lady Sybil was unhappy I had bound the girl and seeing the welts on her wrists I saw the lady was right, and regretted it. I told Sybil I was afraid the princess might try to run because the Welsh are like forest sprites, dissolving into the trees. Sybil's Breton maid,

Amelina, who is of a poetical turn of mind it seems, on seeing the princess, said, 'She is very beautiful. She looks like Wales – her eyes like the brilliant blue wind-driven skies and the colour of her hair reminding me of the black rugged mountains.' But Lady Sybil clicked her tongue and told her this was nonsense. 'She looks like a poor orphaned child to me,' she said.

I could see Amelina's fancy though in the Princess' face. I had to force myself to look elsewhere lest she, or worse Arnulf or Sybil, should notice. She has a strong face, not soft and blurred – every feature is distinctive, the nose, the dimpled chin, the expressive dark brows, another dimple that fascinates in one of her cheeks when she smiles, which, poor girl, she has little cause for. The contrasts of her colours are so strong: the dark pink and light brown of her flesh, the brilliant blue of her eyes, the red of her mouth and the deep rich black of her hair and lashes. And a sharp humour ready on her tongue. I should not linger on my memories of her but instead bury this unwarranted interest. The likes of her are not for the likes of me.

'What does Arnulf mean sending her here?' Lady Sybil asked me.

'He said only to request you teach her French and give her an education.'

'Does he mean to marry her?'

'I imagine it could be in his mind, my lady. It would be an effective way of quelling resistance from the local populace for his rule in Pembroke. Such a stratagem worked well for Neufmarché in Brecknock where he wed the half-Welsh princess Agnes.'

'Yes marriage with a local heiress is good policy. Total disinheritance of the local nobility is a foolish and dangerous course. Arnulf is arriving tonight on his way to give King William news from Deheubarth, so I will tell him to be more fulsome and courteous with his requirements. I need to know if I am educating her to be his wife, or if he has some other purpose. Perhaps she will be of use to me in the meantime as I am close to birthing and will have a baby son to care for soon, God willing.'

'There's no royal family of Deheubarth left for the Welsh to rally to now,' I told her.

'So those teeth are pulled. Neufmarché is most assiduous in his murderings in my brother's lands.' She looked to see my response.

'He is.' I exchanged a frank look with the lady.

'Do you think he carries out this massacre of the Deheubarth family intending to claim the territory himself?'

I needed to be circumspect but the lady was astute and voiced my own fears. 'I think Neufmarché is the very pattern of aggressive ambition.'

She bit her lip and considered. 'Yes. I hope you will do your duty and make sure Arnulf is aware of this.'

'I will my lady. And rest assured I will defend your brother's interests to the full of my ability.'

'Good. I trust and believe you will Sir Gerald. King William and my husband will be pleased to hear this news of the advances made. If the King survives.'

I asked her, 'What is the news from Gloucester?'

'The King is slightly improved. He may be out of danger, but if he dies, then Duke Robert will take the throne.'

'Has his brother been summoned to the King's sick bed then?' I asked.

'There is no mention of that in my husband's letters.' Her husband, Robert FitzHamon is King William's leading counsellor so she is well informed about the doings of the King.

The following day, Lord Arnulf joined us at the castle to discuss with his sister and myself the recent events and to take a look at his intended bride. At dinner he told us, 'The King's sickness has been brought on by his debauchery, heavy drinking and the like. Neufmarché took the initiative, deciding to take matters into his own hands in Wales thinking King William would die. The Prince of Powys, Cadwgan, joined with us against King Rhys but he would have taken Pembroke from us if he could.' Arnulf got to Pembroke Castle before Cadwgan and so prevented his intended occupation there. 'When our true king, Duke Robert Curthose, replaces William,' Arnulf said, 'there will be even greater reward for us.' His sister hushed him for reckless treasonous speech. The Montgommery family are adamantine in their support for Duke Robert's claim to the English throne. Their father made them all swear an oath to it and they none of them care for William Rufus and have not gotten the preferments they hoped for from him. I must take care this record cannot fall into the wrong hands and condemn my lord if the King does survive.

Arnulf's sister wisely told him, 'I know your need for your own domain is great, as our father's fifth son, but take care, Arnulf. There are ears in the walls and spies at cracks in the doors, even here, no doubt. King William is not dead yet and looks likely to recover.'

They turned their attention next to the princess who was seated with us, but not comprehending much of the conversation.

'I want to have a close look at this girl,' Lady Sybil told Lord Arnulf. 'At the wild Welsh foundling my brother sees fit to bring into my home.'

Arnulf told her the princess will soon be a fine-looking woman. She wore her mass of glossy black hair shot through with dark red ribbons. Although she has been through a great trauma with the massacre of her family she bears herself with courage nevertheless. She will make my lord a fine wife. The girl has a few words of French already and Arnulf told his sister to work quickly in educating her.

'You think the King will recover?' Arnulf asked sullenly and his sister told him yes, that was the latest news. 'And what about *his* marriage prospects then? He shows no sign of putting aside his affections for the men of his court and taking a respectable wife.'

Lady Sybil coloured and lent down to pet a hound at her knee, to recover herself. It is known, and doubtless the lady has heard it too, that King William is most affectionate with her husband, Robert FitzHamon.

A few days later I returned to Pembroke Castle to set about putting affairs in order here. The garrison at Pembroke numbers around fifty men of varying ability and weaponry. The men are mostly solid but a few slackers had to be disciplined or reassigned. The castle is well sited on a bend in the river, atop the river cliff. It has a curious old cave beneath that lets out to the river, named The Wogan. There are some splinterings and rottings in the wooden palisade that need repair. I will ride out and assess the condition of other nearby places in time but for now my efforts will be focussed on making this base unassailable. Food and water supplies are sound, with ample winter fodder for the horses and livestock. The water way has been silting up and I ordered it cleared. The forest abounds with fuel and big timbers for construction.

There has been little resistance to us here, since most of Rhys' leading men were killed in the battle and his sons all dispatched or captured. His brother, Rhydderch, might have posed a threat. He could have tried to assert a right to the kingdom but he had little support from the Welsh and swiftly gave his submission to Arnulf.

In the nearby port towns of Tenby, Milford and Haverford there is a mix of Norman, Irish, Norse, Welsh and Flemish traders. I will need to review and report to my lord on the matter of their taxes and the revenues he might expect from wool and wood trading, from agriculture hereabouts and from tolls. I have just taken the Michaelmas rents and it was no simple matter since there is no common use of money amongst the Welsh and everything has to be done with barter and goods in kind and then I have to translate this into money to send on to Arnulf. Although it amounted to a goodly sum I suspect there is much that has not been rendered and few records are truly in good order. This I will rectify before the next rent day.

This year has seen a great advance for my Lord Arnulf and for us all in Wales. His father, the Earl, was pleased and Arnulf has gone to his lands in England, leaving me in command. I mean to make my life, my stand here. Now that I have a toehold in this land nothing will shake me loose.

4

The Lay of the Land

Cardiff castle was like a small village and with plenty going on. From my chamber I could hear the shouts of soldiers and servants, the crowing of the cockerel and donkeys braying. I knelt on the chest below my window and watched the comings and goings, provisions being carried into the kitchen, horses led from the stables for exercising. The grassed compound of the lower bailey had several thatched wooden buildings and a well in the central clear space. In addition to the stables and the kitchen, there was a chapel, smithy, bake house, henhouse, pigpen, brew house, armoury, latrines and various storehouses. The hall building that I lived in was much larger than the others and the only one with two storeys.

I decided to see how far I might be allowed to explore my prison. 'May I go anywhere in the castle my lady?' I asked Sybil.

She stared at me for a while. 'Yes, you may go anywhere but not outside the main gate. You are on trust as a hostage here. If you try to do anything stupid Nest you will be punished. I hope you will not put me in the position of needing to do that? I need your word on it.'

'I give you my word, Lady Sybil.'

I strolled out of the hall and looked around. The main gate was kept closed and heavily guarded. It was only opened if the lookouts high in the barbican tower above the drawbridge were satisfied they knew the visitors or tradesmen and they offered no threat. I wandered over to the henhouse, bakehouse and then the brewhouse, smelling their different smells, the chicken shit, the bread rising and the thick malty smell of beer brewing. Servants bent tending vegetable gardens, a boy stood on the edge of the duck and fishpond throwing scraps to the ducks and then he turned with a bucket to feed the pigs. I went to watch them snuffle and grunt their satisfaction, barging each other out of the way, treading on each other's toes to reach the food he threw to them.

In the chapel I admired the golden candlesticks and a jewelled casket on the altar while the chaplain stood at the door keeping an eye on me. The soldiers of the garrison and the servants were curious or friendly to me. A few of them spoke Welsh and that was a relief away from my halting efforts to speak French with Master Richard and Lady Sybil.

I sauntered up the central path that ran through the lower bailey to the steep causeway crossing the moat around the high mound. The causeway ended suspended in air, several feet short of the palisade that ran around the *motte*. It was only possible to enter if the garrison inside the keep lowered the drawbridge. I waved to a soldier patrolling on the top walkway of the three-storeyed keep and he waved back. I decided to save exploring the motte and the keep for another day.

In the mornings Amelina and I were tasked with collecting bread from the bakehouse and large jugs of ale from the brewery and bringing them into the hall. When it was cold she and I lingered in the bakehouse for as long as we could, talking and warming ourselves in the heat of the oven, until the baker decided we were in his way and Lady Sybil must be starving. Amelina told me she had come into Sybil's service when they were both young girls, after the oldest Montgommery brother, Robert de Bellême, raided her village. 'I saw his men kill my mother, my father and everyone I knew in my village,' she said, her eyes suddenly distant and creased with pain as if she were staring into the midday sun. She turned to me, her expression fierce and her fists clenched. 'Sybil is good to me but if I could harm her family I would.' Then her anger deflated as quickly as it had flared. 'In the unlikely event I ever had such a power,' she added.

45

The lower bailey rang with the noises of the smithy and the constant practice and training carried out by the knights, squires and soldiers. Swords and shields clashed, horses galloped towards one another, arrows thudded into the butts set up not far from the foot of the *motte* causeway. Perhaps when I had earned enough trust, Sybil might allow me a bow and I could keep up my archery practice. All the business of the castle was well ordered but I was amazed at how everything and everyone answered to Lady Sybil. Since her husband was absent much of the time, she ran the whole place.

One day the sun was shining and I asked Amelina, 'Will you come with me to look at the view from the keep?'

'Oh no, Lady Nest. Don't ask me that. I'm terrified of being up heights and besides I can't go in there with those soldiers.'

'Why not?'

'They wouldn't lay a finger on you. They know they'd lose those fingers soon as, if they did, but they won't be so particular about me. I'm not going in there.'

'Very well, I will go alone.' She looked at me doubtfully but I walked out into the bailey and moved with determination towards the causeway, wondering how I might gain access to the keep towering above my head, perched on its grassed mound. There was shouting and a commotion behind me and I turned to see the main gates opening to admit a train of carts and loaded pack-horses to the lower bailey. I stepped aside as they made straight up the path towards the causeway. As the last of them moved past me, I slipped in behind them, my hand on the bundle slung from a donkey. We climbed slowly up the steep incline and I had to use the thick rope fixed to solid posts along the side, to help haul me along. The small train of packhorses and carts stopped at the end of the causeway where I peered down with some anxiety at the long drop to the murky moat below and back up at the tall wooden keep. Soldiers looked down on us from the high gallery walk circling the very top of the keep.

For a few moments nothing happened but then there was a creaking and the drawbridge bounced down onto the lip of the causeway, sending wood dust jumping up all around into the air. The small procession moved forward and I with it. Two soldiers stood on the other side regarding me and clearly knew who I was. 'What's your business here, little lady?' one of them asked. 'I wondered if I might take a look from the top of this fine keep,' I said. 'Lady Sybil has told me I may explore where I will.' 'Be my guest,' the soldier said. 'It's quite a climb.'

The keep had three storeys and no way in from the ground floor. I climbed up the exterior stairway to the first floor and entered. Inside there was a small hall with a hearth and trestles and soldiers who stilled the click of their dice and paused with their pottage and conversation, to stare curiously at me. Perhaps I should not have ventured here alone, should have insisted that Amelina come with me after all, but I was here now. I would persist. In one corner of the square hall there was a hole in the floor and a ladder going down to the storage space on the ground floor. In another corner I saw a ladder going up and crossed to it. I could see the sky above my head. The ladder was steep but solid and I emerged into the sunlight on the walkway at the top of the keep. The soldiers up here could see everything for miles around, beyond the castle, and everything happening below inside the castle. They would spot any escape attempt in no time, certainly during the hours of daylight.

I looked at the path down to the postern gate that led from behind the high grassy motte and let out through the castle's main wall to the moat. It was also guarded and there was no bridge to cross the moat there but two small row-boats were drawn up on the bank, outside the gate. Even if I somehow got beyond the wall and over the moat, there was little cover to conceal an escape. Unlike some places I had seen, this garrison consisted of men with their wits about them who were well drilled and conscientious in their duties. After my explorations I could see no likely means of gaining freedom, but I was glad at least to have roamed and seen the extent of my prison and spoken with many people who in time would grow used to me and forget I was a prisoner.

When I woke I often crossed early to the causeway. The soldiers, growing accustomed to my habits would see me coming and lower the drawbridge. 'Being invaded by the Welsh again,' they joked. As Amelina had suggested, they made the most of every opportunity of looking me over, but no one dared to touch me or offer me insult. I would climb to the top of the keep and look across to the silvery black morning light on the river. I loved to see the countryside laid out for miles and miles, and just glimpse the rising sun on the distant sea. It gave me a sense of somewhere beyond the walls of this fortress.

My lessons with Master Richard gave shape, and sometimes interest, to my life, but many days I woke feeling helpless and hopeless and could not concentrate to his satisfaction. He tried kindness and he tried punishment. I wanted to please him but often my torpor overcame that intention. Eventually, exasperated, he took me before Sybil to answer for my failures. 'The girl will not apply herself consistently. I am at a loss how to proceed with her.'

'You Master Richard, at a loss? Surely not,' Sybil said, regarding me intently so that I grew uncomfortable under her gaze. 'What encouragements have you tried?' she said eventually.

'For a short while she progressed well and I congratulated her, but lately she stares into space and will not work, answering me with vagueness or silence. Perhaps she is a hopeless case, Lady Sybil, more or less a simpleton. Perhaps it is her Welsh blood and she is simply not capable of the learning we might expect from a Norman lady.'

I bridled at this insult but kept my eyes down. I expected Sybil to mete out more punishment. My hands throbbed with the lashings Master Richard had applied with a thick strap he kept hanging on a hook in the locusts' room. When I returned after my lessons to Amelina she frowned, ran to fetch butter from the pantry and delicately touched it to my tender, reddened palms so that I had to bite my lip hard not to cry. My lip was near as swollen as my paddled hands.

'Leave us,' Sybil said and I looked up, thinking she spoke to me but saw Master Richard was bowing and leaving the room. 'Sit down here child.' She indicated the space beside her on the bench. It was covered in soft green cushions and gold drapings cascading to the floor. Sybil was more or less immobilised now by her huge belly. I sat next to her and was surprised when she touched my hair and tucked one stray lock from my plait behind my ear. I looked up at her face. 'I know how hard it is to lose your family, child, to feel yourself alone in the world.' I was bewildered by this softness from her. Perhaps it was a trick, a lulling of me that would end in a beating. 'You are safe here now, with me. I have a small gift for you Nest since you arrived with nothing of your own.' She handed me a wooden box carved with an intricate design of vines and flowers weaving around each other. It was the length of my forearm in every direction and filled my lap. There was some weight to it but not so much that I could not lift it.

I gawped at the box. It had a fine metal lock and key. 'Thank you, my lady.'

'Look inside.'

I lifted the lid. The box was lined with blue fabric and on it sat two pale glass beakers, a knife and spoon.

'My lady! They are beautiful.' Carefully, I lifted up one of the beakers. It was the shape of a miniature bucket and the glass was incised with a lion, an eagle and a griffin. I ran my finger around the pattern, and then placed the beaker back on its fabric nest. The knife was small with a straight blade for the dinner table and other domestic uses. It had a wooden handle decorated with a narrow engraved band of silver. The spoon was made of the same pale wood with a matching silver band.

'It's nothing, Nest. You are a noblewoman and must have some equipment. Amelina is adjusting some dresses for you too which she will bring to your room. And you would do me a kindness if you could try to concentrate on your lessons. Will you do that?'

I swallowed, searching for my voice. 'I will try,' I said.

She smiled. 'Thank you, Nest. I know you are no fool and can do well. Take your box to your room then run back to Master Richard.'

I did as she said, placing the box on the shelf of the *aumbry* in my room, next to my shrivelling claw. Amelina had already laid out the dresses that Sybil spoke of on my bed. There were two that joined the dark red one I had worn since my arrival. One dress was a dark blue and the other was grey, both made from fine wool with embroidered cuffs and necklines. Smiling at them, I caught myself up suddenly. Was I so easily seduced by dresses and cups then? I had to remember that Sybil and these

Normans were my enemies, enemies who had ruthlessly killed my family.

Lady Sybil must have instructed Master Richard to use kindness and not strapping on me. Kindness came more awkwardly to him, but he did his best. He had a mountain of his own work that stood on either side of him on our desk, like two squat cream pillars of parchments. Whilst I studied, he got on with his clerking.

He was the leading scribe for the whole Montgommery family he told me proudly. 'Lady Sybil's father, Roger the Earl of Shrewsbury, was one of William the Conqueror's most important men when the Normans first invaded England and he was richly rewarded. The Montgommerys are at the very tip of the Norman elite, the wealthiest, the most powerful family and yet, pride may come before a fall …'. He tapped the side of his nose as if there was more he could say, but he would not. 'At any rate,' he went on, 'Lady Sybil's husband Robert FitzHamon, he is well in with King William Rufus.'

I considered it might be in my interest to learn the lie of the land with the enemy so I listened carefully to Master Richard's remarks. He managed an enormous workload, with letters, reckonings and instructions coming from Shrewsbury, from the Earl and two of Sybil's brothers there, Hugh and Philippe; from Sybil's husband, FitzHamon who was away at the King's court; from her two brothers in France, Robert de Bellême and Roger the Poitevin; and finally also from Arnulf in Pembroke. I gleaned that Sybil's father and her oldest brother, Bellême, were in disfavour with King William, because they had rebelled against him.

Master Richard was like a spider at the centre of his web of papers that came in and out from all sides and he told me cheerfully about it. 'Ah, Nest, today, we have a letter from …' he would say, liking an audience for his labours. To my relief, Master Richard read out one letter from the King's Procurator, Ranulf Flambard, telling Arnulf that King William was uncertain as yet that he would give permission for Arnulf to marry me. 'You are the King's ward now Nest,' Master Richard told me, 'and he is looking out for a good husband for you.' Sybil had informed me the

King would not recognise my betrothal to Owain ap Cadwgan and I should forget about that, and I had informed myself that I would do no such thing.

One morning Master Richard had to leave me alone with the locusts to go on an errand. To still my nervousness at his insects I got up and went to look at his paperwork, sifting through the letters there carefully so that he would not know. I was surprised when I slowly deciphered a letter from Master Richard to Ran ulf Flambard informing on the Montgommerys' comings and goings, their sayings and doings at Cardiff Castle. He was spying on the family that employed him, selling away their secrets. 'The Montgommerys are confident that Duke Robert will take England if our King William dies,' I read. It seemed Lady Sybil had a cuckoo in her nest. The sound of Master Richard's imminent return came from the passageway and I knew I would not have time to get around the huge table and regain my seat, so instead I stepped swiftly to the small arched opening next to the locusts vitrine, looking down the wooden steps there curiously.

'Be careful there, Nest,' Master Richard's voice came behind me. 'That old staircase is badly broken and Lady Sybil has closed it off from use until she can find the money to get it repaired.'

I turned back to face him brightly. 'I'm sorry,' I said. 'My father told me curiosity killed the cat and I was the nosiest kitten he knew.' Master Richard turned his face away to look at his papers as my eyes filled with tears at the memory of my father. I moved slowly around the table, keeping as far away from the locusts as possible, their hundreds of bulbous yellow-green eyes swivelling to watch me, and I sat down again with my books.

In the afternoons I sat in Sybil's chamber sewing, or learning the table manners of Norman ladies. 'Always wash your hands before a meal and wipe your mouth before drinking. You must cut your bread, rather than tearing it. Do not lean on the table, dip your food in the salt, or speak to someone when they are drinking. Never wriggle your shoulders or allow your hands to be touched by a man who is not of the family.'

I nodded, keeping my opinion to myself that I already knew all this as I had been schooled to be the wife of a Welsh king since I could speak my own name.

'A wife should possess wisdom, modesty, generosity, fertility, and give good advice to her husband. Your behaviour should be decorous, your speech genial and elegant, your bearing regal and composed. I expect you to start behaving in this way from now on. Do you understand?'

I could rarely get a word in amidst Sybil's in any case. She was garrulous in the extreme and I often felt her speech was like a waterfall washing relentlessly over me, dashing down on my head. If she momentarily left the room, the sudden hush was a shock.

In my chamber Amelina and I amused ourselves with 'anti-manners': strutting around the room indecorously, wriggling our shoulders in the extreme, tearing up bread and dipping it in a salt-cellar, our elbows plonked on the table. We took it in turns speaking, unforgiveably, at the other who was drinking from a beaker. Amelina, eventually sobering from our game, showed me how to curtsey to the King when he came visiting, which in her case involved revealing a great deal of bosom as she bobbed down low.

'Will he come?' I asked.

'Oh yes,' she said, 'Lady Sybil's husband, Lord Robert Fitz-Hamon is the King's greatest friend. And entrusted with the task of subduing the Welsh.'

I wondered how FitzHamon could achieve that task since he was rarely here. I did not meet him for the whole first year of my stay in Cardiff. 'We have large estates in Normandy, also,' Sybil told me, and sometimes her husband was away there too, taking care of their interests.

'We don't see the lord from one end of the year to the next,' Amelina said, 'so it's a wonder how my lady can get a chance to get an heir. Let's hope it's a boy in her belly right now.'

Most of the household were Normans, speaking French, but a few of the lesser servants were Welsh and I could snatch some moments in my own language, although they were cowed by my status and shy to talk at first. One of the stableboys, Bryn, told me with certainty that Owain and Cadwgan would come to rescue me. 'For sure, lady,' he whispered.

I found I could converse easily enough with Amelina and she was keen to gossip about Sybil. 'Lot younger than her husband, she is.'

'What is he like?'

She shrugged. 'Old. Not bad. But rotten ugly. Terrible teeth.' She made a face like a rat, making me laugh. 'Not as harsh as she is sometimes.'

The castle was well garrisoned and the surrounding plains and castles beyond had been parcelled out to FitzHamon's leading men: Robert de Haie at Newport, Winebald de Ballon at Caerleon and his brother Hamelin at Abergavenny. These Normans had driven the local Welsh people up into the hills and kept them there with constant patrols and skirmishes. My father had killed the king of this region, Caradog, in battle, and they had no strong leader now. Sybil had spies at work everywhere in Morgannwg. They came from the Welsh settlements in the hills and told her of the vaunting and threats of the Welshmen, which she laughed at, especially when they told her old King Caradog's son was known as Owain the Weak. These people, I learned from Bryn, were reduced to hiding in the thickly wooded valleys, in caves and on the hill-tops and yet a number of other Welsh lords I heard mentioned – Iestyn ap Gwrgant and Senghenydd – were holding out against the Normans and seemed to be offering a greater challenge.

I spoke with Amelina about my surprise at Sybil's rule. 'The wife of a Welsh king or noble does not concern herself overmuch with such matters.'

'Things are different with these great Norman ladies. They can inherit land if there is no male heir. They can act as Regent if their husband is away, as Sybil does, or if their son is too young to rule.'

'A woman does not inherit land under Welsh law. Why doesn't a brother or an uncle or a cousin grasp power if a son is too young to assert his rule?'

'That is the Welsh way, but Norman law and expectations are different. A woman has the right if she has the bloodline and the capability of course, as Sybil surely does.'

Sybil's spies and messengers came from the English King's entourage, and they came from Normandy. Slowly I grew to know the complex geographies and eddies of the Montgommerys' world, although I knew, too, there were matters not discussed in front of me, mostly relating to Duke Robert of Normandy. They showed less discretion when they spoke of the Welsh, because they saw us as vanquished. When Sybil or her visiting Norman allies spoke of their contestation with my countrymen, it was mostly Cadwgan's name I heard. If the plan to marry me to her brother Arnulf came about, how could I live my life? I was Welsh and I did not want to be this Norman wife they were trying to mould me into. I longed for my father's *llys* – his court with the bards, the boasting and jokes of his men. I ached for sight of his wise face and the gentle touch of his hand on my head.

* * *

From the Copybook of Sister Benedicta

Westminster, October, 1093

Greetings Benedicta, oh great venerable mistress of the scriptorium, Henry and I continued in England this year. You mention the Montgommery family that your Abbess belongs to at the end of your last letter. I fear they are not on the same side of things as my Lord Henry, so pray do be circumspect in what you discuss with your Abbess. Nothing of me and Henry I beg you, for they might use it against him. I hesitate to ask it Benedicta, and insist that you run no risks, but it would be greatly beneficial to us if you *do* let me know anything of the movements and minds of Bellême and his brother Roger the Poitevin, that you might learn, or anything on the other Montgommerys. Do not tell me anything your Abbess speaks of regarding her family unless you are content that I should pass it on to Henry. I am his man through and through Benedicta.

You wrote of the different spheres my lord and I swing between. Yes indeed! Our shifts are so vertiginous I am well nauseated at it. First I expected to enter Abingdon Abbey as a novice alongside Henry after our schooling at Salisbury with Bishop Osmund, since Henry was the youngest of the Conqueror's ten children. When good Queen Matilda did that kindness to our mother after we lost everything in the flooding at Bruges, placing you at Almenêches, and me in Henry's household, with nothing but a large grin and an overlarge tunic, I expected to soon follow you into the church. After three years labouring at Latin, however, Henry was promoted to third, 'spare' son when his brother Richard was killed in a hunting accident. We ceased to see monks' robes on our horizons and took to arms and chainmail instead. 'I was growing quite attached to the idea of being an Abbot, Haith,' Henry sighed, 'and now we must think again'. I wasn't so sorry myself.

The Conqueror knighted me along with Henry the year before he died and our practise butts at Salisbury were replaced with real battle in Normandy and the Vexin. You raise a query against Henry's nickname Beauclerc and I assure you he is as much warrior as scholar now. When the Conqueror died he left Henry landless and without title. I doubt that was the King's intention but his death was sudden. Henry's brothers, William Rufus and Robert Curthose, should have gifted their younger brother with fitting lands and title in England and Normandy, but they saw him as threat rather than beloved kin, or they did not want to divide their spoils further. They cut him out entirely which he stored up in his heart, salted down with bitterness. 'They give me nothing. Treat me as if I am invisible,' he complained. 'They will find themselves mistaken.' He is a man of extreme passion when it comes to loyalty.

We visited William Rufus' court so that Henry could claim the lands on the Welsh border left to him by his mother, but William told Henry he had given those lands to Robert FitzHamon who earned them through constant contention with Welsh rebels. 'There is no possibility of change about it,' William said decisively. It is mooted about the court that the King and FitzHamon are lovers, so *there* may be another reason. (Forgive me for bringing your blushes Benedicta!)

We made our way back to Normandy, sailing in company with your Abbess' brother, Bellême, but on landing Duke Robert had Henry and Bellême thrown into prison on the advice of his uncle Bishop Odo, who does nothing but stir up one Norman lord against another. Bellême's father hastened from Wales to entreat for his son's freedom so that Bellême's incarceration was short-lived, but who was there to negotiate with Duke Robert on Henry's behalf? I visited him daily, bringing food, wine and cheer but for an antsy man of my lord's disposition enforced doing nothing for months and months was a torture. When Curthose and Rufus are not against Henry, they are fighting and plotting against each other. The Conqueror has left behind him a brood of vipers rather than loving brothers. It was God's will that brought the citizens and Castellan of Domfront to rebel against the unjust rule of Bellême and beg Henry to be their lord. We were content there with my lord building up the defences and churches of the town and enjoying his small children, Robert and Mathilde. Don't ask me of their mothers, Benedicta, for they are two different women, who he has left – enriched – but nevertheless left behind somewhere on our trail. Sadly you and I have good cause to think so, but not all fathers of bastards ignore responsibility for their offspring.

You asked me about the new Archbishop of Canterbury, Anselm. He is tactful with a sweet smile and temper, yet steely in confronting King William's wrongs against the Church and his moral errors. Believe me that takes some great courage for the King is as combative and forceful a man as his father ever was. I quail to see the arguments between such meek holiness and such worldly fury, Benedicta, although Henry says the Archbishop is more like a mule than a meek sheep, a mule with a forceful kick. The Archbishop is a shrewd judge of character and a great deal more adroit than he pretends. He uses composure and quiet reasonableness where others shout and storm and his most endearing characteristic, which you will like Benedicta, is that when arguments rage too much around him, he leans his head back against the wall and feigns to be sleeping to avoid further confrontation. I like him a great deal! Snoring as the weapon of choice in an argument! I will make him my role model in that at least since sleeping is also my expertise. Fare well Benedicta. Your loving brother Haith.

Almenêches Abbey, Normandy, October 1093

Dearest brother, I am no fool. Do not fear. I do not discuss your business or Lord Henry's with Abbess Emma and I will send you news of anything about the Montgommerys I hear that may be of service to you and your lord. The Montgommerys are a dangerous family to be hated by so I pray for your Lord Henry's safety, knowing that your own is wound around his. My task in the scriptorium at the moment is writing out a formulary of letters for others to follow but my coded letters to you will not be amongst the models!

I am fearful when you write of the battles you and your lord have been involved in, the treacheries of the nobles, the wild seas you and Henry cross back and forth, but don't hold back. I would rather know the all of it, your dangers and your joys, my dear 'little' brother. You write of Lord Henry's fierce passion for loyalty and hatred of betrayal. I trust he will one day reward the great loyalty *you* have shown, staying with him always through the vagaries of his career. Take care always Haith, for my sake, Benedicta.

* * *

Confined as I was, I tried to make the most of the compound. Sybil eventually agreed that I could practice at the archery butts. I was in any case constantly under supervision from the soldiers high on the keep or in the gatehouse tower. I also helped to exercise the horses inside the compound and was returning to the stables after trying out a mare that was recovering well from lameness, when the Welsh stableboy, Bryn, unexpectedly helped me from the saddle. 'Cadwgan's visiting up with Iestyn, nearby,' he whispered close to my ear, as I slid to the ground and stood with my hands flat on the horse's hot flank.

I looked around the stable. We were alone. Just the gentle noise of horses chewing, shifting, breathing all around us. 'You ... you could reach him?'

He nodded once.

'I will let you know.' I walked across the bailey towards the hall with my heart thumping. Did I dare venture it? I knew Sybil was planning to send Amelina to Swansea Fair to shop for gloves and spices. She would expect her to be away for a couple of days and would send her with an escort. If I could persuade Amelina to make Bryn her escort, would they have time to slip away to Cadwgan as part of the shopping expedition? Could I trust Amelina? Perhaps her real allegiance was to Sybil and not to me.

Amelina was waiting in my chamber to help me change my clothes. 'You do not smile or laugh enough, Lady Nest.'

'I sorrow for my family and,' I hesitated but decided I must voice it, 'and I sorrow for my people.' I ventured a look at her face. She was staring at me but I could not read her expression. 'I know Lady Sybil's household is my family now as it is yours, but I cannot help feel torn in two nonetheless.'

She was silent for a moment but then agreed, 'I am torn too. It's the lot of women, Nest. I'm torn between my duty to the Montgommery family and my hatred of them.'

I took a deep breath. 'Will you do something dangerous for me Amelina?' I explained the mission to Cadwgan I wanted her to undertake.

'I will think about it,' she said, a frown creasing her forehead. 'Sybil is fond of me but her punishment for treachery would be merciless.'

5

An Heiress

Most of the animals had been slaughtered in advance of the coming winter when we would have no fodder to feed them. Now everyone in the household must contribute to the labour in the kitchen, salting meat and fish and layering it into large barrels, pickling and making jam and sauces with the remaining vegetables and fruit. These were familiar tasks I had undertaken with my mother in previous years so I did not need telling what to do. For days I worked and waited for Amelina's answer, knowing all the time there was a strong chance she would choose to betray me.

I had borrowed an old dress from Amelina to save my good ones from the splashes and smells of the pickling. Alongside the kitchen maids, I boiled cider vinegar and salt in water, with mustard seed and saffron, and carefully poured this brine over jars of garlic and radishes and sealed them. There was a surfeit of red and yellow apples, so I set about turning them into apple jelly, peeling and chopping, boiling the apples in water with cinnamon. It was hot, relentless work but made cheerful by the gossip and singing of the women around me. As darkness was beginning to fall, my arms and back ached and sweat ran on the back of my neck. I needed a break. I removed my apron and stretched my arms above my head to shift my tired muscles. I strolled into the bailey for some cooling air.

The Curfew Bell rang. Satisfied and exhausted with my labours, I leant against the rim of the well in the bailey listening to the creaks of the huge wooden gates of the castle as they were pulled shut. There was no moon so I could see very little in the darkness. 'Alright, I'll do it,' Amelina's voice was right next to my ear.

I jumped out of my reverie and gripped her arm. 'Truly? Thank you!'

'We must be very careful. Act normally. Sybil is very observant.'

'Yes.'

'I will speak with Bryn to find out how we might reach Cadwgan and deliver your message.' She squeezed my hand and went as quietly as she had come.

I gave her a few moments and then walked into the hall. Sybil was sitting there with her gown pulled low around her bare shoulders and a maid standing behind her rubbing a sweet-smelling unguent into her aching neck. Sybil smiled at me as I passed. I made for the stairs and my room. Upstairs, I closed the door softly behind me and sat down to write to King Cadwgan who should be my father-in-law and who, after my uncle Rhydderch, was the closest I had now to an adult male guardian amongst my own people.

To Cadwgan ap Bleddyn, King of Powys from Nest ferch Rhys, royal daughter of Deheubarth, God speed my lord. I write to you from Cardiff Castle where I am held prisoner in the custody of the Normans Robert FitzHamon and his wife Sybil de Montgommery. The garrison here numbers some fifty or more men and they are well drilled and weaponed. The fortifications of the castle are solid and I would guess, even from my poor knowledge of such matters, impregnable. Arnulf de Montgommery who usurps my father's kingdom plans to marry me. I would keep to the betrothal to your son Owain that my father confirmed with you but I am sure they will not give me up to you willingly. My half-brother Idwal lies in chains in a Norman prison but I do not know where. My mother, your kinswoman, Gwladys ferch Rhiwallon, is I believe held at the Norman castle near Carmarthen.

Would Cadwgan rescue my mother who was his close kin, the daughter of his uncle? I was not hopeful he would see any need to rescue me. I was useless to him and Owain now my father was dead. Unlike the Normans, we did not see land and rights as passed through women, but perhaps he would enjoy baiting the invaders by taking me from them. My stylus hovered above the parchment. I decided I would not tell him about my surviving brother, Gruffudd in Ireland, the heir to Deheubarth now, the *Edling*. I could not trust Cadwgan. He would serve his interests only in any action he might take but perhaps it would be useful for him to know what I knew about the Cardiff household. I resumed,

The Montgommery family are committed to the cause of Duke Robert of Normandy, in treason against their King William. Their chief clerk, Richard Belmeis, spies upon them in behalf of King William. I am hoping you can find a way to fetch me to you. For now, I am never allowed beyond the castle walls, but perhaps in time there will be an occasion. Or I have made a survey of the castle layout and think perhaps the postern gate would be the best means of escape.

I signed the letter, folded the parchment small and sealed it with a dab of soft red wax. I doubted Cadwgan could easily free me but at least he would know I wanted to be freed and held to my betrothal. At least I had done something.

In the morning the Prime bell rang and I went down to the hall where Amelina had been up long before me. She was in her travelling cloak taking final instructions from Sybil on what to buy and how much to pay. Bryn lurked in the doorway. When Sybil moved to a casket and turned her back to fetch a purse for Amelina I passed the letter to her. Between our long sleeves and the pouch at Amelina's waist there was no glimpse of it.

Whilst Amelina was away and Sybil was immobilised in the last days of her pregnancy I read to her and Master Richard from a copy of the *Encomium Emma Reginae*. It was good practice for my Latin, Master Richard said, although he tutted at my stumblings. The text was an account of the Norman noblewoman Emma, the daughter of the Duke of Normandy who had first married an Anglo-Saxon king of England and then married Canute, the Danish king who ruled England not long ago. Master Richard demonstrated his scholarship as I read, with exclamations such as 'Ah a quotation from Virgil I believe' or 'ah I detect the influence of Ovid in that part there.' Sybil turned a sour expression on him, irritated by his interruptions, and his commentary petered out.

Amelina and Bryn were away at the fair for four days but at last the sound of horses arriving came from the bailey. 'Is it Amelina returned?' Sybil asked. I walked to the door as calmly as I could and looked out. 'Yes, it's them come back,' I called over my shoulder. I went out slowly and down the steps, not wanting to appear too enthusiastic to Sybil. I watched Bryn lead the horses, loaded with packs, towards the stable. He nodded to me. I turned to Amelina. 'All well,' she said, quietly. 'I'll tell you later.'

We went back into the hall and Amelina began to greet Lady Sybil, swinging her cloak from her shoulders, when Sybil suddenly bent over, one hand, her knuckled whitened, gripping the edge of the table. I heard a rush of water. A pool of liquid was spreading rapidly between her feet. 'Quickly Nest run and fetch the midwife from her gossip in the kitchen. My son is coming.'

Amelina called after me to bring hot water and clean cloths. By the time I returned with the water, the midwife was supervising and Sybil was straining on the birthing stool in her chamber, held up on either side by Amelina and the young kitchen-maid Mariota. 'Set the things down here and relieve Mariota.'

I did as I was told and Sybil's grip was transferred from the white-faced Mariota to me. Sybil gripped me in the crook of my arm with tremendous force so I staggered under her weight, my flesh grinding under her hand, against the bone of my arm. She groaned and swore. Amelina mopped her brow, and the three of us took shifts holding her up and having our arms bruised until finally after many hours the midwife called out, 'I see the baby's head, lady!'

'Is it a boy?'

'No seeing that yet.' After more huffing and yelling from Sybil, the child suddenly slid out swiftly in a slick of blood and ooze, just like the calves and lambs I had seen birthed in the fields. The baby's eyes were tightly shut and its tiny fists were clenched. It was a girl. The midwife cleaned the child's small face and she grizzled and wailed. Sybil sagged with disappointment against me. The afterbirth came out next and the midwife cut and neatly tied the purple cord and handed the baby to the wet nurse, a Welsh woman who had been called in from a nearby farmstead. I watched the whole process with curiosity, knowing I would one day be birthing my own children, and I thought of my mother, hoping she had good care as her own time approached.

'A girl is excellent to cement agreements,' I told Sybil.

'Yes, thank you Nest. I'm sorry if I hurt your arm. You did me sterling service.' We helped her to the bed and the midwife cleaned her and brought the baby to her, though it wailed red in the face at being removed from the wet nurse's breast. Sybil smiled thinly. 'Well she has a lusty set of lungs and will be a pretty one in time.'

'What will you name her?' I asked.

'Mabel, after my mother.' I wiped gently at the tears that matted her eyelashes, thinking that she was not so many years older than me, still a girl beneath her strong, harsh facade.

With the excitement and work of the birth of the child, it was several hours before Amelina and I could sit down in my chamber and she could report on her encounter with King Cadwgan. 'It was a wonderful adventure!' she exclaimed, gripping my hands, her eyes alight. 'Bryn and I were received with honour in the camp and one of the bards made a song about my face. They wanted to give me one of those beautiful Welsh ponies as a gift but how could I have explained *that* to Lady Sybil?'

'Did you see Cadwgan? Did he receive my letter?'

'Yes he has your message. You never told me what you said to him?'

'Does he send me a reply?'

'He said to tell you he is honoured with your trust and loyalty and will look for a way. What does that mean? A way for what? To free you?'

'Did you meet Prince Owain?'

'Yes.' Her face was suddenly flushed scarlet and she looked down at her hands as she placed them knotted around one another in her lap.

'Well?'

'He is handsome, red-haired, blue-eyed, tall for his age, some fifteen summers. *Fyrch*, he told me.'

'*Fyrch*? Freckled?'

She nodded. 'Very handsome. Gallant and naughty.'

'Naughty?'

'Well you know, full of fun.'

'What embarrasses you Amelina?'

'Just that he is so handsome and will rescue you!' She laughed but her laughter rang false.

I regarded her in silence. 'He is lusty then, my future husband is he?'

She shook her head but would not look at me.

'What else? What did you make of the King?'

'He is a great and charming lord. Also handsome.'

'Many handsome men then.'

'I took your message. There was danger to me!' she said defensively.

'Yes. I thank you Amelina.'

There was a strain between us for a few days after our conversation. Bryn also told me, when I asked him, with his eyes round as saucers, all about King Cadwgan's battle camp and his luxurious tent, but he was evasive when I asked how Prince Owain had liked Amelina. 'She gave your message. That nag's lame and needs seeing to,' he slipped past me to his work, a small grin on his face.

Not long after the birth of Mabel, Sybil sought me out in Master Richard's chamber one morning. 'Child,' Sybil's voice was soft and she held a letter in her hand. This augured badly. 'There is news come in a letter from Carmarthen from William FitzBaldwin who commands there, that is of some import for you.'

My mother was at Carmarthen. 'What is it my lady?'

Her face was solemn. 'I'm sorry to tell you Nest that your mother has died after a complication of childbed.'

I swallowed on my grief. I would weep later when I was alone. 'And what of the child?' I asked.

'He writes nothing of a child. I presume it died too,' Sybil said. She looked down at the parchment in her hands. 'FitzBaldwin has written confirmation from Gwladys ferch Rhiwallon,' she screwed up her nose at the unfamiliar language of my mother's name and mangled the pronunciation, 'that you inherit her marriage portion at Carew and Llansteffan.'

I was confused. 'A Welsh woman does not inherit land my lady, though my father would have dowered me for my husband if he had lived.' My losses were beginning to overwhelm me. My father and brothers and now my mother. A strangled sob escaped me and I pressed my hands over my mouth, squeezing my wet eyes shut.

'I am sorry for the loss of your mother, Nest, but at least you are not penniless. That is important for your future, for your marriage, or if you should enter a convent.'

A convent! No such thought had occurred to me. We did not have nunneries in Wales but Amelina told me many Norman women who did not wish to marry or who were widowed or repudiated became nuns.

'In Welsh law, perhaps you would not inherit, but in Norman law you are an heiress. Which would you prefer?' When I did not answer, Sybil's voice softened again as she told me, 'You may leave your studies for the rest of the day, Nest.'

I thanked Sybil and without looking at either her or Master Richard, I ran to my own pallet to cry for my mother and her child. I wished I could have seen her one more time. I wished she had not died in captivity and despair. I wept for all my family, and then I wept for myself. Another slender string holding me taut to any certain identity in my life had been severed so that now I seemed to hang by a mere fraying thread, suspended vertiginously in the air, almost touching nothing, that fraying last thread being merely my baby brother in Ireland. After I had been crying for a while the floorboards and door creaked. Amelina stood crinkling up her mouth and tipping her head to one side in an expression of commiseration. 'May I come in?'

I nodded. 'Does Lady Sybil need me?'

'No, no, stay where you are. She knows you need time to grieve but I thought I might be able to bring you comfort. Lady Sybil understands you. She lost her own mother when she was four years old.' She passed me a fine linen handkerchief to wipe my wet face and blow my nose.

'Thank you, Amelina.

'Would you like to hear about my early days in the service of Lady Sybil, when we first came to Wales?'

I smiled sadly. I knew she intended to distract me from my misery and I wanted her ploy to succeed, even if only for a short while. Amelina was a born storyteller, a *cyfarwydd*.

'We two tiny girls travelled from Normandy, packed off to live with Sybil's father, Earl Roger, at Montgommery Castle in Wales, which was a shock for us what with the weather, the food and the people,' she said with deliberate humour, trying to make me smile. 'Sybil's father had her betrothed to Lord FitzHamon before she was six, and then married off to him before she was sixteen. I stayed with her through it. She's not so bad. There are some softnesses under her carapace. She is one of the better Montgommerys. And Arnulf,' she added as an afterthought, mindful that he might be my future husband. 'Take heart, little one.' She touched the backs of her fingers gently to my cheek. 'The loss of a mother is a great sorrow but she does not suffer anymore and she looks down on you from heaven, proud of your bravery.'

I started to weep again and she embraced me hard, my wet face tangled in her hair.

'I will look out for you, Nest,' she told me. 'I must go back to my duties. You may find there is more ease if you do the same.'

I smiled weakly at her as she left the chamber. Her words lingered with me. Your mother is proud of your bravery. I must find that bravery, dredge it up somehow, now that I was truly orphaned and had become the lady of Carew and Llansteffan. The very name of the second place, sounding in my mind slowly like the toll of a bell, sent shivers through my body. I reached up for the bird's claw on my *aumbry* shelf and ran my fingertip up and down its brittle three digits thinking of the estuary, thinking of Goronwy.

* * *

From Gerald Fitz̧Walter's Day Book

Pembroke Castle, Advent, December 1093

The Norman lords in the north of England, led by Robert de Mowbray have slain the Scottish king Malcolm and his heir. A kingdom where kings are murdered so frequently is unruly. One or other of the Conqueror's son, be it Robert Curthose or William Rufus, needs to take a tighter grip on the reins or we will all descend into anarchy and lose everything we have gained here.

I am lately returned from a visit to Lady Nest at Cardiff Castle since I needed to present her with a seal for the estates she has inherited at Llansteffan and Carew. I had the seal made on Arnulf's orders by a craftsman in Tenby. I needed Lady Nest's signature to documents and her concurrence for my choice of stewards. The seal was a pretty thing, an elipse shape made from heavy silver, showing a noblewoman holding a flower and wearing a crown. It was finely crafted as the face of the lady and the folds of the gown across her belly and knees were beautifully graved. Nest stared at it in wonder when I gave it to her and then at me, when I told her of her new responsibilities.

Lady Nest has made significant progress in her schooling and looks already more like a young woman than the distraught girl I captured at Llansteffan. She expressed herself happy with the arrangements I intend to make for the safeguarding of her inheritance. She is a rich heiress now. If I could aspire to such a wife and such estates I would be advanced indeed but due to the unfair accident of my birth, that is a world away from my true prospects.

I received a letter from my brother in Windsor in answer to my enquiry concerning Nest's imprisoned half-brother, Idwal. He writes that the boy still lives but my brother has lately had to issue an edict to stop the townspeople emptying excrement into the ditch around the prison as several of the prisoners have died from diseases arising from the noxious fumes. This is not information I can pass to the princess and will have to make up a prettier lie on the subject of her brother.

* * *

A week after the news of my mother's death I looked out of the chamber window at the sound of horses below and my heart leapt when I recognised my uncle Rhydderch at the head of a small group of men. 'Quickly find me a dress, Amelina!' In short order I was presentable and hurrying down the steps to the hall.

Rhydderch was seated at the hall table talking with Lady Sybil. He grinned broadly at me. 'Little niece!'

'Uncle!' I embraced him. He was the first sign of my former life that I had seen for months and months, but I was perplexed. What was he doing here? He appeared to be on friendly terms with Sybil and the other Normans in the hall. 'What is your news?' I asked him cautiously.

'Nothing much,' he said. 'All quiet at Carmarthen. I am sorry for the loss of your mother Nest.'

I inclined my head and stared at my lap for a moment and then looked up again at him. 'You are at Carmarthen then.'

'Yes.' So he had given his allegiance to the Normans, to Arnulf or FitzBaldwin. There was no hope of rescue from him and no response had come from Cadwgan either. I swallowed and prepared to give my uncle more friendly hypocritical conversation, realising I was truly thrown onto my own devices, alone.

* * *

From the Copybook of Sister Benedicta

Westminster, Yuletide 1093

Dear Benedicta, we are still in England you see but we plan to return to Domfront as soon as the weather and tides permit. King William, recovering from his sickness was advised to marry forthwith and he took himself off to Wilton Abbey to get a look at the Anglo-Saxon princess Matilda, the daughter of the King of the Scots and through her mother, a descendent of King Alfred. The nuns kept Matilda in a veil and King William declared he could not marry a girl whose face he could not see in case she was misshapen and ugly in the utmost degree. I shock you, I'm sorry. King William is not a man of delicacies.

This is not the end of the sad controversies around this princess Matilda. For then William argued with her father King Malcolm who wanted to marry her to Lord Alan the Red of Richmond and King William would have none of *that* for it would greatly enrich a lord already too rich. King Malcolm of Scotland left the court angry, refusing to give homage to the King of England and took his daughter away from the nunnery.

Then Alan the Red arrived at Wilton Abbey and thwarted of one bride, he stole himself another, Gunnhild who is a beauty by all accounts, and the daughter of the former Anglo-Saxon King Harald Godwinsson and his handfast wife Edith Swanneck, and so an heiress in the lands of the Danelaw. You will know better than me if we can see God's will in what followed or just man's evil. Alan the Red died and his nephew Alan the Black inherited the poor stolen lady Gunnhild. I'm not sure if she was a professed nun or not.

When Mowbray murdered the Scottish King Malcolm and his heir and Malcolm's wife, Queen Margaret, died from a broken heart, that Princess Matilda was all sudden an orphan and at risk because of the struggles over the Scottish throne. Matilda and her younger brothers and sister came to Rufus's court in London for safety. So now we can see the princess' face on a daily basis and in truth it is a plain but pleasant one, and King William seems to have no inclination for it now he *can* see it. We have enjoyed the festivities of the Yule season here although it has been a hard winter and frost candles decorated even the inside of the frigid hall on occasion.

Henry and I look forward to our return to Domfront. Despite the season we are moving down to the coast tomorrow to wait what the shipmen say of the weather in the Channel that we might make home as soon as we can. Henry is anxious to see his children and I am anxious to see you and bring you more inappropriate gifts for a nun. Would you like a silky lapdog perhaps? Or a great jewelled headdress? Henry has another child by the way – a newborn son named Richard, and an Anglo-Saxon mistress, Ansfride in Abingdon, that he is fond of, but still he must leave them behind for now. It's a difficult thing to have a kingdom divided in half by a wild sea. I wonder if Henry's father, William the Conqueror, thought much of that. Fare well my sister with love from your brother Haith.

Almenêches Abbey, Normandy, January 1094

Dearest Haith, I was horrified indeed to read your account of the Lady Gunnhild stolen from a nunnery by one man named red Alan and then forced to the bed of another kinsman named black Alan. All nuns must quail at such goings on, although whether with loathing or longing is a matter for their conscience.

It was just Plow Monday here and I enjoyed the cook's description of the hilarious rioting around the village by the brawny young men as they prepared to resume their work in the fields after the long holiday of Christmas. All is well and at peace here in the Abbey, with my affectionate kisses and hopes that this year will be peaceful for you and Henry, from your Benedicta.

6

Bitter Wives

After Christmas there was a gathering at Cardiff castle for the start of the new year. Following many quiet months where nothing much happened except my lessons, and baby Mabel's grizzling with new teeth, the castle was suddenly crowded with men and I was disorientated anew. The lord had come home, Robert FitzHamon, and with him most of the Montgommery brothers: Hugh, Philippe, Roger and Arnulf, and in Arnulf's retinue came Gerald FitzWalter. The name of another guest made me quiver with anger: Bernard de Neufmarché, who styled himself Lord of Brecknock, the murderer of my father and brothers. The place bristled with my mortal enemies and I had to find ways to keep it from my face and voice, to grow my hatred fierce and silent. Sybil saw me standing at the upstairs window of her chamber watching the guests ride in. 'Do me the favour of keeping a civil tongue in your head, Nest,' she warned me. 'Your words can be as barbed as arrows sometimes.' I nodded meekly and turned back to the window where, looking down at the new arrivals, I imagined the tip of my excellent sharp tongue probing the air like a snake tasting for prey.

The stables were full with the visitors' horses, many of them large fierce *destriers* that you could not approach. The servants ran back and forth across the bailey with jugs of wine and ale, narrowly avoiding colliding with each other, trying not to slip on the frosty ground. Soon after the arrival of this great crowd of company, I found Gerald in the stables tending to a dark bay palfrey with scarlet nostrils. I asked him for news of my brother. He told me Idwal was held in a prison in Windsor. 'Is he in good health?'

'He continues well, in truth.'

I smiled my relief. At least I knew Idwal was still alive. He was young and perhaps could survive incarceration until I could find a way to have him freed.

I shuddered to be so close in the company of the murderer, Bernard de Neufmarché, but I also wanted to know my enemy. He was a huge man: tall, with a fat gut, and broad shoulders. His right shoulder was twice the size of his left, from a lifetime of wielding a sword. Perhaps it was the bias of my furiously bitter eyes, but he seemed permanently unclean: his finger-nails over-long and dirty, his black beard smeared with grease or almond milk. His right index finger was missing the top section, and ter-minated in a flat, pink plane, that was the cleanest part of his hand. The sight of that pale, abnormally short digit reminded me of a white worm, uncovered beneath a stone, trying to wriggle away from the light.

Neufmarché was accompanied by his wife who had royal Welsh and Anglo-Saxon blood and whose name was the same as mine, but they had renamed her Agnes whether she liked it or not. If the Normans had not usurped our lands she would have been kin to kings and queens in Wales and England, but now she was the miserable seventeen-year-old pregnant wife of a forty-four year old battle-scarred invader. I wondered if my own fate would be like hers. Lady Sybil kept me and Lady Agnes in her chamber most of the time, away from the men, who talked war and drank the castle wine barrels dry, but there were times when Sybil must leave the chamber to manage the household and then Agnes and I could relax and speak with each other in our own tongue and in sorrow for our ruined lands and hopes. 'Here,' she said, surrepti-tiously passing a small roll of parchment to me, 'you should read this. It was written by a bard in your homelands. Keep it.'

'Thank you.' I lodged the parchment carefully in the crook of my elbow, concealed in my sleeve.

'I hate him,' she declared bluntly when I asked about her hus-band. 'He is a vicious, ugly brute. I am royal, the granddaughter of Llewelyn the Great, King of all Wales and yet I am wed to that ignoble nothing, my piety shackled to his impiety, my freshness to his age and foulness.' In the excess of her anger, spittle sprayed with her words onto Lady Sybil's embroideries in my lap.

I allowed a pause to give her a chance to calm down. 'Is there no good you can find and feel in him then?'

'None, nothing. He is nothing to me.'

'He is the father of your child,' I ventured.

'Hmm,' she said with a sly smile, caressing her rounding belly 'So he thinks. I am his unwilling and coerced wife.' She pronounced the word wife as is she had said whore in its stead. 'He was the father of my first son that died last year sure enough.' I looked away from her and busied my hands with my needle and thread, not daring to allow her to say more. 'Will you take it meekly then?' she asked me crossly. 'Lie in lust with men who have killed your kin and taken your birthright?'

'No,' I stammered, 'I don't mean to. I am betrothed to Owain ap Cadwgan and I will hold to that and must tell it to a priest if they attempt to force me from it.'

She laughed at me. 'You little fool. You think *that* will stop them. They take what they want and do what they will and they *will* marry you to Sybil's brother, Arnulf, who rules Pembroke in your father's place. Soon, I expect,' she said with unpleasant satisfaction. 'I've heard them speaking of it.'

I made allowance for her. She was angry and misused.

'I would prefer death to this life, or at least a nunnery to these couplings,' she declared, 'but I am not allowed even *that* mercy.'

The door creaked and Sybil rushed into the room, berating us: 'I *heard* you speaking your barbarous language. You should both know better. You will speak French at all times!' I took a breath. She had not understood anything we said. 'I hoped for a better model from you Lady Agnes, for the girl.'

'Yes, forgive me Lady Sybil. It won't happen again. I was momentarily misled by the girl addressing me in the old language and slipped into it without thinking.'

I kept my irritation to myself that she blamed me and held no solidarity with me. The horn for the meal sounded and I went to my own room briefly so that I could hide the roll of parchment. I had no time to read it now in full but could not resist partially unrolling it and glimpsing a brief snatch of the words written there in Latin. The poet was Rhygyfarch from Saint Davids in Deheubarth.

> *The people and the priest are despised by the word, heart, and work of the Normans. Families do not now take delight in offspring; the heir does not hope for paternal estates. But instead the broken spirit falls, weighed down by lethargy, and, immersed in shadows, does not know what day it is.*

'Sybil urges you to hurry down.' Amelina was at the door.

'Yes, I'm coming now.' I put the parchment in the casket on my *aumbry* shelf and went down with Amelina to the hall, joining the company who were sitting down to eat. Sybil had ordered the rushes changed and the scent of rosemary was strong in the air. A fire burnt bright and furious, keeping the frigid weather outside at bay, although during lulls in the conversation we heard the wind swooping round the corners of the buildings and the candle flames guttered with the draughts. The men who accompanied the lords were ranged on trestles and benches stretching the length of the crowded hall. Piles of weapons stood on either side of the hall door where the guests had disarmed. The chairs and benches at the high table were spread with red embroidered coverings and cushions and slung with grey and white wolf furs. Wine, mead and ale swilled in casks and great bowls set on each table. A bustle of servants went constantly to and fro refilling beakers. Meat was served on skewers and roasted geese on silver platters lined the centres of the tables, ready for carving. Candlelight glinted on the gold, silver and ivory of Sybil's best crockery. I looked nervously at these lords and soldiers with their big hands, hoping they would be careful and break nothing. If any of Sybil's goods were shattered it would be me and the servants who would feel the brunt of her anger.

Sybil and Robert FitzHamon sat in the centre of the high table. To FitzHamon's left sat Sybil's brother Hugh, then Neufmarché's wife Agnes, then Sybil's brother Roger, and then myself. Arnulf was seated on the short side end of the table, with his knees pushed up against mine. To Lady Sybil's right were Neufmarché,

Roger's wife Almodis who was heiress to the county of La Marche in France, Sybil's brother Philippe, Gerald FitzWalter and then Master Richard, who again was seated on the end side of the table facing Arnulf down the length of dishes and candles. It was like looking at the pedigree of the Montgommerys I had drawn up, come alive. All were here except the oldest brother, Robert de Bellême, who remained in Normandy. It was a lot of new people to take in but I needed to know them, these Montgommerys, since they were my captors, and might be my kin if I were forced to wed Arnulf.

I was curious to finally meet Sybil's husband. The men of the castle obeyed FitzHamon gladly and everything seemed to work even more smoothly with his presence. He was not tall, shorter in fact than his wife. As Amelina had said, he was not a pretty man, aged around forty with hair a mundane brown colour. His most prominent feature, and his worst, were his teeth which protruded at the top making him look like a coney in its warren. Despite his rodent appearance and the rigour of his command of the household, he gave me only fair words and looks and I did not fear him. I felt he was a man who would talk straight to me.

The speech of Lady Sybil's four brothers, on the other hand, oozed with double meaning and self-interest, and was all of politics, power and wealth, in Wales, in England and in Normandy. There seemed to be nothing straight about them, and the gathering of them here all together simply underlined that impression. The older brother, Hugh, enjoyed humiliating and paining others. When servants approached with sauce or wine he found reason to belittle them, so that their hands shook and they foundered in their duty. He was scathing to his own brothers, especially Arnulf, amusing himself by remarking that a fifth son could not hope for much and was usually sent into the church. Arnulf bristled beside me. I saw the effort in his face muscles to resist rising to his brother's crude bait. 'Yet *I* am master of the lands of Deheubarth and not he,' he muttered under his breath, beside me. That was not a topic of conversation I wished to engage in with him.

Roger de Montgommery, seated on my right, was, he told me, nicknamed 'The Poitevin' because of the French lands of his wife.

He was cheerful and pleasant. He and his wife Almodis were grand in very fine clothes and ate with most particular manners.

And then there was Neufmarché, with his overloud voice. A crevice of a scar on his face pulled down the edge of one of his eyes and most of the ear on that side of his face was missing, healed into a gnarled lump I was grateful there was a barrier of several people between him and me. Gerald caught my eye down the length of the table, offering me a glance of reassurance. I smiled, wishing I were conversing comfortably with him, rather than with Arnulf and Roger.

The Montgommerys and FitzHamon talked of the King's Christmas Court that they had recently come from, and of the events of the last year. I listened carefully, pretending I did not notice Arnulf's knee-jostling and his chivalrous service of food to me. They talked of King William's conflicts with churchmen, his argument with the King of the Scots, and the murder of that king and his son. My royal family was not the only one cruelly treated.

Talk turned next to the conflict between King William and his brother Duke Robert and now I could feel the undercurrents of careful veilings, since there was not a consensus on this topic at the table. The Montgommerys, I knew, were for the Duke, whilst FitzHamon was the King's man. The Montgommerys had to be indirect about their position, but the glances they exchanged with one another spoke volumes nevertheless, and FitzHamon was not deceived and knew he sat in a nursery of traitors.

There had been a truce between the two brothers, the Duke and the King, and a mutual agreement, since both were unwed and without legitimate heirs, that King William would be Duke Robert's heir to Normandy and Duke Robert would be King William's heir to England, until such time as one of them did produce their own son. The truce however soon cooled and at the last Christmas Court Duke Robert sent a declaration reneging on the undertaking. 'So more war and no heir,' said Sybil, rounding things up succinctly.

'I thought King William meant to wed the Saxon princess, Matilda of Scotland, the daughter of the murdered Scottish king,' Hugh said to FitzHamon.

'Yes, it was so but William was not much taken with the lady.'

'No?'

'He said he did not want a nun in his bed, and she looked and acted like a nun.'

'No good at all,' remarked Arnulf, looking pointedly at me.

I felt uncomfortable to be so physically close to him. I was thirteen but I knew I could find myself in his bed before too long. My brother Goronwy had found it amusing to describe to me what the marriage bed entailed when I was betrothed to Owain. Arnulf was the most handsome of the Montgommery brothers but he had attacked Llansteffan, imprisoned my mother, been present when Goronwy was murdered. I answered his compliments and attempts at conversation with monosyllabic replies. Feeling his attentions rebuffed, he tapped his glass for more wine with increasing frequency. In this company he was reduced to the junior brother and I did nothing to ease his discomfort.

The discussion turned to the poor health of their ageing father, the Earl of Shrewsbury. 'I imagine the King will not bear Robert as father's heir to the earldom and the Montgommery lands here in England and Wales?' Hugh asked FitzHamon. Despite his absence, Robert de Bellême felt like a strong presence in the room.

'No, Bellême scuttled any possibility that he would inherit the Earldom with his support for your Uncle Odo's rebellion against King William,' FitzHamon responded.

The Montgommerys held an awkward silence for a while and I studied them as they ate. Hugh resembled his sister, Sybil, with fair colouring and a broad face. Philippe's looks were darker and he was the slightest of the brothers. Sybil had told me Arnulf was twenty-eight years old. He was lavishly dressed in a black tabard intricately embroidered with gold thread at the neck. His leather shoes were fastened with two gold bosses in the form of lions. Roger seemed the most cheerful of all the brothers, talking about his estates in Lancaster. 'Good wool land,' he declared to me brightly, spooning plum sauce onto the duck on my trencher.

I did my best to look and behave like a woman in this company and not a child. I was tall for my age and Amelina had dressed me in the dark blue gown that matched my eyes. Since I was an unwed virgin my hair was uncovered, loose and long on my shoulders. Amelina had woven silver thread with tiny embroidered flowers into the thick black of my hair and I wore a delicate silver circlet on my brow. 'Oh what a Celtic beauty!' she told me as she dressed me and I had giggled with her. I felt Arnulf's eyes roaming over me all the time, and thought perhaps I should not have allowed Amelina to deck me out like this. I should have hid in drab instead, yet I wanted them to remember that I was a daughter of the royal House of Dinefwr, and I was not vanquished.

Neufmarché talked about his castle building in Brecknock, disparaging the Welsh efforts to resist him. 'Wales is ours!' Arnulf called down the table to Neufmarché, raising his beaker.

Neufmarché was in the process of returning the salute to Arnulf when FitzHamon's voice interrupted his movement, and Neufmarché replaced the beaker on the table, leaving his meaty hand wrapped around it. I turned my eyes away from the sight of his dirty fingernails and the repugnant, truncated index finger. 'Not quite yet,' FitzHamon said calmly but with assurance. 'Whilst you and I,' he said to Arnulf, and then turned his face down the table to the other guests, 'your father and brothers, and Neufmarché here, hold the south and borderlands, the north and heartlands are swarming with insurgents. It is unfortunate the Earl of Chester allowed the northern Welsh pretender to escape. The Welsh rally to him and he threatens our gains. King William has been greatly displeased.'

'Gruffudd ap Cynan you mean?' asked Gerald.

'Aye.'

I looked down at my trencher swiftly so that no one would see my expression. Gruffudd ap Cynan was no pretender. He was the rightful King of Gwynedd and had been mouldering in the Earl of Chester's prison for years. My heart leapt at the news of his liberty. If he could escape from a Norman prison, then so too could my brother Idwal, so too could I.

'The sons of Bleddyn will keep him busy,' Arnulf said.

'Perhaps,' said FitzHamon, 'or perhaps they will join forces with Gruffudd ap Cynan and keep *us* busy.'

'Bring it on!' shouted Neufmarché in a voice so loud it jarred the ears. 'Sooner in the field, sooner slaughtered!' He raised the beaker in his fat grip in Arnulf's direction. I was startled as the men seated in the hall began to thump their knife handles on the table, louder and louder, raising their goblets to Neufmarché's aggressive words. I tensed my jaw. Gerald was studying me but I looked away from his attempted commiseration.

'Is Flambard still holding sway as principal adviser to the King?' Roger asked FitzHamon when the racket had died down.

'Aye, Flambard has a wizard way with lucre and the King likes and needs that.'

'For sure,' Roger grinned into his wine. He appeared to be admiring his own reflection there.

'No good will come of this appointment of Anselm as Archbishop of Canterbury,' Hugh stated. 'He's an uncompromising bastard, a reformer, and will soon be at loggerheads with the King.'

'Already is,' FitzHamon said.

I was shocked that they would speak with such disrespect of an Archbishop. When everyone had eaten their fill and the men were leaning back, their stomachs bulging, their faces growing red with wine, the soldiers in the hall began to make their own entertainment, singing with the village girls that Sybil had enlisted as extra maids for the feast, taking out whistles and starting up harmonies, staggering out the door to relieve themselves. Lady Sybil and her family exchanged gifts with one another for the New Year: cloth, hounds and jewels. Sybil surprised me by telling me she was giving me a horse and ordering Gerald to see me get used to riding the mare and not break my neck. 'Gladly,' he said. 'Anyway Lady Sybil, Lady Nest apparently rides better than I ever will,' he said, grinning at me. I blushed, surprised that he remembered what I had said to him last year.

After dinner each of the Mongommerys stood one at a time and told a tale. Despite myself I enjoyed the stories and the vivid pictures they created with their words. Arnulf's performance, I admitted reluctantly to myself, was the best. 'Now you, Nest,' Sybil shocked me, calling down the table. I felt suddenly sick. I had to refuse, run from the hall. I looked to Gerald and he raised one eyebrow cheerfully, his face alight with encouragement, then my glance passed over Neufmarché.

They thought the Welsh were easily beaten, trodden under-foot. I stood abruptly, knocking over my beaker and a trickle of red wine soaked swiftly through the tablecloth, ran between the wooden planks of the table and dripped onto Arnulf's fine tabard. He made a small irritated sound in his throat. I looked away from the dripping wine, staring into the blazing hearth, trying to forget everyone else in the room. I imagined I was at my father's court, surrounded by old familiar faces, by the faithful warriors of his *teulu*. I recalled the face of my playfellow, the bard's son, who had told me so many winter tales and who had died at Llansteffan.

'My story ...' I began and my voice was small and shaking at first, but then gained in power as I moved into the wellworn grooves of the tale. I had been celebrated for my precocious nar-ratings at my father's court, but now I must speak to these aliens in their alien tongue. 'My story is of the Dogs of Annwn who about this time, at the Yuletide, come from Hell to hunt down wrong-doers.' They were all looking at me. The soldiers and servants in the hall stilled their activities and listened avidly as I hooked them in. I gestured dramatically up to the ceiling above our heads. 'The Dogs can be heard at night passing through the air overhead in full cry, leading the Wild Hunt of King Arawn and his fairy horde, all dressed in white and translucent gowns, all insubstantial as the river mist.' Lady Agnes shivered. 'The hooves and paws of their horses and hounds and the feet of their servants run through the air. And with them,' I shouted suddenly so that Lady Almodis jumped in her seat, 'rides the hag Matilda of the Night.' Now I went on rapidly. 'That hag is dressed in black rags and looks like a bony skeleton risen clagged and damp from a grave. Alongside those ghost riders come the hounds, the hounds of Annwn!' I looked all around again and saw they were gaping at me. 'Those great howling white ghost hounds with their red ears, and their huge fangs, foretell the death of *all* who hear them.' I swept my arm around the room, my pointing finger lingering at Neufmarché and then at Arnulf, modulating my voice up and down with the lilt of the tale. I looked emphatically into the faces of each of the other Norman enemies seated there: Hugh, Roger, Philippe, FitzHamon. 'On the night of the new year their growling grows softer and softer as they approach, hunting down wrongdoers

80

until …' I dropped my voice to an intimate whispered finale, '…
they can run away no more.' Silently I cursed that the Dogs might
visit *them,* these Normans, eat them alive, drag them down to Hell
where they belonged. Lady Almodis stopped eating the pink and
yellow sweetmeats piled before her, her hand stilled in horror
halfway to her open mouth. My tale ended, I thumped back down
into my seat, shaking like a storm-tossed sapling.

There was a moment of silence and then my performance was
greeted with enthusiastic clapping and thumping on the tables. I
took a deep breath and looked up smiling at Gerald who laughed
with me.

'Well! And here she has another talent, along with her come-
liness eh?' Arnulf shouted beside me, as the hubbub began to
subside. 'She tells a good tale!'

Everyone in the hall shouted back their agreement to him, and
I flushed hot scarlet, amazed at my own courage, shifting in my
seat, lifting my refilled beaker to my mouth to reassure myself,
seeking to find some way to make myself inconspicuous again.
Master Richard nodded his grey and ginger head at me, with a
smug expression that said, there she is, my masterwork – telling
you a gripping tale in word perfect Norman. I wished intensely
the Dogs might come and feast on their innards and their sweat-
ing, drunken grinning faces, excepting perhaps Gerald FitzWalter
and Sybil.

'I could be wed to her by now,' Arnulf said to FitzHamon,
turning suddenly angry and aggrieved. 'It would legitimate the
succession of my heirs in Pembroke. I've offered the King 500
pound of silver. Would he accept a higher offer?'

I felt furious at his words, that I, a royal daughter, should be
bartered for in public by this younger son of a nobleman. His
desperate need to compete with the successes of his older brothers in marrying rich heiresses, and hang on to his gains in Deheubarth, was evident.

'The King has said no, for now,' FitzHamon told him in a firm,
cold voice. 'He may relent in time, or you may look elsewhere.'

I kept my eyes down but I felt Arnulf's gaze on me. 'She is my
prize. I took her.' He was beginning to slur his words, his tongue
coated with wine.

'She is the King's ward. Do you plan to gainsay the King?' asked FitzHamon. His voice was soft, but there was threat in his calmness, and everyone fell silent to hear Arnulf's response. I lifted my head and saw Sybil was looking with anxiety to her youngest and dearest brother.

'Of course not, FitzHamon. That is not my meaning.' Arnulf subsided, leaning back in his chair and no more was said on the subject but he continued to stare at me, making me uncomfortable.

Agnes and Almodis rose to retire, and passed behind me. 'That one *will* have you,' Lady Agnes leant down and whispered in my ear, but I had decided by now to ignore whatever she said. Yet I looked at Arnulf with dread and wondered if Agnes' life might be my fate: if I could not love him, would I have to marry a man I hated like her, to keep my affections and loyalties covert for the rest of my life, to live with a smile on my face amidst the conquerors who had murdered and displaced my kin.

'How do you like it here in Cardiff, sister?' Roger asked loudly, deliberately shifting the direction of the conversation.

'It rains constantly, my gardens writhe with fat, black slugs and the winds are over-boisterous. In the winter the clouds are almost continual, but at least the air is healthy,' Sybil told him, laughing.

Go back to your own lands then, I thought, and good riddance. I decided to excuse myself from the table and leave the hall, following after Agnes and Almodis.

'Sleep well, my beautiful Nest,' Arnulf murmured to me as I rose. 'I hope you have not taken any distress at our conversation here?'

'Goodnight, lord,' I said, making no response to his question.

The next morning I sat close to the window at my needlework in Sybil's chamber. Agnes, Almodis, Sybil and Amelina were my companions. I observed that Roger had many reasons to be cheerful. Almodis' hair was golden and she wore an expensive gown of pale blue and white textile, edged with gold embroidery. Sybil shifted with envy in her chair every time Almodis mentioned 'my little son.' Almodis played tenderly with Mabel and I joined her. I had grown fond of the child, in the gulf left by the loss of my own younger siblings.

'Fetch more wine for us, Nest,' Sybil said in her abrupt way.

I looked at her in surprise. Why did she order me and not Amelina to this task?

'Yes, you,' she said. 'You have legs.'

'Yes, my lady,' I said meekly, determining to make what hay I could during my freedom from her surveillance. Amelina told me later that Sybil meant nothing by it and I should not take insult. 'She does show off a bit in company,' she said.

I took what I thought of as my secret route to the pantry, down the passageway from Sybil's chamber, past my room and through Master Richard's empty room (excepting his locusts), down the broken narrow back stairs that nobody was supposed to use. I had ventured exploring down the staircase several times before when Master Richard left me alone and found that since I was slender and surefooted I could edge myself fairly easily around the broken, splintered part with its gaping, jagged edges above a dark, deep fall to the undercroft that ran beneath the hall. I thought of the broken staircase as my respite from them all. Nobody knew where they could find me when I lingered in its cool embrace and inhaled its earthy, damp smell of neglect. Besides it meant I could get to the buttery, off the hall, without passing one of the men on guard at the main stairway who I did not like. He always tried to make a mock grab at me when I passed, growling like a bear. Although he pretended it was a jest, I felt he would be happy to truly grip me and rub his grubby hands over me if he could. I had just sidled past the broken steps and was about to skip down the rest when voices came from the buttery beneath Master Richard's room. I put my foot down carefully, soundlessly, on the next step which brought me to the edge of the doorway that let into that room. To hear, I had to stand hugging the wall very close to the doorway.

'Duke Robert has delivered an ultimatum, and is taking war to King William.' It was Hugh de Montgommery's voice.

'We will be ready to support him.' I recognised Neufmarché as his companion. 'Will all your brothers rally to us? Including Bellême?'

'Aye, all,' said Hugh. 'It was the oath my father swore to the Conqueror, to defend the rights of his oldest son, and it is the oath we have sworn, each one of us, to *our* father. Let's hope Duke Robert does a better job this time than the ham-fisted invasion in eighty-eight that nearly cost us all so dearly.'

So they were plotting against their King William again. I could tell FitzHamon but I did not like the idea of helping any of them. Hugh and Neufmarché moved out of the room and I passed into the buttery thoughtfully. Ten minutes later I was returning up the steps again, a wine jug balanced in both hands. At the top of the broken stairway I drew back quickly, realising Master Richard's room was occupied now and was the scene of another secret exchange. Master Richard was reporting on the household to FitzHamon. 'They are in treasonous collusion with Duke Robert,' he said. 'Another rebellion is planned in support of the Duke and they are all of them in it up to their necks, the Montgommerys.'

'Do you have written evidence of this?'

'I do.' I heard a rustle of papers.

'Is my wife involved?'

I set the wine jug down meaning to inch a little closer to the doorway and hear Master Richard's answer, but I misjudged the uneven surface of the step. The jug teetered and then fell silently for a moment, with its contents, down into the deep hole where the staircase was broken, before finally striking a step and shattering into wine-stained fragments. The sound of its striking and shattering was loud to me and I knew they must have heard something in the room. Opposite me was a narrow recessed window that gave light onto the stairway. Swiftly I stepped into its embrasure, pulling my skirts close around me, leaning in hard against the wall.

'Pigeons!' came Master Richard's voice. From the sound of it, his head was poking into the staircase aperture above me. I held my breath. Could he see the edge of my skirt or arm? It was dark if you looked down into the staircase from the brightly lit room. No more sounds came and after waiting for five minutes, I crept up to the doorway and heard nothing. The room was empty and I dashed across it and back to Sybil's chamber, my heart pounding. So there was no need for me to tell tales, since Master Richard was already doing so himself. In any case I felt torn by my growing affection for Sybil. Did she know her husband set spies on her?

Should I tell the tale to her? Perhaps she had her own counter-spies and was aware of Master Richard's treachery. 'Keep your enemies close,' she said often. I had my own very close.

When I returned to the room, Sybil was flabbergasted that I had 'forgotten' to get the wine. 'It's what you went for, you idiot,' she said, humiliating me in front of Countess Almodis and Lady Agnes. I knew her well enough by now to realise this was merely her blunt manner and not a deliberate intent to wound me, but I saw Agnes smirk at it.

'I will go. Don't worry yourself,' said Amelina, getting up, and weaving her needle carefully in place for her return.

Most of our visitors, with the exceptions of FitzHamon, Arnulf and Gerald, left a few days later and the castle returned to something like its usual rhythms and capacities. I could discern little affection between Lady Sybil and her lord. I heard him at her in the evenings in the chamber next to mine, but he did not stay through the night with her, always rising after his gruntings and returning to sleep in the hall below with the other men. There was scant speech between them. Sybil's marriage seemed little better than the couplings of dumb animals in a barn. FitzHamon was uninterested in Mabel. He merely stared at the baby when Sybil dandled her on his knee. 'Have you considered a husband for her?' he asked.

'Not so far, my lord, she is young, not walking yet.'

'Aye, well we will speak of it next time I'm here. She needs to be betrothed before too long, since she stands as my heir for now, till you quicken with a boy. We will gift the Abbey at Tewkesbury and ask the monks to pray for your conception of our son,' he told Sybil and she nodded meekly at her failure. Before he left she was vomiting again in the mornings and I prayed she would be able to satisfy him with a boy this time.

I considered sending another message to Cadwgan telling him the Montgommerys and Neufmarché conspired against King William, intending to support Duke Robert's invasion. Yet I felt reluctant to send Amelina again into Owain's company. I did not like the way she spoke of him, with an air of ownership. It seemed clear something had happened between them.

In the morning I rose early and stood waiting in the chilly air by the window watching the bailey. Before long I saw Gerald's fair head emerge below me from the hall door and he made towards the stables. I moved swiftly down the passageway, down the stairs to the hall and sidled out into the bailey and then into the stables close to where I knew his horse had been housed so that neither his men, nor the few servants of the household already up, should see me there. 'Gerald!' I hissed in a low whisper and his horse stomped and blew through its nostrils at my unexpected intervention. Gerald's face appeared around the horse's head, staring quizzically at me. 'Lady Nest? Are you …'

Overnight I had wondered whether it might be my best option to marry Arnulf. At least then I could take my rightful place as Lady of Deheubarth, Chatelaine of Pembroke Castle and the rest of my father's *llys* that Arnulf held. At least I could do some good for my people then. 'Sir Gerald I would have a word with you. It's a terrible secret though …'

He moved swiftly around the horse and stood close to me. He put a comforting hand on my shoulder. I could feel the heat of his hand through my cloak that only covered my thin nightshift since I had not dared to dress in case I disturbed one of the female guests or Amelina and they wondered why I was up and what I was about so early. 'What is it, lady? You can trust me. As far as I am able I will assist you.'

I swallowed and looked up at him. I was not sure what I was about but I needed to trust somebody. 'It's Belmeis,' I said.

A look of fury began to spread across his face. 'He has not offered you …'

'No, no!' I gripped his hand to regain his attention away from such a thought. 'No.' I shook my head. 'Nothing like that. I am treated well here.' Did I dare? 'He is spying on the Montgommerys. For FitzHamon. Despite his trusted role in Lady Sybil's household he passes on damning information on her family.'

Gerald stared at me for a moment with his mouth open. 'How do you know this?'

'I am with him learning my letters every day and he is undertaking his correspondences there. I … I accidentally read some of his papers.'

Gerald grinned and looked impressed.

86

I blushed. 'And I heard him, talking with FitzHamon. I fear they mean to harm Lady Sybil and your lord.'

He looked at me for a long moment. 'And do you care if they harm Lord Arnulf?'

My blush deepened and I stammered, 'No ... I ... I am fond of Lady Sybil. She is good to me.'

He looked earnestly at my face a little longer. 'Thank you for confiding in me, Lady Nest. I will do what I can to see that no harm comes to Lady Sybil,' he hesitated, 'or her brother Arnulf from this. You did the right thing, Nest. But please, promise me, you won't take any risks. I couldn't bear to see harm come to *you*.'

'I promise you. Thank you.'

He kissed my fingers and I felt the softness of his mouth against my skin. 'Go back quickly before you are missed. You must not be seen here like this,' he told me.

* * *

From the Copybook of Sister Benedicta

Woodstock, All Saints, 1st November 1094

My dear Benedicta, I am in England again with Henry, spending our time between London and Woodstock. King William has a great new hall under construction at Westminster and I hear hammering and taste stone dust everywhere I turn. We are here, together with Hugh d'Avranches, the Earl of Chester, who is called the Wolf, but is more like an old, very fat bear these days. We are in England on request from the King, with Henry acting in all but name as Regent, since King William has found himself absent for most of the year campaigning against Duke Robert in Normandy. I hope that war does not come too close to you Benedicta? Let me know what is occurring there. You probably hear news of King William's dealings before I do.

Henry is looking around him with an air of taking stock. I've seen this before. It's his 'now let's get this mess sorted out' manner. Doing it in the county of the Contentin was one thing, doing it in the citadel of Domfront was another, but now he is looking around thinking like that for the whole of England, Wales and Scotland. He flabbergasts me sometimes. He must think there is a strong chance he might inherit the crown otherwise he would not waste his time considering it.

'I counsel that best policy, Count Henry,' Meulan told him, 'is to keep your temper in public and draw potential enemies to your side with loving persuasion and generous promises that can afterwards be broken.' (What do you think of that Benedicta?)

Meulan has been doing his best to advise William too but the King is not exactly biddable. He seems only truly happy on the battlefield and has no real interest in the peaceable management of his realm. It's all simply resources for war to him. This has been a long campaign in Normandy and he had need of cash to pay wages to his mercenaries and *familia regis*, his personal army, to fodder the horses, to pay for the ships crossing the Channel. The King and his chancellor Ranulf Flambard recently perpetrated a shameful thing on the English people that has exasperated Henry. 'This is the kind of thing a king is not forgiven for,' he says, 'that earns him rebellion and the hatred of his subjects who should give him only love.' That's another new thing – Henry's philosophy of kingship that he speaks of often now.

But you want to know what *was* the shameful thing. Flambard summoned the English *fyrd* to muster at the south coast to aid the King in Normandy. This *fyrd* is an honourable Anglo-Saxon custom since the times even before King Alfred, where each shire, each village, will send a set number of armed men at the king's summons. It was this *fyrd* that fought off the Great Viking Army under Alfred, that fought off Hardrada's fierce Vikings in 1066 under Harald Godwinson, and that failed shortly thereafter to defend England against Henry's father, William the Conqueror. It is a venerable and honourable tradition here that speaks of the ties between king and people, and of the people's love for their land and willingness to die in its defence. These men, they duly came in their thousands, and Flambard took all money and moveable wealth they had about them and sent it to William in Normandy, and he sent those honourable fighting men home in destitution. Some of them had marched to the King's aid from the far north of the kingdom and now they return begging for food and shelter. Henry says he is ashamed if this is his brother's order and knowledge rather than an act Flambard has effected on his own cognisance. D'Avranches, Warwick and Meulan are also shocked at this mean-spirited act. Without Flambard's knowledge, Henry sent letters to all monasteries along the major routes in England asking in the name of the King's brother that they give aid to these humiliated travellers as they return to their shires. He has done what he can to rectify the wrong.

When Henry and King William are in company together there is a *rapprochement*, an affection, between them, but whilst William lives and thinks only for today, Henry does not forget and he looks so far forward it makes me spin sometimes. He does not forget the earlier wrongs his brother has done to him. I know how dangerous and simmering Henry's long, long memories can be. Sometimes I watch him and think he has two or three different men lurking beneath his skin.

On a happier note, he has been spending time in Abingdon with his mistress Ansfride and their children, Richard and Juliane, who is his newest baby daughter. Henry is negotiating with King William and Edgar Aetheling to contract an honourable betrothal for himself. He wishes to marry the Anglo-Saxon Princess Matilda, but there is a competing offer from William de Warenne, Earl of Surrey and the King, from everything I know of him, will be inclined to take the highest bidder which will be the Earl I fear, for Henry is richer in brains than cash at the moment. The princess herself, I would say, is more inclined to Henry.

Write soon to tell me you are safe and about your new duties in the scriptorium. And if you have any pertinent news on those devious Montgommerys. Your loving brother Haith.

Almenêches Abbey, Normandy, Martinmas, mid-November 1094

Dearest Haith, Thank you for your letter which reached me swiftly since there is a constant to & fro of traffic & messengers across the Channel & throughout Normandy because King William is here warring with Duke Robert. (I have adopted ampersands now since I am a venerable scriptorium mistress.) It is good to hear of these new buildings you write of. We must commend things accomplished to the notice of our successors inspiring them with example & not lazily neglect something worthy of memory to future times. We receive God's mercy according to our works.

King Philip of France gave Duke Robert his assistance against William, the King of the English, in the fighting in Normandy this summer & besieged Argentan close to here but the scene of the fighting has moved off further to the north now. We succour its refugees daily – women raped, children orphaned, villagers who have no homes left to them, soldiers maimed beyond any further use in battle. They are a sorry sight & a reminder of my own good fortune in health & security, & the love of my sisters here, & of my brother.

It is the blood month & we have been slaughtering our animals & laying up pickles, jams, fruit wines & smoked fish for the winter. I have grown overfond of a cherry liquer which our Buttery nun is expert in making. It keeps the cold at bay.

I have been developing my scripting skills & am learning to write in miniscule but I will not use it for your letters (not even those that contain my informings if I ever have any worthwhile) for I know you would have no patience with it & would ask me: is this written with the feet of a tiny, tiny mouse? I have been making ink too & have trouble washing its brown stains from my fingers & apron. I was given permission by the Abbess to go out of the Abbey Haith! to gather my own oak galls for the ink, provided I did not stray far & returned long before the Curfew Bell. I relished my freedom for those hours strolling through the woods, I can tell you, though it rained on me. The air & the rain tasted sweet on my lips & the wet grasses soaked my hem & sandals like the most luxuriant bath. So, so long since I had been out in the world.

Now I have a big pot of ground oak gall, ferrous sulphate, gum arabica & rainwater stewing together. It will be ready to use in a few weeks. I have no more gum left & it is hard to get. If you have a chance at some I pray you send it to me for I am using up all my good ink on you instead of the Lord's work! I have newly made quills lined up in the scriptorium for our copying work although my figures are bleeding with plucking and trimming them all. We have a gaggle of geese in the Abbey that provide us with the quills, so I take good care of those fowl. I rule & prick out the parchments in advance of each day's work. You will laugh when you hear that for colours on my manuscripts, in addition to carmine, cinnabar, ochre, verdigris, woad, chalk, charcoal, a little gold leaf, a little silver, I am advised to also employ rust, urine & earswax! Let's not think too much about the collecting of that last ingredient! With the winter closing in we have few hours of daylight each day for our labours at the ink horns, but I am satisfied all is as well ordered as I can make it. The outcome of things is measured by prudence.

So you see I am a woeful spy earwax to whisper in your pristine ear-hole.

You move in exalted circles indeed Haith. Your lord Henry sounds a good man, but you know that vaunting ambition will fall. The wheel of fortune as you know goes up & then crashes down, so take care of your soul always. While we know the beginning we do not know what the end may be. Farewell to you with a world of affection, Benedicta.

* * *

From Gerald FitzWalter's Day Book

Pembroke Castle, Yuletide 1094

The geese came in early this year. Early geese mean a hard winter and the nights are truly colder, the dark longer. The escape of Gruffudd ap Cynan, though Neufmarché and Arnulf make light of it, is a big set-back to our advances in Wales. The Welsh rally to Gruffudd and he is little by little taking back areas in the north, in his former kingdom of Gwynedd. This does not affect us directly here in the south, but it gives all Welshmen heart and hope to carry resistance to us. In the summer old Earl Roger of Shrewsbury died and the Welsh wasted no time in attacking Montgommery Castle on the back of it, so that even the long established

91

marcher areas of Wales are still not subdued. The attackers laid waste to the town but could not penetrate the defences of the castle itself. I sniff the machinations of Cadwgan in many cases of Welsh attack, but can gain no absolute proof that he leads or orders them.

King William has been away fighting in Normandy most of this year and rumour says his younger brother Henry had been acting more or less as Regent in England in his absence. With the King away the Welsh are encouraged to raid against us and there have been upheavals too in Scotland. It has been a struggle to hang on to the progresses we previously made. I worry at the Montgommery allegiance to Duke Robert and where their treasonous support might lead them, and hence me. I assess that King William is the superior commander and ruler and it could end badly for us, but there is no arguing with the oath my lord and his brothers have sworn. I advised Arnulf that he should take the Welsh uprisings seriously but he is inclined to dismiss them as an unorganised rabble – which they are not. 'Just as a Welsh hound will only catch a hare if it happens to find one asleep,' he said to me, 'so a Welsh rebel only succeeds if a Norman is snoozing.' This is surely false thinking on both the hound and the rebel. I have considered writing to Lord Henry on the matter, that someone in high authority might realise how things are going here, but for now I cannot break my allegiance to Arnulf in such a way. I would not wish to see us lose in Wales all we have fought for and for myself, everything is invested here. As a younger son I have only what I take through my own efforts and if this venture should fail I could easily slip to become merely a mercenary in another man's army, spilling my lifeblood for another man's gain.

I decided it was best policy for my sake and for hers not to pass on Lady Nest's information regarding the spying of Belmeis. If the King should be victor in his struggle with the Duke which seems possible, then I would be more firmly identified with the traitors if I betray Belmeis, and there is no safety or benefit for me in that. Prevarication seems my best path for now. Further I don't like the idea of Arnulf thinking Nest is taking risks in his interest, and wish she would not do so.

I celebrated my eighteenth birthday and Christmas at the King's court at Winchester where I accompanied Lord Arnulf to see his brother Hugh confirmed as the new Earl of Shrewsbury. It was a shock to be in the bustle of the court after the long months of near solitude at Pembroke where I do nothing but work and sleep and talk to my horse. The King was delayed by bad weather for crossing the Channel and Lord Henry conferred the title on Hugh as the King's proxy. He was supported in the King's absence by Hugh d'Avranches, Earl of Chester and the Beaumont brothers, Henry Earl of Warwick and Robert Count of Meulan, who are all smart men. What a great thing it might be to be an Earl if my accident of birth had been different. Or if I had been my father's eldest son I would have been given the castle of Windsor, or if Arnulf had been an elder son, then at least I would now be the knight of an Earl.

Arnulf is still put off by the King's chancellor on his petition to marry Nest and furious at it. The surviving members of the Scottish and Anglo-Saxon royal family were at the court in Winchester including Princess Matilda. She had her head bent close with Lord Henry's often. It is said she has refused marriage to Warenne, the Earl of Surrey, so I suppose she is angling for the King or the King's brother instead for who else is higher? She is a rather plain young woman compared to my Princess Nest.

Part Two

1095–1098

7

A King

Sleepily I lifted a hand from the bedcovers to scratch an itch on the end of my nose and my fingertips encountered a soft velvet texture. I opened one eye to a glorious pink bloom pushed up close to my face. I sneezed violently and heard Amelina laughing. She stood with an enormous bunch of pink, white and yellow peonies in her hands and had been gently brushing the tips of the bouquet against my nose. 'My! It takes a lot to wake you up! Happy Birthday!' I struggled upright in the bed. 'They're from Lord Arnulf,' she said, with a suggestive leer, and set about arranging them into a vase of water on the table.

'They're beautiful. It's not my name day.'

'No. It's your birthday. Fifteen, Nest,' she said, nodding her head meaningfully. 'Fifteen flowers and you have fifteen summers.'

'Amelina?' I raised my brows to her insinuation.

'Time to be a wife?'

I swung my legs out of the bed and she began to undress and dress me. 'Is he here?' I asked.

'No, but he sent a messenger with the flowers, to show he thinks of you on your anniversary.'

I looked at the flowers. They were beautiful, lavish, and in a few days they would wilt in the sultry summer heat. Yes it was time I was wed. I was impatient to become active in the world as a wife, but Arnulf's wife? I knew it was likely. Nothing had come of my covert message to Cadwgan. Despite the numerous successes of the Welsh against the Normans last year no rescuer came for me. All my family, with the exceptions of Idwal in prison and Gruffudd in Dublin, had been killed by the Normans, by Arnulf's people. I was suddenly overwhelmed with memories of the affection, smiles and gifts of my father and mother, my lost brothers Cynan and Goronwy, on my nameday celebrations every January. I felt the loss of my family more keenly with each passing year.

As Master Richard had predicted I was speaking Norman French now as if I had been born to it, but I took every opportunity to speak secretly in Welsh and hear news of the resistance against my captors. The Norman invaders have built their wooden and stone castles on hills all around me, killed many Welsh leaders and usurped their territories, and yet they do not own our land. As FitzHamon feared, Gruffudd ap Cynan has made himself king again in Gwynedd and grows stronger all the time.

Last summer Cadwgan led a Welsh army in rebellion against the Norman invaders whilst King William and FitzHamon were away in Normandy. I suppose Cadwgan and Owain have been too busy to think of me. My kinsmen, Uchtryd and Tewdwr, the sons of Edwin, marched against Arnulf at Pembroke. I was sure they would prevail and Cadwgan's son might come to get me after that victory. I looked expectantly at each Welsh visitor to the castle thinking they might be carrying a secret message but no word came.

Eventually there was news but it was bad news. My kinsmen failed to take Pembroke. Hugh, who is Earl of Shrewsbury now, and Arnulf, regained control and drove Cadwgan into hiding. Yet fierce fires do still spark against the Normans, despite what Lady Agnes thinks of their invincibility. My kinswomen, Angharad and Crisiant are royal Welsh wives, and so will I be in time, I tell myself. Surely there is still time, still hope.

Sybil was overjoyed when she had birthed a son the previous autumn. She named him Haimo and I could not help but be relieved for her. Haimo was nearing one year old now and thriving. The year was advancing into September and I was in the bailey dandling Haimo on my knee and watching Mabel running unsteadily on fat, little legs when a rider clattered in through the gate, his horse lathered in dirty white sweat. Sybil came out,

Amelina close behind her with a water jug. I sat down on the steps, keeping an eye on Mabel. 'Well?' Sybil said, when the man had taken a long draught of water, thrown the rest of the jug's contents over his sweaty head and unlaced his jacket. He bent, grimacing, to his knee to give her a formal greeting.

'I have ridden from far north, my lady, a few days ahead of the King and your husband. He sends me to you with news.'

'You can stand. What news?'

He rose to his feet and Amelina handed him a fresh jug of water that he gulped at greedily. His face and clothes were smothered with dust and streaks of dirt. 'Grave news, lady. King William went north to deal with rebellion.'

I glanced at Sybil and then looked again. There was fear in her face. She knew something, something bad.

'The King besieged the Morpeth, Tynemouth and Bamburgh. Robert de Mowbray and his steward, who undertook the evil murders of the Scottish king and prince, have been arrested. The steward was questioned. Hard. They plotted to replace King William with his cousin, Stephen de Aumale.' The man paused for another gulp at the water and Sybil suppressed her impatience. 'The steward blabbed in exchange for his life and limbs.'

'Blabbed what?' Her expression suggested she knew the answer to her own question.

'The steward gave up details of the plotters.'

Sybil looked at her splayed feet. 'Well, is there more?'

'The King is in high dudgeon, lady, with the conspiracy and with the Welsh who continue to give so much trouble. He is on his way here now to begin reprisals against the rebels, and to subdue the Welsh.'

'Reprisals?' Sybil said quietly.

'That is all I know, my lady. All your husband told me. Except to say you should ready to receive the King.'

'Were any of my brothers in the north with the King?'

'No, lady. They were not there.'

She turned on her heel abruptly and moved to re-enter the hall. 'See to the needs of this messenger and his horse, Nest,' she called at me over her shoulder. I was irked at the way she spoke as if I were a serving girl. I was fifteen, a woman. The glances of the men in the castle told me that. I was a royal woman. She should not treat me like an insignificant girl. Nevertheless my irritation was overcome with anxiety for her and her concern for the fate of her brothers in this rebellion.

Dinner in the hall was uncomfortable in the extreme. Sybil sat in silence but the wheels in her brain were turning. She stared often and with a stony face at Master Richard. He talked far too much and of far too little, unnerved by her glance. I considered that if the Montgommerys had been implicated in this plot against the King, then Arnulf's suit for my hand in marriage, would certainly not succeed. The tension emanating from Sybil was only relieved by the frantic bustle of the servants making preparations for the King's visit.

As the messenger had promised, he was followed two days later by the arrival of Sybil's lord, Robert FitzHamon, in the company of King William and a great entourage that could not all find room within the castle, so that the lesser of them camped outside the walls, along with the King's army that numbered some hundred knights and perhaps five hundred archers and foot soldiers. When the riders came into the bailey they were covered in armour and wore helmets so I could not see the King's face until we sat down to dinner later in the day. Everywhere I went in the castle I had to squeeze around people, baggage and horses. I carried Mabel for fear she would be trampled underfoot.

FitzHamon came hurriedly to Sybil's chambers after washing. He looked for a long time at his son in the cradle as if he were slaking a great thirst. Finally he looked up smiling warmly at his wife, for the first time that I had ever witnessed. He gestured to a servant in the doorway who handed a gift to Sybil, a bolt of costly pale brown silk, but FitzHamon did not linger long in conversation with her. Sybil looked at the door where he had exited and back to me. 'Finally, he approves of me,' she said and there was no affection, happiness or satisfaction in her voice. The bell for Nones rang, so we had no further time for discussion. 'Help me in the hall, Nest.' I stood and followed her down to check on the final preparations for the grand supper she had prepared in the King's honour.

The harvest was not long gathered in and there was food in plenty spilling from sacks and barrels in the castle pantry and buttery and Sybil had spared nothing in her arrangements. She nodded with satisfaction to the hall marshal and all the servants waiting nervously to begin the royal feast. Those members of the household and people of the town who had been lucky enough to be invited filed in first, their weapons handed to the servants at the doorway, and they took their seats as directed by the marshal. I stood waiting with Lady Sybil on the raised dais. She told me the King and FitzHamon had gone to the keep. She turned her head to the hall door and I followed her gaze. A man – the King – walked towards us, with FitzHamon and several other men close behind him.

The King was in the prime of his life, somewhere towards forty years of age I guessed. He looked very strong. His hair was fair and parted cleanly in the middle of his head, revealing a large, white forehead and his beard was red and cut close to his face. The complexion of his cheeks and nose was very ruddy, like a brick baked in an oven. Disconcertingly his eyes were different colours: one blue and one light brown. The King had presence: there was a verve and dash about him. He was not especially tall, rather stocky with a large paunch that pushed at the lacings of his tunic. His clothes were costly and his cloak was lined with a variegated mass of furs: sable, beaver and fox, that seemed to writhe together as if alive, keeping him warm against the Welsh draughts and damp.

The King sat in the centre of the high table with FitzHamon and Lady Sybil to either side of him. His procurator, Ranulf Flambard was seated to the other side of Sybil and the other lords of the King's entourage were ranged beyond the centre according to their status. I sat at the far end of the table next to Master Richard. The King drank a great deal and was loudly jovial and boastful with the men at the table, paying scant attention to Sybil. I began to wonder if he were slighting her on purpose. His administrator Flambard was red-headed with bright, pale brown eyes that scoped each person at the table, including me. He looked like an inquisitive fox.

I was amazed at the ebullient informality of the King's humour. When one of his men said something he found amusing, he shouted, 'By the face of Lucca!', thumping the table and making Sybil's fragile crockery jump up. Everyone hurried to do his bidding and hoped for the reward of his laughter at their quips. When he laughed he exposed a mouth missing several teeth, from battle perhaps, or merely too many sweetmeats. The King talked with FitzHamon and Flambard concerning his plans to take reprisals against the rebels William d'Eu, Odo de Champagne and Roger de Lacy, who had plotted to murder him. He turned suddenly to Sybil. 'I see you are anxious to know about your brothers, Lady Sybil.'

'Why should I be anxious, my lord, they ...'

He held up a hand. 'Save your breath, lady. I know of the extent of their involvement in this rebellion and this is the second time. I forgave the first offence, on the pleading of your father, who had given great service to my own father. Your oldest brother, Bellême, has wisely stayed out of my kingdom.'

Sybil swallowed, opened her mouth, thought better of it, and waited in silence to see what the King would tell her.

'Rebellion was proved against your brother, Philippe,' he told her. 'He is in prison now awaiting my sentence. I am of a mind to be merciful and banish him from my kingdom, requiring him to go on pilgrimage to the Holy Lands.'

Sybil waited with her head down.

'I have had speech with the Earl of Shrewsbury, your brother Hugh. He was also implicated in this abominable plot against me.' He paused and all in the hall were listening. If the King stripped Hugh of the earldom, the Montgommery family would lose their status here entirely, and their enormous wealth.

'Hugh has assured me of his renewed loyalty,' the King told Sybil, patting her hand. 'I have forgiven him for a second time, but I will not forgive him or any more of your family if there is another occasion.'

'Thank you for your mercy, sire,' Sybil murmured, her face as red as the King's own. She told me later, with resentment, that the King had fined Hugh the enormous sum of 3,000 marks as the price of his mercy.

After two days in Cardiff, the King, FitzHamon and the army marched into Wales 'to subdue the natives' as the King put it. He boasted that he intended to leave not so much as a Welsh dog alive. That autumn was one of the worst I had known for years for rain, wind and storm surges along the coasts. The King's campaign against my countrymen floundered in mud and floods. They tried and failed to pursue the Welshmen up into the frigid mountains. After a month the King and FitzHamon had had enough and they returned to Cardiff frustrated.

The tense meals and overcrowding in the castle resumed. Sickness broke out amongst the soldiers who were clustered miserably outside the castle walls under canvas. The doctors declared the sickness to be typhoid fever and Sybil took what measures she could to prevent it from spreading. Bryn came down with the illness and was one of the first to die. Amelina and I sat with him in the hayloft above the steaming horses, holding his hands as he struggled for his last breaths. We looked at each other mutely, our eyes wet with tears, cloths wrapped around our faces, covering our mouths and noses.

The following day Sybil's little Haimo began to cough and cry. He burned with fever. 'No!' Sybil paced her chamber as the doctors examined the baby in his cradle. 'No! No!'

'Amelina, take care of Sybil, and I will do what is needful for Haimo,' I ordered in a low voice. Amelina nodded and rose to do her best to comfort Sybil. I carried out the doctors' recommendations as calmly as I could, trying not to cry and show the welling pity I felt for the child and for Sybil. FitzHamon sat downstairs in the hall wringing his hands and looking up with a pitable hopeful expression every time Amelina or I came down the stairs.

In the end there was little we could do. The remedies made no change in Haimo's condition and he died quickly. I could not believe that the life I had seen grow slowly inside Sybil and then arrive to delight us all, could so swiftly stop and still. Amelina and I held Sybil tightly as she shuddered and sobbed against us when the priest came to take the poor baby away for burial.

The King and FitzHamon were with us another week after Haimo died. A few nights after his death, I sat up in bed and looked to Amelina, lying on her side on her low bed. We heard raised voices in Sybil's room next door and then the unmistakable sound of a man taking his pleasure. Amelina shook her head silently to me.

Sybil's grief at the loss of her son was so great she could barely function. She moved around like a woman walking to her grave. I took charge of the orders for the household and told Amelina to stay with Sybil at all times. I kept Mabel strictly quarantined from anyone who had been amongst the soldiers and the sick. 'Lord,' I ventured, finding FitzHamon sitting miserably in the hall, 'it would be wise, perhaps, to decamp and go away from here, for the safety of the King, to outride the sickness, and for the safety of your daughter and wife.'

He looked at me bleakly. 'Yes. The King must be taken to safety. You are right.'

The King himself showed scant compassion for Sybil's loss. There was a final supper before his planned departure. 'I hear bad news of your brother Bellême,' he told Sybil.

'Surely not, my lord,' she responded. I sat close to Sybil ready to intervene if necessary for she was not herself.

'His wife has left him, claiming great cruelty.'

'Who can say what happens between a man and his wife,' she said lightly, placing her hand on her husband's as it rested on the table.

'Many can say, my lady. Very many. Your brother shamefully kept his countess locked up at Bellême for years, refusing her the right to rule in Ponthieu as her father's heiress.'

'I know nothing of the matter,' Sybil murmured. FitzHamon removed his hand from beneath hers.

'Your brother's wife sought refuge in the household of my sister, Adela Countess de Blois, and will not return to Bellême,' the King said. 'So you see, I have it on good authority.'

'Well I am sorry to hear it,' said Sybil, not making it clear which part she was sorry to hear about: her brother's mistreatment of his wife or the fact that the poor lady had escaped her husband and would not return.

'Your mother was murdered for cruelty to her tenants, I believe,' the King said, his expression revealing it was his deliberate intention to provoke.

'That is a false lie!' Sybil exclaimed and her husband frowned her to silence.

The King spoke to FitzHamon, taking no notice of Sybil's

indignation. Perhaps it was a good thing that she should be pricked out of the torpor of her grief. 'Bad blood, FitzHamon. Keep a weather eye on your wife and daughter. Now where is this Welsh princess?'

I was startled to find myself so abruptly the subject of interest. Sybil gestured in my direction but the King ignored her.

'Stand up and speak to your king, Nest,' FitzHamon told me.

'I am Nest ferch Rhys, sire,' I said, rising to my feet and facing him.

He lent back in his chair regarding me with a smile on his face. 'I can see why Lady Sybil's brother is so keen to gain my permission to wed you,' he said finally when he had finished his top to toe perusal of me.

He turned to Flambard. 'Is she the heiress or not?'

'There are rumours of a surviving legitimate heir in Ireland,' said Flambard. How did they find out about Gruffudd? I kept my expression neutral. Perhaps my uncle Rhydderch had betrayed the information of Gruffudd's whereabouts to them.

'Well find out. What of the son in the prison at Windsor?'

'He is illegitimate sire.'

'Find out more Flambard.' He roved his eyes over me again. I was shocked to realise he was thinking of marrying me.

'Yes sire, I will do what I can as fast as I can. She has only her lands at Carew and Llansteffan, if there is a surviving brother.'

The King continued to regard me for a while and then told me, 'You may sit, child.'

I felt Sybil's gaze boring into me, but kept my head down, refusing to meet her eyes. I knew she was thinking that my fortunes rose unfairly as hers plummeted.

8

A Queen

After the revelation that King William was thinking of marrying me, I lay sleepless staring at the dark beams in the chamber ceiling, considering that I was buffetted helplessly like a fragile raft from rock to rock, from wave to wave. First I should be Owain's wife to seal a peace between my father and his, and yet his father had betrayed mine; then I should be Arnulf's wife to help him usurp my father's lands, yet he was implicated in the slaughter of my family; and now it was mooted I might marry this old foreign king to birth an heir for the Normans. I did not like him. The thought was repugnant. Did I have no power at all over my own life? Could I do nothing? All of these suitors meant nothing but ill to my family and yet what was this family I clung to. Tatters. Shreds. Shards.

Could I find a way to free Idwal if I should learn how to flirt with the King? There was no sense in trying to get word to Gruffudd in Ireland since he was hardly talking or walking yet, and might not survive his childhood in any case. There must be something I could do to find the helm of my own life. Lying in the darkness, my resolve gradually grew that I should push aside my physical dislike and my romantic notions of marriage, and accept this old king as my husband. I should be a queen. By that means I might gain some power to impact on the fortunes of my country.

* * *

From the Copybook of Sister Benedicta

Rouen, Martinmas 1096

My dear Benedicta, you bewilder me with your ampersands, on top of your code too! Have you become the Venerable Bede now? I am spending piles of candles deciphering your tales and have black circles round my eyes like a hardworking clerk. I am not getting anything like my necessary nightly quota of fifteen hours sleep. Nevertheless, despite your exactions, I am enclosing a small gift of gum arabica and another gift to help your little brown, sore hands.

Here is a report of a politic conversation for you Benedicta, of the kind I am all times surrounded by now. One morning early in the year when Henry and I were lately in Domfront, Mculan arrived straight from Curthose's court, and it was clear the Count was brimming with some news longing to be out of his mouth.

'The Duke is unlucky in love,' he began.

'How so?' asked Henry. The two of them have been worrying for some time at the issue of whether or not the Duke would marry and get himself an heir, which would not suit them at all.

'His first betrothed wife, Margaret de Maine, died long ago when they were both very young. Starved herself to avoid the marriage they say.'

'Yes I know of her death of course.'

'But do you know your father had intended to betroth Curthose to Matilda of Scotland?'

'No? How would that be possible? He is her godfather.'

'Yes but that was not the intention when your father and Robert went to Scotland together years ago, in 1080. Your father hoped to find a replacement for Margaret de Maine there for his heir.'

'In truth? No I never knew *that*.'

'Queen Margaret and King Malcolm of Scotland had no desire to make such a tie. They negotiated Curthose down to godfather – with the utmost politeness of course.' Both men laughed briefly.

'Well what does Robert propose now for a wife?' asked Henry.

'As I said, he is unlucky. Agnes de Ponthieu, the heiress, would have been a good choice but since your brother was at war with your father, Bellême was able to be there before him.'

Henry was getting impatient. 'Tell me something I don't know Meulan. What glee is lurking on your face? I see it.'

Meulan was unwilling still to let go of the drama of his telling. 'Then Roger de Montgommery beat him to another heiress, Almodis de La Marche. Wait! I'm arriving at it.' Meulan, laughing, held up a hand to Henry.

'Arrive faster Meulan.'

'Curthose thought he might settle for the second daughter of the Scottish King, Mary, and was encouraged in that hope by her uncle Edgar Aetheling who is great friends with the Duke. Mary is of marriageable age and Curthose needs to shift to get himself an heir soon. The Aetheling says he holds Curthose dear, but nevertheless his main interest is to see his nephew on the Scottish throne and King William gives best hope of achieving that.' Meulan spoke rapidly but Henry was still winding an index finger in a circle in the air to indicate more speed was required. Meulan took a breath and proceeded. 'So Curthose is thwarted over Mary of Scotland too and the Scottish princesses are at William's court now, as you know. Finally he alighted on the daughter of Hugh de Vermandois, Elizabeth.'

'Ah!' Henry looked surprised and nodded slowly. 'A good choice. She is niece to the French King and has Charlemagne's blood. I was thinking about her myself.'

'Don't say anything else on that matter sire! I have married her.'

'What! Isn't she a child still?' Henry leant back in his chair to regard Meulan.

'Yes. Eleven years old.'

'Alright, you have me flabbergasted now.'

'When I was lately at his court Curthose discussed the thorny problem of his necessary marriage and heirs with myself and Bellême. After all these deliberations that is where we ended up – a choice between Mary of Scotland or Elizabeth de Vermandois. Knowing he stood no chance of succeeding with the Scottish offer, I hurried to Elizabeth's father, who is great friends with my father. Hugh de Vermandois was preparing to leave on Crusade and wanted to safeguard his daughter before he left. I suggested myself as husband and of course that I would wait to consummate the marriage until the girl gains her maturity. He agreed forthwith and his overlord and the girl's uncle, King Philip of France, was content with the match.'

A delighted shout of laughter burst from Henry and Meulan joined him. Eventually Henry wiped a tear from the corner of his eye and said, 'Meulan! Meulan! Sometimes you amaze me. You stole the girl from under Robert's nose!'

'I'm afraid so.'

'And what is his response?'

'Sadly I couldn't witness that. I came directly here, after I had made arrangements for my child-bride. I've placed her in the care of my brother's wife until she becomes a woman. She is an exceedingly pretty girl.'

'And exceedingly royal to boot! You have done well my friend.' Henry clapped Meulan on the shoulder and I poured wine for us all. We raised our beakers and slopped them together at Meulan's successful intrigues and nuptials.

'So William plays this card with Edgar Aetheling and the Scottish princesses?'

'I have advised him to do so.'

Henry grinned briefly. 'Of course you have.' He thought for a moment. 'William would still be well advised to marry one of these princesses himself no? And certainly not to give either of them to Robert. Their symbolic significance is too great – the blood of the Anglo-Saxon kings – and their political significance with Scotland is greater for William as King of the English than it is for Robert as Duke of Normandy.'

Meulan nodded. 'I have strongly advised William not to agree to any marriage offer from Curthose for either of them. As to King William's own marriage – he shows no inclination.' Meulan paused. 'He is happy with FitzHamon and wants no disruption to that from a queen at his court. A female queen.'

Henry frowned. 'Do not go too far Meulan. He is my brother.'

'I apologise my lord.' Meulan shifted uneasily in his seat.

Henry waved his hand. 'I know you speak truth but let's be circumspect. It makes me shudder to wonder what my father would have made of William's … preferences.' He looked at Meulan, his eyes wide.

'Indeed. The fact is sire, the Conqueror would have gutted William and his paramour and thrown them both in the sea. Sadly the Conqueror is no longer with us. My informants tell me there is a Welsh princess that William and Flambard have under consideration.'

'A *Welsh* princess?' Henry retreated back into his own thoughts for a while. 'And Curthose? Does he have other ideas for a wife?'

'At present he has none. He is also happy with a paramour.'

Henry raised his eyebrows.

'Agnes de Ribemont,' said Meulan. 'Agnes is managing her husband's estates in Normandy whilst her husband operates in England. Agnes and your brother the Duke enjoy a little risky adultery. Agnes is a strong woman and holds Curthose fast to her. I doubt she will want to see him marry unless she herself becomes a widow.'

Henry and Meulan smiled long and slow at each other, satisfied with their latest information.

But then came the great change you will have heard about, Benedicta, when Duke Robert decided to take the Cross, answering the Pope's call to crusade in the Holy Lands. This resolves many things, both for Henry and for King William, at least temporarily. Henry and I witnessed Duke Robert vowing at Mont-Saint-Michel to carry the Cross against the heathens into the city of Jerusalem and never to return until that deed was done. He has just handed his duchy over to his brother William in Rouen in exchange for a truly vast pile of William's silver that will fund the Duke's journey. Normandy is in the hands of Rufus now and I pray that it is safe there, since you reside within it. Flambard wrung this huge sum of silver that King William used to 'purchase' his 'caretaking' of Normandy from the hard-pressed English. Many other men of Normandy will accompany the Duke including his uncle, Odo de Bayeux and Rotrou Count de Perche. It seems a fitting conclusion to the contention between the brothers and the problems with Duke Robert's rule of Normandy. The theory is King William will caretake Normandy until his brother's return, but in practice, I cannot imagine William has any intention of ever handing Normandy back.

William has promised to restore Henry as Count of Contentin. In the meantime we have been visiting with Henry's sister, Countess Adela in Blois who has birthed a third son, Stephen. Henry is fond of all children, and took his own junior entourage of Robert, Mathilde, Richard and Juliane to play with their cousins. The Countess' husband is also an absent crusader but his wife is more than able to rule in his stead. Adela was educated alongside myself and Henry in Salisbury and aside from our military training she was Henry's equal in all else – in Latin, reading, construing. She is like him with her strategic head. Her oldest son unfortunately had a problem at birth and he has not grown well in his mind, but her second son Theobald looks lively enough, and this new third son, Stephen, thrives. Write to me how are you and the events in your Abbey dear sister. With great affection, Haith.

Almenêches Abbey, Normandy, Holy Day of the Immaculate Conception, 8 December 1096

Lazy, lazy Haith! Fifteen hours sleep indeed when seven hours will suffice you together with a plunging of your great yellow head in a basin of icy water. You must suffer my ampersands for I am a great expert dauber & scriber now of manuscripts I assure you. Thank you a thousand times for the gifts – the gum arabica &, though you joke on my sore fingers, thank you so much for the soothing unguent you sent to succour them. It smells so wonderful! Like an exotic place far away over miles & miles of sunlit sea. I dream of such a journey.

It is an excellent thing that so many great lords, including our own Duke Robert of Normandy, have heard the Pope's call to take the Cross & regain the Holy City for Christendom. We are busy all the time receiving wives, sisters, daughters, small sons, treasuries, into our keeping for safeguarding for those who go as crusaders. We should have peace now in Normandy for some time do you think? We won't know ourselves.

My duties for the Abbey have changed again & wrought a great alteration for me. Perhaps sensing that my enclosure was weighing heavy on me, Abbess Emma saw fit to entrust me with the Abbey's business out in the world so I have been allowed out of the cloister & become a great traveller to compete even with you & your Henry.

The Abbess was concerned about arrangements during Duke Robert's absence. She had me travel to visit with Bishop Serlo at Séez to confirm the existing grants for our Abbey & to arrange exemptions of some taxes. Don't be alarmed. I was not alone. Matilda de Montgommery was my cheerful companion on the journey & we were guarded by the Abbey's lump of a gatekeeper with his gigantic sword. I confess I gloried in the charms of the countryside & could not get my fill of gawping at trees, streams & hills & the apple & pear trees. When we arrived in Séez swarms of black-clad monks were issuing out of the church. We found the Bishop himself in the large garden in front of his palace giving directions to his gardeners. He was helpful in our business & a congenial dinner companion. The following day we continued our travels on to the Abbey of Saint Evroul where some of the documents relating to our case had been lodged. At the Abbey we were taken care of by a young deacon named Vitalis. I found him in the library surrounded by cartularies & charters up to his very ears because he has recently begun work on extending the history written by William de Jumièges, *Deeds of the Norman Dukes*. Vitalis told me he was born in England, near the Welsh border & christened with the name Orderic. His father was a chaplain in the service of the Montgommerys & his mother was an English woman. I found him excellent company & now I am returned to Almenêches, though I am of course glad to be home & surrounded by everything familiar, I am also feeling a little dull after my late adventures so send me news for I know you always have plenty. Nothing useful to report I'm afraid although I listen at keyholes and door jambs at every opportunity (not many such). With affection & & & & & & & & & etc Benedicta.

* * *

Soon after the King's last campaign in Wales and its disastrous consequences for my poor lady and her tiny son, Sybil found she was carrying a child again and she birthed a girl who she named Hawise. Her husband returned home briefly only once after the birth of his second daughter, simply with the intent it seemed of seeding himself another son. He stayed a mere week. 'Too long,' Sybil said glumly and was soon strolling around the castle again with a stomach several inches before her. It is her permanent con dition. She has lately birthed this child and again it was a girl and named Cecile. Now Amelina and I have a motley collection of three little girls in our care: Mabel who is brown-haired, mischievous and confident; Hawise is black haired and prone to sulkiness; and Cecile, the new baby is fair-haired, like her mother.

Mabel and Hawise waddled around behind me as I did my morning chores as if they were my brood of ducklings, and Cecile was slung securely on my back. I was showing Mabel and Hawise how to lift water from the well. It was a cold morning despite the advance of summer. We had been expecting the arrival of King William again. I looked up at the clatter of hooves and there he was looking down at us with his bi-coloured eyes, with FitzHamon at his side. 'Lady Nest, little ladies,' the King said pleasantly. We curtsied to him, the girls wobbling and looking nervously to me to check they were doing it correctly.

Seeing the King in person, I flinched at my resolve to marry him. After they had ridden past to the stables, I stepped towards the hall and caught sight of myself in a puddle and stared at the image as it wavered and blurred with the cold breeze crossing the bailey. Who was I? Who was that woman, considering marriage to a Norman, claiming herself Welsh. The black of my hair, the blue of my eyes, melted together, faltered treacherously on the trembling surface of the water.

9

Inaction

As we dressed for dinner Sybil told me, 'Beware, Nest, the King's usual patience and good humour are stretched at the moment.' She had been exceptionally pleasant to me lately, after the suggestion that I might become William's queen. I had been born and trained to be a king's wife and determined to use my charm on him. If Sybil could tolerate marriage to FitzHamon, surely I could tolerate marriage to the King if it gave some control of my own life and perhaps the future of my lands. Amelina set out my finest clothes whilst shaking her head and assuring me I would be happier with Arnulf in my bed.

Sybil had ordered dresses made for us in the new *bliaut* style. The bright red wool was tight against my body from shoulders to hips and puckered with honeycomb smocking across my abdomen. The voluminous skirts of the dress swirled from my hips when I twisted and turned like the petals of a great blossom blowing around its own stem in the wind. The sleeves were tight to my elbows then widened and draped to the floor. My long fingers were laced with rings that Sybil gave me as a birthday gift, my black hair was lustrous on my shoulders and glittered with a single red ribbon dotted with tiny garnets, that was woven into the top of my head and curled at the side of my face. Sybil perceived my efforts. 'Don't rush to embrace an old man, Nest,' she told me. 'It may not bring you what you hope for.'

I ignored her advice and at dinner I did my utmost to entrance the King yet, unlike the other men who could not take their eyes from me, he seemed to barely notice I existed. I smiled at the cross old man, asked him questions about his hawk and horse. He answered but did not seem overly interested in anything I had to say. Despite his smile when he arrived King William was indeed in an angry mood. I kept my breathing calmed as he told Lady Sybil he intended to kill every male inhabitant of the Welsh mountains.

The harshness of the King's reprisals against the rebels the previous year had shocked Sybil. The Welsh successes in pushing back his Norman colonists were infuriating him. My countrymen, led by Cadwgan, had despoiled the town of Pembroke, and the Norman garrison near Carmarthen had been forced to withdraw. I imagined my father's former *llys* standing broken with battering rams again. I thought of the scenes of happy meals I had shared there with my family, those halls now standing in ashes. My lands, Carew and Llansteffan, were fired, the people driven out from their homes and fields. The King's knights and foot soldiers camped outside Cardiff castle and the next morning King William and FitzHamon led them out in the direction of my homelands.

No news came through to us during their absence. I tried to settle to designing a tapestry I was working on with Amelina. We planned to use it to teach Mabel and Hawise to sew, but my mind kept wandering in anxiety to what was happening in Deheubarth, and my fingers stilled for long distracted stretches of time. 'What will be, will be,' Sybil told me, seeing my concern, and guessing at its cause.

To take my mind away from my worry she allowed me to accompany her into town – my first time outside the castle walls for four years! We required needles and various spices that Sybil wanted to select herself for the kitchen. The wind knocked back my hood as we rode across the moat, accompanied by a small armed guard, and with Amelina leading a rouncie that would carry our shopping home. I gloried in my freedom, looking avidly at everything all around, slaking my starved eyes and stifled mind. We rode slowly up the narrow streets of the town. I pinched my nose closed as we passed a butcher slopping a glob of entrails into a bucket. We had to wait in a narrow alley as two of our escort dismounted to move aside some discarded barrels. Around the four sides of the market place shops stood with their shutters open and goods displayed on external counters. Small boys were employed to keep an eye on the clientele and make sure nobody ran off with the wares. Sybil concluded her business with a mercer and was pointing out a decorated belt to me when a man came up behind us greeting the shopkeeper in Welsh, 'Your braies and your balls be blessed Gwyn!' I stifled a laugh and shook my head at Sybil's enquiring glance. The man's face coloured scarlet when he saw there were ladies nearby.

It was the start of the Whitsuntide holiday when the labourers had a week without working and the festive spirit was building all about the town. Sybil and I sat on our palfreys behind a small crowd gathering at the foot of the steep main street. 'What's happening?' Sybil asked a man standing next to her horse. The man looked up at her blankly and I repeated her question in Welsh. 'Cabbage Race,' he said, which left me no wiser. I repeated his words to Sybil but then we were enlightened as a crowd of men and boys came hurtling down the hill, pursuing cabbages or trying to control them with their feet. Several tripped and fell. Others lost their cabbages to the crowd where they were quickly concealed under someone's cloak, but one father and son made it to the bottom of the hill with their battered cabbage footed to and fro between them and were declared the winners. Sybil and I laughed at the spectacle. 'I hope they feed those cabbages to the pigs now, rather than wasting them,' she said.

Riding back into the confinement of the castle after this brief glimpse of elsewhere was hard but I told myself it must be the beginning of more such freedoms. I was sixteen and could expect to be married very soon. Whilst I still felt that I should be married to Owain, a Welsh prince and my betrothed husband, there had been no news from Cadwgan. I was impatient to be active in the world so if I *had* to marry a Norman man, the King or Arnulf, at least I would gain that from the marriage.

The King and FitzHamon rode back into Cardiff less than five weeks later and I drew in a breath of relief seeing the King's long face. The campaign had been a disaster again, with the Welsh taking to the mountains, the terrain and rain defeating the Norman punitive force once more. The land loved us and not them. It hid us in its folds, waiting for when we could reclaim it from these foreigners. They would never conquer our land as they had conquered the lands of the Saxons. The King's army, that rode into south west Wales so shiny and strong, was now a chaotic jumble of exhausted, dirty men whose food and water supplies had run dry, who had seen friends shot in the back by invisible archers in the trees, who feared they might be the next to contract a lethal dysentry. The King and FitzHamon led the dispirited men back to Cardiff, and riding alongside them into the bailey came Arnulf, his own attire pristine as usual.

At dinner the King sulked and FitzHamon tried to reassure him. 'Peace here is brittle and short-lived but we will prevail.' The King made no response.

'I have a tale to cheer you if you will hear it, sire?' Arnulf said. It seemed that he, at least, had weathered the King's displeasure against the Montgommerys.

'Go on …' said William.

Arnulf told how he had ordered Gerald FitzWalter to hold Pembroke in his behalf and shore up its defences. Pembroke, it transpired, was the only Norman fortification that had withstood the Welsh attacks. 'Morale was low and the situation was desperate,' Arnulf said. 'Gerald fooled the Welsh attackers into believing Pembroke Castle was well supplied and needed no reinforcements.'

'What!' spluttered the King, banging his goblet down on the table, making Sybil flinch.

'Yes!' Arnulf had to pause his story to control his laughter. He wiped his mouth with two fingers, smoothing his brown moustaches, first one side and then the other. 'Gerald slipped out of the castle under cover of night from the great cave that lies underneath the castle and gives out onto the river.'

'The Wogan,' I said.

Arnulf turned to me and smiled. 'Yes, Lady Nest, you know it of course. The Wogan as it is named by the local people. Gerald slipped along the dark river and left a spurious letter, sire, where he knew it would be found and taken to the Welsh leaders. It convinced them their assaults on Pembroke Castle would be hopeless against such strength and abandoned the siege!'

The King thumped on the table with the blunt end of his knife. 'By the face of Lucca!' he shouted, and laughed with tears in his eyes. Even though it was a story against my countrymen I felt some pride at Gerald's ingenuity. Looking at the King's wrinkled red face and hands and thinking of valiant Gerald's curling blond hair and his kind pale blue eyes, my resolve to charm the old King faltered. I touched my hand to the unfamiliar *couvrechef* that I was wearing for the first time to cover my hair now that I was of marriageable age. It was a small square of cream linen that Amelina had tied on for me with my red ribbon studded with garnets, and matching my dress. I saw Arnulf watching me and dropped my hands back to my lap.

'Now,' Arnulf told the King, turning back to him, 'Gerald is raiding the lands of the Bishop of Saint David's in Pebediog.'

'Take care of that one, Arnulf. He is serving you well,' the King said, recovering from his uproarious laughter. 'Where's he from?'

'He is the younger son of your forester at Windsor sire, Gerald FitzWalter.'

'Well, I shall reward him for his initiative when I get the chance.'

Later I sat in Sybil's chambers sewing and looked up to see Arnulf hovering in the doorway. 'May I, sister?' She smiled her assent and he came and sat close to me where he could look at my needlework. 'This is very fine work, Lady Nest.'

'Thank you.'

Hawise clambered onto his knee, looking earnestly into his face. 'Nest sings us beautiful songs in Welsh,' she told him.

'Indeed! Does she?' he laughed. 'Do you think she might sing us one now?'

'No, no, lady!' I protested, looking to Sybil who arched her eyebrows.

'Why not, Nest. Hawise is right. You have the voice of an angel and would do us all a kindness to sing for us.'

I blushed furiously. I did not want to sing in front of Arnulf, but Sybil said no more and looked at me with an expression which I knew meant she would not relent. I searched in my head for a short song but in the end I found the one I knew the best, that I knew I could sing the best. I stood and Arnulf looked up at me, hugging Hawise to him. I sang a song for *Calan Mai*, the first of May. 'Welcome, welcome, first of May, sweet May Day ...' When I finished I slapped back down on my stool, looking at my knees. Arnulf, Sybil, Amelina and the girls clapped enthusiastically.

'You were right, Hawise,' Arnulf said, tickling her and making her giggle, 'Lady Nest does sing beautifully.'

In the evening I rose from the supper table to go to bed, taking a small candle with me to light me up the staircase and along the passageway. The King was accommodated in the guest room next to mine which Sybil had furnished with all her best fabrics. I turned at the sound of footsteps behind me, thinking it was perhaps the King, but saw instead Arnulf close behind me. He was allotted a place in the hall to sleep, but perhaps he sought the garderobe. I frowned as he passed the door to that room and came on instead towards me. 'Nest,' he whispered softly in the gloom and took hold of my shoulder. 'Thank you for that song today. A May Day song is a wooing song is it not?'

'No,' I stuttered, suddenly worried by his proximity. 'It was a song welcoming the spring.'

'Ah, nevertheless, spring is a time for wooing, Nest.' Gently he pushed my shoulder back against the wall. He took the candle from my hand and hooked it to the candle-hook in the wall above my head. 'Now I can see your face properly.'

'My lord, pray let go of me.'

'Of course,' he said, instead, standing very close to me, and placing the tip of his little finger in the small indentation in my chin. 'Won't you smile for me and show me that other dimple?'

I tried to twist my shoulder and face away from him but he gripped me, pinned me there. His body pushed hard against mine. My girl's strength and willowy height were no match for him. Despite myself, I felt a thrill of pleasure pass swiftly through me at the warmth and weight of him.

'I could make you very happy, Nest, if you will let me. Your eyes are like azure pools to drown in.'

I tried to be angry with him. Yes drown, drown, I thought, your lungs heaving and flattened like empty pigs' bladders. Gasp for air and find none. But as I looked into his dark brown eyes heat

119

spread prickling across my face and neck. I fought my body's urge to respond to him. 'Let me go! The King will be displeased!'

'The King!' Arnulf laughed. 'Don't imagine there is anything for you there, Nest. The King is more interested in me than he is in you, I can assure you.' I was confused at his meaning, and seeing my confusion he enlightened me. 'Yes,' he told me crudely, 'he is more interested in my arse than in yours. So forget about him. You are ready for our marriage bed Nest. I will be gentle and loving to you, I swear it.' He leant towards me intending to kiss me. My body reacted without my will, without my conscious intention. I opened my mouth and relaxed the struggle of my arms and thighs against his body. His face came close to mine, and his lips touched mine. I opened my mouth and felt his tongue slide into my mouth, filling it. A stab of desire coursed through me. I twisted my head away. A candle was coming down the passage, and Master Belmeis' face emerged above it. Arnulf let go of me and took a step back.

'Lady Sybil is asking for the child, lord,' Belmeis said meekly, pretending he had not noticed what Arnulf was about.

Arnulf smiled at me wolfishly. 'Then she must go to Lady Sybil,' he said langorously. Master Belmeis moved into the garderobe and closed the door behind him. I reached for my candle and Arnulf brushed his hand down from my armpit against my breast and I took in a quick breath at his touch. 'Not a child, a woman surely,' he said. He leant close and whispered in my ear. 'Will you meet me later, Nest? With Master Belmeis' locusts perhaps?'

'No,' I said.

'Nevertheless I will wait for you there in an hour, in case you change your mind and would like to continue our … interrupted conversation.'

I went back down to Sybil, doing my best to collect myself. I feared that the heat of the kiss and my lust might be visible. Later, when I was alone in my chamber, my face washed with shame that I been prepared to seduce the King, and that I had been so naïve about him, and then that my body had warmed so easily to Arnulf. I thought I could use my power as a woman, and yet I was just a stupid girl.

A memory of my brothers in Llansteffan teasing me on my betrothal to Owain rose in my mind and filled my eyes with hot tears. 'Lord only knows what Owain will make of you, you little hoyden,' Cynan laughed, tickling me under the arm, as I bent giggling and twisting away from him.

'He will make her a woman!' Goronwy yelled, falling against Idwal's shoulder laughing, whilst I tried to look as if I knew what they meant and glared consternation at them.

I stepped out of Cynan's reach. 'Owain will make me a queen!' I declared, sticking my nose in the air, daintily picking up my mud-encrusted skirts and strutting from the hall, which only increased the chorus of my brothers' laughter behind me.

I flung my wooden beaker away from me, frustrated at all this waiting and not knowing my future, all this inaction. So I would not be a queen. Arnulf had disabused me of that idea. If I married Arnulf I would have the kind of responsibilities and powers that Sybil exercised. I looked at my nightclothes laid out on the bed. I looked down at myself in my fine new dress and stood suddenly, stepping to the door. The passageway was dark and deserted. I tiptoed past the guest room where the King was snoring. Opposite the guest room was the door to Master Belmeis' locusts. I stared at it. I wanted to know if Arnulf really was there waiting for me as he promised. I knew I should stay away, but curiosity, desire, frustration mixed in turmoil within me. I turned the door handle and peered in. The room was empty, lit by moonlight that slid in a broad strip across the locusts, the floor and the desk loaded with its parchments and rolls.

I took a breath in relief but suddenly Arnulf was behind me. 'Quietly,' he said, gently pushing me in front of him into the room and closing the door behind us. I had not meant to keep this rendezvous. I was just curious. Now what would I do. He thrust me up against the locust vitrine, one hand on my breast and kissed me hard. I responded to him, feeling suddenly unable to think, my body and mind become liquid. He swept the *couvrechef* from my hair and caressed my head, kissing my neck. 'I didn't think you would be here,' he said. His mouth moved back to mine. The kiss seemed to go on forever. I knew the locusts were seething behind the glass I was pressed up against but I did not care.

121

There was a persistent tapping at the door. 'My lord! My lord Arnulf!' The servant's urgent voice whispered outside the door.

'Dammit!' Arnulf disengaged himself reluctantly from me. The sudden absence of contact with him made me acutely aware of the heat of my desire. My mouth, my hands, were suddenly bereft. Lust ached between my legs. I stared at him.

'The messenger from Neufmarché cannot wait any longer, sire. I'm sorry to disturb you.' Arnulf's servant called softly through the door.

'Sorry, but will you wait for me a moment?' I had paled at Neufmarché's name and he noticed my reaction. 'What is it?'

'Neufmarché is the murderer of my father and brothers, of Goronwy. I cannot forget that.'

'Will you wait for me? I will be swift.'

I nodded. He was half out of the door and then turned back to me, a small perplexed frown on his face. 'Goronwy? At Llansteffan?' I nodded and held my breath. 'Neufmarché's men were not there.'

'That raid was all your doing then, all *your* men?'

He pulled an apologetic face and shrugged. 'It was war, Nest.' His expression brightened again. 'I will be back before you have time to blink three times!'

He was gone and I was alone with the moonlight, the locusts, the sound of my rapid breathing and a growing sense of horror that he might be the murderer of Goronwy. Of course Neufmarché's men had not been at Llansteffan. Why had I made that assumption? Gerald, I thought, Gerald had told me it was Neufmarché's men. I must get back to my room before Arnulf returned and bolt the door. I picked up my *couvrechef* and opened Master Belmeis' door a crack but saw the King's door opposite was also opening. He must be going to the garderobe. Soundlessly I touched Master Belmeis' door closed again and cast around the room desperately. I moved to the broken staircase where I could hide, moving down so that I was just above the broken part and could not be seen from the room. Moments later Arnulf returned and I heard the door close again behind him. 'Nest? Nest?' he whispered. 'Dammit!'

I held my breath. Surely he would leave, but instead his footsteps approached the broken staircase. I moved down further, sidling around the hole in the steps. I could hear him on the steps above me. What if he should fall to his death and I was blamed. I moved swiftly and silently down and down, beyond the ground floor passageway, down to the vast, dark undercroft, full of enormous barrels. Feeling my way around the girths of the barrels, I held my skirts from the ground as best I could. A thin needle of moonlight pierced the room through a hole in the wooden panelling that ran around the top of the space. The barrels were like fat giants in the darkness, looming at me, about to come alive. If Arnulf did come down the stairs and into the undercroft I could clamber onto a barrel and squeeze through that hole but I thought with regret of my new dress that would be completely ruined by such a venture.

'Nest? Are you down here? I won't hurt you.' His voice told me he was a few steps from the bottom of the staircase, peering into the gloom. I squeezed as tightly as I could to the barrel I hid behind. 'Dammit!' I heard him climb back up the stairs and I let out a long, slow breath. After a while, I moved down the whole length of the undercroft to the other safe staircase and back up to the hall. I was relieved to see Amelina still sitting talking with Sybil and went to join them.

'I thought you'd gone to bed ages ago,' Amelina said.

'Will you come with me now?' I asked and together we regained the safety of my chamber and did not encounter Arnulf again that night.

In the morning Sybil told me her brother had been obliged to leave early on an errand commanded by the King and sent me his regretful farewells. 'He left you this gift, Nest,' she said, holding out a fine blue hood to me, lined with silver and grey wolf fur.

10

The Cheated Saint

On the King's last day at Cardiff Castle, Sybil's two older girls were summoned to dine with us as a treat and to delight the King, although both he and FitzHamon seemed not in the least interested or delighted by them. Mabel and Hawise sat wide-eyed and over-awed by the unprecedented occasion. The King presented Sybil with a beautifully made map of Normandy.

'It's my way of apology, Lady Sybil, for taking your husband away so much. At least you will be able to look on this map here and see where he is.' The King regarded Mabel and Hawise who were looking at the map in excitement with their hands hugged under their chins as Sybil had told them they may not touch it and risk mucky fingerprints on the precious parchment.

'Congratulations, Lady Sybil,' the King said. 'You have the makings of a fine brood here and another girl in the nursery I hear.'

FitzHamon frowned mightily in the direction of his daughters. 'I would ask leave, sire,' he said 'to take my wife on pilgrimage to pray for an heir at the shrine of Saint Benignus in Glastonbury.'

'For sure, FitzHamon, and then rejoin me as soon as you can.'

The King left the following day accompanied by the bedraggled army. Sybil told me I was to go with her and her husband on this pilgrimage and the girls would be left in Amelina's care.

* * *

From the Copybook of Sister Benedicta

Westminster, Easter 1097

Greetings wayfarer, politico, inkblotter! We are in England again whilst King William is on campaign in Wales but we will return to Normandy later in the summer. King William has been busy with a great deal of building work in London and Henry assists by continuing the supervision of this work. He is happy since building is one of his very great interests, along with collecting relics and interpreting dreams which he has me speak of with him all the time. Tell me some dreams Benedicta, nothing too saucy or womanly, that I can pretend are mine, because I can't remember my own and he is impatient with me.

'You sleep all that time Haith and still you can't give me some interesting dreams to ponder on!' So he berates me. I need to sleep a lot because my limbs are so large, clearly, and I work so hard during the scarce hours when I am awake.

The new buildings we are supervising in London are a curtain wall around the White Tower, King William's vast new hall at Westminster and a new bridge across the Thames to replace the one that was shattered by a hurricane. King William and Edgar Aetheling have succeeded in their enterprise to drive Donald Bane from the Scottish throne and install young Edgar instead as the new King of Scotland, who is brother to that princess Matilda I told you about, so she is pleased with that. My lord Henry's wooing of the lady is progressing quite well. She likes him (and indeed he seems to have a fascination for many ladies) and now *she* is sister to a King while *he* is brother to a King. Although she is not the greatest beauty I have ever seen she can spar with him in words and he likes that. How are your books and scrolls little sister? Or have you been about more secret missions for your Abbess? With all my affection, your sleepy brother Haith.

Almenêches Abbey, Normandy, Whitsuntide 1097

Haith! I should take umbrage at your jokes on my saucy dreams but I will ignore you. Often that is best. Make up your own dreams. My dreams just consist of seeing your face soon. You can't tell that to Henry! Or I dream that you will find a wife and give me nieces and nephews. Tell me, is this a true premonition? I wish your lord Henry well in his wooing. I have heard Princess Matilda is a most pious lady. Will I see you when you are in Normandy next my dear brother? With my love Benedicta.

* * *

On our journey to Glastonbury we wore plain clothes and broad pilgrim hats and Sybil's servants distributed alms at every stop. In the evenings FitzHamon and Sybil knelt in prayer for nigh on an hour, requesting God's intercession for their heir. Sybil rose with the impressions of small, sharp stones deep in her knees and I sponged them with a cloth dipped in warmed camomile water. Perhaps I thought, as I soothed her flesh, I could pray at the Saint's shrine for a Welsh husband and my freedom, after all Benignus had been a Briton like me and might listen to my pleas. We crossed the broad Severn river by boat from Cardiff to the Devon coast where we stayed in a small monastery and then made the day's ride to Glastonbury. I was on English soil for the first time, and the land rolled gently and green before us.

We stopped to look at the Saint's cell at Meare about three miles before Glastonbury. The priest pointed out the lake, spring and shady tree that Saint Benignus had conjured with his prayers. FitzHamon gave the priest a purse to distribute as alms to the beggars who huddled nearby and we moved on through lush fields of green wheat towards the town which clustered outside the walls of the abbey precinct. We rode past a water mill and vineyard and down Great Street towards the abbey hearing the clack, clack of looms in many houses. The looms made a rhythm of sorts with the hammering of smiths and stone-masons, and as we neared our destination, the clangor of the midday bells was added to the cacophony. We covered our noses passing the stench of tanneries, fullers and dyehouses. Carts loaded with stone quarried in the nearby hills lurched slowly down the street ahead of us, giving me time to look around. Glastonbury Abbey is the richest monastery in the land and the town was crowded with other pilgrims. Two

126

stood arguing with an inn-keeper on the threshold of his tavern. He repeatedly poked one and then the other in the shoulder, prodding them each time a little further into the street, his feet and bulk planted confidently to bar their entry.

When Prior Herluin heard that Lord Robert FitzHamon, the King's right-hand man, had arrived on pilgrimage, he came rushing to greet us, pushing aside the crowd of other less important guests. We were shown to the comfortable guest quarters attached to the prior's own house, while other pilgrims crowded into the abbey's dormitory, wrangling over which bed or piece of floor they might occupy.

After we had washed away the dust of the road, the Prior returned to show us the church. The building was half-finished and masons chipped at the porch sculptures. They briefly stilled their chisels as we stepped in past small hillocks of stone dust and tool bags littering the doorway. First the Prior led us to the tombs of the Saxon kings and then to the shrine of Saint Dunstan, and finally he led us out of Saint John's Church to the Chapel of Saint Benignus where he showed us the marvellous reliquary holding the Saint's bones.

Saint Benignus rested in a long coffin made from ivory, standing on four short golden legs with lions heads for feet. The ivory was decorated with intricate golden metalwork covering the lid and ends of the box entirely. The gold was studded with jewels and pearls and the exposed ivory sides were decorated with enamels showing blue and yellow birds and scenes from the Saint's life. I had never before seen anything so gorgeous. 'The reliquary was given to the Abbey years ago by King Harthacanute,' Prior Herluin told us, 'but it was only five years ago that the Saint was finally moved from his hermitage at Meare and housed here in Glastonbury in this church. When the Saint's bones were moved a miracle of healing occurred. The sign of the cross was drawn in the air above the bowed heads of the crowd with one of the holy bones and the sick, blind, mute and lame were cured. Those with internal diseases vomited up their sickness onto the ground and were never troubled again.'

'You are most kind with your exhaustive informations,' FitzHamon said, with barely concealed impatience, wanting to get on with the business of ensuring his wife would bear him a male heir.

'Is this your beautiful daughter?' Herluin asked, turning to me.

'No. This is Lady Nest, a noble Welsh hostage in our guardianship.'

'Ah.' Herluin turned his back on me. I was no longer of interest. In fact I was positively distasteful, his expression seemed to say. After a little more conversation on the chapel and a little more explicit show of impatience by FitzHamon, the Prior left us to our prayers, promising to see FitzHamon for a meal being prepared in his honour.

The Prior gave us over to the attentions of the priest who tended the Saint's shrine. 'I will be giving a great land grant for the Saint's good favour on our prayers,' FitzHamon told him. The priest reverently lifted the golden lid of the reliquary. FitzHamon and Sybil stooped to kiss the Saint's bones and then knelt, their hands joined together, in silent entreaty for their heir. I approached the reliquary and the priest nodded to me. The skeleton was dressed in a simple monk's robe with a hemp belt. His skull grinned at me from inside the rough brown wool of the hood. The bones of the Saint's hands, folded across his chest, protruded from the sleeves, slender and showing patches of discoloration. I bent and kissed his knucklebone. Saint Benignus, I said silently in my head, I am Nest. I am a Briton like you, daughter of Rhys who was the King of Deheubarth. My family is all murdered, and my brother and I are disinherited of our Welsh lands by these Normans. I pray, grant me a royal Welsh husband and a Welsh heir to fight and gain back what is ours and not theirs. The ancient skull stared back at me in silence.

FitzHamon went alone for supper with the Prior since they had business to talk and Sybil sent me in search of a clerk who could loan me ink and a pumice stone. When I returned I was shocked to see her set about erasing the title of the large, fertile estate in Gloucestershire that her husband meant to give to the Saint, and changing it instead to a small parcel of bumpy land in Glamorgan.

'But my lady …' I protested.

'What? Keep your mouth shut about this Nest. It's all nonsense anyway,' she said. 'Old bones will not make me a son.' Should I betray her? No, I had more sympathy with her plight as a woman expected to breed heirs, than with her lord's disgust at his female brood.

'But if there is even a chance it might help you conceive a son … or if the Saint should be offended and transform a boy-child into another girl?' I said.

Her hand hovered above the tampered parchment. Looking at her handiwork, we could both see it was too late to change things back.

Sybil dropped the pumice and stylus, suddenly slumping back in her chair. 'Oh lord what am I to do!'

'My lady?'

'He will repudiate me for sure if I have another girl and then what will become of me? I will end up a nun like my older sister and never see my girls again. Or you, Nest,' she added with characteristic Montgommery cunning, to ensure my self-interest was engaged. 'Do you think I have ruined my chances?' she asked, looking aghast at the parchment.

'No, no,' I reassured her, since there seemed little else to do. 'You're right. It's all nonsense.'

After two days in Glastonbury we took a boat back down river to the Bristol Channel and crossed towards Cardiff with Sybil puking over the side. 'The Saint has already granted our prayers,' FitzHamon told her, and sure enough before her husband left to rejoin the King, Sybil's stomach was swelling again with a child, and her ankles and fingers grew puffy and fat. Her feet too, seemed flatter and bigger as she hefted herself around. 'It's a boy this time,' she said confidently.

Master Richard greeted us on our return with news that King William had agreed to give a loan of money to his brother, and erstwhile enemy, Duke Robert of Normandy who was going on crusade. The King would go to Normandy at the end of the year to caretake his brother's lands and FitzHamon would go with him. I wondered at this Duke Robert I knew little about, for it seemed doubtful King William would be giving back his brother's rights if the Duke ever returned from the Holy Lands. First he fought to keep it against William and then he gave it to him. These men seemed to play at war as if it were a game, whilst good people bled. Perhaps the King's brother in Normandy was a very great sinner that he must take the measure of a crusade to wash his soul clean. Perhaps he would die in those sandy desert lands and then the war between the brothers would be over, and the possible exposure of Montgommery treachery would no longer keep my Lady Sybil in a miasma of stress.

Meanwhile I waited and waited for Saint Benignus to help me – for news of my own brothers Idwal and Gruffudd or of my betrothed husband Owain. For time out of mind, the royal daughters of Deheubarth had married the princes of Gwynedd or Powys. What did Owain look like I wondered. Idwal and Cynan had been sixteen and eighteen when I last saw them, proud young men just shy of boyhood. Perhaps Owain looked something like one of them. I remembered my brothers riding out of Carmarthen with my father, turning to smile and wave to me. Whose hand had slaughtered my dear brother Goronwy on the beach? I needed to know. I tried, and failed, not to dwell on the images in my mind of Idwal shackled, starved, filthy, in a prison with no hope of seeing the sky and freedom again, or of Cynan struggling for his last breath in the murky waters of a lake, whilst Neufmarché, laughing, held his head down, as my brother's face turned to the blue-white pallor of things underwater, his eyes bulging, the very last feeble bubbles of air departing the corner of his mouth.

* * *

From Gerald FitzWalter's Day Book

Pembroke Castle, St John's Eve, Midsummer 1097

The King's last campaign here that was mooted as a decisive and final action to bring the Welsh to heel was no such thing. As many campaigns before, it was defeated by the weather and the effectiveness of the Welsh archers and their tactics, making good use of the forest and mountain. Wales will not be subdued in typical Norman fashion and needs new ideas. To conquer Wales would require the full attention of the King for at least one whole year and he will not afford it.

King William has been in Normandy campaigning in the Vexin with his brother Henry and negotiating with Duke Robert who has taken the Cross and gone on crusade. The King levied harsh taxes to raise the cash his brother needed for the crusade and as a consequence William now has control of the Duchy. There have been a run of bad harvests so in Wales and England the working people suffer from these taxes for the constant exigencies in Normandy. I had to import corn from England to give aid to the families hereabouts who would otherwise die of starvation. If they all died there will be no one to work the fields. My lord Arnulf and all his family are loyal to Duke Robert but I sometimes wonder if this Duke is the very pattern of a fool. His invasions and efforts to regain England from William were paltry and merely served to kill and injure those lords who were loyal to him. If he thinks King William will return the Duchy to him, *if* he returns from the Holy Lands, then he has dogs' balls for brains.

My lord Arnulf is in a fury that his petition to marry Lady Nest is stalled over and over on the King's behalf by Ranulf Flambard and there is even rumour now that the King might marry her himself – poor tender girl. The thought of her in the arms of either my lord or the old debauched King fills me with irrational rage.

This summer when Pembroke Castle was the only Norman defence that wholly held against Welsh attacks Arnulf said he woul reward me. It seemed a hopeless situation. Everything else had fallen around us and we suffered a long siege and diminishing supplies. My men began to desert, flopping silently over the palisade at night and running into the darkness to take their chances elsewhere. I was left with only a few days supply, little water and mostly young, unblooded squires but I would not surrender and find myself with nothing again.

I knighted the squires and rallied them with speeches. I ordered the four pigs we had left, slaughtered, only partially butchered the meat for our use, and flung the remainder over the castle wall where the Welsh attackers would find them and think, I hoped, that we had so much food we could afford to waste it. I had my scribe write out a letter and pressed my wax seal as Castellan of Pembroke Castle onto it.

I waited for the moonless night and then made my way down into the Wogan cave beneath the castle that gives out onto the river, loaded my grim cargo into a small boat and pushed off. In the blackness I paddled silently inland on the Mill Pond with my companion – the corpse of one of my men recently killed in the siege. I heard horses chomping and sighing near the water's edge and crossed to them. They were the tethered mounts of Welsh fighters sleeping in a camp there. I could see the smoke of their fires just beyond the bank but they had set no watch over their horses. I cut a mare free from the ropes and gentled her as I slung the corpse over her back and led her away from the camp.

It was a short ride from there to the Bishop's Palace at Lamphey where I staged my scene in the middle of the road. The corpse had been dressed in Montgommery livery and carried a satchel with a few letters so that he appeared to be a courier from Pembroke Castle. I put my fake letter in his satchel. It was from me to Arnulf informing him I had no need of relief at Pembroke since I had enough men and supplies to last for many months. I shot the horse dead with an arrow and put another into the corpse. The bow and arrows I used were Welsh. I left horse and man lying in the road, as if they had been ambushed, to be discovered in the morning. The Bishop and his servants are Welsh so I hoped they would take my letter to the Welsh leaders. I made my way stealthily back to Pembroke and to my scared new knights to wait and see if this ruse might save us for we could not hold out much longer and I could think of no other way.

The Welsh continue with bravado in their attacks and successes under the leadership of Gruffudd ap Cynan and Cadwgan. Norman garrisons have had to withdraw at many other places including Carmarthen Castle where William FitzBaldwin recently died. His prisoners have been transferred to me including the small boy named Hywel that Lady Nest's mother birthed after I took Nest from Llansteffan. Nest is unaware of his existence and so it must stay since the boy was in a sorry condition. FitzBaldwin had him castrated soon after birth and once he could walk he was kept mostly in a wooden cage hanging in the castle courtyard in all weathers. As a result his limbs are crippled but he has had the resilience to survive all that nonetheless. I suppose it is true enough that there would be no use to either myself or Arnulf in the future if there were a legitimate Welsh male heir to Deheubarth growing straight and tall, but I have taken pity on the boy and given him into the care of a Welsh woman in the castle who is a healer of sorts. He has the freedom of the castle and a job in the kitchen. He can do no harm here and nobody, including himself, is aware of his identity.

11

Salt-Worn Lovers

Lady Sybil was nearing the time for the child in her belly and FitzHamon came home for the birth, confident that their gift to Saint Benignus would at last give him an heir. During the time of her confinement I continued to take care of her girls. Mabel was five and studying alongside me with Master Richard for a few hours each day. She did not like the locusts any more than I did. Hawise was four and Cecile two years old, so they were still mostly with their nurse but I would play with them in the hall and the bailey, and keep an eye on them when the nurse fell asleep, snoring in front of the fire. Mabel liked to put a feather underneath the nurse's nose and watch it gently lift and fall, lift and fall, whilst she and Hawise giggled as quietly as they could.

At the children's bedtime Amelina sat and told them tales and I often crept in and sat beside Mabel's bed to listen to the stories myself. Mabel liked to twiddle my hair around and around her fingers as she grew sleepy. Amelina told us tales of the King of the Britons, Arthur, who would one day return and drive the foreigners from his lands, back into the sea whence they came.

'Have you heard tell of the Drowned Court?' asked Amelina

I looked around the children's faces and we all shook our heads.

Satisfied with our enthralled response to her opening gambit, she continued, 'Thousands of years ago there was a great, low-lying and fertile kingdom ruled by Lord Helig and called the Plain of Gwyddno, but now the citadel, all the people in its sixteen villages, all their lush fields and vineyards and their church, lie drowned under the waters of Carmarthen Bay. When the tide is very low you can see the splintered trunks of the sunken oak forest that surrounded the northern parts of the kingdom, standing in the sand, sodden, black like ebony, and you can hear the church bells ring beneath the waters in times of danger.'

'How did it all get under the water?' asked Hawise.

'A maiden named Mererid who tended the well was sick with love for a man named Seithininn, who was the night guardsman for the sea dyke. One dark night Mererid and Seithininn drowned in each other's eyes, in each other's love.'

I closed my eyes on the sudden recollection of Arnulf's dark brown eyes as he pushed against me in the passage, but then those eyes yielded to the memory of pale blue eyes like seawater. Gerald FitzWalter. I blinked my eyes open and refocussed on Amelina.

'Mererid neglected her duties at the well and allowed it to overflow, and overflow, and overflow.' She spread and waved her arms all around us so that we envisaged the water toppling over the stones at the lip of the well. 'The water began to trickle down the streets, to lap at the walls of the houses, to saturate the fields, to sweep the bellowing cows along with it.'

I laughed behind my hand and the sleepy girls giggled softly with me at Amelina's theatrics.

'And Seithininn neglected his duties also because he was rolling his beloved Mererid in his arms.' Amelina mimicked the lascivious lover's actions with her own arms making us laugh. 'Seithininn failed to shut the water gates of the city against the high spring tide that lashed higher and higher against the sea walls of the kingdom. The fingers of salt water reached up the streets to join the well waters, carrying fish and seaweed into the houses, and the waters together swelled and rose and roared. And the golden plates of the lords and ladies, their embroidered clothes, their wine barrels, bobbed in the fast waters and the wild sea covered the land with its crashing waves.' Amelina stared at us with wide eyes. Hawise bit her lip.

'A few of the nobles, along with Mererid and Seithininn, sought refuge at the highest point of the citadel but the waters came on relentless and only the seabirds circling above their heads heard their cries, and in the end none of them could save themselves.' She paused to take breath, and we all took a breath with her. 'Now the drowned ghosts of Mererid and Seithininn must walk hand in hand forever, in grief and guilt, on the sea-bed, their salty tears feeding the salty sea, their flesh, wan and textured like old sea-rock, salt-worn, tide-worn.'

Hawise and Cecile sat with their mouths agog.

'Have you heard the church bells ringing beneath the waves?' asked Mabel.

'No,' Amelina told her.

'I have,' I said suddenly, startling them all. 'I heard the bells under the waves when my father and brothers were killed, when I was on the beach at Llansteffan.'

'Truly?' said Mabel.

'Truly,' I said.

Amelina regarded me for a while. 'Lyonesse was a land between Cornwall and my home Brittany that also sunk below the green translucent seas. And the Breton city of Ys was similarly engulphed by a wave as high as a mountain.'

'The sea is close here,' Hawise said nervously.

'Don't worry,' I calmed her. 'There is nothing to worry about here.'

At night I dreamt of my dead brother Goronwy, his body thrown into the sea off Llansteffan. I dreamt that the land of Deheubarth was the Engulphed Court of Gwyddno, waiting under the sea, to return, when a saviour would appear, my brother, Gruffudd ap Rhys, the Prince. And yet, I thought waking, I would not want my brother to harm my girls: Mabel, Hawise and Cecile. They were Normans. In the morning I told Amelina about my dream and my perplexities. 'Your bards say that prophecy is the history of the future,' Amelina said. 'The future is not determined, it is decided by the free will and actions of many people. Perhaps perpetual hatred for one race against another is not the future. It may be so if many of us imagine it that way.'

The following day we dined in the hall and I listened anxiously to the faint sounds above of Sybil's cries in labour. FitzHamon, seated next to me, sat with his fist clenched white around his drinking horn. I was not attending Sybil at this birth since she asked me to take care of her girls instead. Mabel had heard it all before but Hawise and Cecile were wide-eyed and wanted me to tell them why their mama was crying. 'She is bringing you a little brother.'

After several hours the wrenching cries had stopped and the nurse entered to show the baby to Lord Robert. 'It's a fine girl, my lord,' she told him quickly. He looked briefly at the baby, his face grim, his buck-teeth resting on his lower lip. He gave the midwife a silver coin then left the hall without speaking. I saw little of him before his departure to rejoin the King, and Sybil said nothing to me about how things were between them. Not good, for sure. There was a hush around the castle as if we had just experienced a death rather than a birth. When FitzHamon left it was a palpable relief for the household to return to normal, not having to walk on eggshells anymore around the lord's displeasure.

News filtered through that the Kings of Gwynedd and Powys, Gruffudd ap Cynan and Cadwgan, were continuing to harass the Norman usurpers and they in turn continued to take vengeance for my countrymen's stubborn resistance. Since Cadwgan's son might be my husband, I needed more information to know where I could focus my loyalties and interests in these struggles. I determined to find out what I could about the two Welsh rulers from any of the servants or Welsh travellers passing through the castle who would talk to me about them. One day I found what I thought must be a treasure trove on this topic in the shape of a tinker. The soldiers were turning him away at the tips of their spears, jeering whilst he shouted and whined pathetically at them in Welsh. 'What does he say?' asked Amelina as we stood by the well, watching the scene outside the gateway.

'He says he has threads and pins and the ladies would like to see.'

'Quick!' She gripped my arm. 'Shout to them to let him in!'

'But ...' I was about to tell her that judging by the state of the tinker, his wares would not be what she was looking for, but she was already gone, clattering down the path towards the gatehouse in her loose pattens.

'Hoi! Hoi!' I called out to the soldiers.

They all looked back towards me, including the filthy tinker, who was covered from head to foot in rags, wrapped around every part of him, so that he looked like a moving clothes bundle.

'The ladies *do* want to see his stuff!' I shouted as loudly as I could. The soldiers were cupping their hands to their ears, not hearing me, but then Amelina reached them. Moments later the soldiers reversed their prodding and herded the Welsh tinker inside the bailey. I accompanied him and Amelina into the hall, curious to see what he had in his pack.

Amelina had the old man lay out his wares which were much better than I had expected. There was good quality thread of many colours, needles of all sizes and a few other things besides, such as a silver thimble, and two ladies' belts made from fine green-hued leather. Amelina made him comfortable in front of the fire with a small jug of beer and a hunk of bread. She, Mabel and Hawise studied the threads, exclaiming at their bright colours and discussing where they might be effective in the tapestry we were working on. I sat down opposite the tinker and he paused in his noisy slurping at the bread that he was dipping into the beer. Probably it was too hard to eat it without some softening as he most likely had very few teeth. His bright eyes peered at me from a dirty face. There was a musty smell coming from him. He returned to eating and sipping but kept his eyes on me. 'Greetings,' I said in Welsh and saw surprise register in his eyes. He set the beer and bread down.

'Lady. Greetings to you.'

'Where are you from?'

'Me? Everywhere? I'm from everywhere? Never knew where I grew up. Can't remember that.'

'Oh.' I stared at him, wondering how to continue the conversation.

'Can tell where you're from,' he said, a smile in his voice.

'You can?'

'That's a Dyfed accent, for sure,' he said, meaning the southern tip of my father's lands.

I laughed with pleasure that he could still hear my kin in my voice. 'Yes! I was born in Pembroke.'

'For sure you were.'

'I wonder if you might tell me something about the Welsh kings? About Cadwgan and Gruffudd ap Cynan.'

'Kings!' he laughed, and took another gulp of beer and finished off the bread. 'What would I know about kings.'

I was disappointed. 'Oh. Perhaps you do not travel so far to know of them.'

Now he bridled at my assumption. 'Travelled so far. 'Course I travelled that far. 'Course I know of them, the kings of Powys and of Gwynedd. I know, I know!' he told me crossly. 'I'm travelling all over Wales from the north to the south, from the Irish sea to Offa's Dyke. All over.'

'So you are,' I soothed him. 'Some more beer?' I picked up the jug.

'Aye. Great deal of dust on the road.'

I stepped to the dresser against the wall and refilled his small beer jug and poured some into the beaker he held out in a grubby, shaky hand.

'Well, let me see. What does a lady like you, from Dyfed,' he said mischievously, 'want to know about those lords? You're from the household of King Rhys I suppose?'

I nodded but didn't enlighten him any further.

'All gone, now,' he said. 'Rhys' family. All dead.' He looked at me, waiting to see if I would contradict him, but I said nothing. 'Well, in the north now there's King Gruffudd ap Cynan … came back from a Norman prison to reclaim his birthright to Gwynedd. No prison could keep him in. But Cadwgan, now, well, and his brave son Owain, he's the real card. He's the one we're all hoping …' he lowered his voice to a whisper and bent his smelly head closer to mine. 'You know,' he hissed.

I nodded, shifting back from him. 'I know,' I said.

'Come closer,' he beckoned.

Reluctantly I shifted my stool back closer to his knee and bent my head towards his, trying not to breathe his scent too deeply.

'Sorry Lady Nest for the horse dung,' he said in a voice suddenly changed. 'I've overdone it rather. I'm quite overwhelmed by it myself.'

I gaped at him. His voice was young, cultured. Looking around carefully, he briefly pulled the filthy rags down from his nose and mouth revealing a young face, besmirched, and underneath the grime there were freckles. Up this close I realised the lines on his forehead and around his eyes were drawn on with charcoal. 'Speak low,' he said and raised the rags back around his face.

'You're the son of …'

He nodded but said rapidly, 'Don't speak my name. I am your promised husband and I am truly sorry that *this* has to be our first meeting.' His eyes brimmed with laughter. 'I will come for you, if you will still have me?'

I looked around covertly to see if we were observed but Amelina and the girls were occupied with his pack and the hall was otherwise deserted, the servants all about their chores. Amelina had not recognised him but then he must have grown considerably in the five years since she took my message to his father.

'You mentioned the postern gate in your letter to my father?'

'Yes,' I said hesitantly.

'I think you're right. I've reconnoitered and that is the best way. I will wait for you there at the next new moon, when the night is full black.'

I stared at him, my eyes wide, wishing I could think of something intelligent to say. It had been years since I wrote that letter. Why had he not come for me before now? So many things were changed now ….

'Will you be there Nest?'

'Yes.'

The young blue eyes in the old face above the filthy rags smiled at me.

'What's going on here!' Sybil's strident voice made me jump back on my stool, her demand breeching the peaceful murmur of Amelina and the girls, the crack of the fire and my low conversing with the 'tinker'.

'Just buying some thread we need from this tinker,' Amelina said.

Sybil looked in my direction suspiciously. The 'tinker' knocked back his beer and stood to finalise the transaction with Amelina. One of the guards came to see him out under Sybil's disapproving eye. He gave me a little wave with his bandaged hand as he shuffled out, bent and lame. 'Go with God's grace,' I told him in Welsh.

12

Phases of the Moon

The waxing crescent moon meant the next black night was near
enough a month away. I tried to act as normally as possible. I went
to the keep a little less than usual. I allowed myself to study the lie
of the land between the hall and the postern gate only twice. How
could Owain get to the postern gate without being seen by the
lookouts on the top of the keep, even on a dark night? It seemed
impossible. How would I get from the hall to the gate? Could
I sidle down past Master Richard's sleeping form in the locust
room, down to the undercroft and then crawl through the hole
in the panelling I had seen when Arnulf chased me? It seemed a
better chance than risking the drop from my window or trying to
get out unseen past the many people sleeping in the hall.

What would happen if I were caught? I supposed it would
hasten plans for my marriage to Arnulf or perhaps I would be
taken out of Wales and kept in close confinement in Bristol or
Gloucester. I thought of my brothers Cynan and Goronwy but
I did not think Sybil would allow me to be executed. I had never
heard of any Welsh noblewoman executed. I supposed if I stood
at the postern gate in the dark Owain would throw a rope over
and haul me up, catch me the other side, row us silently across
the moat further down, out of sight of the keep. What would
happen if the plan succeeded? I would be married to Owain and
live at the court of Cadwgan, return to the Welsh ways I knew
from girlhood, but I had been living amongst the Normans now
for five years ... I would lose Sybil, the girls, Amelina. Sybil would

be shamed if I escaped and Amelina would be punished, most likely turned out destitute .... After a while I realised I could plan and worry no more. I had given my promise for the betrothal and the escape. When the night came I would put on my dark brown dress that might conceal me in the dark and go and wait for Owain to come for me.

I watched the nightly changes of the moon from gibbous to waning with an increasing sense of dread. Part of me did not want to go but to remain here with Sybil and Amelina, even with Arnulf. This was the world I knew and I knew nothing of Owain and his father, how life might be for me in Powys, but he had risked his life and liberty once for me and would again. I could not let him down.

Wash Day came and I knew tonight would be the moonless night. My heart was heavy, though I sang my usual Welsh washing songs, as I stripped the linens from the beds with Amelina and the girls, as I carried them down to the vats in the bailey, as I pummelled and rinsed, my hands and forearms chafed red with soap. Sybil helped me carry a heavy sodden load to the line and peg out the sheets, nightdresses and shifts. Smoothing my wet hands on my apron, I watched the wet clothes wave at me in the wind, looking as if they were bidding me farewell from my life here. Surreptitiously I looked with grief at Sybil bending, a hand to the small of her back; Amelina flirting with the cook who dabbed at soapsuds on her nose; Mabel and my girls giggling and slipping in the puddles left by our ablutions.

Dead of night, I slipped out of my room without waking Amelina. I could take nothing with me – not my fine dresses, nor my splendid glass beakers. I wore all my jewellery since I might need to hock it in my new life. My claw and knife were in the pouch at my waist. I could not risk a last glance backwards at Amelina from the doorway. The passage was silent and pitch black but I knew my way around every inch of this castle now. Slowly I lifted the latch on the door of Master Richard's room and peered in. He lay snoring and I sensed rather than saw the locusts' myriad eyes bulging at me as I traversed the room and gained the broken stairwell. Down I went and through the undercroft to the place I had seen with the broken panel. I stood on a barrel and felt for the gap but began to panic. I could not find the hole. It *must* be here somewhere! My fingers felt a different surface. The hole had been mended, patched up in an effort to keep the rodents from the stored food and goods, but the patch was rudimentary and using my knife I managed to prise it up and open the hole again. It was barely big enough for me to squeeze through. I took off my cloak and bundled that through first and then struggled through the gap, getting caught at my hips and having to roll left and right violently to free myself, tearing my dress and scraping my shoulder and fingers badly. Once through I crouched next to the building in the dark and reclasped my cloak about me, listening.

All was quiet. I kept to the edges of the buildings, waiting to run between them, listening carefully for sentries. I knew where to avoid dogs that might bark and holes in the ground that could be stumbled into in the darkness. Eventually, little by little, I reached the postern gate. There was an occasional snatch of voices from the sentries high up on the keep and the creak of wood as they patrolled up and down. I peered through a knot in the wooden palisade trying to see signs of movement on the moat or the far bank. I shivered uncontrollably, despite my thick dark cloak. Once a patrol came close to where I stood and I lay flat with my face in the wet grass praying they would not see me. I waited, waited and waited, through the long, cold night, startling at the squeaks of bats and the hoot of an owl, peering through the knot at the splash of a frog or rat in the moat. But Owain never came. When the cockerel crowed and the glimmer of dawn was appearing I made my way back to my chamber, the way I had come, before I was seen by the guards.

Amelina sat awake and dishevelled on her pallet bed staring, as I crept in. 'Oh Lord, Nest! I was so afraid when I saw your bed empty. What's happened? Where have you been? I thought best to wait for first light before I looked for you or told Sybil.' I fell into her embrace sobbing, telling her my sorry tale. 'You'll catch your death of cold in those damp clothes!' She began to strip them from me. 'That was him! The tinker! I didn't recognise him at all! He is so brave and naughty, I told you! But you meant to go without me! There is a reason he didn't come, Nest. There must be a reason. Perhaps he has been injured or captured!'

We stared at each other in alarm but there was nothing we could do except wait to hear news. We sat in the hall with Sybil and the children, sewing, talking as usual and I was relieved at the end of the day that no news came. At least we knew then that he had not been captured or killed attempting to gain entrance to the castle.

What hope did I have of rescue now? My brother Gruffudd ap Rhys was still a child, only a little older than Mabel. It would be years before he returned to Wales, if he ever did. What would the shape of my life be now? Saint Benignus, angry at Sybil's deceit, had let us both down.

Sybil received her own bad news soon after: her brother Hugh had been killed in Anglesey, pursuing Gruffudd ap Cynan and Cadwgan. My curse of the Dogs of Annwn was starting to work. First Philippe de Montgommery had been disgraced and sent on crusade, FitzHamon was thwarted in his hopes of an heir to inherit the Welsh kingdom he had stolen, and now Hugh de Montgommery was dead. Roger de Montgommery, Arnulf, Neufmarché, they were still under my curse waiting to work its magic on them. Excepting Gerald FitzWalter and Sybil de Montgommery I repeated firmly in my head, to ensure that the Dogs understood who to hunt down and who to leave untouched.

'Do you know what became of Cadwgan ap Bleddyn and Gruffudd ap Cynan?' I asked, thinking there might be an answer to the mystery of Owain's failure to appear at the postern gate in those events.

'They are fled to Ireland.' And perhaps Owain with them then, I thought.

'Who will be Earl of Shrewsbury now, lady?' I asked Sybil.

'I don't know,' she said. 'Roger was implicated in the last plot against the King and has more or less retired to Countess Almodis' lands in France. It seems likely the King will appoint Arnulf.' Her face expressed her pleasure. 'And that would put the seal on your marriage too, I imagine. He will make you a very good husband, Nest, I assure you.'

I kept my expression neutral. I resolved with myself not to think too much, to wait and see, but how feeble my resolve was. The image of Arnulf's mouth coming close to mine, the heat and weight of his body pressing against me, came unbidden to my mind. If I married Arnulf, if he were made Earl, I would be mistress of Pembroke, my father's *llys*. It would be a return to my rightful status, of sorts, but I had cursed him. Should I, and how could I, lift my curse against him? But was he Goronwy's murderer?

Sybil laid out the large map of northern France that the King had given her. On the hall table she placed heavy pebbles strategically at its corners to keep it unrolled. She and Amelina pointed out places so that we could follow news of the King's campaigns with FitzHamon and see the locations of the exploits of her oldest brother Robert de Bellême, that we heard of from their letters.

'Here is where I was born,' said Amelina, her finger on Brittany in the north-west of the map.

'Here is where I grew up and first met Amelina,' said Sybil, pointing further south, to Alençon.

Hovering above France on the map was the coast of England and then above Cornwall and Devon, there was the southern coast of Wales. I looked but did not point to Pembroke where I was born, or to the ravaged lands of Deheubarth that belonged to my family.

Listening to the constant battles for territory in Normandy and the contentions there had been between the sons of the Conqueror, William Rufus King of the English, Robert Curthose Duke of Normandy, the third brother Count Henry, and between the other Norman barons, it explained something to me about why their race were here, harassing the lands of others, first the kingdom of the Anglo-Saxons and now the Welsh. Their homeland seemed to be in ceaseless turmoil and contention. They knew no other state.

* * *

From Gerald FitzWalter's Day Book

Pembroke Castle, Whitsuntide, May 1098

Lord Arnulf's brother Hugh, the Earl of Shrewsbury is dead, killed in Anglesey by a lucky shot through the eye-hole of his helmet by the Norse king Magnus Barelegs who had arrived off the coast as a kind of spectator on the struggle between Gruffudd and Cadwgan and the Earls of Shrewsbury and Chester. Gruffudd and Cadwgan have been driven to Ireland and failed in their latest attempt to force us out of the land but King William must act fast to appoint the new Earl of Shrewsbury or else they will be back taking the advantage again. I fear the King is occupied in Normandy and will not turn his attention to our needs here in Wales.

Arnulf has arrived at Pembroke and is waiting to hear what follows his brother's death. He is certain he will be granted the title. 'Who else?' he told me at dinner. 'The King will not appoint Robert or Roger who are proven traitors. No treason has been evidenced against me. I held Pembroke loyally for the King, thanks to you. Who else? You are looking at the next Earl of Shrewsbury and Pembroke, Gerald. And you will be my man.' He clapped me on the back and ordered the best wine brought out for supper and we made a toast to our future.

My own fortune will rise with that of my lord. That is the positive. But the negative is that his elevation will inevitably lead to his marriage and I dread that day when I have to see Lady Nest taken to Arnulf's bed.

We broke bread together in the morning in the hall and drank ale to settle our sore heads from the previous night's carousing. 'Will you take a wife when you are made Earl, Lord?'

Arnulf swallowed and put down his beaker. 'Indeed I will. It is high time that Welsh princess was writhing beneath me don't you think?' He gripped the back of my neck and I flinched at the sourness of his breath as he came close.

'The Welsh princess?' I said, feigning surprise. 'An Earl might look to a better prize.'

He raised his eyebrows in query.

'The King's court is littered with Norman and Anglo-Saxon heiresses who would bring you wealth as well as fine blood lines.' He was silent looking at the table and I thought to go on. 'Adeliza of Huntingdon, for instance, the heiress of that Earl Waltheof who was executed by the Conqueror for his treachery. You could ask King William for her hand perhaps? She would bring an enormous dowry.'

Arnulf considered this. 'The King will be concerned not to create an overmighty lord. I have already seen that in his dealings. And the Welsh princess shores up my position here with the local population. Besides I have seen her and she is well worth the plowing but this Adeliza or some other heiress could have the face of a horse, no!' He slapped me hard on the shoulder again and I feigned to share his amusement. I decided to take the next opportunity to tell Nest that Arnulf murdered her brother Goronwy on Llansteffan beach. She can never know the truth of it. She has mellowed towards Arnulf of late. If she grows a hatred for him it may not prevent the marriage but at least it will prevent her loving him.

Part Three

1099–1104

13

Pentecost

'Nest!' Sybil stomped through the door of Master Richard's chamber and looked at his locusts with evident distaste.

Master Richard was startled and dropped his pen, splattering ink on the parchment he had been carefully working on. 'Tch!' I passed the little sand box to him to soak up the ink before rising from my chair to face her. Sybil rarely came along the passageway to this room. What had I done to merit such a visit?

'Lessons are finished for today,' she said, pressing her hand to her ample breast, still out of breath from climbing the stairs from the hall. 'You have to be measured for new dresses.'

'New dresses!' whined Master Richard. 'My lady, I hardly think that warrants the interruption of the child's study.'

'She is no longer a child, Master Richard,' she told him. 'She is eighteen and her lessons with you will soon be over. Her lessons as a woman are about to begin and new dresses are certainly pertinent to that. Come downstairs, Nest. We have received an invitation to the inauguration of the King's new hall at Westminster for the Pentecost Court. The King orders specifically that you should come so he must mean to confirm your marriage.'

I took a deep breath. It seemed certain then that I would be given to Arnulf.

'And you will meet your countrymen there too. Peace has been negotiated with the Welsh kings and they will attend the ceremony, carrying the King's swords in the procession.'

Gruffudd ap Cynan and Cadwgan ap Bleddyn subjugated to King William? I did not credit it could be true. I realised that Owain would very likely also be at the court.

Sybil, Amelina and I set off with a small armed escort on the long journey to London in mid-May in the year 1099, the twelfth year of the reign of William Rufus. We crossed the Severn to Bristol by boat and met FitzHamon at his townhouse there. We continued the onward journey in his company with the coolness between FitzHamon and Sybil still evident.

We were six days more on the road. The inns we stayed in at Chippenham and Reading were well kept and comfortable but the place we stayed in Newbury left something to be desired. The rushes in the hall smelled of mingled shit and lavender I did not like the smell of lavender anyway. A large group of monks, travelling together on abbey business, crowded the inn and the kitchen could offer us nothing but pease pottage that looked as if it had been simmering in the pot for weeks and that dust might be its key ingredient. Sybil and I shared a bed and rose in the morning itching. We had little sleep since the talbots, the great guard dogs in the yard, barked half the night with the late comings and goings of other guests.

The road was in poor repair in some places, with great holes gaping where villagers had dug out clay for their pots. The landscape of England unfurled before us, so different from the mountains and coasts of Wales. I missed the big skies, brilliant light and rapid changes of weather in my homeland. From Reading we embarked by boat towards London, sailing fast with the current along the Thames, passing through the villages of Sonning, Henley, Marlow and Cookham, sleeping onboard.

At Windsor we disembarked to spend the evening with Gerald's brother, William FitzWalter. This was where Idwal was imprisoned. I would find a way to speak with him if I had to sell Amelina's non-existent virtue to do it. We arrived late in the day and learned that Gerald's elderly father was unwell and had already retired. We were greeted by Gerald's mother, Lady Beatrice, and his brother William and Sybil presented Beatrice with a large salmon she had purchased at the wharf. I was pleased to find that Gerald himself was present, Along with his brother

Maurice and his wife Egidia, and Gerald's sister Alice. Looking at Alice I remembered Gerald telling me he had a sister my age when I was trussed in the cart after the raid on Llansteffan.

FitzHamon and the FitzWalter brothers exchanged news. William FitzWalter described his toils here, keeping the forest laws: 'Last week I had to blind one of my peasants who killed a hart, and the year before I was obliged to hang that same man's brother, caught carrying a bow in the forest, and with dogs that weren't hambled. You'd think they'd learn wouldn't you? My men conduct regular searches of the villages looking for evidence of poaching: hides and deer, boar and hare flesh. They always find some. And on top of that there are those who try to shirk their duty assisting the hunt,' he complained.

FitzHamon and Gerald made sympathetic noises, and William went on, 'We lately had the King's brother, Count Henry here, hunting. Our woods are teeming with wild animals as a consequence of my strict enforcement of forest law. Count Henry is a great lover of the hunt and was well pleased with our chase.'

'He is a great lover ...' Maurice said and glanced at Alice.

William frowned and exchanged looks with his mother. 'Our little sister here is lately betrothed,' he announced.

Gerald put down his spoon and looked at his sister in surprise. 'Who?' he asked her.

'Robert of Windsor will be my husband,' she told him.

'Robert, the son of Walter the Deacon who holds lands in Essex?' asked Gerald.

'Yes,' said William. 'It's a good match. They are a family who are going up in the world, like our own. Count Henry was kind enough to assist us with the match.'

Alice blushed but looked up to smile reassurance at Gerald. I surmised she was not unhappy with her betrothal.

'How are things at the Abbey?' Gerald asked, meaning Abingdon which was not far away and had ties to the family.

'The monks are still complaining that part of their rightful lands are in the forest. The Abbot is frail and will leave us for his eternal rest soon. Count Henry is of a mind to propose Faricius from Malmesbury for election as the new Abbot.'

'Faricius? Do you know much about him?' Gerald asked.

'He is cellerar at Malmesbury and a good friend of the Count's. A physician of skill apparently. An Italian – from Tuscany, with the thick accent of that country. I have trouble understanding a word he says but many hold him in high esteem.'

'He is the Count's midwife!' burst out Egidia, laughing behind her hand.

'Egidia, please!' her husband hushed her. I supposed she meant Count Henry had illegitimate children and his friend, this Italian monk healer, aided the mothers of these children. I looked anew at Gerald's sister, wondering about Maurice's inference that Count Henry was a great lover. I saw from Gerald's worried expression, and glances at his sister, that he had made the same guesses.

'What is your business at court, Gerald?' William asked.

'Arnulf requested my attendance. The King wants to meet me apparently, to hear about my defence of Pembroke and listen to my report of the current situation in south-west Wales.'

'You are growing indispensable, brother, I see,' William smiled.

'And the Welsh kings will be there making their peace with King William so it's useful for me to encounter them,' Gerald said, 'and I have my own other motive for the journey, also. I wish to study the new stone buildings: the White Tower in London certainly, but I've also arranged to visit the building sites at Rochester with Bishop Gundulf and Colchester with Eudo Dapifer and speak with their masons. I've recommended to Lord Arnulf that we build new stone fortifications at Pembroke so I need to discover the costs, find who might be best for such a building commission. I'll stop off at the stone fortress of Striguil also on my return journey.'

FitzHamon looked up from the roasted duck he was dissecting. 'That is of interest to me since I've been considering building stone keeps at Cardiff and Bristol. Will you share your findings with me, FitzWalter?'

'Of course, I would be happy to discuss it with you and take your advice, for you have a great deal more battle and siege experience than I and have seen the stone castles of Normandy. May I continue on the journey with you to court tomorrow?'

'Of course, your company is always welcome.'

We rose to retire and I plucked at Gerald's sleeve in the doorway, holding him back and waiting until the others were out of earshot. 'Is it possible for me to see my brother Idwal, Sir Gerald?'

'I'm sorry, Nest, the King has moved him to Shrewsbury Castle. He's no longer here.'

'Oh.' I let go of his sleeve. My arms hung limply at my sides. The wind was knocked out of my sails. I had been so intent on this and had thought of nothing else all through the journey here and through the meal this evening. Seeing I would say nothing more to him, Gerald patted my shoulder kindly, bade me goodnight and walked up the passageway.

From Windsor we rode the last day of our journey to London, since the river was crowded with traffic and teeming with tolls. Gerald conversed easily at my side for most of the day. 'Lord Arnulf tasked me to speak with you on the subject of appointing a new steward on your estate at Llansteffan. The previous man got a tumour. His neck swelled up like a pig, and unfortunately he died,' he told me. He described the new man he wished to recommend.

'I trust your judgement and approve your choice, Gerald.'

The sun was low in the afternoon sky when we crossed the river Fleet and rode down Watling Street to enter the city by the west gate. At a crossroads just before the gate, men hung from gallows in varying states of decomposure, ranging from fresh death where their once cheerful and now ghastly features could be discerned, to corpses riddled with maggots and flies, to skeletons laced with strips of flesh pecked at by birds. I pulled my headveil round to cover my mouth and nose and looked up at the eighteen-foot high walls and the Newgate portal to the city towering before us. The guards recognised the FitzHamon livery and prioritised us past the grumbling queue of carters and pedestrians.

As we emerged from under the shadow of the gates, I heard bells and the song of monks on either side from the monasteries and churches of Saint Martin Le Grand and Saint Peter. The smells of fish and horse dung were pungent in the air. We

155

continued down Watling Street, past street vendors and a surgeon's shop, past beggars, slow packhorses, rowdy taverns spilling their unsteady customers onto the street, past stinky rills of sewage, past priests and monks wearing black, brown and white robes, apprentices struggling with buckets of water, a mass of men and women clad in bright blues, reds, greens, yellows, all rushing purposefully about their business. I heard French, English and Flemish shouted around me. On either side of the wide street we rode down were warrens of narrow, dark alleys with tall slivers of houses jumbled together at erratic angles. My horse's hooves trod in mud glittering with raw sewage and entrails. Rats, dogs, cats and wild pigs rummaged in piles of rubbish. Over my head hung gaudy shop signs of luxuries: goldsmiths, silk merchants, spicemongers. 'Don't pause,' Gerald warned us, 'or the beggars will be all over you like Master Richard's locusts and strip you down to your braies and bones.'

The great broad river came into sight on our right with the King's new wooden bridge. After the bridge we saw the White Tower up ahead. Work was nearing completion on the high keep, built in grey-brown and white stone. Since FitzHamon was one of the King's leading counsellors we were given lodgings close to the Tower and Gerald prepared to part from us as his lodgings were elsewhere and our roads diverged. FitzHamon and Sybil turned their horses after his farewells and promises to see us at court the following day. Gerald lent close to me in his saddle, handing me a small packet. 'A gift for you, Lady Nest, if you will accept it, now that you are of age and entering the world.'

I was surprised that he should give me a gift and looked towards Sybil's broad back, as she rode on unaware. I took it from his gloved hand. 'I thank you, Sir Gerald. I … must catch up with Lady Sybil.' I kicked my horse on, cross with myself that I should be so awkward and ungracious.

Our lodgings were comfortable but rather dusty and noisy from the stonework going on all around us. We stowed our finery as best we could and went to Mass in the new chapel of the Tower where the stones of the great rounded arches and the thick columns were suffused with golden light. The service was crowded with nobles, knights and squires gathering in the city for the King's court and the opening of his new hall. Robert FitzHamon was a man of the first rank so we were seated in a pew not far from the royal members of the congregation. I recognised the fair hair and ruddy features of King William and exchanged a greeting with Ranulf Flambard as he took a seat in front of us. FitzHamon leant to Sybil's ear and told her 'The King's brother is in attendance.'

'The Duke?' she asked, surprised.

FitzHamon shook his head, frowning irritably at his wife's error. 'No, no, Count Henry. The King's younger brother. Blue tunic,' he said in a low voice, indicating the broad back of a dark-haired man standing in the front pew alongside the King. Sybil and I looked but our view was obscured by the press of people and we could not catch any further glimpse of the man pointed out to us.

That night, in the privacy of the blankets on my pallet bed, I unwrapped Gerald's gift. It was a small ivory cross with an embossed silver stud at its centre and four more studs at the termination of each arm of the cross; simple but exquisite. I looked at it, smiling, and then carefully rewrapped it into the soft green woollen lining.

The following day FitzHamon decided we would travel to Westminster on the river rather than ride through the crowds and smells of the city again. It was a fresh morning with a light mist rising from the water in the early sun. We embarked at the steps near the water gate. Looking downriver, we could see the new abbey at Bermondsey on the south bank being constructed for the Cluniac monks and near finished. I was amazed at the traffic on the river, which seemed no less than the bustle of the city streets. Stately swans weaved their way on waves that spread and rolled in the wake of hundreds of boats of all sizes. We stepped into a small boat being held at the bottom of the steps. The boatman was about to push off when there was a shout from above our heads. 'Hold please!' Even in those few words it was obvious this man was a foreigner. His French was heavily accented with an intonation I recognised as Flemish. The boatman held the boat against the steps as the man clambered in.

'Haith!' said FitzHamon, reaching up an arm.

'My lord! You save my bacon!' Haith gripped FitzHamon's arm at the elbow to steady himself in the boat, and they greeted each other warmly.

'Sit, before you scupper us, sir!' Sybil told him tetchily, and indeed the boat was wobbling violently from side to side as he squeezed around us to take a seat, but he seemed not the least concerned, at home on water legs as practised as the boatman himself.

'Apologies, lady,' he said greeting her acid expression with his own utterly sunny one. This Haith was a striking man: very tall, over six feet, with immensely long arms and sloping shoulders so that he looked as if he could wrap his arms around you at least twice. His thick, straight hair was a rich buttery colour with glints of dark gold, cut in straight neat lines in a fringe, and below his ears and at the base of his neck, unlike the new Norman fashion where men wore their hair long and flowing. Haith was clean-shaven and the strong cords of his neck showed above the low round collar of his tunic. I guessed him to be not long past twenty-five years in age. He had small blue eyes that twinkled cheerfully like shards of topaz in the dark weathered brown of his face.

'Well met, Haith,' FitzHamon said, evidently on good terms with this man, who wore a fine quality sword and clothing. 'Haith is a knight in the service of Count Henry,' he told Sybil in order to ensure she was adequately polite. She inclined her head slightly to Haith and then turned her face away in disinterest.

'I oversleep!' he told me laughing, 'and Count goes on without me. Bad habit I have that he try to cure me for many years. Hopeless though!' He shrugged his shoulders and spread his great long arms, holding his palms up theatrically in mock apology. I was fascinated by his physical presence. It was like watching a player presenting some mime or play, his gestures and facial expressions exaggerated, perhaps to compensate for his pidgin Norman.

'This is Lady Nest,' FitzHamon told him, 'and my wife Sybil.'

'Delighted,' he said brightly and I could not help but smile back warmly at him, although Sybil did not turn from her contemplation of the river. Shouts from men working on the wharves rang out as we passed. The river banks, like the city streets, were strewn with detritus. After the White Tower, the other forts, Baynard's

Castle and then Montfichet's Tower, stood proud of the mass of small buildings, defending the city against seaborne attackers or rebels.

The river curved sharply to the left and suddenly we saw the island of Westminster up ahead with the splendid Abbey and palace and there was the King's imposing new hall surrounded by marshy land. There had been a great deal of rain so the river was brown and fast, lapping against one side of the hall. We were handed from the boat onto wet steps. My foot slipped on green weed strung against the stone and Haith, disembarking behind me, caught me by the waist and easily assisted me up the treacherous steps. 'Alright now,' he said.

'Thank you, sir.'

'Haith! You're late again. The Count calls for you!' a man shouted up ahead, waving his arm to beckon him to hurry forward.

Haith bowed hurriedly to us and joined his fellow, quickly striding towards the hall. Sybil looked with distaste at the ground and huffed crossly. We had to lift our fine skirts and see our best shoes become caked in wet red clay as we made our way to the great arched doorway.

The doors of the hall were intricately carved with lions, dragons, eagles and warriors. Entering, I paused with my mouth open, amazed by the size and height of the hall, the complex arcade and windows high above us, and the crowd of colourfully dressed people before me. A babble of different languages ricocheted off the walls: Norman, English, Latin, Flemish, Spanish, Italian. Near the doorway we sat on a bench and Amelina pared the worst of the clay from our shoes with her small knife.

After Amelina's ministrations I stood smoothing down my gown, feeling womanly in the new dress Sybil had instructed the seamstress to make for me. It was a deep blue fabric with a high round neck, elaborate embroidery around the neck and cuffs and a similar band of golden stitching at knee-height. The sleeves were very wide and lined with pale blue silk. I wore a narrow brown leather belt with a long tongue hanging to my knee ending in an ornate metalpiece of woven gold and silver filigree, which Lord FitzHamon had given to me last Christmas. Arnulf's blue hood with its wolf fur lining hung back from my cloak. My *couvrechef* was fine bleached linen held in place by a blue strip of cloth edged with gold thread. I wore no wimple at my neck since I was unmarried. I preferred to feel the air on my face and neck, and thought I would be stifled when I was married and had to don a wimple like the one Sybil wore.

The ivory cross Gerald had gifted me, hung on a long silver chain loaned from Sybil, and rested just below my breasts. Sybil was puzzled that Gerald should give me such a gift but after some frowning she decided it was acceptable for me to wear it. 'He cannot mean anything by it,' she concluded. 'You are a woman of the first rank and he is the younger son of a lesser noble. He means to curry favour with the future wife of his lord, of Arnulf.'

Arnulf was one of the first people to approach us, with Gerald at his side. 'So, the King will announce the new Earl of Shrewsbury today,' Sybil said. 'I hear King William is well pleased with you, brother.'

Arnulf feigned a modest gesture in response. Gerald looked with satisfaction at the cross and I smiled my thanks shyly to him.

'The King told my husband he judges you to be a competent and efficient administrator,' Sybil said smugly, 'and that you have a well-earned reputation for probity.'

'I am lucky in the King's good opinion. He has recently seen fit to grant me a very large parcel of land in Lincolnshire and Holderness, in addition to my lands around Pembroke.' He narrowed his eyes provocatively at me when he spoke of the lands of my family as his.

'Keep your back straight and your head up and look like the noblewoman you are, Nest,' Sybil told me and began to move forward into the melee of people. I made to follow her, but Arnulf took hold of my elbow and held me back a moment. Gerald hovered uncertainly and Arnulf waved him off with a peremptory gesture.

'Lady Nest, you look very fine.'

'Thank you.' I was suddenly tongue-tied, embarrassed by my memories of our last encounter. He looked fine himself. The

160

embroidery on his dark brown tunic showed an intricate pattern of twining leaves, inlaid with tiny pearls. It was time I was married. Looking at him I reflected that if it came to that today, to him, perhaps I should not be too sorry. I suppressed a smile at the memory that surfaced of Amelina telling me, 'I would …!' But there was my suspicion that he was Goronwy's murderer knawing at my heart.

'I expect a positive answer from the King today on the matter of our marriage,' Arnulf said, close to my ear, 'and then, I will be finding many ways to fill up the boredom of your days.'

Bridling at the self-assurance of his tone, I said, 'I have my own life. It does not need filling up with you.'

He was angry at my rebuff. 'I will be filling you up, Nest, rest assured, before too long.' His earlier pleasant tone had vanished. I pulled my elbow from his grasp and followed in Sybil's wake, catching up to her and watching her stolidly placing her ungainly feet at forty-five degrees to one another.

I let out a slow breath when I suddenly noticed the Welsh princes, distinguished by their dress and short hair, standing on the opposite side of the vast space. The sight of them brought back so many memories. I met Cadwgan at my father's *llys* once when I was very young and thought I recognised him. The two other men must be Gruffudd ap Cynan, the King of Gwynedd and perhaps his son. The tall, red-haired young man standing next to Cadwgan had to be Owain, although I could make no reconciliation between this fine man and my 'tinker'. Owain was looking keenly at me.

'Might I speak with the Welsh princes?' I asked Sybil.

'Very well,' she said, 'but I will accompany you.'

Cadwgan saw us coming and his eyes lighted on me curiously. Sybil and I swept them a curtsey and they bowed in return. 'May I introduce Lady Sybil de Montgommery, wife of Lord Robert FitzHamon in Morgannwg,' I told them in Welsh. 'I am introducing you,' I said to her rapidly in response to the irritation that flared on her face when she could not understand me. They bowed politely to her and she returned their greeting.

'Tell the lady we speak no French,' Cadwgan said to me and I relayed his words, though I doubted they were true. Sybil pursed her mouth. I turned back to Cadwgan. 'And you, lady?' he asked. 'You have not told us who you are?' I guessed he already had an inkling who I was but liked to play in his conversation.

'I am Nest ferch Rhys, sire.'

He surprised me by suddenly taking my hand in both of his, his eyes immediately brimming. 'My dear, my daughter,' he said. Perhaps I had been mistaken about his betrayal of my father. Tears welled in my own eyes and I struggled to control myself. I felt Sybil's gaze on me.

'This is my son Owain,' he said, plucking him by the sleeve and drawing him forward.

'Lady Nest.' Owain swept me a lavish bow that gave a view of his unruly thick red-blond hair. As he rose from the bow, his startling blue eyes played consciously upon me. Drawn to his height again his limbs appeared ungainly in unfamiliar finery. 'I apologise profusely,' he said. 'You may have heard we encountered a little trouble in Anglesey and were obliged to vacation for a while in Ireland. I was unable ....' He shrugged and I nodded, understanding what he referred to. A look of surprise slipped almost too rapidly to notice across Cadwgan's face. He had not known about Owain's plan to rescue me from Cardiff then.

'That's enough,' Sybil told me brusquely, not understanding, but intuiting that the conversation might be moving where she did not wish it to go. I took my leave of Cadwgan and his son, feeling the joy of my own language in my mouth and reluctantly returning to the different shape of French.

'Lady Nest.' I found Gerald at my shoulder, speaking in a low tone and turned to him smiling. 'So the King may give you a husband today?'

'Perhaps,' I said, looking down at his boots.

'I wish you well, lady, always.'

I looked up at him again. 'Thank you. There is something I want to ask you, Sir Gerald.'

'Please do.'

'Do you know who killed my brother Goronwy?'

He looked away.

'Was it Arnulf?' I persisted, although as I asked, it occurred to me that I had not seen his distinctive red tabard on the beach.

I had only first noticed Arnulf in the fort, when I sat with my mother.

'Perhaps. It's hard to say. It's a possibility.'

'I just realised …' I began but then a hush suddenly fell over the hubbub as King William entered wearing a splendid crown and tunic and the procession began to form up behind him. My conversation with Gerald had to be cut short. Edgar, King of the Scots, came first in the procession, bearing the sword of state for King William. The Welsh kings were due to do the same, walking behind Edgar but when the servants bearing the swords on cushions approached them, four of the English barons stepped in, jostling the Welshmen out of the way rudely, and taking up the swords and places intended for the Welsh royalty. At first I saw Gruffudd ap Cynan was deeply offended but Cadwgan smiled and whispered in Gruffudd's ear, who nodded and changed his expression. Owain grinned openly. I guessed Cadwgan suggested that the barons' eagerness to insult them had in fact saved them from a display of subjugation and meant they need not bend the knee to the foreigner. I noticed a tall, stocky man with a broad chest and floppy black hair regarding me and regarding the tussle between the barons and the Welshmen. He also seemed to guess at the cause for Cadwgan's pleasure. He saw what I saw and was amused by the small drama.

'Who is that man?' I asked Sybil quietly, showing who I meant with a small indication of my head. 'The one with black hair.'

'That is Count Henry, the King's brother and the Conqueror's youngest son. He rules Western Normandy and has been now a supporter of one brother, Duke Robert, and now a supporter of the other, King William, as it suits him. Inconstantly. Stay away from that one, Nest.'

I raised my eyebrows.

'You see the woman standing next to him? The Saxon?'

A straight-backed handsome woman, nearly as tall as he, stood beside him. She had two long, neat, corn coloured plaits showing beneath her headveil, draped to fall over her shoulders and the front of her dress, dangling to touch the ornate belt at her waist. 'Yes.'

'That's his current mistress, Ansfride of Abingdon, a widow. And he has two bastards, at least, by two other mistresses.'

Intrigued by her account, I looked back at Count Henry who, to my embarrassment, noticed my interest and gave me a smile and then a formal bow. I curtsied and Sybil huffed beside me. 'Oh for goodness sake, Nest. I told you to stay clear and here you are immediately flirting with him.'

I opened my mouth to protest I had not intended to flirt but the procession was beginning and I was forced to stifle my defence. I gripped my hands around one another. My future would be decided now. Most likely Arnulf ... or even ... the King himself was still unmarried, but surely if he continued to think of me, there would have been some indication, some negotiation beforehand. Yet considering FitzHamon was so unforthcoming with his own wife, it was possible I would not be given the courtesy of any warning ... I stopped my busy brain in its track and focussed on the King. I would know soon enough.

After King William was seated on his throne the business of the court began. Ranulf Flambard was created Bishop of Durham. A great crowd, some three hundred squires, presented themselves before the King to be dubbed as knights. There was a collective gasp from the assembled company when a large contingent of these young men knocked back their hoods to reveal their hair shorn close to their skulls. It was extraordinary to see all these naked, stubbled heads, like sheep after a shearing. The King struggled to control the expression on his face and then spluttered into loud laughter, shaking his head.

'What's this all about?' Sybil asked FitzHamon.

'A protest from Giffard and his boys,' FitzHamon told her, 'that they were kept waiting so long by the King before being made knights.'

Sybil snorted.

'It is an affront to the King?' I asked confused.

'Well, a complaint,' FitzHamon said. 'An amusing one.'

I frowned. 'If the men of a Welsh king behaved so they would soon find themselves dangling by the stomach from the point of his sword.'

'A Norman king has no call for such violent display,' FitzHamon told me smugly, his buck-teeth resetting softly on his moist bottom lip. 'The opinion of his barons is important to him and must be nurtured. They have their own status and pride to maintain and are not merely his minions but his valued and noble advisers.'

Flambard read out a treaty confirming the peace agreed with the Welsh kings, and Gruffudd ap Cynan and Cadwgan ap Bleddyn stepped up to place their marks on the document. Owain searched over the heads of the crowd and found me, an expectant look on his face. The King confirmed that the daughter of Picot de Say was given in marriage to Cadwgan as part of the peace agreement, although the young woman herself did not look best pleased about it.

The ceremonies and the business droned on and I watched a dance of three flies against the lower panes of a stained glass window. My stomach rumbled on air and my feet ached but my attention was gripped when the King announced that Robert de Bellême, the eldest Montgommery, whom I had never met, would be the new Earl of Shrewsbury. I looked swiftly to Sybil who stood with her mouth open, and then my glance passed over her to FitzHamon who stood with a smug look on *his* face. He had known and not bothered to tell her. I looked beyond them to Arnulf and watched him fight for control, his fists clenched, his body rigid. His face was an unnatural red hue and his cheek muscle twitched like a palsy. Gerald was looking at his lord with some concern. I wondered what this appointment of Bellême as the new Earl of Shrewsbury could mean. Bellême had always been a supporter of Duke Robert and not the King. No doubt Master Richard would be even more busy now carrying tales of the Montgommerys to Ranulf Flambard and FitzHamon, and Bellême would be the new jailer of my brother Idwal at Shrewsbury Castle.

'In the matter of the petitions I have received regarding the marriage of my ward, Nest of Deheubarth ...' the King pronounced in a loud but lazy voice, and I jumped at my name, pivoting back to face him. '... It is my decision that she will continue in the guardianship of Robert FitzHamon for the time being. I do not grant these petitions.' He enunciated the last sentence emphatically. The King smiled warmly to me and I curtsied to him.

I absorbed it slowly and let out a breath. He was refusing permission to Arnulf although he did not name him. For now at least. 'Why did he say petitions, plural?' I whispered to Sybil who turned to answer me but we found Count Henry at our shoulders and there before her with a response.

'Didn't you know, lady?' Count Henry said. 'Cadwgan *also* petitioned the King on behalf of his son Prince Owain of Powys for your hand in marriage but it seems you will be a virgin a little while longer. Forgive me,' he bowed again. 'Lady Sybil.' He bowed to her and she curtsied back. 'How rude of me,' he declared, not meaning it at all. 'Won't you introduce me properly to your charge? I understand you already met my knight Haith on your journey here this morning.' The tall Fleming from the boat was alongside him and several other men who formed his entourage.

Reluctantly Sybil introduced me to the Count. 'Do you know anything, Count Henry, of the King's surprising decision to appoint my brother Robert to the Earldom?' she asked.

He inclined his head. 'My brother, the King, was reconciled with Bellême in Normandy because he captured Count Helias of Maine, and then joined forces with William to besiege the Count of Anjou in Le Mans.'

Sybil bit her lip and the Count watched her face, then suddenly he took my hand and began to tow me into the crowd, calling over his shoulder, 'May I take this exotic princess for a tour around the vast new hall?' He did not wait for her response.

I remembered I should not let a man, who was not of our household, touch my hands but there seemed little I could do about it. I looked nervously at him but surely I could come to no harm amidst all these people. I looked back over my shoulder and saw Haith staring after us, his ubiquitous smile replaced with a mildly worried expression. Count Henry was somewhere around twenty-eight or nine I guessed, and though not an especially handsome man, he was striking and had an easy grace and confidence. The Count's mother, Queen Matilda, was reputed to have been a kind of dwarf whilst his father, the Conqueror, had been a giant, but this Henry was of a reasonable height, with no dwarfishness about him.

'Didn't you know about the proposal for your hand from Owain ap Cadwgan, as well as, of course, the long standing one from Arnulf de Montgommery?' he asked me.

'No, my lord.'

'It can't be a surprise to you that all of these lords are desperate for you,' he said, looking me up and down in a deliberate fashion, 'but none of *them* are worthy.'

He was laughing at me. Provoked, I spoke without thinking: 'I was betrothed to Owain ap Cadwgan by my father and it seems an appropriate marriage ... but of course I am subject to the King's pleasure and command.'

I thought he might be angry at my forthrightness but instead he seemed pleased and smiled voraciously. 'Yes, Lady Nest, you are subject to pleasure and command,' he said.

What could I say to such open and inappropriate flirting? I looked around me desperately.

'Have you heard of the curse against Neufmarché?'

I stared at him aghast. 'No!' How could he know?

'You see the pious new bishop there?' he asked in a sarcastic voice, jerking his head discreetly in the direction of Ranulf Flambard. I nodded. 'His mother is a sorceress.' He raised an eyebrow to me and I couldn't help but smile at his expression.

'Indeed?'

'Oh yes. It is the secret of his success, and she has pronounced a curse against the fat, black Neufmarché.'

I failed to suppress my amusement and a choked laugh burst from me as I looked at him expectantly for more.

'She declares the old rogue warrior will die emasculated and with no heir, even though he currently has two sons and a daughter,' he whispered, bringing his head close to mine. 'She is *never* wrong. What do you make of that, Lady Nest?'

I was relieved to see FitzHamon approaching with a young woman at his side. 'Count Henry, I see you have met my ward, Lady Nest.'

'Yes,' Henry said. 'Your wife has done well in her educating.'

I felt pleased that someone of his stature should appreciate me. FitzHamon took my hand politely from him. 'Thank you,' he said bowing and smiling. 'Here is another lady you know, Count Henry. Princess Matilda of Scotland.' Henry greeted her with delighted courtesy. FitzHamon smiled and swivelled to take me back to Sybil, his expression changing to annoyance as soon as his back was turned to Henry. I could not tell if he was annoyed with me or with the Count.

Sybil left me in no such uncertainty and blamed me entirely for the encounter. 'Don't be so foolish as to attempt to ingratiate yourself with that one. He is not simply a suave courtier. He is dangerous.'

I looked back over my shoulder towards Count Henry, trying to imagine how he could be dangerous. He gave me a small wave, his dark eyes alight with a sardonic humour.

'You introduced the Saxon princess to the Count?' Sybil asked her husband.

'They are already well acquainted. She has lately refused a marriage offer from William de Warenne, Earl of Surrey, much to his chagrin. King William cannot be brought to that match, although it would be good policy for him to ally with a woman who is the descendent of the Anglo-Saxon royal line, and who could bear him an heir.' He left us abruptly and Sybil scowled. The word heir, even in connection with another, could not be pleasing to her these days.

Sybil did not allow me to go to court on the following days that we remained in London, and I sat in the lodgings with Amelina working on my sewing. Each morning I was amused to see Haith bundling himself out of the door of the lodging, always running a little late, tucking his tunic into place around his belt or pinning his cloak brooch as he ran, calling out to the boatman, 'Hold there I beg you!'

Amelina tutted at me to stand back from the window as I jumped up to watch him. 'People will gossip about you,' she said, 'that you are ogling the Fleming, though I can't blame you.' Amelina never missed an opportunity to voice her connoisseurship of good-looking men.

On our final evening in London, when Sybil and FitzHamon returned from court I overheard them speaking about me. 'Why does he not give permission to Arnulf?' Sybil asked her husband. 'It's high time she was wed.'

I could not see them since they lay in bed in the inner chamber and I was on a pallet near the half-closed door. There was a silence and I imagined FitzHamon shrugging in response.

'Does the King still have an interest in marrying her himself?' Sybil persisted. 'It's high time he was wed also.'

'It is not your concern,' FitzHamon told her coldly. 'Roll over.' I pulled the covers up over my ears to avoid hearing the subsequent gruntings and gasps of their congress.

I was relieved to see nothing more of either Count Henry or Arnulf before we left for the return journey to Cardiff. FitzHamon remained at court with the King and entrusted us to Gerald's escort who was a great deal more pleasant travelling companion than Sybil's taciturn husband. He interested Sybil and I immensely with his animated talk of the stone buildings he had been studying. I had hoped to resume my conversation with Gerald concerning the murder of Goronwy but no opportunity to speak with him alone presented itself. I felt some guilt that I had accepted Gerald's gift and doubted Sybil's interpretation of what he meant by it. It was a rash act on my part to take it, showing him a significant favour, but I loved the cross. It seemed like the only thing that was truly mine, that had been given to me in genuine, disinterested affection and I did not want to have to give it up.

I was confused about my feelings as I returned to Cardiff still unwed: my feelings about Arnulf were ambiguous; a marriage to Prince Owain was appropriate but it was unlikely the King would give permission; King William had been friendly but there was no further mention of any interest from him; Count Henry seemed to like me and he was certainly intriguing. The King would have to make a decision soon or I would be an old maid, past childbearing, just winter forage. I returned to Cardiff full of stories to tell to Mabel about all the new people I had met and the sights I had seen.

After the Pentecost Court in Westminster Sybil's husband went to Normandy again with King William. He wrote that during a siege at Mayet a man standing next to the King was killed by a stone flung by the defenders and there was a hue and cry that the King had been almost killed. Sybil kindly wrote to her brother Bellême asking that he show leniency to *my* brother Idwal imprisoned in Shrewsbury. She received no reply to this letter but assured me he would take note of it.

* * *

From the Copybook of Sister Benedicta

Winchester, May 1100

To the most venerable and excellent Benedicta, superbus mistress of the scriptorium from Sir Haith known as valiant or sleepyhead. Yet a joking beginning is not right for this letter that I send you sister, since I must tell you there has been a sad accident here. Robert, the bastard son of the Duke of Normandy, who has been a member of his uncle King William's entourage for some time, was alas killed today in a freakish accident in the New Forest – accidentally shot. There were witnesses and they are all sure it was an accident, nevertheless the man who loosed the fatal arrow fled to a monastery for fear of the blame. It is a great sadness to see such youth lost and the Duke will be inconsolable at his loss.

We gather the Duke is on his way home from crusade with a rich new bride, Sybille de Conversano, and is vaunted as a hero. Have you heard news of this, Benedicta? The Duke's expected reappearance is fuelling dissent again amongst King William's barons who are always torn between their lands and allegiances in England and those in Normandy. King William has decided to caretake Aquitaine whilst his friend, Duke Guillaume, takes the crusade route. Meulan is discontented by this and complains to Henry that there is no serious ruler in either Normandy *or* England.

We were joined at dinner yesterday by Walter Tirel who is kin to the Clare family and lord of Poix in Normandy. There was discussion of these problems regarding the rule of Normandy and England, and of the sorry death of the boy Robert in the forest. Tirel who is a famed archer discoursed at length on the question of whether or no the boy's death was an accident, boring me rigid with his theories of stags running between trees and sun in the eyes of an archer. Fare thee well, little Benedicta, from your loving brother.

Almenêches Abbey, Normandy, Midsummer, June 1100

To my dearest brother from your sister, greetings. I am sorry to hear of Robert FitzDuke's death. We also hear rumours of the

Duke's imminent return with his new wife but he has not arrived yet. Tell me, Haith, if I might risk my sister's prerogative, have you any inclination to marry? It is your blood sister who asks, not your holy sister. You never write of women in your letters. Perhaps you are protecting the blushes of your sacrosanct sister? But I should like to know the affairs of your heart & I should like very much to be an aunt one day! Fare well my dear little brother.

14

The King's Wedding

Sybil received a letter from her husband telling her he was not likely to return home soon since King William was planning to give a loan to another crusader and caretake the state of Aquitaine, but in August, around the time of Lammas in 1100, everything changed, although it took some time for the news to reach us.

Hearing shouts in the bailey we came outside into the sunshine to see a messenger riding through the castle gates. 'The King is dead, my lady,' he gasped to Sybil from the saddle.

'What! Nest, fetch water and a towel.'

I went quickly, not wanting to miss the news. The man dismounted and took the water and towel from me, gladly swilling the dust from his throat and wiping it from his face. 'Killed hunting in the New Forest,' he told Sybil.

'An accident?' asked Sybil.

'It has been declared likely an accident,' the messenger said, 'though Walter Tirel loosed the arrow and has fled.'

'Walter Tirel!' Sybil was quiet for a moment, thinking. 'Has Duke Robert been crowned King? Is he here already?'

'No, my lady. King William's younger brother Henry has taken the throne. He has been crowned by the Bishop of London, and your lord has sworn allegiance to him.'

'Henry! And my husband now in *his* service? So fast!'

'Yes, my lady. Your husband, Robert de Meulan and Henry, Earl of Warwick, were amongst those who supported Henry in taking the crown, along with Hugh the Earl of Chester, Richard de Redvers and Roger Bigod.'

'Well! This is a turn around.' Sybil fumbled behind her and found the top of a bench. She sat down unceremoniously.

'Yes, my lady. The new king seems to have a good grip.'

'Does he indeed.'

News tumbled from the messenger's mouth as if he feared he might forget it. 'Your brother, Robert de Bellême, Earl of Shrewsbury has given his homage. The new king has imprisoned Ranulf Flambard in the White Tower. William Giffard has been removed as Chancellor and Henry's priest, Roger d'Avranches, takes charge of the new king's business. William Giffard is to be Bishop of Winchester.' He paused for breath. 'Your lord requests your presence at court, my lady, and the Lady Nest, too.' He briefly looked in my direction. 'For the King's wedding and the crowning of a new queen.'

Sybil looked at me in panic. 'And who will be the new queen?'

'It is not known for certain yet, lady, but the King has made it known he will wed before Christmas.'

'Well,' said Sybil, staring into space for a few moments, still trying to take it in, weighing up the impacts this change might have on her brothers. Then she looked at me. We did not voice it but we were both wondering if there was a change for me implied in the message. King Henry would certainly make me a more entertaining husband than William Rufus. 'Well, Nest, we had best begin our packing and preparations.'

In the privacy of her chamber, when just me and Amelina were there, Sybil voiced her suspicions about King William's death. 'It is strange is it not, that Duke Robert of Normandy's natural son died in this same way in this same place just a few months ago?'

'What are you thinking?' asked Amelina.

'That perhaps the death of Robert FitzDuke during the hunt in the New Forest was a mistake … or a rehearsal … or a way of ensuring that competition was out of the way.'

'The boy was illegitimate though …' said Amelina.

'As was William the Conqueror, the father of Duke Robert and King … Henry. Walter Tirel is well-known as one of the best marksmen at the court.' She shook her head. 'Anyway speculation is pointless. Henry is our new anointed king in the eyes of God. Although now Duke Robert has returned from crusade surely this cannot stand. I cannot believe the Duke will rest content with it and surely will challenge Henry for the crown of England that was rightfully his.'

In the morning Sybil's chambers were in chaos, strewn with clothes and undergarments for our hurried packing. 'Make sure to pack that blue gown for Nest,' she pointed it out for Amelina. 'And her best red one there, and … where is your jewellery casket Nest? Let me look at it.'

I handed it to her. There was very little in it besides Gerald's pearl and silver cross, my rings and my jewelled belt-tip. 'Well this won't do,' she said. 'Amelina, fetch my casket and let's see if I have anything for Nest, to match with her clothes.'

Our packing was interrupted by the arrival of another messenger, this time from Sybil's brother Bellême, the Earl of Shrewsbury, telling her he had crossed the Channel to greet Duke Robert on his return from crusade and to meet the new Duchess.

'He is playing both sides then?' I asked.

'His allegiance is undoubtedly to Duke Robert, but he's playing safe for now with Henry, to see how the wind blows, I suppose. It's very difficult for the Norman lords with lands both sides of the water, and different rulers in each land,' Sybil said.

I wish you would all pack up and go home then, I thought, not for the first time, and knowing full well that wish would not be granted.

* * *

From the Copybook of Sister Benedicta

Salisbury, Michaelmas 1100

Dearest Benedicta, this letter follows hard on the heels of my last for a reason. How strange are the twists and turns of our fortunes like the bends of a river. I have stayed with Henry through thick and thin, through every vicissitude, and now I am the man of the

King of the English! Probably you have already heard the news. I send you a gift together with this letter as sign of my newfound importance.

We were in that fateful hunting party in the New Forest when King William was killed at Lammas. We heard an anguished cry: 'The King!'. It came from our left and we forced a path through the brambles to see what had happened. There was the terrible sight of William Rufus' lifeless body pierced by an arrow. Try to picture the glade, Benedicta, with the sun striping the grass and birds twittering all around as if we were in paradise, and Fitz-zHamon kneeling there weeping beside the bloodied king, trying to find life and failing. He stared up at us, his face white and anguished. 'The houndsman says the arrow is Tirel's. That Tirel has fled,' he said, his voice filled with disbelief at what his eyes were looking upon.

Meulan looked at the King's corpse one instant and turned to Count Henry the next. 'The King is dead, long live the King.' He knelt to my lord. His brother the Earl of Warwick joined him and I fell to my knees alongside them. FitzHamon looked at us and Henry looked at him. FitzHamon stood up from William's body, staggered over and joined us on his knees in homage to our new King.

'Rise,' Henry told us.

'We should ride with all haste to Winchester,' Meulan said and that is what we did, leaving King William's poor corpse to the ministrations of servants.

At Winchester there was a small gathering of lords in the hall. Meulan strode on ahead of us and declared in a loud voice that William was dead and Henry was acclaimed king by his barons. After the initial shock and disbelief at the news of Rufus' death had died down, William de Breteuil, fingering the treasury key at his belt, argued. 'By which barons? By what right? We are all oath-bound to the older brother, Duke Robert. He is surely our dead king's successor?'

'He is across the seas on crusade and may not return,' Meulan asserted.

'He is en route to Normandy now, returning, the hero of Jerusalem. We all know this,' Breteuil said, looking around himself for support. What was unsaid was that every man in that room, including Breteuil, knew Henry to be the more competent contender for the throne.

'Who here declares for Henry?' Meulan called out. Again his brother, FitzHamon and I cried aye and now we were joined by others, by de Redvers, d'Avranches, Urse d'Abitot, Roger Bigod, Eudo Dapifer and Haimo Dapifer. Seeing this was the majority opinion Breteuil ceased his opposition and knelt in homage to Henry, holding the treasury key up to my lord. You can imagine this scene, Benedicta, and my excitement to be playing a role within it.

Henry, Meulan and I rode with all haste then to Westminster and Henry was consecrated as king a few days later. It has been a whirlwind, Benedicta. Now Henry sits in court in Salisbury and begins to be about those reforms of the realm that I know he has been brewing for a long time. He means to marry before Christmas he tells me, but as yet has not announced who his bride will be. Had you ever thought to see your brother so exalted, little Benedicta? As to my marriage that you ask about, well yes, I mean to do it some day, and to make you an aunt, but you must be patient. I do not have a great deal of free time on my hands right now! There was a woman I saw and could easily love but she is much above me and no doubt betrothed to another man. She is not for me I'm sorry to say, but trust to your brother's lust. I will make you an aunt, I promise! With love and haste, Haith.

Almenêches Abbey, Normandy, All Saints, 1 November 1100

My dear brother, what events! What changes everywhere. I am thrilled & terrified at this shift in your lord's fortunes. That you should be the right-hand man of a king! How could either of us ever have dreamt of *that*, when we sat in Bruges as little children, watching our mother work her loom every hour of daylight excepting Sundays, trying to sustain us, her bastard children, unacknowledged & unsupported by their father.

Thank you a thousandfold for your gift of the exquisite book of hours. Abbess Emma, Sister Matilda & I have been pouring over its illustrations with stupendous delight for many of our own hours.

The Duke & his new wife, Duchess Sybilla, are lately returned to Normandy but wearing mourning for the death of their newborn son on their journey. All Normandy mourns for them & hopes the Duke's marriage will bring us peace & good governance. There is chatter on what the Duke may think of his brother Henry seizing the English throne, but no sign as yet from the Duke himself.

He has been occupied with taking the banner of the heathen Vizier that he captured in the Battle of Ascalon to the Abbey of Mont-Saint-Michel & receiving benediction there for his role in the reclamation of the Holy City. The banner they say is a great silver pole topped with a golden apple & the Duke was a soldier without fear when he took it, slashing his way right & left amidst the heathen horde. Tales of the Duke's valour are ringing everywhere – even here in the middle of the pots & pans & jams of Almenêches. My Abbess & I are greatly proud of the Duke. It is rumoured about that he has been changed by his experiences fighting against the infidels & seeing with his own eyes the Holy City & the place of Christ's passion. Perhaps all things will change now in Normandy, as in England. I am so excited for you, Haith. Write & tell me everything that occurs! With love & blessings from Benedicta.

15

Nearness to the King

In early November in the year 1100 the ground was already frozen hard and the trees bare but the Great Hall and Abbey of Westminster were decked for the royal wedding with red and gold banners everywhere, wafting in the breeze created by hundreds of milling people. Count Henry … King Henry I mean, looked very fine in a purple silk tunic, the long cuffs all embroidered in gold and red silks. The thick gold band of his crown was studded with precious jewels: blue, red, yellow, orange gems flashed in the pale winter sunlight as he stood before us on the top step in front of the Abbey doors, with Archbishop Anselm in a sumptuously embroidered cope, and the woman who would be the new queen. Despite the rules of etiquette that were supposed to govern where people stood, the courtiers jostled one another, straining to get the best view of the couple.

I held fast to Sybil's hand as she elbowed her way to the front. With my other hand I held up the hem of my red dress trying to avoid some clumsy person stepping on it and ripping the fabric. At the front of the crowding people I was surprised to see Henry's Saxon mistress, Ansfride, her belly clearly rounded with a child.

Two Norman ladies behind us were not impressed with Henry's betrothed wife. 'Look at that dress! A fashion as old as the hills! We are to be ruled it seems by an Anglo-Saxon rustic – a very Godiva.' I turned and recognised the speaker as Elizabeth de Vermandois, the young wife of King Henry's main counsellor,

Robert de Meulan. Sybil had introduced us the previous day and told me Elizabeth was a lady of the very highest rank.

It was true that Princess Matilda of Scotland's gown, though made from beautiful pale red and green silk fabrics, was in the old fashioned, shapeless style with tight sleeves. A mantle and cloak further draped her body. Sybil and myself, like most of the other ladies pushing and shoving here, were wearing the new style *bliauts*, tightly fitted to our hips with side-lacings, full-skirted with low slung girdles and sleeves wide at the wrists. Nevertheless I admired the gorgeous Anglo-Saxon gold thread decoration of Matilda's dress that wound around her neck in heart-shaped leaves on a curving bough. She wore a gold and garnets cross on a long chain that was also fine Anglo-Saxon metalwork. Matilda appeared to be consciously proclaiming her Anglo-Saxon heritage and King Henry must have concurred with this as an appropriate gesture to his new courtiers.

The previous week the new king had taken Princess Matilda's case before a court of bishops and she had to prove that she had never been a nun. The Archbishop supported the marriage and a deputation of sisters from Wilton Abbey came and swore the Princess had not taken holy vows. I felt foolish in my own expectations about Henry and did my best to conceal how I felt from Sybil and Amelina.

Matilda's face was rather plain but she carried herself with grace and modesty. She was twenty years old and I reflected that before Henry chose her as his queen there had been very little difference between us. We were both native princesses, whose families had been subjugated by the Normans. She was a descendent of the West Saxon Kings and could trace her bloodline to King Alfred and beyond. All agreed Henry had made a clever and politic choice of wife. The blood of the House of Wessex and of the Conqueror would flow through the veins of Henry and Matilda's children. She had been well educated, first at the Scottish court, and then at the abbeys of Romsey and Wilton. Although her first language was English, she spoke perfect French and was rumoured to be able to read and write in both those languages, and in Latin besides. She brought the King a small dowry of lands in the north, but he had vastly enriched her with his wedding gift of estates all over the country and especially in London, where the people clung to their Anglo-Saxon traditions.

I was surprised to find myself seated next to the King at the wedding feast, some distance away from where Sybil and FitzHamon were placed. 'My two beautiful ladies of the Britons,' he said turning to each of us as we took our seats, since Matilda was both English and Scottish and I represented Wales. When Matilda was occupied in conversation with Archbishop Anselm who sat on the other side of her, the King leant close, his mouth grazing my ear, and whispered, 'I regret I had to choose the Saxon princess over the dimpled one'.

I was momentarily stunned. He had only been married for one hour yet sitting alongside his new wife and Archbishop, he flirted with me? I should reprimand him, yet that was impossible since he was the king, and anyway my vanity ached for such recognition. I felt a certain attraction to his shamelessness, enjoying his naughty delight in me. 'The dimpled one is also regretful.' Had I actually said that? I shocked and thrilled myself, wondering where this would lead. Henry's eyes lit up and his gaze roved deliberately over my face, the pulse at my neck, the curves of my breasts in my red gown.

'Perhaps you would be kind enough to visit me one day at my palace in Woodstock,' he said. 'Do you hunt?'

'I like to ride and I am not bad with a bow, I believe.' I looked boldly at him. His hair was very black, his skin pale but pink with wine and heat, his large dark brown eyes drew me in. His mouth was red and moistened with wine and it started to curl now with the start of a new remark but then his wife claimed his attention. I turned to my other neighbour, Richard de Redvers, and beyond him the knight Haith. Between them they kept me occupied with a stream of animated anecdotes about their shared youth with the King, until the time came for Henry and Matilda to be bedded.

I joined Sybil and we accompanied Matilda to the bedchamber, watching her maids remove her fine clothes until she stood in a thin linen shift, a young woman like me. I imagined myself in her place, waiting for the arrival of the King, waiting to couple with him and produce an heir to the throne. The groom's party arrived making a riotous noise, with Henry in their midst in a nightgown.

His calves were browned by the sun and the top of his chest, visible above his carelessly laced gown, swirled with curling black hair. I envied Matilda. Henry's humourous eyes sought out mine but I looked away. It was not *my* bedding with a king.

A week after the wedding, Sybil and I returned to the Abbey to witness the Queen's coronation. Archbishop Anselm anointed and crowned Matilda and presented her to the crowd of people to be acclaimed. A great shout rose up and I joined my voice to it, feeling stabs of jealousy and resentment. We followed in procession to Westminster Hall where Queen Matilda was ritually enthroned alongside Henry, holding a sceptre in one hand and an orb in the other, and she declared in a confident voice that she would be the mother of the King's people. 'He has chosen well,' Sybil said, with grudging admiration. 'He shows more sense than his brother William already. She is participating in his councils and my husband tells me she is capable and wise in her advice to the King.'

'He had to choose Scotland or Wales and I think he has done the best he could with the dilemma.' Sybil and I turned to Elizabeth de Vermandois' voice behind us. I looked at her perplexed and she smiled, took my hand, and drew me away from Sybil to a window seat. Elizabeth had taken a liking to me and I, in turn, enjoyed her lively company, although Sybil said she was feckless and untrustworthy. It was hard to believe such an assessment when confronted with her extraordinary beauty. She was only fifteen but had already been married five years. She was a wise old young woman. She had pale creamy skin, lightly sprinkled with tiny freckles, a mass of dark red hair and turquoise eyes. She was the niece of the French king and told me she could not care less what anyone thought or said about her.

'But what did you mean: he had to choose Scotland or Wales?'

'Don't pretend to be silly, Nest. I know you are no fool. Marriage is always politics, not sex or love. Hardly that!' she laughed. Her own husband was forty years older than her. She told me his knees made the most awful creaking noise like boughs rubbing together in a high wind when he rose from prayers at their bedside to come and do his marital duty by her. 'If it were sexual attraction, Henry would have chosen Wales without a doubt.'

'But what do you mean exactly?' I persisted, my cheeks warming at her flattery.

'Matilda brings him her brothers, the King of Scots and his nobility and therefore their allegiance. That just leaves him two frontiers to worry about instead of three – Wales and Normandy.'

I nodded. It made sense.

'And even if he had succumbed to your superior charms – he said that to me by the way – verbatim – you would not have brought Wales in peace to him would you?'

'No. Wales consists of more kingdoms than my father's.'

'Quite. Not to mention the wolf pack of Norman lords that roam around it, staking their autonomous claims regardless of the King.'

I was mollified to hear the King had at least seriously considered me and saddened to hear her apt description of the state of my homeland.

Sybil and I remained in London for over a month, staying on for the Christmas Court, and this time lodging in a house the King had loaned to FitzHamon. The new queen was accompanied everywhere by her chaplain, Ernisius. I wondered the judges at the tribunal *had* found her not to be a nun since she attended matins, mass and vespers daily, observing the full office in her chapel and joining in the recitation of the psalter, nevertheless Matilda and Henry seemed genuinely happy with one another.

I spent more and more time with Elizabeth despite Sybil's disapproval. Elizabeth was on very friendly terms with the King, giving me opportunity to observe his character. He was a curious mix: shrewd and severe, obviously intending to give no room to doubt his ability to rule. As Sybil told me, he was an intellectual, enjoying debates with the scholars and artists at his court. I never met anyone with such enormous curiosity. He had endless probing questions for the scholars but his curiosity extended also to all the people around him, even the servants. He would worm your life story out of you, persisting until he thought he understood your motivations and aspirations. He had a piercing mode of questioning relentlessly until he had gotten at something that seemed to surprise even you, and *then* he was satisfied.

I was sitting with Elizabeth in the courtyard watching the children of the royal nursery playing at blowing soap bubbles from a pipe. The nursery comprised King Henry's illegitimate children, orphaned wards in his care, and the sons and daughters of barons that he was fostering. I was surprised when Henry suddenly appeared in the courtyard, looked around, and sat down next to me. He smiled and we continued to watch the children playing for a while. 'I was the youngest of ten children, you know, Lady Nest.'

'Yes, my schoolmaster had me write out the genealogy of your family.'

He seemed amused at that. 'My oldest brothers, Robert and Richard, were grown men and outside my world as a child. I was closest to my sister, Adela. And you?'

'I was closest to my brother Goronwy but my older brothers, Cynan and Idwal, were heroes in my girl's eyes.' I stopped. 'I find it hard to speak of my family, sire.'

'Forgive me. You have some brothers who live I believe?'

I shook my head. 'Well, Idwal is my half-brother. He is imprisoned, sire.'

'I heard there was a brother in Ireland. A younger brother?' he asked, his great brown eyes gentle and concerned.

'I don't know if he lives. I ....'

'Lady Sybil's family has been like your own lately, I imagine?'

'Yes, I am greatly fond of Lady Sybil and her daughters. Much of my life has been spent in her household.'

'What is your youngest brother's name?'

'Gruffudd.' I bit my lip, realising, too late, that his trick was to seem to show something of himself to you, but then, somehow you ended up revealing a great deal more than he ever did. 'But he is likely dead. There is nothing heard of him,' I ended lamely, cross with myself for speaking of him.

King Henry watched the children, he laughed and called out to them and I surreptitiously observed him, thinking about what I knew of him. He was surrounded by a small group of men who were old and loyal friends and the affection between them appeared very strong. Richard de Redvers, Hugh Earl of Chester, his chaplain Roger and the Flemish knight Haith, were amongst this group. Henry was openly loving to his bastard children, Robert, Mathilde, Richard and Juliane, and warmly affectionate to both his wife, Matilda, and his mistress, Ansfride who was not concealed. Henry spent a great deal of time with his heavily pregnant mistress and she was treated with deference and respect by his friends. She was importuned, gifted, flattered and lobbied for assistance by nearly as many petitioners as the Queen. Matilda turned a blind eye to this aspect of her new husband's court.

Sybil told me the King would betroth me now to her brother Arnulf, but I was not so certain of that. Henry was very attentive to me, taking every opportunity to compliment me. He turned back to me suddenly now and I had a sense that he had been perfectly aware of my study of him all along. 'Cadwgan has asked for your hand in marriage for his son Owain again,' he said.

'Sire?' I asked cautiously.

'I'm afraid I have had to refuse him, Nest,' he said. 'It would do no good from my perspective to have the Welsh royal line of Deheubarth joined, in your fair person, with the royal line of Powys would it?'

I did not reply to his question, but after a moment, I said, 'I would like to know about my half-brother, Idwal, sire, who is imprisoned at Shrewsbury. He is illegitimate and no threat to you.' This was not strictly true since I had no doubt that if Idwal were freed the men of Deheubarth would rally to him and chase the Normans from our lands.

'Indeed? I will see what I can do for him,' said Henry, looking earnestly into my eyes and kissing the tips of my fingers, as he rose. He called out affectionately to the bubble-wet children and strolled off to return to his business for the realm.

A feast was in preparation in the great hall of Westminster because Robert de Meulan had arrived at the court with Prince Louis of France who had come to see King Henry and Queen Matilda as a gesture of recognition for their new regime. I was delighted to see Gerald arrive in the hall and he sought me out for conversation. His father had recently died and the King was due to give a ruling on the inheritance. Gerald's brother William had been confirmed as Constable of Windsor by King Henry. 'The King is very attentive to you, Nest,' he said. I groped for a response but the need evaporated when Gerald's name was called out by the King's usher.

'Step forward Sir Gerald FitzWalter,' King Henry said.

Gerald stepped forward and dropped to his knee before the King, looking earnestly at him. 'God speed, your grace.'

'I heard from my brother William,' Henry said, 'and from Arnulf de Montgommery that you gave us good service in Pembroke, in the far reaches of Wales.'

'Thank you, sire. I strive to do my duty.'

'I am granting you a vacant manor in reward for your service Sir Gerald. It is in Berkshire, the manor of Moulsford, half-way between Windsor and Woodstock. I expect you know it from your childhood?'

'Yes sire! Thank you sire! I had not expected such generous reward.' I was pleased for Gerald and he turned to me smiling. I noticed Henry watching the exchange of smiles between us with interest.

The night was advanced, the feast consumed, the wine well soaked up by the guests, and my eyelids grew heavy with the lazy strumming of the musicians after their earlier energetic performances. 'Lady Nest, I wonder if you would favour me with a word.' I startled myself fully conscious and looked into the new queen's face. 'Of course,' I said, a little flustered. Why would she wish to speak with me? Had she noticed her husband's attentions. I flushed hot at the idea. 'I am retiring now,' she said, 'perhaps you would take a final cup of wine with me in my chamber?'

'Of course.' I rose and anxiously followed her to the winding stone steps leading up to her room, where her maid placed a tray with two fine gold goblets and a jug of wine and left us.

'I need to talk something over with someone,' she said, looking earnestly at me, 'someone who does not have their own agenda and might seek to advise me wrongly. I thought of you.'

'I'm flattered and will do what I can. If it is within my power.'

'My husband is facing a difficult decision and he asks my advice, you see. I needed to mull it over with someone sensible. It's so early in our marriage and such an important thing and I want to make a good choice. Since it concerns another queen, my lord Henry says I may have the right answer for him.' For a moment I saw an uncertain girl in her features before they resettled into her usual decorous expression.

'Another queen?'

'Yes.' She regarded me for a long moment. 'I must ask for your complete discretion, Lady Nest.'

'It is yours.'

She stared at me again for some time, clearly wondering if she could trust me, whilst I wondered that she should single me out. Yet she had few other allies at court, at least few other women. Most of the Norman ladies scoffed at her in a barely concealed fashion and no doubt she was aware of this. The King's friends were more familiar and at ease with Ansfride. It was our shared background as native princesses, as outsiders in the Norman court, I supposed that led her to try me.

'Believe me, if you betray me, Lady Nest, I will seek and find vengeance for it.'

'I …' I was flabbergasted by the sudden vehemence of her expression and her words. I swallowed some wine and set my goblet down carefully and then turned my eyes back to her. 'My word is my honour. I will not betray your confidence if you choose to speak to me now.' I waited.

She plunged in. 'Henry has received a secret missive from Queen Bertrada of France.'

My eyes widened. Thank God, it was not me and Henry then that worried her.

'Bertrada urges Henry to imprison her step-son Prince Louis.'

'Imprison him! He is an honoured guest! The heir to the French throne!'

'Yes. She seeks to displace him and make her own son heir.'

'That is wickedness, surely?'

'Yes. I think so too. You think I should advise Henry against it?'

Again I was flabbergasted that she should place such confidence in me and such trust in my advice. 'May I ask, my lady, why it is you feel I can advise you on this? I am not a woman of the court, practised in these political subtleties. I know nothing of the politics of the French court, and very little even about the English situation. Perhaps you would do better to speak with Elizabeth de Vermandois?'

She looked down at her hands in her lap for some time. 'I have discussed it with my spiritual advisers of course,' she said, meaning her chaplains, and perhaps even the Archbishop. She looked up again and her expression was candid. 'I can't speak with any of these Norman ladies. They think me a fool. A bumpkin.'

'I'm sure that's not the case,' I said, although I knew that it was.

'Yes they do. You, at least, do not look down your nose at me because I am not Norman. I thought your advice would be disinterested, heartfelt. That is what I want.'

'Then, my Queen, I advise you to follow your heart and your first instinct. King Henry would surely be well advised to stay out of these machinations of the French court. Louis is likely to gain the crown soon, and if King Henry allies with Queen Bertrada in this and her plot fails, he will have gained an implacable enemy on the French throne.'

Matilda clapped her hands together. 'Exactly my thinking! Thank you, Nest. I hope that we can be friends, that you will be at court often.'

'I fear I am returning to Cardiff Castle with Lady Sybil tomorrow, but good friends, yes,' I said enthusiastically, although my attraction to Henry, and his to me, lurked guiltily behind my words.

Sybil, Amelina and I returned to our routines in Cardiff after the excitements of the wedding and the court. I felt a mixture of regret and relief to take leave of Henry and his attentions. Mabel, Hawise, Cecilia and Amice were delighted at our return and were of an age now to afford me some company and conversation. Mabel, who was eight, rode out with me most days when the weather was fine. Master Richard was occupied with business and my lessons with him were frequently cancelled. Often when I arrived at the door of the locust room with my books and scrolls balanced in a neat pile, he would shoo me back down the passage. 'Not today, not today, Nest. I have far too much work in hand.' Evidently, he did not want anyone overlooking that work.

On those days the girls would join me in my chamber and we sat working together on the King Arthur tapestry with Amelina. The tapestry showed the King, his Queen and his mounted knights. Arthur and his Gwenhwyvar wore jewelled crowns and decorated clothes, their heads bent towards one another in love. Banners flew from the towers of the castle. Arthur's court was surrounded by a meandering river, edged with marshy ground, where stately swans floated serenely and boats plied up and down. Flowers, vegetation, birds, trees, vineyards emerged beneath our fingers and needles, crowding and twining around the scene. I imagined this to be my court, mine and Owain's in Powys perhaps. Or even mine and Henry's. I briefly allowed myself that illicit thought.

'Are you going to marry soon?' Mabel asked me, jarring my daydream. I was twenty now, past my prime, and still not betrothed. All the little hands around the edges of the tapestry draped across our knees were suddenly stilled and all the little faces turned to me expectantly. Even the youngest, Amice, who was only three and not old enough to join our sewing, was sitting with us. Amelina kept her busy playing with bits of wool and thread. 'Mother says you will marry my uncle Arnulf and then you will be my aunt?' Mabel said cheerfully.

'I don't know, Mabel. My marriage is at the King's pleasure, since I am an orphan. He has given no commands as yet. He has been far too busy with many other matters in his new reign to give much thought to me.'

'Can we be your bridesmaids?' Mabel persisted. 'Carry your train and throw petals in your path.'

I smiled at her, but pictured myself marrying Arnulf with those petals spotted with the blood of my father and brothers. 'We shall see what the King decides eventually.' I pointed to a bluebird on the tapestry. 'Look, we could make two birds together, another mating pair to echo the king and queen.'

The first year of King Henry's reign was turbulent, since his brother, Duke Robert challenged him for the English throne and there was war. Aside from the absence of Sybil's husband about the King's business however, the distant events did not touch the calm humdrum of our existence until FitzHamon returned the following January with much news, a summons, and a boy.

* * *

From the Copybook of Sister Benedicta

Windsor Castle, Martinmas 1101

Dearest Benedicta, I am sitting here in the draughty old castle of Windsor listening to the pitiable squeals and human-like screeches of the animals being slaughtered before winter. Perhaps you are doing the same in Almenêches or perhaps you are stirring, stirring jam until your wrist burns like fire, looking with satisfaction on your rows of clean pots readied for your concoctions.

There was a terrible conflagration in the city of Gloucester in June and it is near enough burnt to the ground. Henry was forced to move his Pentecost court to Saint Albans where a new Abbey is under construction. Soon after the court we moved down towards the coast where we expected the invasion of Curthose, trying to take back the English crown, and Henry mustered a great army. The Duke landed towards the end of July and we marched resolutely to meet him. The Duke, despite his vaunted deeds as a crusader, had no stomach to meet us in battle and instead, you will be glad to hear, a peace was negotiated between Robert and Henry and the Duke has formally relinquished his claim to the English throne. I think perhaps, the Duke was just going through the motions of making a bid for the English throne to satisfy his belligerent barons, and he always meant to conclude a peace with his brother. My lord Henry is victorious and England will see many changes for the better now. I am sure of it. The treaty was drawn up at Winchester and has just been formally signed and witnessed here at Windsor. King Henry is saddened right now by the news that his steadfast friend Hugh d'Avranches, Earl of Chester has died. He was enormously fat and could not even walk at the end they say. My lord is in need of good and loyal friends for he is surrounded by a slavering pack of nobles who will pounce if he shows any weakness. More soon, in haste Haith.

Almenêches Abbey, Normandy, Yuletide 1101

My dear brother Haith is always in haste these days! I prayed for three days without stop on my knees on the cold stone flags of the church when I heard the Duke would invade England because I knew you would be there in the front rank defending your King Henry. I even had to put my armwarmers out of sight, under my pillow, because I could not bear their red colour for fear they presaged your blood spilt in battle.

I have shed *such* pools of tears in relief that you have come to no harm & there was no battle, only peace, & I thank God's mercy over & over that this was his will. Take care every day, every hour, every minute, my Haith, with love from your sister Benedicta.

* * *

From Gerald FitzWalter's Day Book

Cardiff Castle, Yuletide 1101

It is with immense irritation at the mismanagements of men supposedly greater than I, that I must record how Gruffudd ap Cynan has regained control of all of Gwynedd and the Norman advances in the north are lost again. Now Henry is king I do not know where my best chances lie. Lord Arnulf and the Montgommerys of course support Duke Robert's claim to the English throne and name Henry a usurper. But now Duke Robert's mooted invasion has failed (and this for a second time), he has formally relinquished the crown to Henry, and his supporters are left high and dry again. Arnulf says he will keep his head down and gradually regain the favour of the new king but from what I saw of this Henry when I was at Westminster, he is not the sort to forgive disloyalty, nor is he the fool that his brother Duke Robert has shown himself to be. I fear my colours are nailed to the sinking mast of the Montgommery family. I cannot lose everything I have gained.

My father died last year and my brother William inherited as Constable of Windsor Castle whilst my brother Maurice inherited the family lands in Eton. What should I be left with if Arnulf falls from King Henry's favour? Lady Sybil invited me here to Cardiff to celebrate Christmas with her family. I need to safeguard my position and so I sought out Belmeis for, thanks to Lady Nest, I know his role in all of this.

I found Belmeis in his ridiculous locusts room, contemplating the piles of papers before him as usual. Nest and the older FitzHamon girls were with him, reading their Latin primers. I smiled warmly to the princess. 'Might I have private speech with you, Belmeis?'

He grinned in that irksome patronising fashion he has and shooed Nest, Mabel and Hawise from the room.

'I look forward to speaking with you at dinner,' I told Nest as she squeezed past me in the doorway, her fragrant black hair inches from my mouth. I closed the door behind them.

'What can I do for you, Sir Gerald?'

'Perhaps I can do something for you.'

'I am intrigued.'

'I know you feed information to FitzHamon, to the King, on the goings on of the Montgommerys.'

He blanched and began to protest against my statement. I held up a hand to stop his babbling. 'Don't argue, Belmeis. I know. But I'm not here to confront you with it, rather to join you in it.' That stopped his whining denials abruptly.

'Er … Sir Gerald, how do you mean?'

'I am loyal to my lord Arnulf as I can be, but I am also the King's man now. Now the Duke has relinquished the throne.'

He looked at me and gestured that I should take a seat opposite him, steepling his fingers beneath his chin and regarding me, greatly calmed since moments ago. 'Indeed. We are all the King's men now.'

'Not all,' I countered, 'as you know.'

'How can you … contribute to my efforts.'

'Not all the Montgommery correspondence goes through you. Some comes straight through Pembroke and out to Normandy with seaborne couriers.'

He shifted in his seat, leaning forward with an interested expression. 'Yes, I have been aware of that and nothing I could do about it. Particularly the correspondence of Bellême comes in, and of your Lord Arnulf, goes out to Normandy, in that way.'

I nodded.

'You do not read or write yourself, Sir Gerald?'

'I read and write well enough,' I said. 'My father intended me for the church in my early days and I was educated at Abingdon Abbey. And besides, I have a loyal clerk, loyal only to me.'

'Any man can be bought.'

'Not this man.'

'Then we have a new partnership I believe.' He stood, reaching across the broad table and God help me, for I must help myself, I shook his oily palm.

16

The Summons

The boy that Lord FitzHamon came home with in the January of 1102 was named Robert. He was around eleven years old and he was King Henry's oldest bastard. The King had placed him in FitzHamon's household for training. He was a cheerful addition to our community and soon great friends with me and the girls, although Lady Sybil regarded him sourly, unhappy to be landed with 'the King's droppings' as she put it when her husband could not hear her. Gerald joined us for the Christmas and New Year's celebrations but a worried expression slipped down over his usual cheerful face whenever he thought himself unregarded. I resolved to ask him if he had some trouble.

FitzHamon took me by surprise, handing me a letter from the King with my name carefully scribed on it. Princess Nest of Deheubarth, it said. Gratified that the King gave me this title but fearing it might be the order for my marriage I opened it. King Henry told me in gentle language that he had enquired after my brother Idwal, and found him dying in prison. I was surprised the King had remembered my request, and brushed at the tears that clouded my eyes so that I could read his account. The King wrote that he moved Idwal to the gentle care of his own physician, Abbot Faricius, but he had died last month. 'Nest, I am truly sorry for your great loss, and regret I was unable to do more for your brother,' wrote the King. I tried to control myself but a loud sob escaped me and my face ran with tears. Another of us cut down. Only me and Gruffudd left now to avenge my father and reclaim his lands. I felt the weight of it settling on my shoulders anew, whilst I wept for Idwal. FitzHamon stood awkwardly, regarding my emotion, but Gerald stepped forward and held me hard, my face squashed against the prickly green wool of his tunic, as I shook and sobbed.

Sybil allowed me to keep to my room after the news of my brother's death, but after a few days had passed, she knocked and entered. 'Nest, I'm *so* sorry. I know how fiercely I love my own brothers but believe me the best treatment for such grief is to keep going. Won't you come and assist me with the feast?' She held out her hand to me and I took it and rose from the bed. She bent to the bowl of water on the table, dipped a cloth and brought it gently to my face. 'Poor girl, poor girl,' she said, which only made me weep anew. She led me down to the hall.

His first few days back, FitzHamon rested from the journey and conducted business but now Sybil had the hall buzzing with preparations for the Christmas feast. Later that day I took my seat next to Sybil and Gerald was seated between FitzHamon and Belmeis. The boy Robert FitzRoy was seated next to me and Mabel beyond him. 'It's been a year,' FitzHamon opened the conversation with evident understatement. There were rumours flying that the Montgommery family had been implicated again in rebellion, supporting Duke Robert against King Henry, and Lady Sybil was sick with anxiety. It was typical of her relationship with her husband that he had chosen not to give her any of this news that touched her so closely in the privacy of her own chamber.

FitzHamon recounted King Henry's arrest of Ranulf Flambard soon after the coronation and how Flambard had been confined in a room at the very top of the White Tower. During King William's reign Flambard had been hated for his onerous taxes, and his arrest had been a popular move on King Henry's part.

'He escaped,' FitzHamon told us dramatically. 'A rope was smuggled into his room in a wine cask.'

I tried to imagine the portly, fox-faced, and no longer young bishop shinning all that way down the high tower on a rope, and had to feign a coughing fit to smother my giggles.

'He got to the coast and took ship to Normandy to traitorously join Duke Robert. His mother, a one-eyed sorceress, joined him, with the haul of his ill-gotten treasure.'

I frowned at FitzHamon's account. 'A one-eyed sorceress?' I said sceptically, remembering Henry's jokes to me about her.

'Yes,' he responded flatly. FitzHamon had no sense of humour whatsoever. 'She was nearly shipwrecked in the Channel and arrived on the shores of Normandy naked.'

'A *naked*, one-eyed sorceress with treasure,' I said.

FitzHamon looked at me, uncomprehending why I repeated what he said, and continued his story. 'Whatever we might say about Flambard ...'

'Or his mother.'

'Nest!' Sybil warned me sharply and I looked down and sideways at Gerald, exchanging a surreptitious smile with him. Next to me Robert was laughing and it was a laugh remarkably like his father's, the King's.

'Whatever we might say about Flambard, he is wily and astute. He gave the Duke good advice and backbone and the Duke invaded in July, coming ashore at Portsmouth, instead of Pevensey where Henry was expecting him. When the Duke landed many of the barons defected to his side. He turned to Sybil. 'Including your brothers.' Sybil stopped eating.

'What happened?' said Mabel, her eyes round in her round face.

'The two armies met at Alton, near Winchester,' her father told her and the rest of the hall, raising his voice, since everyone was transfixed by his story now. 'But a peace was negotiated and no battle took place.'

'Did you negotiate the peace, father?' Mabel asked.

Her father looked surprised at all these questions from a mere girl-child but reluctantly acknowledged her presence. 'Yes, myself and a number of other barons mediated between the brothers and eventually an agreement was reached. The Duke acknowledged Henry as King of the English. In exchange King Henry agreed to give the Duke an annuity of 3,000 marks ....' There was a collective gasp at the huge amount. '... And to give up most of his lands in Normandy to Duke Robert, apart from Domfront.'

'And what of the barons who had supported the Duke?' asked Sybil.

'King Henry and Duke Robert agreed there should be no reprisals. That each man, regardless of which side he had chosen, would retain his lands on both sides of the Channel.'

Sybil looked relieved.

'But ...' FitzHamon, carried on, 'Henry and Robert agreed that if one brother should find reason to charge any man with treason in the future, the other brother would support that charge, and also regard that man as a traitor.' I pondered this and heard the shrewd manoeuvring of Henry in it. I was fast becoming an admirer of Henry's politicking. 'King Henry and Duke Robert celebrated the peace treaty in September at Windsor,' FitzHamon said. 'We had good hunting in the forests there, thanks to your brother,' he told Gerald who nodded distractedly, the worried expression back on his face.

'The Earl of Surrey, William de Warenne was disseised of all his lands and left England with Duke Robert,' FitzHamon continued. 'And your nephew, William de Mortain, is in the King's displeasure,' he said to Sybil.

'I hope he will regain the King's trust, then,' she said quietly.

'And is there news of the Queen?' I asked. We all knew that Queen Matilda was carrying a child.

'She fares better now,' FitzHamon responded. There had been rumours she was ill and likely to miscarry at the time of Duke Robert's invasion. 'Abbot Faricius has been attending her for months with his potions and remedies.' He made a small grimace of distaste at having to discuss women's troubles, yet an heir to the throne was of paramount interest to everyone. 'We hope there will be a boy in the royal nursery soon.'

'Along with all the bastards,' Sybil said, glancing down the table at Robert FitzRoy who blushed and looked down at his trancher.

'Unfortunately ...' FitzHamon demanded his wife's attention with a loud, irritated tone, 'since the peace treaty, your brother Bellême has formed an alliance with Duke Robert that Henry regards as a breach of the peace terms. He has declared all of your brothers to be traitors and summoned them to the Easter court at Winchester to answer the charges.'

Sybil paled, put a hand to her chest, suddenly breathing in loud heaves.

'Mama?' Mabel asked.

'The child should go to bed,' FitzHamon said.

Amelina stepped up, took Mabel's hand, and led her away, quietening her bewildered questions. 'Your mama will be alright.'

Sybil's face was ghastly pale and I felt furious with FitzHamon that he should torture her like this in front of everybody. I poured a glass of water, and gave it to Sybil, who took it from me in a daze, her hand shaking. Gerald's eyes were on me but FitzHamon continued oblivious or uncaring about the state of his wife. I noticed the boy, Robert FitzRoy, oberving all these exchanges with an intelligent look in his eyes.

'You need to see to your own position, FitzWalter. The King will not allow those who have proved disloyal to go unpunished,' FitzHamon told Gerald.

'Thank you Lord Robert for the warning, but I am sworn to the service of Lord Arnulf and must take the slings of fortune as he sees fit to command. He commands me, for the present, to hold Pembroke Castle for him.'

Glancing again at his wife, finally acknowledging her shock, FitzHamon told her, 'It was going to happen sooner or later Sybil, since your brothers could find no loyalty to their King in their hearts.'

'They were loyal to Duke Robert, the eldest son,' she said. 'They were sworn to it.'

'Then they were in the wrong country,' FitzHamon told her quietly. 'Are you also in the wrong country, wife?'

'No, Robert,' she said quickly. 'I love my brothers and mourn their losses and disgraces but I am true to you, and to King Henry.'

I felt sorry to see her so humbled. Since she had given him no heir she was in a very weak position and another lord, one less straight than FitzHamon, might have used the fall of her family as an excuse to put her aside and take another wife who would prove more fertile ground for sons. He might do so yet.

FitzHamon told us Lady Sybil and I were also summoned to the King's Easter Court at Winchester.

'Nest?' Sybil asked. 'Why does he summon her?'

'She is a woman now and the King will dispose of her.' I looked up at him but he said nothing more. Either he did not know the King's intentions regarding me or he had decided not to tell us. If Arnulf had been tainted as a traitor then he was surely an unlikely candidate for my husband now.

17

The Fall

King Henry's Easter Court in that year, 1102, was held in Winchester, the ancient seat of the Saxon Kings. It took us near a week to reach the city, travelling by river and road. The cross-shaped layout of Winchester, with its four gates in the old walls and four main streets crossing in the middle, made it easy to find your way about. Houses and shops clustered outside the walls. The royal mints and forges were busy, the sizzle of metal smelting and the hammering loud in the street. The royal treasure was kept here in the palace, heavily guarded. Pilgrims crowded the city visiting Saint Swithun's Priory and the Saint's shrine and they gawped at the King's finely dressed courtiers, riding down the streets. The tombs of the West Saxon and Norse royalty: King Alfred, King Canute and Queen Emma, had been moved from the Old Minster to the new Cathedral recently built by Bishop Walkelin. William Rufus was buried beneath the new tower of the cathedral and remembering his loud brashness, I wondered that it was stilled and silent now in a stony grave. The cathedral's font showed the miracles of Saint Nicholas, the kindly children's saint and I studied the images carefully so that I could describe them to Mabel and Hawise when I returned.

The mood at the court was sombre and nervous after the recent rebellion. Sybil and I entered the hall and moved through the crowd of people slowly, trying to make our way nearer the front. I was glad to see Elizabeth who plucked me by the sleeve and pulled me forward and close to her, tucking my arm under hers. Henry and Matilda were seated on thrones and the King's Justiciar, Roger Bishop of Salisbury, stood before them making announcement of the King's will. I had expected Henry to catch my eye with his previous flirtatious humour but he did not look in my direction. Queen Matilda had been delivered of a healthy baby daughter two months before and looked well.

Archbishop Anselm attended the court but FitzHamon told us he was in conflict with King Henry on the matter of the King's powers to invest Bishops. To everyone's surprise Ranulf Flambard appeared and was restored as Bishop of Durham. Obviously that wily man had played fast and loose between the two brothers in the recent war and done well in a deal to switch to Henry's side. I searched in vain for sight of his sorceress mother but I did glimpse Haith in the crowd of knights close to the King and he lifted his hand to me in greeting. I disentangled myself from Elizabeth and dropped him a curtsey, smiling at his cheerful face. Elizabeth elbowed me. 'See Ansfride?' She nodded her head discreetly towards the King's mistress who was seated in a place of honour. 'She has borne Henry three children; all being cared for in the royal nursery. Richard, Juliane and Fulk. What do you think our pious Queen thinks about it?' I offered no response but took Sybil's hand as she came up alongside us. She was looking around but there was no sign yet of any of her brothers. Master Richard Belmeis, very splendidly attired in a bright yellow tabard that did not suit his sallow complexion at all, stood not far from us, at the side of the crowd.

Roger de Montgommery and Arnulf, it transpired, had chosen to disregard the King's summons. Roger had cut his losses in England, forfeiting his vast lands in Lancashire and returned to his wife's county in France, preferring not to risk the King's ire. Arnulf was reported to be in Ireland. I feared what the outcome of this defiance might be for Gerald. Roger of Salisbury announced that Arnulf's non-appearance was confession of his crimes and the King therefore stripped him of his rights in Wales and in England, and my family's lands were given into the stewardship of a knight named Jordan de Saye. I knew nothing about this knight, who was not at court. I was relieved to find he had already started on the journey into Wales, because my first fear had been that I might be awarded to him as wife along with my father's lands.

'Ah!' said Elizabeth, in a tone of warm satisfaction, and I followed her eyes to where the crowd was hushing and parting before the advance of a tall, well-muscled man with black hair, flecked with grey. Sybil gripped my hand. Robert de Bellême strode confidently into the court to answer to the King, exchanging a brief acknowledgement with Sybil as he passed. His glanced flicked over me. At the front of the crowd he sank to his knee before Henry. Sybil's expression brightened with confidence that her eldest brother would rescue the fortunes of the family. I had seen a resemblance to Arnulf in his face but thought his mouth cruel, like the stories about him. After King Henry and Duke Robert, Bellême was the richest nobleman in both the kingdoms of England and Normandy. He wore that knowledge in his stance. 'Handsome, isn't he,' Elizabeth whispered in my ear.

The King twitched his fingers to Bellême indicating that he should rise.

'There are forty-three charges of malfeasance against you, Robert de Bellême,' Bishop Roger told him, ominously not using his title of Earl.

'Forty-three!' said Bellême. 'Then may I have a servant fetch me a chair?'

A titter of amusement ran around the hall but was quickly killed when the King spoke for the first time. 'No you may not.'

Bellême raised his eyes to the King's face and they stared at each other. The temperature in the hall seemed to drop several degrees. All gossip and whispering ceased. Even the dust motes in the beams of light piercing the hall appeared to pause in their dances.

Bishop Roger began to read the charges in a droning voice. As the list progressed Sybil's fingers locked tighter around my hand and she looked angrily several times in the direction of Master Richard. At first Bellême took the litany of charges with a sceptical, surprised expression bespeaking innocence but when Bishop Roger produced a number of letters written in Bellême's hand and bearing his seal, Sybil's brother began to lose his swagger, and he also turned to stare hard at Master Richard, flexing his hands as if trying to decide which of them he might use to kill the clerk. Master Richard avoided the eyes of both the Montgommery siblings. At last the list of charges was completed and a great hush ensued.

'Well?' said King Henry.

'My lord, I am astonished at this calumny against me. I beg leave to consult with my own counsellors before answering these ridiculous and false charges.'

Henry stared at him for some moments and finally responded. 'Very well. You have until tomorrow morning to do so and then I will hear your defence and give my ruling.'

Bellême bowed and backed away from the King, walking swiftly from the room, not glancing this time at his sister.

The following morning I comforted Sybil when we discovered her brother had fled to Shrewsbury and would not appear to answer the charges. King Henry proclaimed Bellême stripped of the Earldom of Shrewsbury, sent word to all Normandy that Bellême was declared a traitor, and gave orders to ready an army to march against the castles of Arundel, Tickhill, Bridgnorth and Shrewsbury itself. My curse against the Montgommerys had come true. There was only Neufmarché left for the Dogs of Annwn to hunt down.

Bishop Roger of Salisbury announced the King's orders that Richard Belmeis should go into Sussex to seize the vast Montgommery holdings there for the crown. Master Richard nodded his acknowledgement to the King, and left without exchanging so much as a glance with Lady Sybil, in whose household he had lived for so many years. Sybil turned her head and spat on the ground as he passed.

'He deserves castration,' I whispered in her ear, 'but there would be little point in it.'

She clenched my hand gratefully.

'Lady Nest ferch Rhys.' The King spoke to me directly, instead of using the mouth-piece of Bishop Roger.

I stepped forward, my heart pounding. 'Sire.' Taken up with Sybil's distress I had forgotten that I too was summoned for a decision today.

'I am aware there is the disposition of your marriage to be put in order.'

I kept my eyes on his face.

'I can no longer allow you to continue in the household of Sybil de Montgommery,' he said. Sybil opened her mouth to protest but thought better of it. 'Of course, you have done an excellent job with my ward so far, Lady Sybil,' the King said swiftly in a conciliatory tone. 'However, Lady Nest is of royal blood and needs to be at court where I can look about for a satisfactory match for her. She will enter service as one of the ladies of Queen Matilda for now.'

'Yes, sire,' we voiced together. Sybil looked deflated, shrunken, her loud, garrulous voice dimmed. I turned to her with tears in my eyes and we held each other's hands. 'You have been my dear sister,' I whispered to her, 'and will always remains so'. I had grown a new family in her and her daughters and now I had to lose my family all over again. We exchanged a long embrace and then, after our years together, she was gone. Suddenly I was alone, defenceless and unloved again amongst strangers.

18

The Character of the Badger

The Queen's court did not stay at Winchester for long. 'Nest, would you oversee the packing of my bed and other items from my chamber?' the Queen asked, as we began preparations to return to Westminster.

'Yes, my lady.' I curtseyed and moved to her chamber, wondering what this duty might consist of. Everything in my new life was unfamiliar and uncertain, although I had been allowed to keep Amelina with me. In the Queen's chambers two men stood awaiting my orders. 'Everything is to be packed up carefully to be moved to London,' I told them, hoping they had more idea how to go about it than I did. They bowed and began stripping the furs and sheets from the bed and folding them carefully into chests. They rolled the great mattress, roped it and carried it from the room to the waiting carts in the courtyard below. I moved around the room packing small items and stowing them into the chests. The two men returned and began to dismantle the bed, removing the carved wooden supports at the four corners and breaking the strung frame down into sections. Everything was moved down to the growing chaos of packhorses below readying for our departure to my new life at the royal court.

Over the summer, King Henry was away, campaigning against Bellême, and I spent time growing accustomed to my changed circumstances with Queen Matilda. Unlike her energetic husband who constantly moved between palaces and hunting lodges across the country, Matilda liked to spend as much of her time as possible, static, in London. She rarely moved around with the King, only travelling when necessary for the Easter, Pentecost and Christmas courts. King Henry had granted rich incomes to the Queen from the city including the port taxes of Queenshithe and the citizens of London took her warmly to their hearts, calling out affectionately in the streets, whenever she ventured outside the palace.

The Queen's entourage consisted largely of priests and clerks and only a few Anglo-Saxon ladies. Emma, Christina, Cille and myself, were her only regular female attendants. They spoke to each other and the Queen in English but occasionally Matilda would recollect that I could not understand and commanded that they switch to French. The Queen was no more stylish in her dress now than she had been at her wedding and coronation, and the Norman ladies of the court did not, on the whole, consort with her. One morning I entered the Queen's chambers with Cille and was delighted to see an array of the best Anglo-Saxon embroidery, jewellery and metalwork laid out.

'Look, Nest!', Christina exclaimed. 'These artisans have come with such exquisite examples of their work for the Queen to see. She intends to buy some for herself and to purchase other things as gifts for her friends.' I picked up the Queen's baby daughter, Maud, from her cradle and walked around, showing Maud the fine things draped across the chests and tables. The merchants had sumptuous silks and velvets in a dazzling array of colours. One man showed the Queen an extraordinary bestiary and seeing me admire the book, the Queen purchased it for Maud. 'You can read it to her, Nest, and show her the pictures.' The Queen was pleased I was able to read and write and could share the pleasure of books with her since the other ladies' schooling had been more rudimentary than my own.

I put the bestiary on a low table, and sat before it with Maud on my knee. It was written in Latin and had beautiful ink drawings of many creatures. 'Look here is the Lion, the King of the Beasts, who sweeps away his tracks with his tail and sleeps with its eyes open. He reminds me of Sir Haith!' I laughed, looking up at the Queen, who smiled back to us. I turned the page. 'And here is the

Hedgehog which rolls on the ground at harvest time to gather grapes on its spines and feed them to its young.'

Elizabeth sauntered in, looking for me. She glanced around at the textiles and jewels with little interest and sat beside me. 'This is the Amphisbaena which has a head at each end of its body and can roll along the ground like a hoop,' I continued, pointing it out to Maud, 'and here is the crocus-coloured Crocodile, that weeps after eating a man.'

'Also crocodile's *dung*,' interrupted Elizabeth, 'is an ointment to make old women and whores beautiful again.'

I glanced with a small smile at her.

'Well that is hardly something the little princess needs to know is it, Countess Meulan?' the Queen said, mildly irritated.

'Here is a fox feigning death,' I went on, hoping to avoid an argument, 'and a unicorn resting its head in the lap of a virgin.'

'And there,' pointed out Elizabeth, turning the pages, speaking in an ironical babyish lisp, 'is a hunter chasing a beaver who is biting off the hunter's testicles, quite rightly, and a delightful hyena feeding on a corpse.'

Hurriedly I moved past those pages.

'Isn't it beautiful,' Matilda said to me, ignoring Elizabeth's perverse humour. 'It's based on the *Physiologus* and Isidore of Seville's *Etymologiae*. All God's creations provide examples for us to consider the correct way to live.'

Elizabeth and I exchanged glances. Later I would consider with her, the examples of the hounds I had just seen mating in the yard, and the Queen's very fat lapdog that sat on a cushion, being fed candied sweets by Christina. Its skin was stretched taut over its rotund body, looking like an over-filled pig's bladder fit to burst.

'If you could add an animal from Wales to this bestiary, Nest, what would it be?' Elizabeth asked.

'A badger.' I looked up and saw blank faces. 'You know. It's big and has a black and white stripy head and waddles.' I imitated its movement, wobbling from side to side, my hands before me like paws, making the baby chuckle, her eyes bright upon me. The Queen and the ladies still looked blank. 'Well it mostly comes out at night.'

'What does it teach us, Nest?' asked the Queen.

I thought of its pungent black excrement that Goronwy had trod in once barefoot and the smell persisting for days despite many scrubbings; of a badger he and I watched galloping in a field; of the big badger setts humping at the side of the path that we walked past in the daytime knowing they slept deep down there wheezing.

'Well they sometimes eat rotting fruit and get drunk, and they eat hedgehogs, chickens and occasionally lambs. Their fur makes a very good shaving brush.'

They looked at me doubtfully. 'Yes but what is their best characteristic, Nest?' the Queen persisted.

I thought about it for a while. 'They are often underestimated. When they are cornered they are fierce fighters and will see off larger animals.'

Queen Matilda reminded me of FitzHamon in her lack of humour, but she was learned, intelligent and interested in literature. She was astute and practical and Henry did not demure at leaving serious matters of state in her capable hands. She frequently had her head bent about business with her chancellor Bernard, her chamberlain Aldwin or her chaplain Geoffrey. Besides these men, her brother David was with her most days and other men attending on her included Robert Malet, Gilbert the Sheriff, William Warelwast and Michel de Hanslope. On one occasion her sister Mary, who had recently married the Count de Boulogne, came to visit. Matilda was closely interested in the affairs of her siblings, especially the Scottish king, Edgar. I was, however, disgusted to find Master Richard Belmeis in the Queen's favour. He had the temerity to speak with me, friendly-fashion, as if I had not witnessed him being a great liar and traitor to my dear Sybil.

'Lady Nest, what a pleasure to see you here, displaying the fruits of my labours in your education, so wonderfully, in the Queen's household. You are indeed, an ornament to the court,' he gushed, reaching for my hand.

I took a step back from him, keeping my hands rigidly at my sides.

'How are your educational assistants?' I asked him.

His smile grew a little hesitant and he looked from my face to the Queen's in confusion.

'The locusts,' I said. 'Those creatures that step over each other, squashing the heads and feet of their own relatives and patrons to feed themselves.'

'Are locusts really so badly behaved?' asked the Queen innocently, but Master Richard took my meaning and made his excuses to depart soon after.

The Queen was extremely pious and spent much of her time in prayer, reading and speaking with her spiritual advisers. At Lent she wore a hair-shirt beneath her royal robes and walked barefoot between the palace and the church. Her deceased mother, Queen Margaret of Scotland, was being mooted as a saint and Matilda had aspirations to emulate her. She commissioned the writing of a *Life of Margaret* which she was using to train herself in the offices of good queenship. She corresponded frequently with Archbishop Anselm and Bishop Gundulph of Rochester, but Abbot Faricius, who had seen her through the birth of Maud, continued her favourite, and she showered him with gifts to enable him to repair and expand the Abbey at Abingdon.

'I knew the King for some time before our marriage,' the Queen confided to me and Emma as we sat sewing with her, 'when he was Count Henry, and we liked each other well.' She smiled warmly to herself. I kept my own thoughts silenced, that Henry, in truth, seemed willing to like any female he encountered.

Her chambers were always bustling with writers, priests and canons who came to discuss new monastic foundations with her or repairs to existing churches and abbeys. She met with masons who presented building plans for new bridges and hospitals. An endless crowd of petitioners waited outside her chambers, hugging gifts for her, hoping for her gracious intercession. The Queen loved music and a different musician performed for us each evening. Rahere, who had been King William's minstrel, and William LeHarpur were both frequent guests.

The royal nursery and the King's foster children were under the Queen's supervision. Henry's oldest illegitimate daughter, Mathilde, was eleven and being brought up at court and the

Queen was affectionate to her. Nobody (but Henry of course) seemed to know who her mother had been. Ansfride's three children by Henry were also cared for in the nursery: Richard, Juliane and the new-born Fulk. In addition to this shoal of illegitimate royal children, Henry had a number of foster sons training at the court, including Brian FitzCount, the illegitimate son of the Count of Brittany; Olafr Godredsson, younger son of Godfred Crovan who had been King of Dublin and the Isles; and William, the orphaned son of Robert of Rhuddlan, the Norman lord who had tried to rule in north Wales and been killed by the men of Gruffudd ap Cynan.

Queen Matilda was anxious to see some integration of her own court with the Norman court of her husband and so she encouraged my friendship with Elizabeth de Vermandois. 'Let's walk in the garden,' Elizabeth said to me, and the Queen absent-mindedly nodded her approval, her head bent over a religious book. Elizabeth was vivacious, confident and gorgeous. We were of a similar disposition and I relished her company. She was excited at the news that the Queen's brother, Edgar King of the Scots, had received a camel from one of his warriors returning from the Holy Lands and King Edgar had sent it in turn as a gift to the Irish King Muirchertach Ua Briain. 'Imagine the bewilderment of that poor animal, Nest!' she exclaimed. 'Taken from the broiling hot desert first to the windy slopes of Scotland, then tied down in a rocking boat across the stormy Irish Sea to their rainy bogs there in Ireland. Henry has one too, you know. A camel. At Woodstock!'

Her sense of fun and reckless mischief reminded me of my brother Goronwy. I asked Elizabeth about her marriage, intrigued at the great age gap between her and her husband. 'When I was eleven years old my father was leaving on crusade and married me to his good friend, Robert de Meulan. Robert was *forty* years older than me.' She paused but diplomatically I made no remark. 'He is *so* old, Nest,' she laughed, 'that he fought at the Battle of Hastings with the Conqueror!' I smiled but refrained from comment. 'I am fond of him,' she went on. 'Greatly fond. He is intelligent and kind. He waited until I was a woman before he took me to his bed.'

'I like him a great deal,' I said honestly, although I could not say I would have felt the same if he had been my husband, and I had to bed with such an old man. Elizabeth's new-born daughter, Isabel, was also being cared for in the royal nursery. Elizabeth was more engaged with the politics of the court even than the Queen and she was close friends with Henry. She became my guide and able teacher in my new milieu.

Towards the end of a hot summer I was surprised to receive a message from the King, conveyed by Haith. It read: '*I would be grateful for your aid, Lady Nest, in my current negotiations with the Princes of Powys. Please oblige me by coming to me with all haste to Bridgnorth in the company of Haith who will take good care of you.*' The King's seal was fixed to the scroll. Henry was besieging Bellême at Bridgnorth. Why did he summon me to a battlefield?

19

The Chase

I supposed that the Welsh princes were siding with one or the other or both in King Henry's contention with Bellême. 'But why does he need me?' I asked Haith, bewildered. 'He must have Welsh translators and mediators more fit for the task than I? And if I am to take an absence from court, what should I tell the Queen?'

Haith wore his usual cheerful expression. 'Suggest to tell her …' he paused, thinking. 'King is sending you on mission to give a gift to Abingdon Abbey. She's always happy for gifts for Faricius.' He nodded enthusiastically at his own suggestion.

'But … you recommend I should lie to her?'

He said nothing, only looking at me and shrugging his shoulders. Then, 'King's orders,' and another shrug.

'Haith, is my … virtue … threatened? Tell me the truth.'

He coloured. 'The King likes you of course. I like you!' He beamed his huge smile at me, trying to make light of things as always. His expression sobered. 'He would not force you. He never does that!' He looked at me and I could not disbelieve him. Haith was loyal to Henry but I felt he would not lie to me for him. 'Really does need you for negotiating with Welshmen,' he added.

I could not find a way to refuse and I was, in truth, curious, flattered, keen to escape the stifling daily habits of Matilda's court. The idea of riding with Haith to a battleground on the Welsh borders, of speaking with my countrymen, of being important to the King, seemed a great adventure. I packed a saddlebag and told my lie to the Queen who accepted it with a small frown. 'I see,' she said. 'You will be accompanied by Amelina? You will take great care of her, Haith?'

'For sure!'

It felt wonderful to be out riding after the months of sewing and praying and always being on my best behaviour. Haith was a ceaselessly cheerful companion and kept us both amused on the journey, although the road was often awash from flooding and full of deep holes that were like deadly small lakes for the unwary. We were riding at dusk through a thickly wooded part of the road when my horse shied and Amelina screamed. Haith turned his horse quickly to us. I looked with horror at what had spooked my horse and maid. On a fence at the side of the road, ten large greying tongues were nailed in a row and beneath, the decapitated bodies of wolves lay on the ground. 'No worries,' Haith said. 'Village and inn just up ahead. We'll get there before nightfall.' But even he looked worried.

We reached the King's encampment at Bridgnorth Castle on the second day. The war camp spread out before the castle walls like a parasitic plant strangling a tree. Haith led us through the camp, with its ramshackle tents, piles of weapons, tethered horses, wagonloads of supplies. Dishevelled women and dirty children moved amongst soldiers who were eating and cleaning weapons. Small campfires burned everywhere, choking me with the smoke from damp wood, tantalising my nose with the smell of roasting rabbits and birds. Soldiers stood in small groups, many in a state of partial undress, their faces grimed, staring at me. I raised my hood against their stares.

The King's tent was a splendid architecture of swooping red and yellow brocaded silks. At the top of the tent pole, a red banner with two golden lions whipped in the wind. Inside, the tent had all the comforts of a royal chamber. Henry's face lit up at the sight of me. 'Princess Nest! I thank you profusely for answering my strange request. You may leave us Haith, and your woman ...' He gestured at Amelina. Henry was wearing dark battledress and it suited him.

Haith glanced at me and murmured, 'I am always at your service, lady. Just ask.' I smiled my thanks to him. Amelina frowned but I waved my hand to indicate she should go with Haith.

'Please do sit,' Henry indicated a cushioned couch beside his own. Wine, bread and cheese stood on a low table. I reached to the water bowl and towels washing my face and hands, removing the dust of the road. Henry held out a beaker of wine for me which I took gratefully, shaking my head for now as he indicated the food. 'You must think it a very strange request to bring you here.'

'Yes, my lord. I imagine you have plenty of Welsh translators to draw on and do not need my service in that.'

'I have Welsh translators yes, but what I need is an astute and knowledgeable head. And someone I can completely trust.'

I tried not to show my pleasure too much at this assessment. I reflected that the enemy was Robert de Bellême, Sybil's brother, but I had no reason to be loyal to him, whereas the shape of my life was very much in the hands of King Henry.

'You will recall that Cadwgan's son Owain has asked for your hand in marriage?' I reached for the wine goblet to mask my extreme interest. Henry filled it for me again. 'I make no promises to you on this score, Nest. It's complicated. You are of great significance to the Welsh princes. My assent would depend on the political situation, but I *would* consider it.'

'What is it that you need me to do?'

'The Princes of Powys are allied with Bellême, but Cadwgan has given me his word that he will stay aloof from the conflict. His younger brother, Iorwerth, however, seems willing to commit more in assisting me. I would like you to be present at my meeting with him tomorrow. Advise me. Ensure that I am understanding the nuances of the language.'

'Yes, I can do that.'

'There is the matter of your accommodation,' Henry said. 'There is a curtained section of the royal tent that might suit you.' He nodded towards one corner of the tent.

'I ... fear that would not be fitting, sire. I am an unmarried woman and should be accommodated separately, with my maid, and an older female chaperone.'

'Of course, of course!' he said, waving an arm, attempting to conceal an expression veering between irritation and disappointment. 'Haith!' he shouted and the knight stepped in through the

213

entrance flap of the tent. 'Lady Nest is in need of her own tent, and a female chaperone. Sort that out will you.'

Haith's face showed his confusion at the thought of where he would find such a female chaperone in the war camp, but he bowed and retreated to set about his task. After I had passed a few hours of pleasant conversation with Henry, Haith returned, having erected a tent and found an elderly widow at a nearby manor who was willing to act as my companion. Henry kissed my hand with a dramatic expression of regret on his face. 'And must I really part with you, Nest?' he whispered.

'I fear so, sire.' I knew Henry was flattering me and yet I felt a ridiculous pleasure in it. Haith held the tent flap open and I followed his lantern across the uneven ground to the comfortable quarters he had prepared, and to the comforting safety of Amelina, and the widow who greeted me but was soon bundled into blankets and snoring on her straw pallet. Amelina stood smoothing out some clothing for me for the next day. 'Were you looked after?' I asked her. 'What have you been doing with yourself?'

'Oh organising things here. Haith kept me amused.' She gave me a complicit smile and I raised my eyebrows at her incorrigible lust. She pouted. 'Mind you, he's more interested in you than me. Did nothing but ask questions about you. If you would be comfortable enough here, and so on and so forth.'

As I lay on my pallet-bed trying to sleep, I recalled the touch of Henry's lips on my hand. I should not have come. Sybil would have counselled me against it. I had hastily conferred with Elizabeth before my departure and she had breezily told me I should go, it would be an adventure, but I realised now I was here and it was real, that I had made myself vulnerable to affront and embarrassment. Haith assured me Henry would not force me, but I recalled the anxious expressions I had seen flitting across Haith's cheerful face when he thought I was not looking. I had prevailed in securing myself a chaperone and refusing anything improper, however. I turned my thoughts to tomorrow. Perhaps I really could influence the outcome of the conflict, of Henry's relationships with the Welsh princes, and perhaps he really would allow me to marry Owain ap Cadwgan.

When Haith conveyed me, along with my ancient chaperone, back to Henry's tent in the morning, Prince Iorwerth had already arrived with a small entourage. They were all seated and rose at my entry. Iorwerth was a man in his late forties, with greying hair and a lined face. 'You honour us, Lady Nest,' he told me in Welsh. 'Tales of your great beauty and grace have not been exaggerated and *any* Prince of Powys would be swooning in bliss if he were rewarded with you as a bride.'

I was confused at his words and my confusion showed on my face because Henry quickly asked, 'What does your countryman tell you, Princess Nest?'

I conveyed the last part of Iorwerth's words to the King, passing over his reference to my beauty and grace. 'Sire,' I added forcefully, 'if you are using me, my marriage, as a bargaining token, I should like to know it, and with whom.'

Iorwerth looked anxious at my tone. 'You are confusing our guests,' Henry said, with a cheerful smile on his face. 'I assure you I am not about to give you away in marriage right now. Please tell Prince Iorwerth that he will be richly rewarded if he will lend me his aid against Robert de Bellême.'

I translated the King's words and saw that Iorwerth assumed I was part of this proferred reward. It was a reasonable assumption given my presence there. I saw now what Henry's game was in bringing me as his translator. Iorwerth might be important to Henry now, but it was his older brother Cadwgan who had the upper hand in Powys and it was Cadwgan's son, Owain, I felt, who would make the most appropriate husband for me. The negotiations proceeded smoothly and after an hour Prince Iorwerth and his retinue left, with many expressions of love to King Henry and myself.

'Excellent! That went very well,' Henry beamed at me.

'I should like to return to the Queen, now,' I told him.

'Already! I thought you might stay another night, by my side, bringing me cheer in this bleak time of war.'

'Your invitation honours me,' I said frostily, 'but the Queen is anxious for my return.'

'Very well, very well.' He was cross at my resistance. 'Haith! Convey Lady Nest back to Westminster as soon as you can make ready. She is anxious to leave me.'

I decided that no response to his words was my best policy and before long, Haith, Amelina and I were returning on the road we had come along a few days before. 'All good?' Haith asked.

I looked at him, wondering what exactly he meant. 'Yes, all good,' I eventually responded.

* * *

From Gerald FitzWalter's Day Book

Near Cardigan, The Assumption of the Virgin, 15 August 1102

All is lost. I am landless and lordless. The Montgommerys have played treason too far and too many times and they and I suffer wholly for it. They are all disseised of their English and Welsh lands and banished the kingdom: Robert de Bellême, Roger the Poitevin and Arnulf de Montgommery. Their father, the Old Earl, and King Henry's father, the Conqueror, would weep to see such an outcome of their own close friendship and ventures in the conquest of 1066, to see such lack of love between their sons. How much the Montgommerys have lost. And tainted with them, I have lost near everything, excepting Moulsford if the King will allow me to keep it. He may not.

The King sent Jordan de Saye as Castellan of Pembroke in my place and all my care and work there is of no substance any longer. I was ordered by the King's courier to wait at Pembroke for the arrival of de Saye and to handover whatever he needed in the way of keys, men, information, to enable him to take command. In return I was given leave to go free rather than walk into Pembroke's dungeon. It was a bitter moment to give up everything I have worked for these last nine years. As I mounted my horse to ride out of the castle that had been mine, Lady Nest's brother, Hywel, came out with a few others to wave me off. He is nine now and a little crooked but still an affectionate and a capable boy around the kitchen. His identity is still hidden so he should be safe enough there. I rode out free but to where and to what?

216

Of the Montgommery brothers, Bellême and the Poitevin have returned to their rich estates in France. Arnulf however has no lands beyond the kingdoms of England and Wales. He should have knelt to King Henry as I advised him rather than support the hopeless case of Bellême's war, but he was too proud to admit an error, or too afraid of the King's punishment. The Welsh Kings laugh at us, able at last to play us off against each other and see our hold in Wales weakened. In time King Henry will send in new men but Wales was in effect the Kingdom of the Montgommerys and now that is gone.

My only hope is that the service I have done to Belmeis in sending him copies of Bellême and Arnulf's correspondence with Normandy will protect me, perhaps even raise me. Belmeis himself has of course done well out of the tragedy. The King has rewarded him with lands and made him Sheriff of Shropshire with an overview of Wales, filling the vacuum left behind by the Montgommerys. That such a weasel should be so raised up, but I must stay friendly with him for now. I have written to ask for his protection in return for the treacherous favours I did for him.

Arnulf, in desperation, sent me to treat with the High King of Ireland, Muirchertach Ua Briain, offering his swordarm to him against his enemies in exchange for land. I crossed the boisterous Irish sea, sailed up the Liffey and landed at Dublin where I was greeted by the haunting cries of gulls and a dark grey sky. A large number of longships were moored at the landing place and a man teetered at the top of one of the masts. The town was established by Vikings and feels so still. It was surrounded on the river bank side by a high wooden palisade atop an embankment. Once I was given permission to disembark and climb the steps up and through the palisade, I found streets made from wooden logs lashed together and laid over the boggy ground as a boardwalk, and a mass of thatched long houses each sitting within its own fenced plot and belching gouts of smoke from the roofholes. A priest walked by, muddied to his knees, clanging a large rectangular handbell, calling people to mass.

After two weeks of negotiations with King Muirchertach I returned from Dublin to Arnulf who waited, hiding out near

Cardigan, to hear the outcome of my negotiations. 'I have bettered even my commission, sire,' I told him.

'How so?'

'King Muirchertach Ua Briain will take your allegiance and give you lands, ships and men … and his daughter Lafracoth in marriage.'

'What! Are you insane, FitzWalter!'

'It was the seal on the agreement required by Muirchertach. There was no negotiating on it.' This last was not entirely the truth but whilst I was at the Irish court Muirchertach gave his other daughter Bebin in betrothal to Magnus Barelegs' son Sigurd, and it occurred to me, seeing her sister seated beside her that it would be a way to ensure Lady Nest no longer ran the risk of an uncertain marriage to Arnulf.

'What do I want with an Irish hoyden!' Arnulf yelled at me. 'I want the Welsh princess that was promised to me all this time, not this … this Lafra …'

'Lafracoth, sire. She is no hoyden I assure you. A beautiful and cultured young girl, sire, in truth. We all know that we do not marry for desire, lord, but for allegiance and wealth.'

'Yes, yes,' he said sullenly, waving me off.

He was crazed with the news for several days but had to grow reconciled to it. He has no other options. He can never have the Welsh princess and her father's kingdom now. Arnulf sails to Ireland tomorrow and he will find his wife is not without beauty, though she is not Nest. I do not sail with him since he has given me my promise of fealty back. I told him I knew only England and Wales where my kin are, and must chance myself there, not in Ireland. He was reluctant but eventually admitted I had served him long and well and deserved the granting of my request for release from his service. He is morose, as well he might be, with his losses and his prospects.

One stroke of luck occurred whilst I was in Dublin. I was invited to dine at the hall of the Norse lord Ragnall. I made my way up Fishamble Street to his hall where it seemed most of the household were out hunting when I arrived, perhaps too early, and there was not so much as a stableboy to greet me. I called out hallos in vain and then watered and tethered my own horse. I left my swordbelt at the doorway and ventured in. A fire burnt well in the hearth and I could smell the scents of a meal in preparation.

'We heard you, sir, but are at a crucial moment here!' Two young men sat at the table in the hall, with beakers of ale, playing at Hnefatafl. The red-haired man, who I recognised as Owain ap Cadwgan, had called out to me in Welsh, holding one arm up to stay me from an interruption. He and his contender kept their eyes fixed upon the game and not upon me. I approached them and saw Owain was taking the role of the attacker with white pieces. 'Submit!' he exclaimed as he captured one of the defender-pieces. The other, younger man, was black-haired and defended with the red pieces. His king-piece still stood in the castle in the centre of the board. A serving lad looked up from stirring a pot and brought me over a beaker of ale. I lent against the warm stone close to the hearth and watched until their play was concluded with Owain finally capturing the king of the dark young man. They shook hands laughing and then looked to me apologetically. 'Much was riding on it!' Owain exclaimed. 'I won a fine horse here from my friend Gruffudd.'

'You are Welsh, my friends,' I said, using their tongue.

Their faces were more guarded now and their glances took me in. 'And you, Norman,' the dark-haired boy said, looking at me with blue eyes. There was something familiar about him.

'Aye. I am invited here by Lord Ragnall to dine. I am Gerald FitzWalter, until recently, Castellan of Pembroke Castle.'

The dark-haired young man leapt to his feet at the sound of my name, reaching to the empty scabbard at his hip. Owain gripped him and pushed him back down into his seat. 'Easy! Our friend here is a guest of Lord Ragnall.'

'No friend to me,' the dark young man exclaimed, looking angrily at me.

'Give me your names that I can understand how I have offended,' I begged them, hoping all the while that Ragnall would arrive before too long and calm down the situation which I had not expected at all. I looked to check there was little distance between me and my sword leaning in the doorway. Though the young boy had no beard, was perhaps only fifteen or sixteen years old and I had the advantage of age and experience on him, nevertheless I had seen such youths made dangerous before in their eagerness to prove themselves, and I would not underestimate him. Owain I knew to be a bloodied warrior, and if it came to a fight he was bound to support his fellow Welshman and friend.

'I am Owain, son of King Cadwgan. You know of me no doubt.'

I inclined my head politely. 'Indeed Prince, I am glad to meet with you.'

'And my friend here, who alas you anger with your trespass on his lands, is King Gruffudd ap Rhys.'

For a moment I floundered. I could not think what was meant by it. 'I ...'

Seeing my confusion Owain enlightened me further. 'Gruffudd is the heir to Rhys ap Tewdwr who was slain by Bernard de Neufmarché at Aberhonddu.'

'Gruffudd ...,' I said, turning to him, 'then you are the brother of Nest, Princess Nest.'

'What do *you* know of my sister? How is her name in *your* mouth, Norman?' The young man's face was flushed and he growled his words at me beneath a furious brow.

'Take ease, Gruffudd,' Owain soothed him, holding him down in his chair with a heavy grip on both his shoulders.

'I have had the honour of knowing your sister for some years, lord. You will be glad to know she fares well. She is in England, at the court of King Henry. She is treated with honour, sire, as she merits.'

He looked a little mollified and raised his beaker shakily to me. The serving boy approached tentatively and refilled Owain and Gruffudd's beakers. I shook my head at his proferred jug. I judged they were both a little drunk, despite the early hour.

'Is she wed? Nest?' Gruffudd asked me, his face and tone shifting mercurially to a friendly enough façade.

'No, sire. Not as yet.'

The two Welshmen exchanged a look.

'And ...' Gruffudd began, but then I was relieved to hear the hunters arrive back in the courtyard beyond and to know I would soon have Ragnall between me and these two young pretenders to Welsh crowns. It was a stroke of luck to come across Nest's brother. He is a fine young man who has been reared and trained in Ragnall's warrior household. He and Owain both are wont to boast there of their intended inheritances as kings' sons. With Arnulf and the rest of the Montgommerys out of the way in Wales it would be a good time for such boasts to be acted upon. Nest would look gratefully on news of Gruffudd ap Rhys, but so would King Henry, and I am in needs to buy my way back into the King's good graces. Evidently Gruffudd means to make an attempt to reclaim his kingdom at some juncture if he could ever find himself adequately equipped with men and ships. Ragnall keeps him dangling on such a promise I have no doubt, but I see no likelihood of its fulfilment for the moment.

* * *

At Queen Matilda's court, news filtered through to us that Bel-lême, betrayed by his Welsh allies, had been forced to surrender Shrewsbury to Henry, and had fled the kingdom. Sybil's family, that had been the greatest in the realm during the rule of William the Conqueror, was reduced to nothing in England and Wales. Prince Iorwerth had captured his brother, Maredudd, and Henry had imprisoned him, but then Iorwerth had approached Henry for his promised reward and despite Henry's assurances – which I was certain had included me – the Prince found himself also incarcerated at the King's pleasure, so Cadwgan was now unchallenged ruler of Powys. It had doubtless been the agreement between Cadwgan and Henry all along.

Henry used me, dangled me as bait for Iorwerth, and perhaps hoped to conquer me himself too. The sooner I was honourably wed the better. I decided to work on Queen Matilda to see if she could intercede with the King to find a suitable husband for me. Why not Prince Owain? Could it really make a difference to Norman rule in Wales? Grudgingly, I admitted to myself that yes it could. Cadwgan was already as powerful as Henry was prepared to allow any Welsh prince to be. My alliance with Owain would present a significant rallying symbol for the Welsh resistance, and would give Cadwgan and Owain every reason to expand their control into Deheubarth, against its current Norman rulers, who were insecure as yet after the dismissal of Arnulf. If Henry would not consent to a marriage to Owain, then who *would* he bestow me upon? I determined to discuss this knotty problem with Elizabeth.

* * *

From the Copybook of Sister Benedicta

Westminster, Midwinter 1102

Dear Benedicta, forgive my tardiness in writing to you. There has been much afoot. Last year as you know William de Warenne, the Earl of Surrey, left Henry's court in the company of Duke Robert. Henry has been setting his house in order as I told you he would, creating an aristocracy around him that is loyal as they never were in the reign of his brother William. He disseised Warenne for allowing his men to inflict private warfare on villagers in Norfolk and refuses all his treaties for restitution. Ivo de Grandesmil has had to hock his land to Meulan and go on pilgrimage for similar reasons of offence against the King. No doubt you will have heard from your Montgommery Abbess that Henry has dealt with that family harshly. The Montgommerys are all disseised and banished from England. Their nephew, William de Mortain, continues to be a concern. Henry is giving him a chance to show loyalty since he is young and a kinsman to Henry also, but I doubt that will end well either. Slowly Henry moulds his raptor barons to his own needs. If you hear news of any of the Montgommery brothers it could be useful for Henry to hear it.

Your favourite, Archbishop Anselm, has been holding council and doing a similar job of cleansing and shaping on the Church much to the discomfort of some bishops and abbots who gained their positions through bribes to William Rufus, and to the unease of those married clerics that Anselm chastises and orders they must set aside their mistresses and children. Friction continues between Anselm and the King regarding the controversy over investiture of bishops and this has no prospect of resolution for now. I am lately returned from campaign against Bellême at the Welsh borders with Henry and have been kept busy conveying beautiful young ladies through wolf-infested forests and the like. How are things in Normandy? From your brother, with love, Haith.

Almenêches Abbey, Normandy, Yuletide 1102

Dearest Haith, all is calm here at the Abbey for now although we expect trouble with the return of Bellême. He is a turbulent man & peace does not follow him. You will have heard of the sad death of good Count Etienne de Blois on crusade. His wife Countess Adela, sister to your King Henry, is ruling Blois as Regent for her young son Theobald & doing an excellent job of it to all accounts. Duke Robert & his wife Sybilla have cause for celebration with the recent birth of their son William Clito. We are all praying that this son will live, & that Duke Robert, steadied by a wife & heir, will find a good rule of the Duchy now. Beautiful young ladies you say? I send you all my affection & this gift of warm woollen hose that I have knitted for you to wear in your draughty palaces. I hope they are not too small for your great hooves. Benedicta.

* * *

The Christmas court was held in Westminster so the Queen could stay put, as she liked. We heard the sad news that the wife of Duke Robert had given him an heir but died soon afterwards and the Queen has sent both her congratulations and her condolences to the Duke, who is her godfather. Henry has lately arrived back with his household and amongst the members of his entourage swelling the palace, were his adviser Robert de Meulan, Elizabeth's husband; Henry, Earl of Warwick and Meulan's brother; Bishop Roger of Salisbury; William d'Aubigny, Henry's butler; William de Courcy, Eudo and Haimo who are Henry's stewards; Aubrey de Vere, his chamberlain; Ralph Basset, one of his justiciars; William Warelwast who acts as a diplomat to Rome and the sheriff Urse D'Abetot. Elizabeth schooled me in the names and roles of everyone. I was disappointed that FitzHamon did not come to court, thinking Sybil might have come with him, but FitzHamon, Henry told me, had business in Normandy.

Henry also brought with him the scholars, Petrus Alfonsi and Adelard of Bath, since he was very interested in their latest discoveries concerning counting and astrology. Adelard, who had travelled widely in the Holy Lands, had a table set before the King and was demonstrating his new invention. The surface of the table was divided into units and counters could be moved around the table to add and subtract. 'I am also, sire, writing a treatise on the illnesses of hawks, from their heads to their toes.'

Henry nodded his head up and down earnestly, equally interested in the counting and the hawk diseases. 'Excellent, Adelard. Truly excellent.'

I was surprised to see Gerald in the crowd of people thronging the hall and raised my hand to catch his attention but he did not see me. Before I had a chance to step to him and ask how he did, the King's herald shouted his name: 'Gerald FitzWalter!'

Gerald stepped forward and knelt to the King, his head bowed.

'You were vassal to the Montgommerys and Castellan at Pembroke Castle?' Henry asked Gerald.

'Yes, sire.'

'You travelled to Ireland on Arnulf de Montgommery's behalf to ask for help for the rebels against me from the King of Munster and negotiated an unsanctioned marriage for Arnulf de Montgommery with the Irish King's daughter.'

'Yes, sire.' Gerald's head stayed down.

My mind raced to comprehend what I heard. Arnulf was married! And Gerald ... Gerald was accused before Henry of treasonous acts. I looked in panic at Henry's face trying to read Gerald's doom there. I had seen him issue warrants for hangings and maimings for much less.

20

An Old Maid

Henry contemplated Gerald's bowed head and looked out across the crowd of people, his gaze alighting on me. 'However …' Henry began.

I did not think but suddenly found myself standing next to Gerald in front of the King. I was aware of Gerald turning to look up at me in surprise, but I did not look at him. 'Please, sire, grant Sir Gerald FitzWalter clemency as he gave me compassion when my father, the King of Deheubarth, was slain by Bernard de Neufmarché. I know that as steward of my father's conquered lands, he has treated all with fairness and justice. Even the Welsh would say so.' I had stepped up and spoken in a rush and now I was alarmed at my temerity, wondering where had it come from, but shouldn't a princess be able to speak to a king?

I was relieved to see a smile blooming on the King's face. 'My dear Lady Nest. You plead eloquently for Gerald FitzWalter.'

I wanted to say more but my legs were shaking terribly and I feared my voice would also shake.

'No more words, my lady?'

I shook my head.

'Well, FitzWalter, since you have such a fair champion, who could gainsay her?' The King appeared to be highly amused but he sobered his expression and voice to pronounce his decision on Gerald. 'You will stay here at court for now, FitzWalter, where I can watch if your tendencies are as rebellious as the Montgommerys or no, and then we shall see.'

'Thank you sire. You will find me loyal to you. I thank you greatly, Lady Nest,' Gerald turned to me, his face scarlet. The King waved his hand for the next business and Gerald walked quickly from the hall, glancing back over his shoulder at me.

With Henry back at court I noticed that he showed a great deal more affection for his wife and baby daughter than FitzHamon had ever shown to Sybil and her daughters. The Queen was pregnant again, but unlike Sybil who was always so sturdy in her pregnancies, Matilda was constantly unwell. The King invited me twice to Woodstock but I found reasons to demure on each occasion, using the excuse of my duties to his wife. I was not such a fool as to risk myself there with him, nevertheless I was surprised and, I had to admit to myself, a little jealous, when Elizabeth told me Henry had taken a new, and very young, mistress, named Sybil Corbet. 'She is exquisite,' Elizabeth said. 'Like a doll.'

'Well, if a full-grown man must play with dolls ...,' I said waspishly.

Elizabeth herself might be described as exquisite, with her red hair and strange coloured eyes, but there was nothing doll-like about *her*. The white flesh of her arms and shoulders were softly padded, and her breasts swelled substantially in her bodice. I was a little jealous of that since my own body was still rather boy-like. 'But you haven't started bearing babies yet like me!' Elizabeth exclaimed. She had lately discovered she was pregnant again and her body was blooming fast.

At the beginning of May the court moved to Windsor for Pentecost where a controversy occurred because Duke Robert and William de Warenne arrived to attend the court without giving notice to the King. Henry was furious with his brother and refused to see him. Eventually the Duke admitted, using Meulan as his mediator, that he should have asked leave from the King before landing on English soil. It was embarrassing to see how Henry and Meulan manipulated the Duke into humiliating himself, particularly since he had come, selflessly and with great courtesy, to plead for the reinstatement of Warenne. This pleading then did not get off to a good beginning. I think it is Henry's deliberate policy to put his opponents on the wrong foot from the outset.

The Duke is a peculiar looking man – very short and round like a small wine barrel but very courteous and genial. I liked him. Warenne is an extraordinarily handsome man – tall, fair-haired, with the pronounced shoulder breadth of a practised warrior. After a few days of bandying accusations and apologies back and forth, Henry finally summoned the Duke and Warenne into his presence to explain their business in England.

'I come to plead with you, brother, to reinstate William de Warenne to his English lands,' the Duke declared, his face wreathed in anxious smiles.

'Those lands were disseised on good grounds of offense against my laws.' Henry's demeanour made no concession to them.

'I humbly beg your forgiveness and forbearance,' Warenne told King Henry graciously. 'If you would accept my fealty I would serve you faithfully for the rest of my years.'

It was puzzling. Why would Duke Robert allow Warenne to jump ship to Henry? Warenne was a powerful and rich baron with a substantial following. Was it a trick? In the Queen's chambers we ladies discussed the mystery of it back and forth, along with the looks of the Duke and the Earl. 'I do believe that we need such a looker as Warenne at the court of King Henry!' Elizabeth declared making us all laugh and even the Queen suppressed a small smile as she kept her eyes fixed on her embroidery.

The Duke and Warenne's audience with King Henry continued the issue on the following day. 'You plead for Warenne?' the King asked his brother.

'I do.'

'What compensation is offered to me should I agree?'

'I will give up the 3,000 marks annuity you previously promised. I make this offer on the advice of my god-daughter, your queen, your peace-maker.'

Henry struggled to keep the delight from his face. He bent his ear to Meulan's advice. He must have known of this in advance. It seemed unlikely that the Queen would act in this matter without consulting with her husband and Meulan.

'We will think on it,' Henry pronounced.

The Duke stayed at court for some time and proved to be good company. He was an excellent conversationalist, enthralling us all with his tales of the Holy Lands. He appeared affable to the point of foolishness, for a Duke, especially given the self-interest he is surrounded by. The Queen was pleased with his company and he spent a good deal of his time with us in her chambers. Alas, we did not see so much of Elizabeth's 'looker', Warenne.

After a few days Henry indicated he would accept the deal offered and so Warenne was allowed back into favour and restored to his rights in England, and the Duke returned to Normandy, inexplicably impoverished by his own hand. I asked Elizabeth what she made of it. 'The Duke is a fool, I'm afraid, Nest, simply a fool. It's possible he meant it as an olive branch to Henry.'

'But they are not at war. Why would the Duke need to offer Henry an olive branch?'

'They are not at war *yet*,' she said. 'But the Duke does, at least, understand the measure of his own brother and what his intentions might be. I suppose that Henry, Warenne and my husband had it all worked out beforehand and simply manipulated Duke Robert and Queen Matilda to their desired course. The Duke is no match for our Henry. And delightfully, now we have the addition of the *unmarried* Warenne to our court!' She grinned naughtily at me and I shook my head at her. 'Well! You did ask me to think on who might be a good husband for you ....'

The Queen was sick constantly with her pregnancy and then hankering in the afternoons for sweetmeats. One morning she sent me to the merchant's shop to stock up the supplies of her favourite treats – marzipan tortes, quince paste, sugar-coated almonds and anise seeds. Returning, I rounded a corner of the garden-wall fast and bumped into the King. Instead of disentangling himself he made a deliberate effort to entangle himself further with me and my packages. 'Off you go,' he said to Amelina, waving her to continue past us alone. 'How is my Queen, Nest?' He juggled my packages behind my back with me inbetween his arms.

Disconcerted, I blurted out, 'A little pained I fear.'

'Pained?' Something like pain appeared in his own expression.

I said nothing further and Henry shifted my packages to one hand, cupping my chin, 'Come now, Nest. You may speak freely. What pains her?' I had more sense than to speak freely on the matter. When I simply shook my head he started guessing. 'Is it Ansfride? Or Sybil Corbet?' and then laughing, 'Or you perhaps?'

I flushed scarlet and made another attempt to extricate myself but the more I pulled away the more he pulled me into an embrace. Flustered and irritated by his playful grappling I blurted again: 'Sire, you think the Queen is oblivious to your mistresses but I fear she does suffer because of it.'

Now he let go of me and his face became serious. He bent down to pick up one package that had dropped to the ground and handed it to me. I was regretting my forthrightness. 'I'm sorry, sire, to mention it, but I …'

'I'm sure you are right, Nest. Thank you for saying this. I don't want to make Matilda suffer, you know. I keep meaning to mend my ways. Forgive me will you?' He took my hand, turned it over and one fingertip stroked back and forth gently across my palm. My face and neck felt heated and looking down at myself I saw that the exposed skin above my neckline was blotching red.

'It's not I who should forgive you, sire. It's the Queen.' Reluctantly he let me pull my hand from his and I moved swiftly back to my duties.

At Westminster I usually slept with the Queen's other ladies in her chambers. On the occasions when the Queen received the King in her bed we all had to be ushered out to sleep in the outer chamber. Henry would saunter in wearing his nightgown, lean to me and whisper, his breath hot on my ear, his skin fragrant, 'The Queen will need some privacy'. He enjoyed my embarrassment and it was always me he singled out from the ladies for this communication. Here at Windsor however, I had been given the luxury of my own small bedchamber, and I revelled in this rare solitude. Even Amelina was accommodated elsewhere. I was sleeping soundly and startled awake. There was scratching at the door. I could see nothing. The room was pitch-black. I sat up in my nightdress and shivered in the cold air after the warmth of my bed. The floor was cold beneath my bare feet. The scratching came again. I moved towards the door. But what if it were Henry? I took a step back.

I would ignore the sound, but then I heard my name whispered in a woman's voice through the keyhole. 'Nest! *Please!*' Quickly I reached out, unlocked the door and heard, rather than saw for I could see nothing in the darkness, Elizabeth hurtle in, fumble for me and find my arm. Softly she closed the door behind her and pulled me to lean against it with her. She was giggling close to my cheek. I could feel the heat of her body through my thin nightdress, the round of her pregnant stomach pushed against mine. 'Elizabeth?'

'Sshh! Lock the door again, quickly.'

I fumbled at the lock. 'I can't see anything!'

'I know!'

The key finally found its slot and clicked into place. 'It's locked. What's happening?'

'Sshh!' She was shaking with suppressed laughter.

'What on earth are you doing? It's the middle of the night.'

She pulled me to the bed and we both fell in. She pulled the covers up over our heads and began laughing in earnest. 'Oh Nest! I was so nearly caught there, flitting in my nightdress! If you had failed to open the door!'

'Caught?'

'Oh Nest you won't believe it. He's so wonderful!

'Who is wonderful?'

'William!'

'Who?'

'Oh Nest. Don't you notice a thing?'

I was bewildered. 'Noticed what? William who?'

She groaned at me and rolled in the bed, drawing her knees up and then rolling back against me. 'William de Warenne of course! We are lovers! Just now. It just happened!'

'But ... I had no idea.' My eyes had grown a little accustomed to the gloom now or perhaps the light of dawn was starting to seep in. I could make out her eyes dancing with delight close to my face.

'Nest, he loves me! And he is gorgeous. To make love with a young man. Darling, it's entirely a different act I assure you.'

I gaped at her. 'But Elizabeth ...'

'Oh don't scold me. If you knew, if you had felt it in your own body, you would understand me.'

'But the child ...'

'... is Meulan's, don't worry.'

'I don't understand.'

'That's the wonder of it Nest. I can rut with my dear William, as he puts it, and nothing can come of it since I've Meulan's child already in my womb. What do you think of that!'

'I think, I think ...' I shook my head. 'I think if you are found out you will both suffer terribly.'

'We won't be found out. And in any case who is going to make us suffer. Henry?'

'Well ...'

'I assure you, not.'

'It is a sin.'

'I will gladly do penance for it.'

'Your husband might discover it and punish you.'

'He won't know. And Henry will protect us.'

'Does Henry know?'

'I think he does. He knows most everything.'

I held her, desperately anxious for her. 'Don't do anything stupid Elizabeth. I couldn't bear to see you hurt.'

'You always look on the bleak side of things. I'm not hurt. My whole body is singing with glee I assure you! If my uncle the King of France may bed whom he likes and ignore censure, why should not I?'

'I don't think much of your methods of matchmaking for *me!*' I told her with a smile, reminding her of the earlier suggestion that Warenne might make me an appropriate husband.

I entered the Queen's chambers the following morning with little Maud in my arms. Henry was standing there with his wife, and Haith. 'Ah Lady Nest, there you are!' the Queen said. Henry tickled the child under her chin, managing to 'accidentally' press the back of his hand overlong against the exposed skin above the neckline of my dress. He looked at me with a playful expression, challenging me to object. I stepped away from him. 'I have a commission for you,' Matilda told me, unaware of the mute exchange between me and her husband. 'Hand my daughter over to one of my other ladies.' I did as she commanded, carefully rolling the child into Christina's arms. 'As you know, Nest, I have been very ill with this new pregnancy and my lord commands that you go to his physician, Abbot Faricius in Abingdon, to fetch some medicines that he is preparing to assist me in this travail.'

I looked at Henry, wondering why it was necessary to send me. The Abbot could simply send one of his monks with the medicines.

'You would be assisting us both greatly, Nest,' he said. 'We are in hopes that the Queen is carrying a male child and we must all do everything in our power to safeguard an heir to the kingdom.'

I bowed my head. 'Of course.'

'Haith here will escort you,' Henry said. 'And your maid.'

Haith stepped forward with his enormous grin surrounded by the buttery sheen of his mane of hair. 'I know that river Thames very well, lady,' he said, 'You don't need no fear, no way, with me besides.' He thumped his chest. I couldn't help but smile at him.

'Can you leave straight away, Nest?' the Queen asked.

'Yes my lady.' Perhaps it was her ploy to get me away from her husband. I felt she might be aware of the King's 'attentions' to me.

Our short river journey from Windsor to Abingdon took us through Wallingford. Haith, Amelina and I shared boat space with messengers, merchants and pilgrims. At Wallingford a party of revenue collectors joined us and when one of our fellow passengers heard we were heading to Abingdon Abbey he told us Faricius was renowned for his skill as a physician. 'Getting gifts left, right and centre he is, not just from the King who favours him, but from all the noble folks round about who've benefitted from his skill – a son saved, a wife aided in a difficult birth.'

When the three of us had some privacy again I asked Haith, 'Have you been in the King's service long, sir?'

'Forever,' he said with characteristic brio. 'Henry and me always like brothers. Years. I was first serving him in Normandy. We both pretty much boys then, and his fortunes very up and down in those days. Good to see him now.'

'Yes,' I agreed. Whatever one might think about some aspects of Henry's character it was clear he was making a good job of being king.

At the end of our journey the Abbey came into view. It had been one of the wealthiest foundations in England but was destroyed by Danes more than a hundred years ago and now was in the process of major restoration. Haith and I stepped off the boat and I wobbled a little so that he grabbed my waist, reminding me of the first time we met at Westminster. 'Careful! Need land legs. They are coming now … steady, steady. Yes!' He reached out a hand and hauled Amelina onto the quay. She simpered her thanks to him. Despite her lascivious hints, I noticed Haith did not seem to reciprocate her fascination with him. Amelina was a good-looking woman but he seemed oblivious to the display of her charms.

Porters on the quay unloaded our two small travelling chests onto a donkey and Haith took its reins. We walked the short distance, skirting the edge of a busy market, to the Abbey Portal. Our entrance was considerably delayed by having to wait for a long line of wagons each drawn by twelve oxen that were being coaxed through the archway, carrying stone from Wales for the Abbey building works. I listened with pleasure to the carters' banter and surprised them by calling out a greeting in Welsh which they returned with a flourish of their caps and cheerful smiles.

The Abbey consisted of a vast complex of buildings, housing around fifty monks and sixty or so household staff. The buildings included an exchequer, the guesthouse, bakehouse, hospital, stables and church. Abbot Faricius came out himself to greet us. He had a heavy Italian accent and a fleshy face with intelligent small black eyes. He was younger than I had expected him to be – perhaps somewhere in his late thirties. After welcoming us he left Haith, Amelina and I with the monk in charge of the Abbey's guesthouse. Haith waved to me and led the donkey off in the direction of the stable. 'This way Lady Nest,' said the monk and we followed the swish of his brown habit. 'We have just one other female guest here at the moment.' I thought I detected a hint of distaste in his voice.

In the guesthouse I was surprised to find a young girl hurling herself affectionately at me. 'Oh thank the Lord you've arrived. I've been so bored here with these monks fussing about and bells ringing all the time and what have you. How is Henry?'

The guesthouse monk raised one eyebrow at me and left me to it. I dropped my leather bag onto a bed and turned back to her.

'Henry? Have we met before?' I asked bewildered, taking her in. She was a beautiful girl with a long, pale, oval face, perhaps sixteen, with light brown hair and large grey eyes. The most noticeable thing about her, however, was her enormous belly. I looked back and forth between her childish face, her thin arms, and the unlikely mound of the child she carried.

'I feel that we have,' she said enthusiastically. 'Henry mentions you quite often. The dimpled one he calls you!' She laughed. 'I'm Sybil. Sybil Corbet and this is little Henry.' She softly patted the side of her rounded stomach. I kept my surprise at her, and my irritation with Henry for duping me again, to myself. The three of us settled down to talk together before dinner.

Haith stayed at the Abbey for one night. With his easy humour and stash of stories about escapades involving Henry, he made Sybil laugh helplessly, holding her hand to her side. He headed back to the river the following day with the medicines for the Queen provided by Abbot Faricius carefully packed in a pouch at his waist. My journey had been a ruse all along for Henry to send me and Amelina to take care of his mistress as she approached the time of childbirth.

The Abbey had a very fine library and when the Abbot discovered I could read he gave me a key to go in and out as I pleased, which I did as often as I could to escape Sybil's chatter and her constant questions about the Queen, which I did not want to answer. I wandered around exploring the Abbey complex. Inside the Church of Saint Nicolas there was a golden wheel hung from the high ceiling on long, fine chains, with twelve lamps and innumerable little bells and a tablet of gold and silver was carved with the twelve apostles. An aqueduct brought water into the Abbey from the river, and fountains ran in a series of courtyards. The water mills nearby churned ceaselessly. The Abbey gardens were flourishing and well ordered with one part set aside for the fruit orchard, another for vegetables, and a third for the medicinal plants for the Abbot's cures.

Faricius took me on a tour of his medicinal garden. 'Rosehips to ward off a cold, elderflower for a chesty cough, willow for a headache, thyme to clean away grease from your fingers and bowls,' he told me. 'Some of the clergy complain about me, I

234

know. They are suspicious about my experiments and the medical work I do, especially that involving my female patients. They are jealous of my friendship with the King and other nobles. I take no notice. Innovation is always resented. You are a curious young woman though I believe, and not a foolish one. Perhaps I might show you something?'

I smiled my assent, gratified by his compliment, and intrigued by his invitation. He led me to his study and when he opened the door I was astonished to see a room littered with books, drawings, models. As I advanced further into the study I began to make out the drawings but could not understand what I was looking at. 'This is a preliminary version of a flying machine,' Faricius told me, pointing out a curious contraption with several flat wings and a basket. In a sketch pinned to the wall above the contraption, birds were shown drawing the structure into the air and a man sat dangling in the basket. 'And this is a new siege engine for hurtling stones and this here is a drawing for an artificial giant iron hand that can be used to grapple soldiers on the battlements of a castle during a siege.' He pointed to the illustration, imitating the grappling action with his own hand so that I could envisage it at work quite vividly.

Enboldened by the confidence he was showing in me, I decided to ask a question that had been burning in my head since I first arrived. 'Abbot Faricius, I believe you tended to my brother Idwal ap Rhys who had been a prisoner at Shrewsbury. The King wrote to me of it.'

He bowed his head briefly and then looked back to me. 'Yes, my dear, so I did.'

'He ... did he suffer terribly?'

'He had been in a dungeon for eight years, child, and was damaged by it through a lack of food, exercise and clean air. He lived only two days in my care and could not speak I'm afraid but I saw the way he smiled at the sky and the passage of birds, looking through the window of the infirmary, how glad he was to be out of the dungeon. The King sent a man who could speak Welsh and that man told him that he was freed as a favour to you, his sister, Nest ferch Rhys, and that you were well. He understood that. At the last I had him carried out on a pallet to lie in the open-air under the sun. He is buried with a headstone in the Abbey grave-yard. I will show you the place.'

I wept copiously at this description and the Abbot, wisely, let me exhaust my grief. He poured a beaker of water for me and I struggled to recover myself.

'Thank you.' I was not finished with the Abbot however, and had another difficult question to ask him. 'Father, do you think it right that the King should be bedding all these mistresses?'

'The King must be right, my dear,' he said, patting my arm, his eyes serious. 'He is God's anointed. If the girl is sick, or her preg-nancy is hard – which it is not – then that would be my business. Nothing else! Nobles always have mistresses. It's a given.'

'Yes, but …' I stopped. There seemed little point in holding this discussion with Faricius. He was delighted by Henry, who was his friend and benefactor, and saw nothing wrong in his behaviour. I had tried asking Sybil Corbet what her parents thought of her liaison but her response had been similar to Faricius'. They were very pleased with her of course, she said, that she was so gor-geous and the King had been unable to resist falling hopelessly in love with her. She told me her father had no son and she and her sisters were joint heiresses. 'Henry has promised to find me a good husband,' she said, 'but not for years and years yet. Not till we have had our fill of one another!'

I looked away, embarrassed at her lust and the image of Henry that it provoked for me.

When Sybil's child came it was a girl and born very small but both mother and child fared well under Faricius' care. Not long after the birth I was pleased to see Haith on horseback return-ing through the Abbey gateway, leading two other horses. 'Lady Nest!' he called out. 'All well?'

'Yes,' I called back, not sure if he meant with me, or Sybil, or both.

'More orders for us,' he said, dismounting. 'Queen at Winchester going to have baby soon. King says Abbot and Nest should go quick to her.'

'Of course. Will we go today?'

'Tomorrow, early. Horses needs some hay today and Haith needs some ale!' His big grin, and the point of his chin, turned his browned face into a perfect series of V shapes. The lines incised on his cheeks were testament to how often he grinned and laughed. He led the horses to their respite and I looked forward to the addition of his conversation at dinner.

Sybil pouted at the news of our departure. 'Well, what am I to do without Nest and Amelina? Who will look after the baby?'

'You will, my dear,' Faricius told her patiently. 'Perhaps the King will send for you soon.' He patted her small hand.

'Of course he will,' she said smugly. I tried not to imagine Henry embracing her gangling girl's limbs.

Faricius packed up his instruments and herbs and we travelled to Winchester for the Queen's lying in. Our journey this time was along the old Roman road through Milton, Compton, Hermitage, Donnington and Newbury where we turned off and went through Kingsclere to the hilltop royal hunting lodge at Freemantle to break our journey for the night. The place was covered in dustsheets and the caretaker and his wife did their best to accommodate us given they had received no notice in advance of our arrival. The following morning we were back on the Roman road, through Whitchurch, Sutton Scotney, King's Worthy, arriving in Winchester as the sun went down.

Only a few days after our arrival Queen Matilda's travail began. Matilda endured two gruelling days of labour, but then at last, gave birth to a healthy boy in August who was named William and baptised by Bishop Gundulph. I fear that without Faricius' skill either the mother or the baby or both might not have survived. There was great rejoicing and bells rung everywhere in the kingdom for the birth of the King's heir. Henry arrived a few hours after his son, and sat lovingly holding the enfeebled Queen's hand, as if he were not a great philanderer. She drifted, exhausted, in and out of sleep. After a short while he caught my eye and gestured with his head that I should speak with him out of earshot of the Queen. 'How are Sybil and my new daughter?' he whispered.

'They are very well, sire.' He nodded his thanks complicitly to me. He baffled me. He was blithely unfaithful and yet genuinely affectionate for wife, mistresses and all his children.

* * *

From the Copybook of Sister Benedicta

Westminster, Martinmas 1103

Dear Benedicta, Meulan has recently returned to court from Normandy carrying bad news of fighting near Almenêches between Bellême and Curthose. I beg you write to me with haste to reassure me you are well.

You know, no doubt, that we had Curthose at the English court last year when he came to plead for the reinstatement of Earl Warenne. We all wondered that the Duke would damage his own cause in such a way but Warenne seems genuinely committed to King Henry now. Henry and Meulan discussed the matter when I was present serving at the table. Meulan stated, disgust in his voice, 'It does not occur to Duke Robert that his genial, easy-going personality might be used as propaganda against him. He simply believes he has the God-given right to be Duke, he is a hero crusader and all will be well with the world.'

Henry answered him, 'So we use the unruly state of Normandy against him? We moot it about.'

'Yes,' says Meulan, 'and the distress of the Norman Church besides.'

'*Is* the Norman Church distressed under my brother, then?' asked Henry.

'It is now we say it is,' Meulan said. (Which is wickedness if not true, no? What say you Benedicta, as a venerable spokeswoman of the Norman Church?)

Henry looked concerned. 'My sister Adela ... she will side with me against Robert, I believe,' he said slowly.

Meulan rushed in upon his thoughts. 'And besides, Adela de Blois' husband gained only a tarnished reputation on crusade. A rope-dancer he was called, for what some saw as a cowardly escape from the walls of Antioch, whereas Curthose is declared a hero. That must grate upon the Countess. You could subtly draw attention to it in your letters to her, perhaps, sire?'

Henry told him, 'I will have to be extraordinarily subtle then. There is no idiocy in my sister.' No, nor in mine, I thought to myself.

238

You will be saddened to hear that after the failure of Anselm's mission to Rome to find a compromise on investitures acceptable to the King, the Archbishop has been exiled to Normandy. The poor man has spent more time wandering than warming his toes in the archbishop's palace in Canterbury.

King Henry has started to set his house in order now in Normandy too. Meulan's recent mission there was to stabilise the situation from Henry's perspective. Since the deaths of William de Breteuil and of Curthose's wife Sybilla, Henry fears instability increases again. Meulan went with a pretty task. Where many men have used swords, silver and aggression to win their arguments, Henry instead prefers to send girls as his secret weapon! Meulan's mission, which he has successfully completed, was to betroth Henry's illegitimate daughter Mathilde to Count Rotrou de Perche who was formerly an ally to Curthose, another illegitimate daughter Juliane, went to Eustace de Breteuil who has inherited there, and Meulan's own one-year old daughter Isabel is betrothed to Amaury de Montfort who stands to inherit Evreux before too long. This is the astute policy of the two of them – the King and Meulan – to bind the nobles of Normandy to Henry, to slowly win them away from Curthose. Evidently Henry's intentions do not end at the shores of England.

I was lately tasked as the King's midwife on two occasions. I am a veritable stork, Benedicta, with all the royal babies I have been assisting to usher into the world. First there was the daughter of the King's mistress, Sybil Corbet, who was birthed at Abingdon Abbey, and then I escorted Lady Nest of Wales and Abbot Faricius from there, to help at the Queen's own lying in at Winchester. The King and Queen rejoice, and all of England with them, at the birth of a son. I, however, am in tremendous anxiety until I hear from you. Tell me the fighting has not come near to you, with love from your brother Haith.

Monastery of Saint Evroul, Holy Day of the Immaculate Conception, 8 December 1103

Dear Haith, first I am safe. Abbess Emma & I have taken refuge at Saint Evroul where the monk Vitalis, who I wrote to you of before, has been my kind companion & support. Alas, our Abbey of Almenêches was indeed in the thick of fighting between Bellême & Curthose. The Duke shamefully used our buildings as stabling for the horses of his rough mercenaries with no care for us. The Abbess acted swiftly to place all younger sisters, including myself, working well out of sight & out of reach in the inner buildings, so that only the older nuns had to interact with these rude men & suffer their insults. Bellême responded to this incursion on his lands & the affront to his sister the Abbess, by arriving to drive out Curthose's men.

Shortly after Curthose and his men had left Sister Matilda & I were summoned to the Abbess' chamber. You can imagine my feelings Haith when I entered the room to be confronted by the sight of Robert de Bellême seated in the Abbess' chair, with my copybook of our correspondence open on the table before him. I stopped in my tracks so that Matilda behind me, bumped up against me. 'Sister Benedicta?' she said, perplexed.

'Yes – Sister Benedicta?' said Bellême, 'Don't dawdle on the threshold, do come in. Do close the door behind you, niece,' he said, his voice & face loaded with sarcastic politeness. Matilda glanced with a worried frown at me, & turned to do as he asked. I stepped up to the table & looked at Abbess Emma whose face was unusually pale but otherwise did not betray her emotions.

'A ciphered book of letters, Sister Benedicta.' Bellême said. We all looked down at the inked gibberish in front of him. 'One of the other sisters saw you scribing the book & hiding it in the library. Quite rightly she reported this to the Abbess and luckily I happened to be here at the time. Your correspondence with your brother, Haith, I believe, Sister?'

I made no response.

'You did not inform me, Sister Benedicta, that your brother is in service to King Henry,' Abbess Emma said, & there was a tremor in her voice that I had never heard before.

'I was unaware that my service to God required the revelations of my family résumé,' I said, but regretted my tartness, since it brought an unpleasant smile to Bellême's face.

'Don't be disingenuous, Sister,' he said. 'You have no doubt

240

been selling secrets to the English King in these ciphers!' He slapped his hand on the copybook.

'I have sold nothing!' I said furiously, 'and I know no secrets.'

'I cannot see what she could have told to harm you,' the Abbess said. 'She knows nothing of your business.' She tried to give me a reassuring smile but I was not at all reassured by the fact that even his own sister was clearly terrified of the man sitting in front of me, accusing me of treachery. Imagine that our jesting with one another to write in cipher should bring me to this, Haith!

'Someone else, in addition to Belmeis, betrayed me,' Bellême said slowly, & looked down to leaf through the ciphered pages,' & here is the answer to that puzzle.'

'I don't believe it,' Abbess Emma asserted. 'Sister Benedicta just does not have that sort of information to pass to anyone even if she wanted to. I believe she is loyal to me, brother, & this is nonsense.'

'It is a book code, I assume,' he said to me, ignoring the Abbess' protestations. I could hear Sister Matilda breathing loudly through her mouth, close behind me. 'Which book?'

Again I said nothing.

'If you are lily-white innocent & these letters are not full of betrayals of me to King Henry, then why withhold their translation?'

'The letters are merely exchanges of cheerful, mundane gossip between a brother & sister who love one another & miss each other's company,' I said, holding his eye, though it was hard to do, because I had heard the gruesome stories of his tortures of prisoners, like everyone else in that room.

He smiled. 'And is there revelation here of Henry's plot to murder his brother, William, the former king, in the New Forest, perhaps?'

I swallowed & tried to keep my countenance neutral, my mind racing all the while to try to remember if there *was* anything in our correspondence that could be evidence against either myself, you or Henry.

'You have a guilty look, Sister. Perhaps you & Sir Haith have been writing to each other on King Henry's plans to attack Normandy hmm? The Duke would be glad to have *that* evidence.'

'There is nothing of the sort that you fancy in my correspondence, sir.'

'So, again, tell me the book that deciphers it, my clerk can set to work & in no time you will be exonerated & I will be shamefaced & full of apologies.' He waved his hand in mock apology.

'I will not be bullied,' I said, looking to Abbess Emma for support but not finding any there. 'The letters are my private correspondence. They contain nothing of import regarding you or affairs of state.'

He sighed & looked down again at my copybook, closing it. 'Sister Benedicta, I am a busy man & do not have time for this.' He stood, came around the table towards me &, oh Haith, my heart was thumping then I can tell you, though I had no intention of giving an inch to the man. He gripped my upper arm painfully, pulled me with him towards the door which Sister Matilda, her face flushed scarlet, opened deferentially.

'Brother! Robert! What is it you mean to do with Sister Benedicta? I'm sure she is innocent of your charges!' the Abbess called out behind us as we stepped into the corridor & he began to hurry me along it. He marched me to the library, his face grim, ignoring the astonished looks of several nuns in the corridor who swiftly moved out of his way.

Inside the library he let go of my arm. 'You are mistaken, Lord Bellême,' I told him, lifting my chin with as much outward bravery as I could muster. 'You are completely mistaken in these accusations.'

'As I have said, there is a simple way for you to prove that. Give me the book that deciphers your letters.' He looked around the library. Two nuns who had been working on a manuscript gaped at us. 'Get out!' he said & they scurried to obey. He clearly had no inclination to proceed with politeness or gentleness. 'Well?'

'No. My correspondence is private & does not concern you.'

One of the nuns had left a candle burning on her desk. He picked it up. 'Sister Benedicta, I grow weary of this charade. You are the Scriptorium Mistress I believe? The keeper of this fine library?'

I said nothing.

'I will count to five & then this candle will be set to these books and manuscripts,' he told me calmly. 'One ... two ... three,' he pronounced slowly, his eyes on me. My mind raced. If I gave him the psalter to decipher the letters surely there was not much in our letters that could condemn me, or you, or King Henry. I tried to remember. *Was* there something that I could not let him have? The psalter in question sat innocently, close to my hand, neatly centred on my workplace which I was standing next to. 'Four ...' The door suddenly banged open & Sister Matilda hurtled through with the Abbess close behind her.

'Uncle, we are certain that Benedicta ...' but she could not finish her sentence as we all looked in horror at the flames licking at the parchments close to Bellême. Sister Matilda's precipitate entrance had caused him to shift a little too close to the manuscripts he was threatening & the fire took no time at all to catch at the dry rolls & boards. It was spreading with alarming speed. 'Fire!' yelled the Abbess, but even as she said it, we all backed away towards the door, knowing it was too late to attempt to put it out. The fire bellowed & bloomed along the shelves, licking into the corners, climbing the drapings, like a beast let out of Hell. I had slipped mother's psalter into the sleeve of my habit as I backed towards the doorway. The Abbess & Emma ran ahead down the corridor raising the alarm to the other sisters & Bellême similarly fled to save himself & his men. I too ran down the corridor, looking back once over my shoulder, to see the flames bursting out from the library door, looking set to pursue me. I ran past the open door of the Abbess' study but skidded to a halt & swiftly retraced my steps, grabbed my copybook from her desk, threw it & my psalter into her satchel that stood leaning against a stool & resumed my flight, the satchel bouncing at my back.

I emerged into the courtyard coughing & fell into the arms of the Abbess & Sister Matilda who gasped their thanks to God that I was safe & had not succumbed to the fire as they had feared as I was the last to emerge from the building. I saw Robert de Bellême mounted on his horse in the gateway. He took a last angry look at me & then turned his horse, to gallop away from the conflagration.

We turned back to the Abbey. There was nothing we could do. The whole place was ablaze, the fire spurting now from the roof & windows. We wept to see our home so swiftly reduced to blackened timbers, haphazardly fallen one upon another.

We are lodged here at Evroul for the time being whilst the Abbess organises the rebuilding of the Abbey. Her brother was remorseful for the trouble to her but remorse does not rebuild the charred ruin of our chapel & library. Still we thank God that we have all escaped with no loss of life or injury & that in time we will return.

It was very strange to come out of our enclosed cloister & to ride freely through the open countryside again & then to speak face to face with Vitalis and other monks here, rather than always everything through a grille. I felt so odd to be leaving the cloister, my home since I was six years old, and not know when I would return.

I fear your King Henry & his counsellor, de Meulan, have judged the situation rightly. There is constant warfare in Normandy now, everywhere, all abouts. Abbess Emma assures me she believes my account of the copybook and trusts my word. Take care of yourself Haith & know that I am well & safe in the kind company of my Abbess & the monks of Saint Evroul. With love Benedicta.

* * *

After a few months, when the Queen had recovered her health sufficiently in the February of 1104, her entourage moved back to London. Matilda was distressed that relations between Henry and the Archbishop were now so strained that Anselm was formally exiled in Normandy and stripped of his revenues from Canterbury. She was glad to return to her coterie of priests and clerks in London and the city received her and Henry's heir with a riot of celebrations. We finally made our way through the rapturous crowds and the Queen, exhausted by the journey and the welcome, lent heavily on my arm as Christina and I supported her up the stairs. Emma and Cille rushed forward to greet her as we entered her chamber and I was shocked to see Sybil Corbet standing with them. Sybil lent and whispered in my ear. 'Nest! I've missed you and now we will be together again.'

'We have a new lady in my chambers, as you see, Lady Nest,' the Queen told me in a neutral voice. I doubted the Queen could be unaware of her husband's harem although she never spoke of it to me or any of her ladies. Perhaps she viewed it as a penance that she had somehow earnt. She had his bastards underfoot all the time in the royal nursery since Henry openly acknowledged his natural children, and the Queen was relentlessly kind to them all. Henry's illegitimate daughter Mathilde, who was twelve, was standing next to Sybil. Suddenly Mathilde began to snivel and then to sob. 'What is it darling?' the Queen asked, bending to loop her arms kindly about the child's neck.

'Papa is sending me away.'

Henry loved all of his children, legitimate or otherwise, and I turned with an expression of confusion to the Queen for an explanation. 'The King has betrothed Mathilde to Rotrou, the Count de Perche,' the Queen said. 'It is an honour and of importance to the safety of your father's realm,' she told the girl gently. 'Dry your tears. You are very lucky the Count has agreed to take you to wife. You will be a great lady, a countess. And he has also betrothed your little sister, Juliane, to Eustace de Breteuil.'

It was admirable that Henry took such care of his illegitimate daughters, but I discerned the care was secondary to their value to him as political 'gifts', helping him to consolidate allegiances. So it was with all fathers, but in Henry's case he had a superabundance of such political gifts. Juliane was only three years old. I suddenly felt a great overgrown spinster, when I thought of a three-year-old and a twelve-year-old being married off, and a seventeen-year-old Sybil Corbet already a mother, whilst I was twenty-three and still unwed. Elizabeth, who was also younger than me, had recently presented her elderly husband with twin sons and was consequently the toast of the court.

Ansfride meanwhile was not discarded by Henry and they could be seen often strolling in the garden or laughing in the hall together. Part of his appeal was that he adored women, so many women, and when he spoke with you he really made you feel he valued you, where many men were disapproving or contemptuous. When Henry spoke to me, I felt as if I were the only one in his gaze, and it was a struggle to keep in mind all the others, and that he made them feel exactly the same way. It astonished me that he could maintain such a complicated personal life at the same time as managing the business of being king but this ableness too, was part of his charm.

'It's a stressful occupation, Nest, being king,' he told me one day. 'I do need help. Your help perhaps?' His fingers strolled teasingly up my arm and my flesh seemed to burn in a series of small fingerprints where his skin touched mine.

21

A Blind Eye

The Queen's household had not been back in London for very long when I noticed that Sybil Corbet's belly was pushing at the folds of her skirts once more. I watched both the Queen and Sybil, on different occasions, looking out from the window at Henry who was strolling arm in arm with Ansfride in the garden below. Their reactions were very different. 'She was his first love,' said the Queen, 'and he is kind to still take note of her.' I kept silent on the issue of Ansfride being his first love given that he had two bastard children before he ever met Ansfride.

Sybil Corbet, on the other hand, leant dangerously far out of the window hoping to catch the King's attention and when he did not look up she turned to me exasperated. 'What does he still see in Ansfride? She is twice my age. An old widow.' Yes, I thought, but nearer his age than you are. 'Well don't you think he *has* to love me the most? I *am* the youngest one?' she asked me, as if this were powerful logic.

At the beginning of Spring I was bending in the garden early in the morning, cutting rosemary to take to the Queen's Chamber and was startled by Henry's hand on my backside. 'Sorry, it was irresistible,' he said as I straightened up quickly, stepping away from him, swishing my skirts and feeling the scarlet heat of my face. He spoke as if his behaviour was nothing out of the ordinary.

'A beast is unable to resist its urges,' I snapped but flushed anew, realising I could not speak so to a king. He merely creased his eyes in amusement at me.

'I'm glad I've come across you, particularly like this,' he said. 'I have to send you to Abingdon again, Lady Nest, if you will? For me?' he wheedled. I could hardly gainsay him and wondered what or who I would find waiting there for me this time. I was happy that I would see Abbot Faricius again and escape for a while from the piety and gossip in the Queen's chambers. Sometimes I woke in the night staring at the ceiling and aching for Sybil de Montgommery, her daughters, Cardiff Castle. Sybil wrote to me often with news from Glamorgan but I longed to see her, to hear her talk without pause for breath, to watch her duck-walk her way across the bailey to embrace me.

Gerald FitzWalter was ordered to escort me and Amelina on our journey to Abingdon on this occasion. I was pleased that he had gradually won his way back into the King's favour and trust. We stopped on the journey to spend a night with his family at Windsor and resumed our travel by river the following day. On the boat he told me: 'I miss Wales, but you are a little bit of Wales to comfort me, with the lovely lilt of your voice.' It crossed my mind that Gerald might have made a good husband if he had not been of such low status. 'You are a great favorite with the King, Nest,' he said, hoping to draw me out in conversation on the topic.

'So are many young women,' I said dryly and changed the subject, pointing out a heron on the water's edge.

The lady waiting for us at Abingdon Abbey this time was named Edith of Greystoke. Gerald left the Abbey after one evening with us, to return to court. 'A very pleasing young man indeed,' Faricius remarked as we watched him depart. Edith was a fractious companion in the last month of her pregnancy, but at least she was a young woman rather than a girl like Sybil. She had a strong northern accent and told me her father was Forn Sigurdson, Lord of Greystoke in Cumberland. I was relieved to find she was not terribly interested in talking about Henry or the court. Her own concerns seemed mostly to do with farming and animal husbandry. I was content to keep her company and speak with her on those subjects while she waited for her child to come. Her labour was fast and as straightforward as she was and she bore Henry a son who she named Robert. The Queen would have more work for her blind eye, another bastard in the bulging royal nursery, being nursed and schooled alongside her own two children, and the sons of other nobles. I remembered my early reflections on the genealogy of the Anglo-Norman family: how I thought they were in danger of dying out. It seemed Henry had the same anxiety and was setting about breeding like a rabbit to the best of his abilities.

At Abingdon a letter from Sybil de Montgommery arrived for me, forwarded back from Westminster, telling me Arnulf had fallen out with his father-in-law the King of Munster, who had deprived him of his wife. Since Henry had stripped Arnulf of his lands he had gone to seek refuge at the court of the Count of Anjou. Arnulf would certainly never be my husband now. I wanted to speak with the King about my marriage but knew he would turn any such discussion in a direction I did not want it to go, into flirting with me himself.

* * *

From the Copybook of Sister Benedicta

Westminster, April 1104

Benedicta, my sweet sister, I am quaking with fear and fury at your news – at your encounter with Bellême. Pray, my darling girl, do not ever, *ever* endanger yourself on my account or Henry's. We can take care of ourselves. And especially do not risk yourself ever with Bellême again. The stories about him are not exaggerations. You have seen that with this terrible fire, but he is capable of worse and I believe he will return to threaten you again. You must come to England. Let me know the best moment and I will come to fetch you. We will find a good Norman convent to house you. Henry will be glad to assist. He sends his kind wishes and concern for you, after I told him of the events at your Abbey and pledges financial aid for the rebuilding. I am sleepless and sick with worry at the thought of what has happened to you. Even the sight of these ciphered letters makes me want to throw them away from me in grief for you. Write back quickly Benedicta with the messenger I am sending who is instructed to wait for your reply and I will come with all haste to you. Your brother Haith.

Monastery of Saint Evroul, April 1104

Dear Haith, I understand your trepidation but I assure you I am safe & have no intention of leaving Abbess Emma at this time of our tribulations over the rebuilding of the Abbey. There is no need for me to turn tail & run. The Abbess does not doubt me & assures me she will protect me. Indeed I believe she feels a great fury at her brother, not only that he burnt the Abbey to ashes but also that he undermined her authority so totally in front of Sister Matilda & myself. The Abbess & I were close before, but we have grown even closer since that terrible fire. We are grateful beyond measure for King Henry's assistance and concern & I am tasked to write him a formal letter of thanks. I am staying put & entreaties will not sway me. Try not to worry, Haith. With love Benedicta.

* * *

I returned to my service with the Queen. Sybil Corbet had disappeared and I followed the Queen's lead in not mentioning it. A few days after my return I woke to a beautiful sunny May morning and was stretching and still in my nightgown when Cille poked her head around the door to summon me to the Queen's Chamber. 'There's a visitor come to see you, Nest.'

'A visitor?' Perhaps it was Sybil de Montgommery allowed at court and come to see me at last. Hurriedly I reached for a blue dress, one that Sybil had given to me.

The Queen greeted me with a warm smile but dashed my hopes of seeing Sybil by saying, 'Your visitor is next door, Nest. Go and speak with him with my blessing and good wishes.'

I was perplexed. What male visitor would I have? I stepped into the Queen's small side chamber where Gerald FitzWalter turned to greet me. My first thought was that he brought me bad news: perhaps Sybil de Montgommery was ill? He was smiling, yet there was a great tenseness about him. His rapidly shifting expressions were contradictory – happiness, guilt, misery. I must be mistaken. 'Sir Gerald! This is a pleasant surprise.'

'I'm glad that you feel so. Thank you.' He subsided into a desperately anxious silence, while I had hoped he might quickly explain his presence and strange expressions to me. 'I never thanked you properly for interceding on my behalf with the King,' he said.

'I was glad to do so, for the reasons I gave.'

'It's good to see you looking so well, Lady Nest.'

'Thank you.' I could not return the compliment to him, since his anxiety seemed to grow worse as we spoke and his face was blanched, green almost. 'Are you … quite well?' I asked him. 'Won't you sit?'

'No!' I was startled by his vehemence. 'You must think me mad. I apologise. I just …' He paced the small room like a bear in a cage and then made a visible effort to pull himself together. 'Lady Nest, I have news,' he did not meet my eyes now. 'The King has given me leave, commanded me,' he hesitated, 'to marry you.' He ventured to look at me now. I gaped at him, speechless, so that he was forced to continue. 'The King commands that I marry you, and I am so glad of it, my lady, that I could fly.'

I could say nothing. I sat down on a chest, just breathing, looking at my hands in my lap, but then I began to smile slowly to myself. I looked back up at Gerald. 'He wants us to marry?'

'Yes. I know I am unworthy of you, lady, in rank, but I will do everything in my power to be a good husband to you in all other ways, if you will give your consent. I believe he means to send me back to command Pembroke on his behalf, with you at my side. With your ….' He dried up, looking with the utmost anxiety at me.

Pembroke. My consent. Was that in any way an actuality? The King had commanded it. I was his ward to dispose of as he wished, and yet I could not believe that he had commanded *this*. That I should marry a man I liked! Liked a lot, I was slowly realising, as I began to absorb what Gerald was telling me. Yes, he was a Norman, but I liked him, had always liked him. He was not as high-born as I, but I knew he was kind, had initiative and integrity. I knew his liking for me was real. It seemed the Queen had been aware of Gerald's intention and gave me her blessing. I was twenty-three and it was high time that I was married. I had started to despair that the King would ever choose a husband for me and feared I might be an old maid and never have my own children. If I *must* choose a Norman man, Gerald would be my first choice.

Suddenly faced with this command to marry I realised how the anxiety over my marriage had ruled my life since I was twelve, since Gerald first wiped my face in the rain as I sat tied and traumatised in a cart. It had been a tension straining taut my every fibre, every nerve for the last eleven years. I was nauseated with the release of that grip.

Gerald squatted down beside me. 'I'm sorry, Nest! I've shocked you. You are naturally horrified at the command. Shall I send for one of the ladies? You look so pale.'

'No, no. Just give me a moment to regain my balance. I'm … I'm not horrified I assure you.'

He waited. I slowed my breathing. Gerald rose and brought me a beaker of water and sat down next to me. I looked at him, at his pale blue eyes full of concern for me, the comely planes of his face, carrying a few small scars now, his blond hair still curling delicately around his ears. Growing older suited his features. I reached my hand to his and he took a deep breath, staring at me, his mouth slightly open. I leant forward and kissed him full on the mouth. When I leant back, smiling at him, I retained his hand. 'Nest?' An uncertain smile hovered on his face and in his eyes.

'Yes, Gerald, I would gladly marry you. So gladly!'

'Truly, Nest?'

I simply smiled in answer. He pulled me to my feet, lifted me up and swung me around in glee. My headdress slipped from my head, my black hair fell loose. He set me back down and kissed me in the curve between my neck and shoulder. I thrilled at the touch of his mouth on my skin and reached to his head to kiss him again but he stepped suddenly away from me.

'I … perhaps we should not. I should go.'

I frowned at him. 'Already?'

'Yes I must go. Thank you for your answer.'

I was bewildered. 'You blow hot and cold!'

'No. No. All hot,' he said looking down at his boots and then up again. 'But I have to return to my duties. To the King.'

'Very well. Where will we live, Gerald? And when shall we be married?'

'If it pleases you, I thought we could be married within the next few weeks, at Moulsford, and that is where we would also live. But as I said, although he has not yet confirmed it, I believe the King means to eventually send me back to Pembroke with you at my side, making a world of difference for the local people.'

'It pleases me, Gerald! It all pleases me!' Llansteffan beach and estuary were in my mind's eye. The Claw. Pembroke. Home.

He smiled, took my hand, kissed my fingers briefly and was gone. I sat back down on the bench, shaking my head, smiling to myself, still feeling the delicate touch of his mouth on my neck, thinking of going home to Wales. I wanted to rush to tell Elizabeth but she was away from court. After a few minutes I became aware of Queen Matilda and her ladies hovering at the doorway, looking to see if they could intrude and offer me their congratulations.

A few weeks later I travelled to Gerald's manor at Moulsford for the wedding. Since I had no family (aside from my brother in Ireland, if he still lived) I asked Henry's knight, Haith, if he would escort me and he readily agreed. 'Married!' he said. 'Married to FitzWalter! Well!' The Queen had been effusive in her congratulations and gave me a gorgeous grey and blue embroidered dress for my wedding day. I did not fool myself that her emotions were not mixed with pleasure at seeing me out of Henry's way. Henry himself sent a brief note congratulating me and the gift of a very beautiful silver bracelet engraved with a bird in flight, but I did not see him in the weeks before I left court.

When I arrived at Moulsford a wedding gift from Sybil de Montgommery was waiting for me on the hall table: a splendid saddle and gold saddle-cloth. Amelina and I ran our hands over the cloth and leather, smiling together. 'Well,' said Gerald, standing awkwardly before us, 'I will have the servant show you to your quarters and give you some refreshments after your journey, Lady Nest.'

Upstairs in my new chamber Amelina prepared a bowl of hot water pungent with cinnamon, liquorice and cumin. She stripped me in front of the fire and first washed my hair in the bowl, pouring jugfuls over my head. She wrapped my head in a dry cloth and then she washed every surface and crevice of my body, making me giggle. 'You're tickling me, Amelina!'

She paused in her swabbings and sat back on her heels regarding me. 'You are very, very beautiful, Nest, and at last you have your man. A good man, I believe.'

'Yes, a good man. But not a Welsh man.'

'No.' Tears sprang to her eyes.

'Amelina?'

'I'm thinking of that Welsh prince, Owain, who was your first betrothed.'

'Yes. You loved him a little yourself, my friend, I think.'

She wiped the tears from her cheek. 'I'm sorry, my lady.'

'Never mind it. That is over with now. I will be the wife of Gerald FitzWalter and the lady of this pretty manor and then we will go home, home to Wales.'

'It's a relief, lady, no? Who knew where things were going before this.'

I nodded vehemently. 'Oh yes, it is a relief.'

She reached for a dry cloth, dried my skin, draped my best clean shift over my head and began the arduous task of combing out my hair.

'Smells good, Amelina,' I said as she tugged at my hair, one hand placed on the top of my head. 'Go gently with that comb. I don't want a headache for my wedding night.'

It was a simple wedding, I suppose, for someone who had once looked to be the wife of a Welsh, or even a Norman, king, but Gerald looked very handsome in a green embroidered tunic, and I hoped I looked well enough. The ceremony took place at the church in Moulsford. It was Maytime and I wore a crown of pale pink and white flowers. Sunny Haith bounded into the hall, exclaiming at my looks, my hair, Gerald's good fortune. He escorted me on the short walk to the church door where he placed my hand in Gerald's. Amelina stood at my side, wreathed in smiles. Gerald slipped a broad silver ring onto the third finger of my right hand. After saying the words of promise to each other, after the priest's blessing and a simple outdoor feast in the field, Gerald and I walked back to Moulsford Manor hand in hand. I rolled the heavy, unfamiliar ring around on the finger of my free hand.

I looked at the small but pretty manor, its façade covered with climbing white roses. It was mine. Not a palace in Powys but still mine. My unexpected safe haven. And Gerald was mine, Gerald, who truly loved me. I looked forward to the prospect of setting about loving him.

'I have to see to some business in the stables and will return to you soon,' he said, leaving me at the doorway.

In the bedchamber I lay my floral crown on a polished table and Amelina and I set to making up the great bed. We stood either side wafting the sheets and then the quilt between us. The quilt was another wedding gift from Sybil in Cardiff. She had stitched the tapestry of Arthur and Gwenhwyvar, that we had all worked on together, onto the quilt. We had just finished plumping up the pillows and pushing them into position when I heard boots at the door and turned to see Gerald again. I smiled warmly and gestured to the servants and Amelina to leave. 'Welcome to our married life, my lord,' I said, when we were finally alone. I had asked Amelina to set out and fill my special glass beakers that Sybil had given to me long ago.

We sat together at the small table and he rolled the beaker in his hand admiring its pattern. He took a long draught of the wine and set the beaker down, smiling thinly.

I frowned. 'Something ails you?'

He ignored my question. 'Are you pleased with this little manor?'

I stood and went to him. 'Yes! It is pretty and yes, it is little, but we will be happy here.' Boldly I insinuated my skirts and myself between his legs, put my hands on his chest, and brought my face down close to his, waiting for him to kiss me.

He stood and disentangled himself from me, holding me at arm's length. 'You look *so* beautiful, my lady.'

I looked quizzical at the extreme regret I heard in his voice. His behaviour seemed immensely odd. He was worried about something. 'I cannot stay,' he said.

'But…' We had to bed now. It was the necessary final part of any marriage. If he left now, we were not truly man and wife yet. I had expected the next few weeks would be our time to grow close to one another. 'The King has surely given you time from your duties, to give your duty to your new wife?'

He shook his head and his eyes evaded mine. 'The King commands your presence at Woodstock. I am ordered to send you there now.'

'The King?'

'Yes, find your best clothes and jewels, Nest, and ready yourself. It is not a long journey and you should leave immediately.' He kept his eyes on his boots. 'He is waiting for you.'

Illumination began to dawn on me and my stomach and mind churned together.

'What are you telling me, Gerald?' I said in a cold voice. 'Speak it.'

'You know it,' he said, finally looking at me, tears in his eyes.

'You pander me to the King! You prostitute your wife!' I could not believe this was happening to me, that Gerald would so deceive me, that my happiness could turn so suddenly to bitterness.

His face was an agony. He held his hands out in supplication to me. 'Please, Nest … calm yourself. He will not treat you unkindly.' I stared at him. He looked away again miserably. 'He is my overlord and yours, Nest. I had no choice.'

'We should consummate our marriage now,' I said desperately, plucking at the laces of my gown, 'then he will not want me and will leave us be.'

He stepped close and stilled my hands. 'We can't do that, Nest. I am sorry but we can't. It was the price I agreed to, your bride-price.'

I gripped his chin and forced him to look at me. 'What do you mean?'

'I asked him for you as wife and he laughed at me. It was a mistake. I should not have asked, but I have been mad with love for you all these years, Nest.'

A chill ran through me at his words. It was what I wanted to hear from him but not like this. 'What happened?'

'He laughed, and then he considered. "A bold and understandable request, Sir Gerald," he told me, "given the looks of the lady, but you reach too high I fear. She is a royal princess, with lands.

You are the third son of a forester, with nothing but your swor-darm.'" He stopped.

'And?' I prompted.

'Then I saw his mind working and then he made me the offer. "You may have her, FitzWalter," he said slowly, "for you have served me well". He held up a hand to stay my thanks. "But I will have her first." And he lent forward with his elbows on his knees and stared me in the face. "I cannot agree to that, sire," I said. "Then," he said, "she will not be your wife and I will find myself another knight for the offer."'

I sagged against Gerald's chest. 'You see how he had me trapped,' he pleaded with me. 'What could I do? Let him offer you around to his *conroi*. One of them would have agreed, Nest. Probably all of them would.'

I staggered back and sat down on the bed, absent-mindedly running my hand over the smiling face of Arthur's queen, Gwen-hwyvar, on the quilt. He dropped into a crouch at my knees and put his hands in my lap. 'I am so sorry, my love. There was noth-ing I could do.'

'And you can bear this?' I accused him.

'No,' he said. 'I cannot. Every inch of me churns at it. But do you see a way out of it?' I was silent. 'He will treat you kindly and he will return you to me ... in time.'

'In time? How much time?' He shrugged. 'Ah, at the King's pleasure. I am to be ... the King's pleasure. Then I should remove this.' I stood, slid the heavy wedding ring from my finger, and dropped it into the dregs in Gerald's beaker, my eyes furious upon his.

Part Four

1104–1107

22

Into the Menagerie

Gerald did not escort me to Woodstock. 'I can't,' he said. I had married a dishonourable coward. I was a fool to think I was anything to any of these men. I was just a gift the King had chosen to give to Gerald and borrow back for a while, with Gerald's compliance. Amelina did not come with me to Woodstock. Gerald told me this was the King's orders, that I should go without women servants. I found her to tell her what was happening and watched the emotions on her face move through disbelief to fury to a stoic recognition. She hugged me tightly, then stepped back gripping my hands, her face grim. 'Courage, little one. You are a princess and you know how to manage a king. Send for me when you have mastered him, as you will.'

Gerald sent me with a small armed escort and a chest of clothes and jewels that did not augur a stay of one night and had not been furnished from his meagre resources. How long had he known of this I wondered? How had he kept it from me and allowed me to naively believe I was simply marrying him. I was an idiot to have cared for him, to have so stupidly and fondly imagined our future life together.

I rode towards the palisade of King Henry's palace at Woodstock which had been built up around one of his favourite hunting lodges. Outside the walls, a vast travelling market that followed the King wherever he went was camped out, calling their wares as we passed. Angrily, I looked to see if anyone had a set of cuckold horns for sale that I might buy my husband as his wedding gift.

As I passed through the shadow of the gates, strange, mournful bayings and growlings came from the exotic menagerie of lions, lynxs and camels that the King kept here. Inside the compound I rode past the stables, the kennels and the mews, and prayed for every second to be long drawn out, for I had no idea how to face this new turn in my fortunes. Haith was standing outside the stables. He looked up at the sound of the horses, recognised me, and immediately dropped his head. So everybody knew why I was here. And did Haith know at my wedding this morning?

The King's usher met me graciously and led me into the palace, pushed open the heavy double doors of the King's chambers and announced me. The King was in the company of several men and women and I was relieved to see Elizabeth and also recognized William de Warenne, Bishop Roger of Salisbury, Henry's close friend Richard de Redvers, and my old friend Abbot Faricius, who smiled reassuringly to me. 'Ah, Lady Nest.' They all rose and bowed to me as if they did not see me as a Welsh whore. 'Let me introduce you to my friends,' the King said. 'You know Elizabeth of course. She is a key member of my *conroi*.' They laughed at his jest. Formally, he introduced the men in the room who I was already familiar with, and one I had not met before, an older man, Roger Bigod from Norfolk, the royal steward. Warenne and Elizabeth sat close together playing at dice with Redvers and I joined them. I was, temporarily at least, relieved to be part of a civilized gathering, where I had imagined on my journey here that the King might immediately put me to his bed. 'Won't you sit and take some wine with us. Do you play?' Redvers asked me. They behaved as if I were an honoured guest and I determined I would not allow any hint of my degradation into my demeanour.

I knew all men and women at court fell over themselves, did anything, to attain nearness to the King so I could not expect support from any of these people if I tried to resist Henry's intentions, not even Elizabeth. They and all the courtiers were constantly petitioning the King for lands, offices, marriages to heiresses, titles, custody of royal wardships, pardoning of their taxes and debts. I was to have the greatest nearness to the King now and they were jealous of me for that.

After a few hours the King declared his intention to retire. Everyone rose and the King placed his hand on mine to make it clear that I should not leave with them. When they had all gone I asked him: 'What does the Bishop think that I am left alone with you sire, unchaperoned.'

'I'm not sure. He has ridden home to his mistress Matilda of Ramsbury. We can ask him when he returns.'

My defences were puny.

'You are so lovely, Nest.'

'What has happened to Lady Ansfride, sire?' I countered.

'She is great with child again, but I am taking good care of her, you may be certain of that. I'm very fond of her.'

'And Lady Sybil Corbet?'

'She is well also, and far away,' he said, looking amused. 'How arch you are, Lady Nest.' He smiled but there was a hint of irritation in his eyes now. 'But, Nest, you and I *are* here and what should we do then?'

I stood up. I could not sit. I could not bear the falsenesses and civilised lies any longer. I backed away from him as far as I could until I felt the cold of the stone wall against the palms of my hands and on my back, through my gown. 'Why did you have to act in this way?' I said angrily. 'Why did you have to make a fool of Gerald and of me!'

He pulled an apologetic face, acknowledging my anger. 'Would you have agreed to become my mistress if I had asked you straight out – without this ruse?'

I said nothing. I was so angry with him I couldn't think straight.

'In marrying you to FitzWalter I intended to protect your reputation.'

'Your behaviour is deceitful and despicable!' I spat the words furiously at him.

Again he waited silently for a while before responding. 'If you truly have no liking for me, I would not force you. I thought perhaps you did.' He stood. 'You are unlike any other woman I have known, Nest. The burden of kingship is heavy. I can never completely put it down, never cease its necessary defences and distrusts but with you I feel I can be myself, just a man. Henry.'

He stepped towards me until there was an arm's length between us, speaking slowly, gently. 'Your Henry? I have desired you for so long, Nest. I want just to love you.' He stepped closer. 'Do you want to leave?' I said nothing. He reached a hand to stroke my hair and then my cheek. I let him. His hand moved to my bodice, to my breast. I let him. I felt the thrill of his physicality, of an exhilaration taut between us like a rope that had just been suddenly caught at full stretch, thrumming, whipping, twisting around itself. I had always felt it. 'Nest?' His voice was thick with desire.

Without looking at him, I cupped my hand to the back of his head, closed my wet eyes, and sought blindly for his mouth. My fury leeched together with my desire and I met his lust with my own in a first coupling that was neither gentle nor slow.

Over the next few weeks at Woodstock Henry and I were equally persistent and insatiable in our love-making. Afterwards he would sleep soundly beside me, snoring softly, and I could not help but feel a growing affection for his sleeping face. He held me folded in a warm embrace and I felt safe. We made love constantly, at night time, in the afternoons in the forest when we rode away from the hunt and his entourage seeking seclusion, before dinner when he watched me dress and then undressed me all over again. He called me his 'wasp' because he said my tongue was more sting than honey and it made him laugh. '*Gacynyn*,' I said, 'wasp.' I tried to teach him some Welsh. 'My words fly like *gwenyn meirch* – wasps.' When I was briefly alone, I lay on our bed admiring the shapely pale curves of my own arms and legs, holding them up to look at them with satisfaction, running my hands over the flat plane of my belly and the curves beneath my breasts.

He read to me, discussed all of his business as king with me. I began to think that perhaps to be a royal mistress was at least closer to the destiny I should have had than to be wife to a mere knight. He knew so much more than I, had seen so much, that he shared with me. There was a bench just outside our bedchamber with a view across a small walled garden full of flowers that filled the night with their perfume and we heard the faint rustlings of mice going about their business. We sat on that bench most evenings talking long into the last glimmers of sunset and the growing darkness, telling each other profound and mundane details of our day, our hopes for the future, our past lives.

He sought my reassurance in his private moments of self-doubt that he showed to no one else. 'Sometimes, Nest, I think perhaps I am a fake at this business of kingship.' He talked to me of his revenues from the royal manors, land taxes and tapping the wealth of churchmen, magnates and towns for his wars in Normandy. He complained about the need to take credit from Flemish merchants and Jewish communities in London and Rouen. 'The aid paid by the towns is not enough.' He talked to me of the Caen stone he was having exported across the Channel for his building projects. Life with Henry was endlessly interesting and he involved me fully in all of it. He had tremendous energy, directing his affairs with the aid of four scribes whose work was supervised by Bishop Roger of Salisbury.

After a week I managed to secure his agreement for Amelina to join me and it was a great relief to see her come through the door of my chamber. 'I see from your looks that you have not fared badly,' she said. She marvelled over the jewels and gowns Henry had given me, at my sumptuous chambers and my splendid Norwegian hawk sitting on her perch in my bedroom with her jesses, her silver chain and tinkling bells. 'Can you sleep with that thing staring at you?' Amelina asked, pulling a face.

I laughed. 'She's hooded at night time.'

'Thank goodness! She looks like she wants to eat me, to grip me with those yellow talons and peck at my tender parts with that fierce hooked bill.'

'*Lots* of people want to peck at *your* tender parts!' I teased her. We looked at the raptor gripping the perch with its tethered claws. Her downy white belly was streaked with fine black lines, contrasting with the dark feathers of her back, head and folded wings. She watched us with round yellow and black eyes, her head swivelling precisely as she followed Amelina's movements around the room. 'Tell me, Amelina, how is Gerald?'

'Distraught. I think he truly loves you, Nest.'

I was still furious with Gerald but her description of his state prompted me to send him a curt letter. '*Sir Gerald*,' I wrote, '*I send you a brief note to reassure you that I am well and, as you told me, well-treated. I hope that you will take ease in that. Nest ferch Rhys, spouse to Gerald FitzWalter.'*

'It's a little spiteful,' Amelina commented.

'He deserves a little spiteful at least.'

A large number of huntsmen and staff attended Henry. His fewterer took care of his pack of thirty hounds: a mix of grey-hounds, mastiffs, alaunts, spaniels, setters and lymers. His falconer took care of his gerfalcon and peregrines. Other staff cared for the menagerie of exotic animals that bayed and howled most extraordinarily at the dawn of every new day and sent their pungent alien scents in whiffs across the courtyard. Unlike a wife who would have to take responsibility for a household, I found a mistress had to do nothing – except of course keep her lover happy. We took a mid-day dinner, entertained by musicians, and then a siesta, when I did not get much sleep. Henry saw the older courtiers in the morning for business and the younger courtiers in the afternoon for more leisurely activities including hawking, picnics and archery in the surrounding woodlands. Henry was skilled at tracking and Warenne nicknamed him Stag's Foot in jest.

Elizabeth visited me frequently to see how I did. 'Well, Nest,' she said, 'here at Woodstock we can be ourselves. Are you not a little bit in love with Henry? Isn't Henry's court a great deal more fun than the Queen's? *You* are a queen here!'

It was often difficult to read Henry's feelings since he kept his true self well protected. Sometimes he feigned anger with his courtiers, using this and procrastination as defences against their constant importuning. He knew how to manipulate the hopes and fears of men and women. I saw that he could be calculating, determined and ruthless, his hatreds and friendships maintained to extremes. In love with him? I could not say that but certainly I was endlessly fascinated by him, addicted to him as a drunkard hugs his bottle of wine to himself.

Haith was as cheerfully friendly to me as always but I was angry with him and eventually had to confront him. 'So you knew too at my wedding to Gerald that it was a sham and you were all laughing at me.'

He looked appalled. 'I knew nothing at wedding. I swear it. Are you alright, lady? Want me to get you out of here. I can hide you in Flanders. Just say a word.'

I shook my head. 'I'm alright. I'm just angry at the deceit, but of course it is Henry and Gerald who deserve my anger, not you. My apologies.' I looked down at the dusty ground.

There was a small stone with one side cut and gleaming like amber. Haith moved it with the toe of his boot closer to my shoe. 'Anytime to Flanders,' he said. 'Just say it.'

I looked into his face. 'I thought you were like Henry's brother.'

'I am,' he said, 'but brother is not always a good lad, and lady has my heart.' He grabbed at his chest, staggering. 'Where's it gone?' He palpated the breast of his tunic comically. He was ridiculous. I had to laugh. 'Lady is like magical mermaid for us all! Singing, singing to all us men on sea of life,' he called out as I turned from him, still laughing.

I was still smiling at Haith's pantomime as I pulled my riding gloves from

my hands and pushed my way through the doors of the King's chambers. Henry was seated with Meulan and Elizabeth. They rose at my entry and greeted me. I went to Henry and he took my hands and kissed them. 'Good ride? Join us, darling.' A servant poured a beaker of wine for me and I took a seat beside him.

'Bellême is allied with Duke Robert again. William de Mortain has left England, abandoning his huge estates here, to join the Duke's court,' Meulan said, continuing a report that had begun before my arrival.

'Mortain is a fool as huge as his lost estates,' Henry said.

'Indeed, your grace. Curthose is backed into a corner. The ineffectiveness of his rule in Normandy is talked and complained of everywhere. Our diplomacy with the neighbouring rulers in Maine, Anjou and Flanders has isolated the Duke.'

'Good. Then all is primed. We will ship to Normandy before too long. The administrators have been collecting heavier taxes in England this year in preparation. We will have ample resources for the army and provisioning.'

My birthday was approaching and I had told Henry that I was born at half past midnight. I had been asleep some hours the night before my anniversary when he shook me gently awake. I looked blearily at him. 'You're dressed?'

'Wake up, my love.'

Beyond Henry, Amelina hovered with a big grin on her face. 'What is it?'

'It's your birthday,' Henry whispered into my ear, kissing my neck. 'So up you get sleepy head.' He pulled me upright.

The night was fully dark beyond the window. 'But it's the middle of the night!' Despite my complaining, Amelina got me dressed and then Henry picked me up, laughing and carried me to a horse that Haith was holding waiting for me. The four of us made the short ride to the bank of the river Glyme.

'What's going on?' I asked Henry, fully awake now. The night was hot and sultry, a half moon gave slivers of light on the pathways and stones. He lifted me from the horse and led me by the hand down the bank to a small boat that was moored there. Haith and Amelina loaded several baskets into the boat and we all stepped in. 'A midnight row?'

Henry put his fingers to my mouth. 'Hush, you are waking the fishes with your constant questions. Wait and see.'

I subsided into silence, enjoying the regular slap and slow pull of the oars through the dark water as Haith rowed us downriver to a small island in the middle of the stream. Amelina busied herself dangling bottles of wine on strings over the edge of the boat into the water, keeping them cool.

On the island they had set up a fairy bower with candles and glittering tapestries spread on the ground and Amelina and Haith unpacked a sumptuous picnic. I thought Henry would command Amelina and Haith to withdraw but instead the four of us sat together eating, drinking and laughing. 'Happy birthday, my love,' said Henry kissing the tips of my fingers tenderly.

'Happy birthday, Nest,' said Amelina and Haith, raising their beakers to me.

After nearly three intense months together at Woodstock, Henry left me in late August to cross the Channel and take a decisive campaign to his brother. Even Henry's smaller, travelling court here at Woodstock was an enormous undertaking. His Master Marshal had four deputies who managed the complex logistics of moving the court. Henry said I was not to return to Gerald during his absence but rather commanded me to stay in his household at Woodstock, and I was very glad of that. I did not wish to have to confront the hypocrisy of my marriage, and in any case, I regarded Henry now as more or less my husband.

* * *

From Gerald FitzWalter's Day Book

Rouen, All Saints, November 1104

I have what I want and yet I do not have what I want. I have only myself to blame, caught in the net the King threw so skilfully over me. I am an utter fool for I glimpsed her love and my own happiness so briefly and now I have lost them completely. She is his and it is my fault.

I am with the King in Normandy where he has been sometimes campaigning against and sometimes negotiating with his brother Duke Robert. Now that I have met the man and spent time in close proximity with King Henry I see even more clearly the folly the Montgommerys committed in choosing to support the older brother. The King's stratagems prevail everywhere. William de Mortain, who continues loyal to Curthose and unruly to the King, is disseised of his lands in England, and the King's nephew, Stephen de Blois, is awarded Mortain's estates.

The King has promised to reward me for my loyalty (which I suppose includes gifting him my wife) but I see no sign of that as yet. Nothing he can give me can compensate for what I have lost in losing Nest.

Duke Robert has come to terms with King Henry and all works in the King's favour. I am out of my element away from Wales. Though my blood is Norman, this is my first time in the Duchy seeing as I was born in Windsor. It feels like an alien world and I long to return to the Welsh coasts and dream that Nest is there with me, but I may never see her again. I write but she does not reply and she will never love me now. I cannot bear to look at the King and yet I have to steel myself to it daily. He rubs my nose in his ownership of her, and keeps me close where he can look at my humiliation, although we do not speak of it of course. There is murder in my heart, regicide, but that would not bring me to Nest or to Wales. I am sick with longing for both.

* * *

Henry returned to me at the end of November in 1104. An owl had been a regular visitor, frequenting a branch close to the window of our bedchamber. There was a full moon and the owl's shadow was projected huge onto the floor. I gestured to it. 'The owl welcomes you home, Henry, as do I.'

'Perhaps in taking the throne I have allowed myself to be manipulated by my own vanity,' he said to me one night as we lay naked on the great bed together and he caressed my loosened hair, 'but there is no way back and I enjoy the work when it goes well and when it does not, I have you, Nest, to console me. My lovely Nest with your flashing blushes and your delightful constellations of dimples, freckles and moles.' He touched his finger softly to the myriad tiny brown marks on my arms and the few on my neck. Somewhere in him I thought there was a small overlooked boy who needed to please, to be loved, for his capacities to be noticed.

'You're tickling me, Henry!'

At times I felt like a fish out of water surrounded by his subtle, practised courtiers, a fish I named in my own head The Gauche as I tried not to blunder and flounder.

I found myself terrified by the depth of the love I was growing for him, as if that love was a deep hole where I teetered on the very edge, afraid I might hurtle into that compelling void.

Just before Christmas we travelled down river to the court at Windsor. Queen Matilda barely acknowledged my existence, no doubt aware I had become Henry's latest conquest, and I was relieved to see that Gerald was not at court. I supposed he remained at Moulsford, unable to confront with his own eyes the outcome of his deception. Henry made light of a second warning of excommunication he received from the Pope but I knew he was anxious about it, especially worrying how to contend with it alongside his plans to take Normandy from his brother. I knew he would soon need to talk it over with me, when he could steal time away from the Queen.

At Windsor I had expected to share Henry with his wife but my illusions of being his *only* beloved mistress were shattered when I saw Henry first with Ansfride and then with Sybil Corbet. My heart plummetted as I stood across the room, watching the way he stroked a stray curl from Ansfride's cheek, and then how he surreptitiously caressed Sybil's arm in a conspiratorial manner. I recognised those moves. I had felt them in my own body. I was bitterly disappointed to find myself sharing him with these mistresses and perhaps with others besides. When Elizabeth came to see me I gripped her arm and hissed at her, 'Are you sleeping with him? Have you?'

'No! You fool!' she said. 'Calm down. You're bruising my arm. Henry and I are the best of friends but we have never found it to our liking to engage with each other in that way. You have no competition from me. Besides, if Warenne found I was sleeping with Henry I swear he would kill him, king or no. He wants me to leave my husband.'

I let go of her arm. 'I'm sorry. Forgive me. I am rendered insane by it all. Will you? Leave your husband?'

'No. It would not be the honourable course, but he asks me over and over.' She considered me. 'You have no options here, you know.' I said nothing. 'You wait for him to return to you. You behave proudly as if you are unaware of those others. He will return to you. He is very faithful, in his way.'

'Faithful! Like a sultan with a harem.'

She shrugged. 'Well, do you still want him?'

I heaved a sigh. 'Yes, the saints help me. I hate him and love him in equal measures. I am hungry for him.'

'Then ...' she rolled her eyes at me. 'Don't you think you have a lot more to offer him than Ansfride who is getting on a bit now, than Sybil who is an inane child, or even than his pious queen who thinks that since she has birthed his heir she need no longer suffer her duties as a wife?'

'You're right. But I won't humiliate the Queen. I won't allow Henry to do so. And I'll not compete for him, like some common harlot.'

Taking Elizabeth's advice, and using Amelina's flair for dressing me, I waited patiently for Henry to notice I was better looking, more noble, more cultured, more interesting and more necessary to him than any other woman. After a few days it was me he sought out surreptitiously night after night.

'Sorry!' he told me. 'I can't be cruel to Ansfride and Sybil you see. I'm just letting them down gently.' I was fully sceptical about that but nevertheless smiled my forgiveness, moving my chess piece to take his pawn. 'Beaten soundly,' he said, lifting my hand and licking my palm with a naughty smile.

After the Christmas court we returned to Woodstock but in February of 1105 Henry received news that FitzHamon had been captured and imprisoned in Bayeaux. Henry was anxious to rescue him and set off with his entourage to muster an army at Romsey so that Woodstock was abruptly emptied. He would be away for several months at least.

Soon after Henry left I found I was carrying his child and sent word to him. I felt extraordinarily tired but knew from my attendances on Sybil that I would feel better in the months to come, after the early stage had passed. One Sunday morning when all the parishioners filed into the church for mass I remained outside on a bench, at first feeling too nauseated to enter and then when I felt better again making a decision to stay outside in the sunshine. The muffled sound of hesitant singing of the first hymn filtered out to me through the closed doors. It might have been good to be singing in there but this morning I needed to drink in the air, all of it, the great expanse of blue sky that arched over the church and its lush hillocky graveyard with its scatter of vivid flowers. I took a gulp of that air, that high blue above the church and laughed aloud, alone with just the graves to hear me. Throwing my head back, stretching my arms along the back of the bench so that I could see only blue, blue, I opened my mouth as if I were singing that sky into existence. I was going to bear the King's child. I was going to have a child. Laughing quietly to myself I dropped my head forward again and looked anew at the church. I felt as if a blindfold had suddenly been removed and I was seeing everything with newly washed eyes. It was the most ridiculous church I had ever seen with an astonishingly ornate doorway that was far too much for the humbleness of the rest of the building and its small village setting. Quite incongruous. That doorway would have looked fine on a cathedral, but here on this tiny village church there was something hysterical about it, hysterically funny. I laughed again, imagining the ambitious young stonemason who had put that vainglorious, that glorious doorway on this tiny church.

To my dearest Nest, Lady of Wallensia, from Henry, King of the English, greetings and affection. What joyful news from my delightful wasp! Seeing a messenger approaching and discerning that the letter was yours I began to read it ardently since the writer is so dear to me. Never do I receive a letter from you but immediately we are together. The measure of my joy is so great at your news that I cannot read your letter with dry eyes. I beseech you to inform me frequently how you do.

I embrace you with an unbounded love and beg God's clemency that you might be safely delivered of your precious freight. I commend you to Abbot Faricius who will take the greatest care of you both.

I desire your lovely self to know I have long held you close in my heart. If it should please you to send to me, who loves you beyond what I can say, some token of your love, I should value it more highly than the whole world. If there is anything you would like to have I beg you not to delay informing me of it through the bearer of the present letter. You are the one possessor both of my body and of my mind. With straining neck and fixed eye I long to follow you and your little burden on your progress to Abingdon. I yearn for you in your absence and yet I burn in your presence. Your sweet name is without ceasing on my lips. I sigh for love of you. Every excellence of mind and body adorns you. Not with me is my heart, but with you and if not with you, nowhere for without you it cannot anywhere exist. We have enjoyed carnal pleasures together from love and not from lust and now here is the fruit of our love.

Here at Romsey the army grows in numbers every day and we will soon embark for Normandy but we suffer from excessive cold and enormous torrents of rain. Yet you may be very sure, dearest, that the messenger whom I send to you, leaves me safe and well. You will certainly see me just as soon as I possibly can return to you.

Alas, the Pope has sent me warning a third time that I am in grave danger of excommunication if the investiture dispute cannot soon be resolved with Archbishop Anselm, and he has taken the regrettable step of excommunicating my dear friend Meulan to reinforce his threat. By God's grace we will yet prevail.
Farewell, my all, sweet wasp.

Henry would be displeased at having to launch his invasion of Normandy with this threat of excommunication against him and Meulan would be fearful at having to go into battle with his soul cut off from the solace of the Church. In April Henry crossed the Channel. News came fitfully of the to and fro of his fortunes but I received no more letters. He succeeded in freeing FitzHamon and together they burnt Bayeaux to ashes. I wondered what would happen to me if Henry were killed. I would be returned to Gerald I supposed and live out my life the lady of Moulsford Manor and Gerald would have to accept Henry's bastard as his own child. How different a life would that be to the months I had just known with Henry. I could not help feeling I was born for Henry's burning love, and not for a narrow, mundane life with Gerald.

As my pregnancy advanced and my stomach sailed proud before me I was saddened to receive another letter.

To Nest, Lady of Moulsford, wife to Gerald FitzWalter, from Sybil of Montgommery, greetings. My chaplain is writing this letter in great haste. My husband has taken Caen for the King, but he has received a grievous head wound in the fighting and is likely to die. In that event, pray for me and my daughters my dear friend.

Sybil said nothing of my relationship with the King in her letter, although she must have known of it.

My pregnancy was easy enough and I travelled the short distance to Abingdon with Amelina in June, staying in a fine house near the Abbey belonging to the King, and feeling unwelcome echoes of my times here with Sybil Corbet and Edith of Greystoke. Faricius had a ready supply of news from Henry's campaign and kept me informed. At the end of May a few of Henry's supporters had defected and he had conducted fruitless peace negotiations with his brother Robert Curthose so the conflict continued.

My son was delivered by Faricius in August. I named him Henry and sent word to the King, together with a lock of my hair and a tiny lock of our child's hair. My baby was black-haired, like me, like his father. He was perfect and I was overwhelmed with the passionate love I felt for this tiny new human being, with his great brown eyes and his miniature fingers and toes. Amelina wept with joy and kissed him over and over. 'You'll drown him!' I laughed.

'Smell his head!' she said in wonder, holding him back to me. 'He smells delicious.'

I nuzzled my mouth and nose softly against the down of his head. 'Yes he does.' I stared long into his face and he stared back at me, all wondering at the world he found himself in. There was something of my father in his face, something of Goronwy and I wept looking at him.

'Oh, Nest,' Amelina said, perching on the edge of the bed, taking him from me again and holding him cradled in one arm as she leant to dab at my face with a handkerchief with her other hand, 'you're all emotion and tears after the birth but you will settle back down to normal in time.'

* * *

From the Copybook of Sister Benedicta

Westminster, All Saints, Christmas 1105

Dear Benedicta, I am glad to hear you will soon return to your beloved Almenêches when rebuilding is completed but I am still horribly anxious for you with Bellême at large. I was lately at a wedding where the bride asked me to give her away. Such a bride, Benedicta, you have never seen! I think she is the most beautiful woman I know, truly. Her black hair was loaded with small bright flowers, her blue eyes dancing. It was a happy day and an honour to me that warmed my heart. Some things came after with my lord that I felt ashamed about, but since she put me in the place of her brother I will always try to give her that care, as I give you. You would love her as a sister if you knew her.

The truce Henry agreed with his brother last year did not hold for long and we embarked for Normandy this spring with Henry intent on taking the Duchy from Curthose and bringing order there. Believe me, if God ever looks kindly on that venture, Normandy would be glad of it but God did not look kindly this year and his instrument was Archbishop Anselm.

You asked for an account of the campaign. We heard FitzHamon had been captured and held prisoner at Bayeux. Henry mustered a vast army at Romsey in England in February and we crossed in March. His intent was more than simply the freeing of FitzHamon. At Easter we were at Carentan where Bishop Serlo sheared off our long hair, starting with Henry and Meulan and then me. I felt as if I were waiting in a queue to have a tooth pulled. So picture me as a kind of shorn sheep. I had bumps on my head I never knew were there before!

So we were an army now dedicated to God to save Normandy but then the Archbishop and the Pope threw a branch into the spokes of Henry's carefully laid plans. The Pope excommunicated Meulan to show he would make good on his threat to excommunicate the King himself if he would not reach a compromise in their dispute. Meulan, who is a Godly man, was, as you can imagine, not at all happy to find himself going into battle for his king as an excommunicate. Worse might have occurred for Anselm set out to reach us and declare the Pope's doom against Henry but he was waylaid by that clever lady, Countess Adela de Blois. She is great friends with the Archbishop, as she is with anyone useful, and told him she was ill and had need of him. She delayed him at Blois and sent word to Henry that the threat of excommunication was dire and imminent.

Meanwhile we freed FitzHamon and burnt Bayeux to the ground. Henry is in terrible mode. We marched on Falaise where FitzHamon has taken a head wound that I fear he will not recover from. We had to look on his brains exposed which was not a pleasant sight I can assure you. Though he breathes and the doctors fuss around him, no doubt making matters worse, he shows no sign of consciousness. He has been a stalwart soldier and courtier for the King, and we were greatly sorry to see him brought to this.

At Pentecost we were in Cintheaux and Henry attempted unsuccessfully to come to terms with Curthose. Receiving news there of Anselm's intention, Henry and I travelled to Laigle where momentously the King has conceded all to Anselm and the Pope on investiture. He could not continue to resist the Pope and be the Holy Saviour of Normandy at the same time, and he is ever pragmatic. Towards the end of summer we returned to England with Henry's intentions in Normandy thwarted, but the wheels are in motion, the momentum is gaining and I believe Henry has no intention to stop now he has cleared the Pope's obstructions from his path. We will be back in Normandy for the fighting season next year. I pray it will end soon, and will end well for all of us.

Here at the Westminster Christmas Court, Bellême had the effrontery to appear as King Louis' envoy. Henry received him coldly and gave him no concessions on his former lands in England or on the French King's demands and Bellême left disgruntled. I wished I could have thumped the man for the grief he caused you and your Abbey but alas I could not. I would soon find myself swinging on a gibbet if I gave violence to a noble, despite the King's affection for me. What is your news, Benedicta? Fond wishes, Haith.

Monastery of Saint Evroul, Yuletide 1105

Dearest Haith, greetings & blessings of the season to you. Almenêches is near-restored now & Abbess Emma, Sister Matilda & I will return there in February & set all to rights, with the aid of our other sisters who will come flocking back from their family homes where they had to take refuge. I will be truly glad to go home, although I have enjoyed my sojourn here, assisting Vitalis now & then with details for his work & discussing it with him. No thumping or hangings I pray you Haith. I go on day to day, comforted with the thought of you out there in the world. I cannot imagine your shorn head makes you look like a sheep. More like a shaved lion I should think. I pray your strength is not in your hair, like Samson, but in your arm & heart. Take care always my dear brother, Benedicta.

23

The Gift

A few weeks after our son was born the King returned to England but he did not come to me immediately at Abingdon where I continued. 'King Henry is very busy,' Faricius told me. 'He has radically reformed the court, setting narrow allowances, forbidding pillaging and molestation of villagers, publishing his itinerary and a schedule of prices that courtiers must pay for provisions to local people. No doubt this is the consequence of his new harmony with the Archbishop.'

'Good. That sounds very good,' I said, thinking he would come soon to see me, and his beautiful new son. I wondered if my letter had missed him as he crossed the Channel and I wrote to him again at Westminster.

In all this time I had not laid eyes on or heard from my 'husband' Gerald, but two months after my son's birth, I was astonished to see him riding into the courtyard of my residence in Abingdon.

I smoothed my dress, commanded Amelina to accompany me, picked my child up from his cradle and walked as calmly as I could to the hall to greet Gerald. After a brief glance at me and the child and a formal exchange of greetings, he did not delay in communicating his errand. He informed me the King had restored him as Castellan of Pembroke Castle and I and my child were to go with him, to Wales.

I looked at him, stunned. 'But … I have received no communication from the King.'

'I am communicating his orders to you now, Lady Nest. I have them by his hand and seal.'

'He sends no word to me himself,' I said, more to myself than to him.

'The King was threatened with excommunication and has had to agree many changes in reaching an agreement with the Archbishop. The Queen is very close to the Archbishop,' Gerald said. I understood his implication. I was quietly discarded and returned to Gerald. I could not believe this could be the end of it. Henry meant to come to me eventually. I was sure of it. If not ... indignation welled within me for my own sake and my son's but yes, he *must* mean to come to me when he could.

I felt furious Henry did not speak with me directly, angry that Gerald could just take me as if I were a parcel to be passed from hand to hand but amidst the welter of my distress, fury, anger, there was delight too that I would go to Wales and that I was allowed to take my son. I had been worrying at that. I knew the children Ansfride, Sybil and Edith had borne Henry were being raised in the royal nursery, taken away from their mothers. Was this a slight to my son? Or a gift to me, that the King did not require me to give him up? Or would he come for him later? I did not care what Henry's motives were, only that he allowed it.

Gerald noticed the way I was hugging little Henry to me. 'I will take good care of you and the little lad, Nest. I swear it.'

I swallowed, looked at him with a brightness I did not feel, began to issue orders to Amelina to ready my household to move, and tried to prepare myself for my move from royal mistress, almost a queen, to the wife of a mere castellan, from Henry's lover to Gerald's wife, a man who I hardly knew now, and perhaps could never like again after his betrayal of me, after the trading of me between men that I felt suddenly sullied by.

With Amelina's help I packed my possessions into two chests and they were loaded onto the waiting horses. We went first to Moulsford to allow Gerald to put his affairs in order with his steward and tenants. I looked with disinterest at the pretty manor on the Thames, that had once briefly, just for a few hours, seemed like my heaven. The delay of several months at Moulsford allowed me a little time of transition although I struggled to hold my head up and to suppress my feelings of grief at the loss of my lover. I tried and failed to feel angry with Henry who I knew, rationally, was the real culprit but I had no trouble in being angry with Gerald and he was to hand. I made no effort to converse with him and he gave me a wide berth, leaving me to my own devices. I immersed myself in my baby, weeping as I fed him, looking into his dark brown eyes, the King's eyes. From the window of my upstairs room I watched the road in vain for a messenger from Henry. 'He's not coming,' Amelina told me repeatedly, risking my ire or the deepening of my depression.

Some days I tasted misery in my mouth. I tried to remember how my love for Henry had felt when we were together but that feeling was overwritten, crosshatched with disbelief and bitterness. Another time I tried to find a rage against Henry. There was a small patch on him, I told myself, invisible to the eye, a wound that could not heal in perpetual need of a bandage, the bandage of a new love and then another and another. He had to discard one love and take another because he did not believe he could fool anyone into loving him for very long. Deep beneath his confident charm there was, I thought, a morass of self-doubt slopping around that rarely blinked at daylight but was lurking there nonetheless.

I was furious with myself too. I had observed Henry, known his characteristics and habits and yet my fury and my knowledge gave no salve to my bruised heart. I had allowed my vanity to fool me into thinking that I was different from all the other women. I had thought I could command a different love from him altogether. At times I was irrationally angry and unkind to Amelina. 'You played me for a fool with Owain, perhaps you have been sleeping with Henry also, or Gerald,' I shouted at her.

'Are you mad, lady?'

I could not believe I had lost him. How had it gone from there to here? I could not fathom it. I had missed that moment when he fell out of love with me. I blinked and somehow he slipped from my embrace. He had sucked the heart out of me like an oyster and left me just the hoary, slatey layers of a discarded and empty shell. Memories of him were everywhere but most of all on my skin.

I went down to the bank to look at the Thames which was high, rising and threatening to flood, muddy brown water slipping fast over the weir, filled with debris, black treetrunks and mats of vegetation that looked like bodies sliding and trapped in the water's turbulence. 'Lady, come away from the edge!' Amelina called behind me. Surprised, I slipped, catching my arm just in time around a tree to save myself from the close rushing waters, one foot shooting up into the air and one blue jewelled slipper catapulting into the slime, quickly hooked and carried off by the swift river. 'He gave me those slippers,' I sobbed, embarrassed at myself even as I said it. Gerald was with Amelina. They had come out together in search of me. He wrapped his arms tightly around my waist from behind. 'I've got you. I've got you, Nest. Let's get you back to the house and dry. Nest. Sweet.' He gentled me, speaking softly against my wet cheek.

Elizabeth wrote from court without mentioning at all my sudden ejection as royal mistress. She wrapped the occasional reference to Henry nonchalantly into the letters. I supposed it was her way of telling me this was how I should act, as if it had never happened. Her letters often made me laugh out loud and I relayed their contents to Gerald when they were decent enough. '*Queen Matilda's piety knows no bounds,*' Elizabeth wrote, cattily. '*She has invited lepers into her chambers and washed their rotting feet and is establishing a leperosarium near London. She is determined to out-saint her mother.*' Elizabeth relayed the information that Duke Robert had come to King Henry's court in Northampton in January to ask for the return of the Norman lands the King had taken but Henry refused. '*Anselm will be recalled from exile,*' she wrote, '*and the King will sail for Normandy again in the summer with a large army.*'

'He means to finish this conflict decisively I believe,' Gerald said.

I failed to care what he meant to do in Normandy and what happened at court. Eventually, having to act as the lady of Moulsford, instructing the servants, I was forced to regain some of my composure and I began to allow sadness to seep and leak into me, remembering my innocent thoughts of making this a home for Gerald and myself, before I knew that I had been bartered.

24

Being Welsh

It was Spring in 1106 when we finally set off for Wales, for home, spending the first night of our journey in the guest-house at Malmesbury Abbey. I avoided Gerald as far as possible, keeping company with Amelina. He made no attempt to lay with me as my husband at Moulsford or at any of the places where we stopped on the journey. After Malmesbury we coaxed our horses onto the ferry boat across the Severn estuary towards Cardiff.

I was overjoyed to break the journey and spend one night with Sybil and her daughters in Cardiff. We rode into the bailey, amidst the richly familiar sights and sounds of the compound. 'Nothing much has changed,' I said to Amelina, but thought of how much *I* had changed since Sybil and I rode out of here four years before to answer King Henry's summons to us and to the Montgommery brothers at Winchester.

Sybil and I ate a little with Gerald, for form's sake, and then making the excuse of my fatigue, we went to Sybil's chamber hand in hand to settle down and catch up with each other's news. Amelina moved around the room quietly unpacking my nightclothes and making up the extra beds. Mabel and Hawise occupied the chamber next door that used to be mine. The girls were supposed to be sleeping but all four sidled into the room in their nightgowns and smothered me with kisses and hugs, then peered fondly at little Henry sleeping in his cradle. We settled into a huddle on the great bed.

'I wish I could just slip next door, into my old chamber, and carry on as before.'

'Nothing is as before,' Sybil said bluntly.

'How is Lord FitzHamon?' I knew Sybil's husband had been carried to Tewkesbury Abbey and was being cared for there.

'He will die soon,' Sybil said and her daughters studied the quilt glum-faced. 'Can you speak to the King for us?' Sybil's dear face wore an expression of unusual and extreme anxiety.

'I ... I fear I don't have any sway with Henry anymore.'

Sybil shocked me by bursting into wholly uncharacteristic tears. 'You were our last hope!' she sobbed. The girls began to weep, alarmed by their mother's emotion. Amelina hugged Hawise and Cecile to her sides, and I took Mabel's and Amice's hands in mine.

'But Sybil! Last hope for what?'

'When my husband dies, Henry will dispose of us all. We're all worthless to him, tainted Montgommerys.'

'No, don't imagine that! I'm sure Henry can't think of any of you as worthless. He will feel he owes it to FitzHamon to take care of his daughters.'

'You really think so, Nest?' Mabel asked.

I nodded enthusiastically. The girls ranged in age now from Mabel's thirteen to Amice's nine. Henry would seek out good marriages for them surely.

'And you think Henry will feel he owes anything to me, to Sybil de Montgommery?'

I looked helplessly at Amelina and made no reply.

The following day we continued our journey towards my lands by boat, sailing past Swansea and the cows grazing on the salt marshes of the Gower Peninsula. Our vessel was a *knarr* with a square sail. I thrilled at the sight of the longed for high, wide skies, the scudding white clouds and the sandy coastline of home. Gerald frequently took little Henry from my arms or Amelina's and walked around the boat, talking to him, showing him what the sailors were doing, or pointing at a pod of dolphins leaping in the water beside our vessel. At first I was wary but soon realised Gerald would do him no harm and that he was growing genuinely fond of my boy.

The final part of our voyage took us across Carmarthen Bay towards the harbour at Saundersfoot. Because of the treacherous waters and sandbanks of the triple river estuary we could not go too close to where Llansteffan Fort stood on the headland, but I saw it from a distance. It stood in ruins still, its timbers blackened and fallen after Arnulf's raid long ago. I looked across to the headland I knew so well, the beach, the mouths of the three rivers – Gwendraeth, Tywi, Taf. It was like looking down a well for I was looking down time, down the fourteen years since Gerald had taken me from here trussed in a cart, ripped from my family. Gerald saw me looking, my eyes shaded against the sun, and came and stood beside me. 'Llansteffan is yours now,' he said, unnecessarily. After a while he realised I did not intend to reply. 'I can order its restoration?'

I turned now to look at him. 'Leave it as it is.' I walked away and stood alone again, further up the boat, looking at the beach where I had lost myself. The Claw. Perhaps I would find myself again now that I was returned to my own land.

When we approached the harbour at Saundersfoot the tide was far out and we had to weigh anchor at some distance to wait for its return to carry us in safely. The great sandy bay stretched for miles. 'Why don't we take a small boat and row to the beach?' Gerald asked me. 'The boy would like to wriggle his toes in the sand after being cooped up on the boat for so long.' I looked with longing at the beach myself and nodded my assent. The small row-boat was lowered into the water and Gerald got in first. Henry was carefully strapped and lowered down on ropes into Gerald's arms which he thought was a grand adventure, worthy of his best chuckles. I hitched my long skirts into my belt at the sides, kicked off my shoes and gingerly felt with my bare feet, one step at a time, down the knotted rope ladder to the boat.

Gerald soon rowed the short distance and jumped into the shallow water to lug the boat to the sand, whilst Henry wriggled forcefully in my restraining arms, excited by the pattern of light on the water. I waved at Amelina watching anxiously from the ship. Gerald pulled the boat aground. 'You hold the boy,' he told me, and then took me by surprise, as he swept me up in his arms and waded to the damp sand with us, depositing us there. I blushed and smiled at my feet, straightening my skirts, my hem already plastered with damp sand patches that scratched against my ankles.

Henry struggled in my arms and I set him down. He had recently learnt to crawl and could make surprising speed at it. He knelt on the damp sand lifting a handful to his mouth. Gerald rushed to him and stood him upright, gently brushing the sand from his face and laughing. 'That doesn't taste good!' He held Henry by the hands, his arms raised up, and walked him along the beach between his knees with Henry giggling, pointing that he wanted to head to the edge of the water where little waves trilled towards him. After a while Gerald corralled him away from the water, carrying him to a rock pool to show him a crab. I looked at my son and my husband. I looked at the blue of the sky and the sea and the great sweep of yellow beach. I lifted my skirts above my bare toes and ankles and walked slowly towards them. Henry was crying out for a crab that Gerald had pulled from the pool with his gauntleted hand and Gerald was shaking his head. 'No, no. It will pinch you hard. You can't touch it!' We laughed together but I turned away swiftly. Tears pricked at my eyes which might have been from the whip of the wind, but I knew they were rather from the whip of regret.

A few hours later Amelina changed me and Henry out of our damp, sandy clothes in an inn. Outside again, I handed Henry to her in a covered cart, and mounted my horse. We took the road towards Carew, which was also my land. Gerald rode up alongside me. 'Nest, can you forgive me for what happened?' he asked in a low voice.

'There is nothing to forgive. You followed your orders as you always do, and I have been happy in the time since I last saw you.'

He received this doubtless unsatisfactory reply in silence. I was determined not to play along with this sham marriage. I knew now not to expect anything more from the King. I was discarded. He had moved on to some other love. I was distraught that he had not even sent me a letter of farewell but I would not voice my distress to anyone, not even to Amelina. My pride was hurt but I told myself I had known this would happen all along.

Somewhere in Henry there was a stone-cold strategist who used his lovers and children as pawns. Making me his mistress and marrying me to a minor Norman, he had deliberately disempowered me, disassembled any symbolic force I might have held for the Welsh or offered to any husband, either Welsh or Norman. He was disingenuous when he told me he had married me to Gerald to safeguard my reputation. I was rather more politically significant than Ansfride, Sybil Corbet or Edith and he was more motivated by the need for a cover against the ire of his allies in Wales.

Gerald interrupted my thoughts: 'The people in Deheubarth will be overjoyed to see you return.'

'It has been fourteen years. They will have forgotten me,' I said sullenly.

'Oh no!' he said. 'You will see.'

As we came into Carew, news of my coming had gone before us. The people came out, lining the road, calling my name, 'Lady Nest! Lady Nest!'. They threw flowers and shouted for my blessing. I was astonished and then overwhelmed with emotion at their affection and to be addressed in Welsh after all this time. I looked with a full heart at the familiar scene – the low walls of lime-washed cob, the narrow shuttered windows and the thick frowns of thatch on the village houses. The thatch was loaded here and there with moss and lichen. Smoke belched from triangular openings. Piles of firewood and water butts stood close to the houses. The smell of beer issued from the village brew house, the smell of bread from the bake house and the cacophony of fowl came from the goose and hen houses.

Gerald smiled at me. 'See, they remember you alright!' I did not return his smile but saved my own smiles for the cheering crowds of villagers. Many of the women held handkerchiefs to the corners of their brimming eyes. I decided to dismount.

'Is that wise?' Gerald asked.

I ignored him and took the hand of a villager standing to help me climb from my horse. 'You honour us, lady!'

'Thank you all for your kind greetings to welcome me home,' I called out. 'How do my father's people fare?' I asked the man who had handed me down from the horse.

'We are your people now, lady, and right overjoyed we are to see you here amongst us. We're faring well enough. A good harvest this year. Life goes on despite these Normans in the *llys* where your good father ruled. Is your brother coming, lady?'

'I know nothing of my brother,' I said, lowering my voice, anxious Gerald would overhear and understand. 'Speak softly of him. Many Normans understand some Welsh now. He will come one day.'

Gerald leapt from his horse and held his hands with the fingers laced together for me to step up and remount. I gripped the pommel with one hand and steadied myself on Gerald's shoulder with the other, avoiding his eyes. I turned in the saddle to watch the Carew villagers waving until we rounded the bend and were out of sight.

'I've started designing a new residence for you at Carew,' Gerald said, 'if it pleases you? Pembroke is a garrison, full of soldiers and few comforts. I thought you might like something more ... courtly.' He coloured.

'Thank you,' I said softly. 'That is kind.' We were like strangers with Henry leering smugly between us at every word and every turn.

As we neared Pembroke its timber-walled hulk loomed above us, fitting the headland as a perfect triangle. Gerald turned to me with a grin. 'Shall we take a boat to the Wogan?'

I meant to show him perpetual disfavour but I could not resist the suggestion. 'Oh yes!' I tried to hide my glee but it was insistent. Underneath the great castle was an enormous cave letting out directly onto the river, that was called the Wogan Watergate. It had been lived in by primitive men and women thousands of years ago. Their bones, stone tools and rudimentary drawings on the cave walls were there still. As a child I was always pestering my father to enter that way instead of taking the ordinary road to the main castle gatehouse. Gerald, pleased to see me at last taking an interest and volunteering to do something in his company, was quick to organise the small boat for us. Amelina continued on the road with little Henry and the rest of the entourage, whilst Gerald and I stepped into the boat.

The tide was flowing out and the Pembroke river was rushing to the sea. 'Do you know how to gain the entrance?' I asked him anxiously. Entering through the cave entrance when the river was turbulent could be a risky procedure.

'Don't worry,' he said. 'I know it and I know this castle at least as well as you do.'

He steered our little craft skilfully, vigorously, across the current and pulled us to the bank at the mouth of the cave. Engrossed in his task he had to forget for a while the tensions between us and I was able to watch him without his notice. How dashing he was, how handsome, this treacherous husband of mine. I enjoyed watching the muscles of his arms and legs battling the water, and then looked at him from the swaying boat as he leapt out, hauling it aground. He grinned at me, exhilarated at his success, offering me his hand. I took it and stepped from the boat, surprising him by retaining his hand when he started to pull it away. We walked towards the yawning cave entrance. Inside it was chill, dank and green with patches of damp moss and streaks of red in the rock, just as I had remembered it. Without a lantern and coming from the brightness of the day, we could not see into its darkest reaches. I stumbled on the uneven ground and Gerald steadied me. He moved to lead me to the stone steps that led up to the castle but I stayed him. 'Gerald.'

'My lady?' He faced me in the gloom, still holding my hand.

'We must try to be man and wife, I suppose.'

He was silent but stepped closer to me. When I did not step away from him, he put one hand on my waist and the other on my cheek. 'I have always only thought of you as my wife, Nest.'

We stood in this awkward embrace for a few moments, looking at each other. 'Let's go in and greet your household.' Gerald led me to the steps that wound up to open out blindingly into the light of the vast bailey at the heart of the castle.

The castle was very much changed since my father's time. The timber buildings of the compound were all restored and new-thatched and some had been enlarged, including the hall, the stables and the chapel. The high wooden palisade that ran all around the triangle of the headland and then across the front of the castle was new-built with a wooden walkway for the garrison guards.

A two-storey gatehouse guarded the entrance to the bailey and the exit across a drawbridge. The gates were open and I saw that a deep ditch had been dug across the front of the castle so the only means of access was across the drawbridge – or through the Wogan. Pembroke Castle looked 'ship-shape', like an embodiment of Gerald himself, whereas before, I admitted to myself, it had been a little ramshackle.

The Pembroke household were out in full to greet us and their reception was ecstatic. Norman and Flemish soldiers, Welsh cooks and kitchen boys alike stood bobbing gaily and calling out welcomes in their diverse languages. A small girl was gently propelled forward towards me from the protection of her crouching father's embrace and held out a bouquet of wood anemones and bluebells to me. 'Thank you, sweetie,' I said quietly, bending to her. Her dimples mirrored my own. Suddenly she realised she was the centre of attention and fled back distraught, colliding with the safety of her father's knees and Gerald and I exchanged smiles.

25

Rebuilding

Our first meal in Pembroke was drawing to an end. 'I've arranged a chamber for you Nest. I hope it will be to your liking. If there is anything you need I hope you will tell me.'

'Thank you.' I gave him no invitation to visit me there this evening. I was tired and although I had already determined that I would attempt to take Gerald back into my heart, I needed more energy and perhaps I needed more time to achieve it.

In the morning I stood on the west wall close to the chapel looking across the river to Monkton, the Benedictine Priory that Arnulf had established in memory of his brother, Hugh. Arnulf was ousted and I was home but who was I now? Was I Norman or Welsh? Was I the wife of Gerald or still the lover of Henry? I had been so immersed in my relationship with Henry and had had no warning that it might end abruptly as it did, that it was hard to shift the flow of my affections, but Gerald was my husband in the eyes of God. I determined not to hang waiting helplessly on Henry but to make the best of the situation now that I had recovered from my initial disbelief at being so easily discarded.

Weeks passed and my relationship with Gerald thawed little by little. He was loving to my son who was too small to ever know Gerald as other than his own father. Amelina liked him and dropped hints every day that I might be kinder to him. I could not deny that he was a capable castellan and conducted his duties with panache, fairness and humour. I started to find myself laughing at his conversation. Our discussions at dinner became more animated. He was a good-looking man and it was evident that he burnt with desire for me, but nevertheless he waited patiently for a sign that I could accept him as a lover.

One night I made a snap decision. It was time I put vain hopes of Henry behind me. He had sent no word and had forgotten my existence and that of his son. It was Henry who deserved the full brunt of my resentment and not Gerald. I needed to resume my life, not waste it pierced over and over with stupid hope for a man who did not deserve my loyalty, when a man who was at least caring was sitting before me. 'Will you join me in my chamber?' I said, turning my eyes on him. I did not smile but I sought for a connection with him.

He held my gaze. 'Can you ever feel for me as you once did? In the first days of our betrothal, the first hours of our marriage?' he asked.

'Yes,' I lied. 'I can. I do.'

'You ... do you really wish it?'

'Yes,' I said, putting my hand on his, searching in myself for how I had felt about him when we were first married, in the short hours before I knew about Henry's ruse, before I knew Henry.

'I could leave you be, Nest ... if you need more time.'

'I need you. I wish to ... be your wife, in truth, in ....' I could not find the right words.

'I understand.'

We rose together and I scraped my chair clumsily, noisily. He took my hand and led me to the stairs up to my chamber. My heart beat and I felt trepidation at the act I was about to engage in, as if I were a maiden.

We stood by the bed. After looking in my face to ensure I was truly willing, Gerald slowly unlaced my gown. He kissed me and stroked a warm hand inside my bodice, cupping my breast and breathing hard. I reached to the lacings of his tunic. He was a passionate, enraptured lover, and I could not doubt the sincerity of his love for me. I liked him, and yet, although I feigned love, I could find nothing more than liking for him. Not love. Thank God, not *that*. I would never again allow that in to hurt me.

If it had not been for Henry's manipulations of us both I could have loved Gerald. If it had not been for my passion for Henry I might have given that passion to Gerald. Since I was a girl stolen from my home, I regarded Gerald as my one kind, true friend but when he married me in my May flowers crown, when he swung me around telling me he loved me, knowing all the time of his bargain with the King, then I had seen a mask slip from his face. His fair hair and his smiling blue eyes were suddenly transformed to a pretty surface I no longer believed in. I saw him as a wolf in sheep's clothing, no better than the rest. I could never regain how I had felt before. The best I could do was like him. I would never trust him.

I felt pleasure at Gerald's caresses and at the lithe, muscled beauty of his body, so unlike Henry's bear-like stockiness. It would have been different if Gerald had not married me knowing he would give me to the King but that fact was always there between us even as Gerald's olive skin slid against mine, as his flesh entered mine.

* * *

From Gerald FitzWalter's Day Book

Pembroke Castle, Easter 1106

God has answered my prayers, and more. I have my sweet Nest and my own Pembroke. And now my glorious wife tells me she is carrying our child! I am building a new manor house for her at Carew with the latest and the best of everything. I studied the options, conferring with my master mason. Carew's hall has a high ceiling and gleaming pale timbers. I have ordered the walls plastered and painted with a scene from the stories of King Arthur that she likes so well. The hearth is so huge you could stable a *destrier* in it and it is edged with fine tiles patterned in blue and yellow. A tapestry I commissioned for Nest's chamber depicts moon and stars and another shows butterflies, bees and flowers. Even the garderobe is a new fangled marvel with a chute to the ditch outside, its boards inside covered with a green cloth and plugged with a cushion.

I had to move the boy Hywel, who is thirteen now, back to Rhydygors Castle so that Nest would not find out about him.

He favours her in his looks and whilst no one has an inkling who he is, they might begin to suspect if they should see them standing side by side. The poor boy is no threat to anyone but I am ashamed of his condition and struggle enough with the reasons she already has to blame me.

* * *

From the Copybook of Sister Benedicta

Almenêches Abbey, Normandy, October 1106

I have no need to copy my letters now to and from my brother Haith, because he is here! In the Abbey's guesthouse! And Abbess Emma, all curious as *I* was, to hear in full an account of the battle between Duke Robert and King Henry at Tinchebrai and its aftermath, gave me leave to come out of the cloister to greet my brother and invite him to dine with her this evening. 'Go now,' she said. 'He is just arrived.'

'Thank you Abbess This means the world to me.'

I rushed out in time to see Haith dismounting and groaning louding at his aches and pains. He did not see me for a moment and I watched him stretching his muscles.

'Oh thank God!'

He turned to see me running towards him. 'Benedicta?' Twenty years since he had seen me, except through the cloister grille.

I fell upon him.

'Benedicta! I'm filthy from the battle. Don't!'

'I don't care! I don't care at all!' Blood and dirt grimed every inch of him but I gladly gripped him and rubbed my face and hands against him, sobbing. 'You're safe! You're alive. I was so afraid for you.' That creased grin that I remembered so well from our childhood, that turned his face, mouth and chin into a series of V shapes; his voice, the blue sparkle of his eyes.

'Yes I think I recognise the little girl I was separated from in Bruges so long ago in this nun here!' he laughed. 'Grown into a fine woman, albeit all concealed in that voluminous black habit and wimple. I'm fine. It's so wonderful to see you Benedicta but you are outside? Outside your cloister?'

'The Abbess gave me leave. Isn't twenty years of separation enough excuse? I am often outside the cloister now. I am the one who carries messages to the Bishop and others, as you know. Haith you are so pale beneath that grime.'

'Forgive me. I am bone tired.'

'Of course. Come and sit by the fire and tell me and Abbess Emma all about it. We have heard rumours and now you can confirm it all.'

Two hours later Haith, washed and fed, looked like he was feeling considerably more human. The Abbess and I looked at him expectantly and he set down the beaker of our best damson wine. 'The battle was swift and there were few casualties before Duke Robert's surrender. King Henry has the Duke and others captive. Curthose's small son William Clito is placed in the care of Helias de Saint-Saens. Henry has been unanimously proclaimed Duke of Normandy and will soon set about restoring order here.'

The Abbess looked down at her hands folded in her lap and then up again to Haith. 'Poor Robert Curthose, to lose everything, but his rule has not been a happy, peaceable one. I am in hopes the new Duke, Henry, will repair all our fortunes. What of my brother, Robert de Bellême?'

'I believe there was some secret negotiation between Bellême and Meulan before the battle.' Haith paused to let us make our own surmises regarding that statement. 'He escaped from the battlefield.'

'Then our troubles are not over,' the Abbess said.

Haith turned to her in surprise. 'Perhaps not quite yet,' he agreed in a low voice.

* * *

A few months after our arrival at Pembroke I found I was carrying Gerald's child. I was as happy as he was, as Amelina was, about it. It felt like I had finally started another life, after Henry. I frequently rode to Carew to visit my holdings and my people there and now that Gerald has finished building the comfortable new manor house it has become my principal residence. I was still unable to bring myself to go to Llansteffan so Gerald's steward continued to take care of my interests there.

Not long after my twenty-sixth birthday, early in October 1106, we received news that Henry had finally succeeded in subduing Normandy. He defeated his brother Duke Robert at the Battle of Tinchebrai, fought on the lands of Sybil's nephew William de Mortain. Elizabeth's husband, Robert de Meulan, and her lover, William de Warenne, had been two of Henry's commanders in the battle. Robert Curthose was disinherited of Normandy and in the custody of Bishop Roger at Devizes. Henry was proclaimed Duke of Normandy as well as King of the English.

Elizabeth wrote to tell me she and the Queen had been to visit the former Duke in his captivity, and that he was comfortable although downhearted and anxious for his son. I tried not to flinch at every mention of Henry's name that was so frequent on everyone's lips, so lost to mine.

Sybil wrote that her brothers, Bellême and Arnulf, had repeatedly petitioned the King for the return of their lands, but were denied. I felt glad of that. If Arnulf ever returned here as Gerald's overlord it would have been an unwelcome complication. The threads holding Gerald and I together were fragile still and we were winding them carefully about each other. But I felt safe. Henry knew better than to ever trust the Montgommerys again. He would not relent.

'Many Normans can breathe easier now,' Gerald told me, 'now that their heartlands in Normandy and England are combined together under one overlord.'

Gerald took me to visit the site of my father's old *llys* near Carmarthen and then on to the castle of Rhydygors where the Norman lord Richard FitzBaldwin had recently reestablished the castle and we dined with him. My mother and her child had died here and FitzBaldwin kindly showed me to my mother's grave where I laid flowers and shed tears. 'Do you know if her child that is buried here with her was a boy or a girl, had a name?' I asked.

'No,' FitzBaldwin said embarrassed by my emotion, 'I'm sorry I don't know anything about it.'

As I was mounting my horse to leave, I noticed Gerald turning a boy around swiftly by his shoulders and pushing him into the darkness of the kitchen doorway. He strode back towards his horse keeping his eyes down on his boots. His face was flushed. He was hiding the boy from me but why? Perhaps he was an illegitimate son? I could not blame him for that when he nurtured my own.

For the first half an hour of our ride Gerald remained silent. I would ask him about the boy another time. 'The Welsh roundabouts live in peace alongside their Norman lords,' Gerald told me, 'and it's largely because of your presence. You are their lady and they are happy. They accept us because of you.'

I was not sure how I felt about that. The King had appointed new Normans to lands in Wales, filling the vacuum left after the fall of the Montgommerys. He gifted the fertile lands of the Gower coast to Henry, Earl of Warwick, and Bishop Roger of Salisbury was building a new stone castle at Cydweli. I had no news of my brother Gruffudd, who I presumed must still be in Ireland if he lived. Perhaps he had accepted his disinheritance and given his swordarm to some sea venturer.

Before the end of the year our son was born at Carew. The bells of the chapel and the town church peeled to greet his arrival. 'I should like to name him Rhys,' I told Gerald.

He pulled a face. 'I think he must have a Norman name, my love. Sorry.'

'I want him to be named Rhys.'

'Let's call him William and when we have daughters they can have Welsh names, hmm? Gwladys after your mother?'

I saw he would not relent despite his gentleness. 'Then our second son will be named for my kin.'

'Perhaps not our second one,' he still demurred, 'but our third son, for sure!' He beamed at me.

I could not win this battle. 'Three sons and daughters! We will be very busy then, my lord.'

'Yes, Nest, my darling love, we will be very busy!' We laughed and gently he stroked our son's cheek.

Some weeks after the Christmas celebrations and the feast of the Epiphany in the new year of 1107 I sat down at my desk and updated my journal. There was a roll of parchment on my desk, tied with a blue ribbon, that I did not recognise. I unrolled it and found a poem written in Welsh.

> *O sea-bird, beautiful upon the tides,*
> *White as the moon is when the night abides,*
> *Or snow untouched, whose dustless splendour glows*
> *Bright as a sunbeam and whose white wing throws*
> *A glove of challenge on the salt sea-flood.*

'Amelina,' I said, looking up as she came into the room with a pile of clothes in her arms. 'Do you know where this parchment came from?'

'No.' She shook her head, pulling a puzzled face. 'I thought you knew.'

'I've never seen it before.' I turned it over in case there was a dedication or explanation written on the other side, but there was nothing. 'A poem. A gift from someone in the castle perhaps?'

She shook her head again and continued folding the clean clothes into a chest. The provenance of the poem was a mystery then, for now.

I reached for parchment and my quill again and drew up a genealogy to show how my blood line, the line of the daughter of the last king in Wales, flowed on in my two sons, Henry and William, and how they are related to the royal families of Briton. Perhaps my sons will lead the Welsh back to their patrimony, despite their Norman names and blood. Perhaps they could marry into the families of Gruffudd ap Cynan in Gwynedd or Cadwgan ap Bleddyn in Powys. I would find out about the daughters of those princes. I am the daughter of a king. My son Henry is the son of a king and kin to princes and I will see he has his due rights.

There is no way back now. My sons are Normans, no matter what I tell them about their Welsh heritage, and my husband is Norman. My own desire to be resistantly Welsh is now necessarily compromised and hedged about by love.

26

The Hobbled Claw

One morning in late Spring in the year 1107 I returned from my ride and Gerald, who stood with his mason in the courtyard of Carew, looked up to smile warmly at me, calling out 'There's a messenger for you in the hall, Nest!'

Inside, I pulled my gauntlets from my hands and Amelina fussed around me, undoing the clasp of my cloak and slinging it over her arm. The messenger put down the beaker of ale Amelina had furnished him, stood and bowed to me.

I took a seat. The messenger held out two scrolls to me. 'Lady.' I took one of the scrolls. It was a letter from Sybil Montgommery.

To my dearest sister, Nest, chatelaine of Pembroke. You may have heard that Henry, King of the English and Duke of Normandy, has lately returned from Normandy and held court at Windsor. I was summoned there and went trembling because, Nest, I am sorry to tell you my husband died a few weeks ago at Tewkesbury Abbey. He never regained his wits. King Henry has made his bastard, Robert FitzRoy, lord of all my lands in Glamorgan, Bristol and Gloucester and intends to betroth Mabel to him, as FitzHamon's heiress.

That insect Belmeis is continuing to enrich himself as Sheriff of Shropshire, usurping the battle-won gains of my father and brothers like a roach. King Henry has sent my Hawise and Cecile as novices to Salisbury and Wilton Abbeys so that all the FitzHamon inheritance is concentrated in Mabel. He tells me nothing as yet of how he means to dispose of me or Amice, but you will know all this soon yourself and we will speak directly of it for he summons you to attend the betrothal in Cardiff. I long to speak with you. Perhaps you can intercede for us with the King? If he sees you in person, your beautiful face, he will not be able to resist, I know it. In misery for the fate of my family. Your dear friend Sybil.

I wiped a tear from my cheek, not at the thought of FitzHamon dead, but for Sybil's grief and insecurity, for her girls. I hoped Hawise and Cecile were treated kindly by the nuns in their Abbeys and determined to write to them there. The King's bastard son Robert would, I thought, be a kind husband to Mabel. Perhaps she and he could intercede with Henry for Sybil since Henry was very fond of Robert, his first-born. Might Henry allow me to bring Sybil and Amice into my household? Henry. I would see Henry in person in Cardiff then, at the betrothal.

The other scroll the messenger held out to me bore Henry's seal and was the summons Sybil had warned of. It was addressed to me and said nothing of Gerald. It informed me that Haith would arrive to escort me to Cardiff. I looked up from Henry's signature to see my husband coming in with a brace of pheasants hanging over his shoulder. He lent and kissed my neck as he passed behind me. 'What do you have there?' He slung the pheasants on a side table and washed his hands.

'A letter from Sybil. FitzHamon has died.'

He sat down beside me and took my hand. 'I am truly sorry to hear that. He was a great warrior, a great lord. One of the first of us to make a bridgehead in Wales.'

I extracted my hand. 'I cannot celebrate that.'

'No … I …'

'And also,' I said, brandishing the second scroll with the King's seal. 'A summons to Cardiff from the King.'

Gerald paled. 'The King …'

'Mabel will be betrothed to his son Robert. I am summoned to attend.'

'And the King …'

'Will be there.' I finished his sentence and looked steadily into his face.

I woke Amelina before first light the following morning. 'We're going to Llansteffan.'

'What?' she looked at me blearily. 'I thought you never wanted to go there again.'

'Come on. We're going. You, me and the boys. We are going to watch the morning tide in the bay and I am going to plan the restoration of the *llys*.'

We rode to the headland near Llansteffan where we could look out across the river Taf behind us, the river Tywi below us and the river Gwendraeth across the estuary, all flowing into the great bay. We could see the blackened timbers of Llansteffan further along the headland. The Claw. My place.

The waters had been receding out to sea for some hours, leaving myriad little rills snaking across the brightening mudflats towards the main channel. The weak light gathered more and more to itself turning from pale to murky yellow-gold, from the merest blur of pink to red-gold. In its transitional roll into light the water sloshed out of the bay to the sea and later would roll back in again.

The bay was a near relation to the morning, with its great opening at the convergence of the estuaries of the three rivers, with its great sky. Its fishes, birds and pebbles all rolled together towards the warming sun. Colour was emerging from the silver greys of old moonlight. Small vivid islands of grass in the sand were surrounded by puddles and pools left behind that would be collected again on the water's next return.

I creased my eyes against the new glare of the pale sun, looking towards the sand of the shifting dunes – The Walking Dunes. I took in the extraordinary empty expanse of the estuary – the greys and silvers and pale yellows stretching around us in all directions – the screams and swoops of gulls, the salt lick of my lips, the breeze on my cheeks blowing strands of hair across my face, the distant fishing boats out in the bay, the tiny dark figures of men and women with their clothes hitched up, out on the mudflats, searching for cockles, mussels and seaweed.

You had to be always conscious of the tides here, the spring tides and neap tides, the weather, the state of the sands, the phases of the moon. I knew how to walk quickly on the sides of my feet across dubious waterlogged surfaces. My brothers had taught me and I would teach Henry and William how to do it.

It was very quiet on the estuary, only the sound of birds and the soft lull of the water, where the wind died down between the headlands. Ahead there were wading godwits, redshanks, oystercatchers and sandpipers, their silhouettes lined up along the edge of the retreating waters, snatching at insects. The sun was on the distant sands on the far bank. I looked at the ghostly yellow shimmer of sandbanks underwater. The sand banks were uncovered at every tidal retreat and then the waters heaved back over them. I looked across the estuary opening out now where the three rivers became the sea. The mist and cloud on the third river, the Gwendraeth was indistinguishable from the whitening sea. The water was several hours past its high water mark. It was flowing back out fast, uncovering more and more mud and sand in the Gwendraeth river mouth. The Cefn Sidan Sands shimmered ahead, now silver, now bronze, the pale early morning sunlight bouncing on the fine grains and pulverised shell. Blithe midge explored the landscape of my ear and neck. A rookery of seals basked on the distant rocks.

Slowly, pausing after each, I said the names of my dead family aloud, rolling them on my tongue as the sea rolled the pebbles. 'Rhys. Cynan. Goronwy. Gwladys. Her unnamed child who died at Carmarthen. Idwal.' Little Henry looked curiously at me, wondering what I spoke of. The hounds of Annwn had hunted down the Montgommerys and FitzHamon but Neufmarché lived and ruled still. They would come for him in time. The tide was almost fully out now and would be turning again soon, rushing back to cover all.

Amelina stood away from the cliff's edge holding the baby, but I knelt close to that edge, holding tight to Henry's waist as the wind buffeted us on the headland. 'This is our land, Henry,' I told him. 'My land, your land, and your brother William's land.'

'Water,' he said, pointing.

I smiled. 'Yes more water than land sometimes.'

I looked all around me. My Claw, my triple estuary, was hobbled with a string of Norman castles, with FitzBaldwin's Rhydygos further up the Tywi, Laugharne behind me on the Taf, Saint

301

Clears high motte castle at the head of the Taf, and Cydweli where Bishop Roger was building, across the estuary, on the Gwendraeth river.

I remembered Goronwy and I laughing together in sunshine as we followed with our swaying heads the wheeling and whistling of the kites above Llansteffan, their forked tails, the sweeping and swooping fingers of their wings, their glorious red and golden plumage, their cruel hooked beaks and far-seeing eyes. They ruled the sky, they owned it, it was theirs. I reached into my pouch and took out the battered and faded claw. I felt sorry for it and for myself. Was the claw the sign now of invasion – the three inlets the Normans had come up into my lands and gripped onto like the kite with its prey, devouring it on the wing, or was it my hand clinging onto the soil for dear life till my last breath was spent, till my hand might be severed at the wrist? I would never willingly leave here now. I had come home. Suddenly I flung the claw from me and watched it plummet to the water far below.

Henry giggled and Amelina screwed up her nose. 'You've had that disgusting thing all this time!'

'It was once part of a proud and beautiful bird, Amelina, that owned this sky, that traced its wings in glorious arcs against these winds. See!' I said in sudden ecstasy, pointing at a pair of kites that appeared as if conjured by my words, soaring above the river, piercing the air with their lilting calls. The *Barcud Cochs* – the red kites, the *Boda Chwiws* – the whistling kites. We watched them loop in wide repeating circles looking for prey. We watched them hang on the wind. One suddenly stooped, striking a small bird that had unwisely crossed the sky beneath them. When the birds had disappeared from view, Henry pointed at the ruins of Llansteffan.

'Shall we rebuild that castle on this glorious estuary, Henry? Shall we mend it?'

'Yes.'

'Can you hear the bells under the water?' I asked him. Henry frowned at me and nestled his face into my neck. 'If you hear the bells, it's a warning of what is to come next,' I whispered into the delicate round of his ear.

Historical Note

The stories of Nest ferch Rhys, Gerald FitzWalter, Haith and King Henry continue in my next two novels, *Conquest Book II: The Drowned Court* and *Conquest Book III: Return of the Princes*. This novel is based on historical research and on evidence concerning the real people and events that appear in it, although much is imagined beyond and around the evidence. The majority of the characters are based on real people with the exceptions of Amelina and Benedicta. The plan of Cardiff Castle in 1093, whilst based in research, is my own imagining.

The story of Nest told in these novels spans 1093–1146 when native Welsh rulers were in prolonged contention with invading Normans. We tend to look at history with hindsight. The Norman conquest of Wales did not in any way resemble the swift conquest of England. For over two hundred years, from 1066 until 1283, when the last Welsh leader was killed, it was by no means certain that the Normans would succeed in subduing Wales. Even as late as 1400 there was a successful Welsh rebellion led by Owain Glyndwr. Nest's nephew, Rhys ap Gruffudd, Prince of Deheubarth, became one of the most successful native leaders against the Normans in the second half of the 12th century.

Early records name the people inhabiting the geographical area of modern Wales as Britons but at the end of the 11th century this terminology began to be displaced with the terms Wales and Welsh (derived from Old English, meaning Other) and Cymry (Pryce, 2001).

The story of Nest ferch Rhys has fuelled reams of fictional and historical writing yet the certain facts about her are few. The death of her father in 1093 and the fates of five of her brothers are recorded. There is no historical evidence that she was betrothed to Owain ap Cadwgan. That is my invention.

Nest was taken by the Normans and married Gerald Fitz-Walter of Windsor, the Norman Castellan of Pembroke Castle, who first served the Montgommery family, and then after their fall, he served King Henry I. One of the initial spurs for my writing of this novel was an irritation at the flippant, derogatory references made by some male historians at how many lovers Nest had, as if each of these was simply a lascivious choice on her part.

Nest's grandson Gerald of Wales asserts that she was the mistress of King Henry I and bore his son Henry FitzRoy. Susan M. Johns argues that Nest married Gerald soon after 1097 and had a relationship with Henry in 1114 (2013). Kari Maund, on the other hand, considers that Nest's relationship with Henry occurred before her marriage to Gerald (2007). She may or may not be part-inspiration for some of the stories of the *Mabinogi*on which may or may not have been written by her sister-in-law, Gwenllian ferch Gruffudd ap Cynan (see Breeze, 2009).

The *Conquest* series draws on the legend of the Engulphed Court of the sunken kingdom of Cantref Gwaelod or the 'Welsh Atlantis'. In chapter 11 when Amelina tells the story of the Engulphed Court, I have transposed the legendary Cantre'r Gwaelod from Cardigan Bay to Carmarthen Bay. There is evidence that thousands of years ago there were many lands that were engulphed by drastically rising sea levels. The legends of the drowned lands of Cantre'r Gwaelod, Lyonesse and Ys, off the coasts, respectively of Wales, Cornwall and Brittany, are thought to be ancient folk memories of land inundations after the Ice Age.

The historian Eleanor Searle has convincingly argued that property and succession claims inhered strongly in women in Anglo-Norman society (1980). Marriage to heiresses did not simply enrich men, it legitimised their position within power-groups, and the status and bloodlines of their heirs, and for the incoming foreign Normans it strengthened their territorial claims.

As far as I know Henry holds the record for the most illegitimate children produced by an English king – at least twenty-four, and he clearly regarded them as valuable and useful for offering in marriage to secure loyalties and properties. One of his illegitimate daughters became the Queen of Scotland, three others were married to Norman barons, and at least three of his illegitimate sons were probably Earls. Not all the details of King Henry's numerous mistresses and illegitimate children are known for certain (see Thompson, 2013 for a discussion of Henry's illegitimate children).

King Henry I was one of the most successful rulers of the early middle ages, taking over the English throne and then the Duchy of Normandy. Historians generally discount the idea that Henry directly had his brother William murdered nevertheless Henry had the most to gain and moved remarkably swiftly after William's death to secure the English throne. Historians are also circumspect on the subject of William Rufus' sexuality.

Haith (or Hait) does appear in the historical record, but his sister Benedicta and Haith's role in Henry's household are my inventions. Bellême did cause a fire that burnt down his sister's abbey at Almenêches in 1103 but I have imagined Benedicta's role in that event. Elizabeth de Vermandois, wife of Henry's chief counsellor, Robert Count de Meulan, was substantially younger than her husband, and did have an affair with William de Warenne, Earl of Surrey. Robert, Henry's first-born illegitimate son was probably mainly educated in the household of Robert Bloet, but he was betrothed to Mabel FitzHamon.

The only significant deviation from historical evidence is that I have renamed Nest's older half-brother for clarity's sake since two of her brothers were called Goronwy. Her half-brother Goronwy, the son of her father's concubine, named Idwal in the novel, fought at the battle near Aberhonddu in which his father and brother Cynan died. He was captured by Bernard de Neufmarché and sent to prison in London, where he died in 1101. Nest's full brother, Goronwy (and so named in the novel), was her father's heir in 1093 and was beheaded by the Normans after his father's death.

In relation to names: fitz was the Norman prefix meaning son of, ap was the Welsh suffix meaning son of, ferch was the Welsh suffix meaning daughter of. Aetheling was the Anglo-Saxon for heir, edling was the Welsh word for heir, Adelin and Clito were Norman designations meaning heir. It is likely that King William II was not nicknamed Rufus during his lifetime and similarly the only evidence for King Henry I's nickname Beauclerc is recorded after his death, however the use of Duke Robert's nickname Curthose and that he was taunted with it by his father are recorded during his lifetime. I have utilised Rufus' nickname in the novel to bring some clarity to the welter of people named William and to distinguish him from his father, King William I the Conqueror. I have called Henry's wife Matilda throughout and their daughter (also Matilda) Maud throughout to avoid confusion. Queen Matilda II was born Edyth of Scotland but sometime before her marriage to King Henry she changed her name to the Norman Matilda. Amongst the Norman barons there was a plethora of Roberts, Rogers and Williams so I have called them by their territorial titles, for instance, Meulan and Bellême. The genealogies at the beginning of the book have been simplified for clarity's sake. A medieval Welsh mile was the equivalent of three miles and 1470 yards in contemporary measurements.

Although stories of King Arthur were not widely disseminated and developed until Geoffrey of Monmouth's *Historia Regum Brittaniae*, written around 1136, and Chrétien de Troyes' Arthurian tales written in the late 12th century, Arthur did feature in several earlier Welsh and English sources. Nest may have known the Welsh tale, *Culhwch and Olwen*, with its description of Arthur's court and mention of his queen, Gwenhwyvar (Guest).

This book was significantly inspired by the landscapes, literature, and history of south-west Wales. Raymond Williams's two volume novel *People of the Black Mountains* (1989 & 1990) was an important early starting point. The poetry in Chapter 6 is from *Rhygyfarch's Lament* written in 1094 (Faletra, 2014). The poetry in Chapter 24 is from 'To the Sea-Gull' by Dafydd ap Gwilym, written in the 14th century (and so anachronistic for this story) (Gurney, 1969). Several phrases in the book come from the wonderful letters of Henry's sister, Adela Countess de Blois (Ferrante, 2014). In the second chapter the phrase 'you never know how the past will turn out' comes from Maria Loh's book on Renaissance artists (2015). In the final chapter Nest's reference to walking on waterlogged sand on the sides of her feet comes from Robert Macfarlane (2007).

I have drawn on biographies of the sons of William the Conqueror by Emma Mason, C. Warren Hollister, Judith Green and William M. Aird; on the biography of Queen Matilda II by Lois L. Honeycutt; on studies of Nest ferch Rhys by Kari Maund and Susan Johns; and on the work of many other historians of medieval Wales and the Anglo-Normans, as well as primary sources such as the chronicles of Orderic Vitalis and William of Malmesbury. A full bibliography of my research is on my website http://traceywarrwriting.com

References

Aird, William M. (2008) *Robert Curthose Duke of Normandy (c. 1050–1134)*, Woodbridge: Boydell Press.

Breeze, Andrew (2009) *The Origins of the Four Branches of the Mabinogi*, Leominster: Gracewing.

Davies, R.R. (1987) *Conquest, Coexistence, and Change: Wales 1063–1415*, Oxford: Oxford University Press.

Faletra, Michael A. (2014) *Wales and the Medieval Colonial Imagination: The Matters of Britain in the Twelfth Century*, London: Palgrave Macmillan.

Ferrante, Joan, ed. (2014) *Epistolae: Medieval Women's Latin Letters*, https://epistolae.ccnmtl.columbia.edu

Green, Judith A. (2009) *Henry I King of England and Duke of Normandy*, Cambridge: Cambridge University Press.

Guest, Lady Charlotte transl., *Culhwch ac Olwen*, http://www.ancient-texts.org/library/celtic/ctexts/culhwch.html

Gurney, Robert (1969) *Bardic Heritage*, London: Chatto & Windus.

Hollister, C. Warren (2001) *Henry I*, New Haven/London: Yale University Press.

Honeycutt, Lois L. (2003) *Matilda of Scotland: A Study in Medieval Queenship*, Woodbridge: Boydell Press.

Johns, Susan M. (2013) *Gender, Nation and Conquest in the High Middle Ages: Nest of Deheubarth*, Manchester: Manchester University Press.

Loh, Maria H. (2015) *Still Lives: Death, Desire and the Portrait of the Old Master*, Princeton: University of Princeton.

Macfarlane, Robert (2007) *The Wild Places*, London: Granta.

Mason, Emma (2008) *King Rufus: The Life & Murder of William II of England*, Stroud: The History Press.

Maund, Kari (2007) *Princess Nest of Wales: Seductress of the English,* Stroud: Tempus.

Pryce, Huw (2001) 'British or Welsh? National Identity in Twelfth-Century
Wales', *The English Historical Review*, vol. 116, no. 468, Sept, pp. 775–801.

Searle, Eleanor (1980) 'Women and the legitimization of succession', in Brown, R. Allen, ed. (1981) *Anglo-Norman Studies III: Proceedings of the Battle Conference*, pp. 159–170.

Thompson, Kathleen (2003) 'Affairs of State: The Illegitimate Children of Henry I', *Journal of Medieval History*, 29, pp. 129–151.

Williams, Raymond (1989, 1990) *People of the Black Mountains,* vols 1 & 2, London: Chatto & Windus.